A SMALL WEEPING

A SMALL WEEPING

ALEX GRAY

First published in Great Britain in 2004 by
Allison & Busby Limited
Bon Marche Centre
241-251 Ferndale Road
London SW9 8BJ
http://www.allisonandbusby.com

Copyright © 2004 by ALEX GRAY

The moral right of the author has been asserted.

'Lucifer Falling' from *Collected Poems* by Norman MacCaig published by
Chatto and Windus.
Used by kind permission of The Random House Group Ltd

A catalogue record for this book is available from
the British Library.

ISBN 0 7490 8330 1

10 9 8 7 6 5 4 3 2 1

Printed and bound in Wales by
Creative Print & Design, Ebbw Vale

This novel is dedicated to the memory of Cathrene Anderson 30.5.47 – 27.10.99

LUCIFER FALLING

The black radiance
was Lucifer falling.
Space grieved for him
shuddering at its own guilt
and moons were never the same
after passing through
the gauze of wings.
The crystal battlements shook
to hear him laughing;
and somewhere amid
the angelic jubilations
there was a small weeping,
forecast
of the time to come.

Norman MacCaig

Prologue

The feather wafted upwards, a fine wispy curve, and for seconds it sailed the air. Slowly, slowly it began its downward journey, tacking and spinning on the currents; slight, light, hovering and shimmering. The dust motes danced against the sunlight like a cloud of gnats as the white feather passed them by. It sank at last in a curtsey and settled on the bed, still as the body below the sheets.

1

There was something appropriate about the fog blotting out everything beyond the station, thought Lorimer as he made his way through George Square. It was as if the natural world was trying to obliterate whatever waited for him behind the swirling curtain of mist. The red surface below his feet was darkened to the colour of old blood, statues loomed out of the mist like silent sentinels and even the tops of buildings were obscured by the pall of dankness, giving an impression of walking through some subterranean chamber. He'd be doing that soon enough. The woman's body had been discovered in the lift between the upper and lower platforms of Queen Street station. Who she was and how she came to be there at all were the questions uppermost in the Detective Chief Inspector's mind.

Lorimer had been woken from a fitful sleep around three a.m. After the Transport Police had alerted the Area Control room in Cowcaddens, the call had filtered through to Lorimer as the on-duty DCI. Now he was rounding the corner of George Street, his eyes drawn to the striped scene-of-crime tape cordoning off the station's entrance. No taxis would be plying their trade up here for a while, that was for sure, he thought, seeing the line of official vehicles parked on North Hanover Street. He'd deliberately left his own car across the square, wishing to approach the railway station on foot as a stranger might have done. Perspective, that's what he'd wanted. But all he'd found was this Gothic landscape.

A spiteful little wind blew along the narrow, cobbled lane across the road. It caught the back of his neck, reminding him, too late, of his wife Maggie's sleepy advice to put on a scarf. The uniformed officer standing outside was shifting from one foot to another, beating his gloved hands across his arms in an effort to keep himself warm.

"Sir?" The police constable came to immediate attention as he recognised Lorimer.

"Been here long, Constable?"

"About half an hour, sir. We were in the area," the PC explained, making a move to unlock the glass doors into the station. They opened with a sigh and Lorimer stepped into the light.

Inside was not much warmer, fog swirling along the tracks from the black hole beyond the length of a parked train. Lorimer stared out into the void, wondering.

"What about Transport? Wasn't there an officer on duty tonight?"

"Supposed to be, but they don't always stay in the station for the entire shift, sir," the constable replied, not meeting Lorimer's eye. Someone's head was going to roll for this all right, especially if the Press got hold of it. But the DCI didn't seem to be in a hurry to lay the blame at anyone's door. Instead he continued to stare down the track as if his vision could penetrate the tunnel's hidden gloom beyond platform 7.

His eyes wandered back along the length of the platform, coming to rest on blue painted plywood sheeting that surrounded the lift area.

"That was quick. Who rigged that lot up, then?"

"It was like that, sir. The lifts are being renovated at the moment."

"So how do we gain access?"

"It's downstairs, sir," the constable replied. "We've got the area sealed off at platform 8 on the lower level."

"The stairs are over by the other side, aren't they?" Lorimer murmured, looking round but making no immediate move across the forecourt of the station. He wasn't squeamish but part of him had wanted to see the station empty and open like this before the body downstairs took precedence in his immediate thoughts. He walked back along the platform towards the lifts then turned to face the building on the opposite side of the rails, the stationmaster's office. Even standing on tiptoe, Lorimer was unable to see the upper windows for the train parked beside him. He nodded to himself, wondering who could have had access to the lifts during the night. There'd be plenty of questions for the stationmaster to answer.

A scattering of traffic cones surrounded the entrance to the lift, a device on somebody's part, no doubt, to assist the Scene of Crime boys when they turned up. Lorimer approached the blue hoardings and peered in. The concertina doors had been pushed aside and he could see a single line of light from the shaft below. Voices murmured beneath his feet. Looking up into the empty socket of the lift mechanism, Lorimer saw only a tangle of cables. With a sigh he turned and headed for the stairs that would take him to the lower level platforms of Queen Street Station.

By contrast to the violet blue gloominess of the upper level, platforms 8 and 9 dazzled the eyes. The walls were wasp-yellow with a lip for seating and between the two platforms ran a central area supported by filthy, black pillars.

A huge bear of a man dressed in a British Rail donkey jacket emblazoned with orange fluorescent panels looked up as Lorimer approached the lift doors.

There was something like relief in the railwayman's expression; authority had arrived in the form of this tall figure whose hand took his in a reassuringly firm grip.

"This is Mr Gibson, sir."

"You're the stationmaster?"

"No, sir. But I was in charge tonight. I'm the supervisor," the man shook his head as if somehow he'd been responsible for the whole sorry mess within his station. "I, well…" he tailed off, raising a hand towards the lift. Then, dropping it with a sigh, he stepped back as if to introduce the main character in this early morning drama.

Lorimer gave the railwayman an understanding nod and turned towards the light flooding out from the lift.

The woman lay in one corner away from the door, her head resting against the wall. For an instant she looked like a rag doll that had been flung down by some petulant child, her legs splayed awkwardly. Long strands were escaping from a plastic clip that skewered her hair. Lorimer could see the gaping mouth that had opened in protest as her last breath was cut off. But it was her eyes that would disturb his sleep for weeks to come. Their expression of terror made his head resonate with her scream. He could hear it echoing around the damp walls of the station.

Lorimer would be glad when a police surgeon came on the scene to close those eyes.

His gaze dropped to the woman's neck. Two ends of a red chiffon scarf hung like banners either side of her chin. She'd been strangled. It was one of the commonest methods of killing that he'd seen in his career. Sometimes it was a domestic gone wrong, other times a crime of passion, but here? Just what had happened here?

He looked again at the red scarf and hoped to hell there'd be some traces for forensics. Lorimer stood back, taking in the dead woman's clothing in one glance; the soiled white jacket, skimpy top and short skirt were like a badge of her trade. She wasn't the first one on the game to be so brutally murdered in this city and she wouldn't be the last. Lorimer had long since learned to control the surge of pity and anger that threatened to overwhelm him in such cases but anyone observing that clenched jaw might see he wasn't yet inured to either emotion.

Lorimer walked to one side of the body, oblivious to the stares of the two men standing outside, then stopped. He hunkered down closer, considering the woman's hands. At first glance he'd thought they must be tied but now he saw that they had been deliberately arranged in a praying gesture, palm to palm, pointing towards her feet. Lorimer bent forward, his attention caught by the unnatural gesture. Was she holding something? Or was it just a shadow? Lorimer shifted his position so that the overhead light showed the woman's hands more clearly. Fearful of disturbing the corpse before the arrival of the on-duty pathologist and the SOCOs, the DCI peered at the space between the flattened palms. Yes, there was something there. Lorimer drew a pen out of his inside pocket and gently lifted one white cuff.

There, like a blossom of blood, lay a single carnation, its stem fixed between the dead woman's palms.

He let the sleeve of her jacket fall back into place, wondering what Dr Solomon Brightman might make of this murder. This looked like the hallmark of a ritualistic killing. Under his gaze the woman was being transformed from a flesh and blood creature to a victim whose death had to be solved. Lorimer had long ago learned the need to detach himself from the horror of a killing. The victim, whoever she was, would become real enough in the days to come, but for now he must force himself to see her objectively. He was looking at a new and complicated case and not just a case for forensics, either. They'd be mad not to use Solly's expertise as a criminal profiler.

Voices from the staircase made him look up. Two figures appeared out of the darkness carrying their kitbags. The cavalry had arrived in the shape of Dr Rosie Fergusson and Dr Roy Young, forensic pathologists. Between the two of them there should be some answers to the dead woman's silent cry for help.

Gibson, the railwayman, caught Lorimer's sleeve as he walked out to meet the two medics, "D'you need me for anything else?" The man's face took on a white glow under the fluorescent light making him look as sick as he probably felt.

"Yes," said Lorimer shortly, "but I wouldn't hover around here if I were you. Stay upstairs in the staffroom meantime." He glanced at the PC who had, until his arrival, been in charge. "Any chance of some hot drinks? It's freezing down here."

"We can rustle something up in the manager's office," Gibson told them both. "I'll show you." He led the constable towards the stairs, his gait quickening. Lorimer smiled wryly. Even the biggest guys were still daunted by the sight of a corpse. Not so this pair, he thought, striding forward to greet them.

"You do pick them, don't you?" Rosie glared at him as if Lorimer had manufactured the murder all by himself. "Here I was all cosy, tucked up with a good book thinking nobody would be daft enough to end it all on a night like this." The diminutive blonde was already delving into her kitbag and pulling out white overalls.

"Don't listen to her," Roy Young laughed. "She'd be out of there like a whippet once the call came in." Lorimer grinned. Rosie's grumbles would stop the minute she set foot inside the locus. Her professionalism was total. Even though she was the senior pathologist she didn't pull rank and always took her fair share of duties. Looking at her now, pulling her hair back into a knot, Lorimer marvelled at how Rosie Fergusson revelled in the business of cadavers and their hidden secrets.

His thoughts were cut off by another voice commanding his attention.

"You beat us to it, then," Alistair Wilson strode across to join him. In the wake of the detective sergeant was a tall young man whose padded jacket made him look like the Michelin Man. Maggie had joked that the boy from Lewis was so new to his role as a detective constable that you could still see the shine. Niall Cameron nodded to Lorimer but immediately looked beyond him, his eyes drawn towards the figures huddled within the open lift.

"Want a look?" Lorimer asked. Both men stepped

forward and Lorimer heard Rosie's "tsk" of annoyance as she stood up to make room for the officers.

"Bloody hell, we've got a right one here," Wilson's voice echoed coldly over the deserted platform. "Put to sleep with a flower in its hand. What d'you think, young Niall? Is it Ophelia or what?"

Niall Cameron glowered down at the detective sergeant, his pale cheeks reddening, aware of everybody's scrutiny. Lorimer watched him, glad to note that the boy was wise enough not to rise to the bait.

"*She* hasn't got a name yet, Sergeant," Rosie snapped, "and if you don't mind we'll not find that or much else until you take yourself off!"

"That's me told, then," Alistair Wilson grinned at the pathologist, totally unabashed. He tried to catch Cameron's eye but the Lewisman had already backed out of the confined space and was looking expectantly at Lorimer.

"This your first murder case?" Lorimer murmured, steering Cameron away from the scene of crime, one hand lightly upon his shoulder.

The lad nodded, a frown creasing the space between his thick, straight eyebrows.

"Don't mind Sergeant Wilson. It's just his way."

"I don't mind. I just don't like to think of her as a *thing*, that's all."

Lorimer nodded. "I know, but sometimes it helps to keep a distance between the victim and the investigating team. A murder investigation is unlike any other. Emotions can run high."

Lorimer shrugged then added, "She probably will be named Ophelia just for the record, you know, now that DS Wilson has given her a soubriquet. At least until there is a positive I.D." Lorimer could see that Wilson's offhand approach had ruffled the lad but despite this Cameron was turning back towards the corpse as if he wanted another moment to see for himself.

"I know Dr Fergusson would be pleased if you attended the post mortem," he told the detective constable. "Only if you want to," he added, watching Cameron's jaw tighten.

"I don't mind," he replied with a diffidence that earned him some points with Lorimer. This one was cool under fire, all right.

"So," Alistair Wilson had caught them up now. "No handbag, no apparent identification. D'you think she was local?"

"Who knows?" Lorimer replied, thinking once more of the railway tracks that disappeared into the mist. "Depends what direction she came from, doesn't it?"

"Want me to ask about?" Wilson persisted. "Try Waterloo Street, maybe?" he suggested, mentioning one of the main haunts of Glasgow's prostitutes. He had thrust his hands deep into the pockets of his raincoat and pulled it tightly across his body against the bitter chill, but his eyes were alight with the desire to be off on the hunt for who-ever had put an end to this poor wretch. His detective ser-geant might seem flippant at times but Lorimer knew it was just a front. Under the surface Wilson was as angry and disgusted as any of them at the waste of a young life.

"Won't do any harm. If any of them are daft enough to be out in a night like this," he added.

"Oh, they'll be daft enough if they need a hit," Wilson laughed mirthlessly.

"Okay. It's worth a try. But make sure you've got an accurate description from Dr Fergusson. We'd certainly be wasting our time waiting for a missing person's report if she was on the game. Meantime, I think DC Cameron should take a statement from Mr Gibson. He was the one who found the body," Lorimer explained, pointing towards a door. "He's upstairs in the staff room," he added.

As if on cue, a constable descended the stairs bearing a tray of polystyrene cups, their contents steaming in the cold air like alchemists' potions. Lorimer retreated to the edge of the platform, observing the tableau around the open lift. An aura seemed to surround the group as though their breaths had clouded together. For an instant he thought about the dead woman's spirit. Then he turned and walked back to the stationmaster's office.

Lorimer was drinking his third hot chocolate of the night as he made his way back to the North Hanover Street entrance. The SOCOs had come and gone, the body was on its way to the mortuary and Frank Gibson had been driven home. His footsteps echoed across the stone floor of Platform 7. It was still as cold as the grave. He'd wandered around the perimeter of the station with DC Cameron, checking out the CCTV cameras. It was most likely the killer had come by car, parking in the car park at the back where no swivelling grey heads recorded the comings and goings of staff vehicles. There was so much to be done. CCTV footage from the area around George Square, North Hanover Street and Cathedral Street was being carefully checked by the night shift at Cowcaddens. The scene of crime people had gone over the area between the car park and Platform 7. It was the only logical way a stranger could have entered the station unseen. The black cab drivers were being contacted to find out about any late night drops or uplifts from the rank at the station door. And what would DS Wilson find from his questioning of the girls along in Waterloo Street?

Gibson's main concern had been for the minimum disruption to the trains. They'd keep the North Hanover Street entrance cordoned off from the public and Platform 7 was out of commission meantime, but the station would open for business as usual. Lorimer yawned. It wasn't yet daylight and he had hours of work still ahead of him. These nine-to-five commuters didn't know they were living.

2

It had been a long day. Rosie stretched out with a yawn that made her jaw crack. It was good to be finished at last, she thought, sinking into the leather folds of her favourite chesterfield in the University staff club. The post mortem had shown death by strangulation and it looked like the ligature was the dead woman's own scarf. Forensic testing would verify that eventually, of course.

Lorimer had brought along his lanky Highlander to observe. Give the lad credit, thought Rosie, swirling the ice cubes at the bottom of her brandy glass, he'd not blanched at the sight of her opening up the cadaver. Some of them simply fainted away, usually the big macho ones that wouldn't flinch in a bar room brawl when glasses were flying. But DC Cameron had watched with an interested detachment as if he'd been one of her senior med. students.

The staff club was quiet tonight, just three elderly gentlemen discussing academic something-or-others over by the fireside. Rosie found the sound of their low voices soothing. She didn't want to make small talk or any other sort of talk until she had to. Despite her tiredness there was an underlying excitement. Solly would soon be here and then she could give him an account of the day's events.

Lorimer had assured her that the psychologist would be invited on board for this investigation. Although he was the Senior Investigating Officer, the Procurator Fiscal still had to be consulted. However, he hadn't shown any worries over Solly's involvement.

The queer sight of that carnation pressed between the woman's hands still bothered Rosie. Straightforward murder was okay but weird stuff like that gave her the willies. She considered the wording of her draft report. She'd outlined the position of the praying hands resting on the woman's vulva. It was a point she'd already endowed with significance in her own mind though the report afforded no room for symbolic speculation. That was the area of expertise that she expected from Solomon Brightman.

Solomon. She gave a tiny sigh. There was something otherworldly about him that she found both attractive and exasperating, his timekeeping, for instance. He was notoriously late for everything and tonight he'd already kept Rosie waiting for the best part of an hour. So why did she do it? Rosie asked herself. She was not a naturally patient person, just the opposite, but since getting to know Solly she'd found herself habitually waiting in the staff club where they'd meet up after work. He didn't drive so Rosie often dropped him off home even though his flat was less than ten minutes' walk through Kelvingrove Park.

Rosie Fergusson was hooked and it surprised her. Solly wasn't her type at all. He had no great interest in socialising other than to sum up his fellow man, but he seemed happy enough in her company even though he'd been a bit shy to begin with. They'd met in the most inauspicious of circumstances, the locus of a grisly murder in Garnethill, and she'd taken an instant liking to him.

The ice had melted in her glass. Rosie slurped the watery dregs, considering whether to have another and leave the car parked overnight. She could always take a taxi home. If she didn't get a better offer, a bad little voice murmured in her head. Rosie grinned at the delicious naughtiness of the thought then looked up to catch the barman's eye.

"Same again, please," she smiled at him, holding out the

glass.

"Rosie." Suddenly Solomon was standing there looking down at her, his eyes twinkling gently behind those horn-rimmed spectacles.

"So sorry I'm late. Had to take another class for one of my colleagues. Fellow I told you about, remember? He's having a bad time of it, poor man." Solly unwound an enormous knitted scarf from his neck as he spoke, his expression somewhere between apologetic and glad to see her, as Rosie noted with delight. "There," he plonked himself down beside her and flung an arm around her shoulders, giving a friendly squeeze.

"Never mind that," Rosie told him. "You're here now and I've been dying to tell you what happened today. Lorimer's got a new murder case and he says you're going to be asked onto the team."

"In that case I'd better have a drink, don't you think?" Solly grinned at her. "Before you tell me the nastier bits."

Rosie waited impatiently as he sauntered over to the bar then returned with a pint glass of orange squash.

"That all you're having? I thought you'd be needing a double vodka at least," she joked.

"Really? Okay, let's hear it."

"Well, it started off this morning. Early. And I mean early. Something like four o' clock. Peter and I were called out to Queen Street Station. It was bloody freezing. Anyway. A woman's body had been discovered in the lift between the upper and lower levels. Strangled. Probably with her own scarf."

"Any idea who she is?"

Rosie shook her head. "Looks like a prostitute and there are plenty of traces of semen. No handbag, nothing in her pockets; young, probably early twenties. She'd been dead long enough for rigor to set in."

"Sounds pretty normal," Solly put in. "Sorry, I didn't mean that to sound callous, but why do they want me?"

"Ah, that's the interesting part. Whoever strangled her

didn't just leave her lying there in a heap in the corner."
Rosie paused for dramatic effect. "Wait till I tell you. They
stuck a flower in her hands then put them together in a
praying position. Like this," she added, placing her hands
palm to palm, pointing down between her legs.

Solomon did not respond for a moment, gazing at
Rosie's hands.

"What sort of flower?"

"A red carnation. One of the long-stemmed sort. Why?
Could that have any significance?"

"Possibly. For the killer, at any rate."

"What about the praying hands? D'you think that might
have some religious meaning?"

"How can I tell? I haven't even seen a report, let alone
been asked officially to comment."

"Okay, let's look at this clinically. We'll say that God created Eve with the anatomical advantage of having arms
that stretch towards the genitals; that might simply be the
way they fell but I don't think so."

"Why not?"

"Wait till you see the photographs. It really looks like
he's made a kind of ritual out of the flower and the hands.
It's been done so carefully. But what I wanted to ask you is,
why place the praying hands downwards like that? Why
not fix them up so that they looked as if they were really
praying?"

"You're hoping I'll make the leap between the genital
area and a sexual motivation," Solomon gave her a half
smile.

"Sort of. I don't know. She'd certainly been sexually
active. There was semen in her mouth as well as in the
vagina."

"Lorimer thinks it's a stranger killing, then? Just
because of the flower?"

"I think so too, Solly. It wasn't like the killer was sneer-
ing at her. It was different. As if… oh, I don't know. As if he
had some sort of remorse, maybe."

27

"A valedictory message, perhaps?"

Rosie squinted up at him. Her excitement had evaporated between waiting for Solly to arrive and his almost diffident response to her news.

"I thought you'd be pleased to be working on another case with us," she huffed.

The psychologist gave a sigh. "I'll be highly flattered to be asked, but my workload right now is pretty scary. With Tom's classes…"

"Solly, you don't mean that!"

"No, of course I don't."

"Then you'll come on board with us?"

"If you're sure I'll be asked. What about Superintendent Mitchison?"

Rosie made a face. The new superintendent was not making himself popular with anybody. Rosie and Solly had met him at George Phillips' retirement dinner, never really expecting him to take over from the Divisional Commander. They'd all seen the Super's job as Lorimer's and it had been a shock when Mark Mitchison was appointed to the post.

"Mitchison would probably ask you to sign several forms in triplicate," Rosie snorted, "but he's not the SIO in this case. It's down to Lorimer. Anyway, I don't think Mitchison would oppose your involvement, especially if it gets the Press off his back. Having a celebrated profiler will give him all the kudos he wants."

"Well, we'll see," Solomon replied, nodding gravely into his orange squash. "We'll see."

"Yes!" Jimmy Greer punched the air and sat back down in front of his computer screen. It had paid off. A bit of chat here, a backhander there, ach, it was all in a good day's work. Tonight there'd be punters tuttutting over the murder of some scummy wee whore but they'd be reading his byline. Jimmy's nicotine-stained teeth grinned out from his moustache as he typed in the copy. The Police Press Conference hadn't given that much away but Jimmy had

28

his own methods of filling in the blanks left by tight-lipped senior officers. So far he'd avoided any brushes with the Press Complaints Commission, though he'd sailed pretty close to the wind a few times.

DCI Lorimer was in charge of this case and Jimmy knew he'd be lucky to get anything off him. Still, there were always hard up coppers who'd tip him the nod whenever there was something salacious enough to tempt the senior reporter.

Greer hunched his long, cadaverous frame over the desk, his reddened fingers tapping out the details he'd gleaned about the murdered woman. She'd still to be identified but from the description the man Gibson had given him, he could tell what she had been, all right. Anyway, no self-respecting woman should have been out in the station at that time of night.

3

The case of Deirdre McCann was headline news for three days. By the end of the first week the political situation in the Scottish Parliament had taken precedence over the dwindling paragraphs concerning the prostitute's bizarre killing. Then there was nothing. Even Jimmy Greer couldn't manufacture a news item from thin air. Oh, yes, the case was certainly still a live one, he was assured, but damn all was happening, or that was how it seemed. He'd managed a piece on her mates for the Sunday supplement. There were lots of photos of the women lounging against walls and smoking. But his text had been padded up by the prostitutes' own stories. Not much was really known about the McCann woman. Twenty-three, originally from Airdrie, a known prostitute and heroin user, she'd been on the game since her mid-teens. There was no family in the background causing a ruckus, which was a pity. Both her parents were dead and her only sister didn't want to talk to the Press. Sometimes the family angle could keep copy going for weeks with protests about police incompetence thrown in for good measure.

DCI Lorimer hadn't forgotten Deirdre McCann though she'd been dead now for almost three months. Intensive police work had uncovered her identity and her manner of death but even with the help of Dr Solomon Brightman there had been no way forward in the case. Unless they were very lucky it would remain unsolved, adding yet another layer of discontent to Lorimer's present mood.

As he sat as his desk, scanning the latest memo from Mitchison, Lorimer wished for the hundredth time that George Phillips' taciturn face would appear round his door, demanding action, demanding results. But Lorimer only saw him whenever the former superintendent called round on some committee business for the Chief Constable. The new man in charge of the division was a different kettle of fish from old George. Fish was right, thought Lorimer. Mark Mitchison was a cold fish if ever there was one. He went by the book, didn't even take a drink or socialise with the lads. Lorimer had nursed some promotion hopes of his own, as everybody knew, so it looked too much like sour grapes to be other than polite to the new boss, but Lorimer groaned inwardly every time they met. Mitchison was a paper man. He generated forests of administration and memos on a weekly and daily basis. Lorimer was fed up to the back teeth with him and had even considered asking for a transfer.

There was a vacancy for a training officer at Tulliallan, the police college, and he had gone as far as writing for an application form. But he knew fine it would end up in the bin next to Mitchison's endless memos. Meantime it was put up and shut up. Maggie had been badly upset by his failure to secure the post of Superintendent. She'd seen it as a foregone conclusion, especially after the successful outcome of the St. Mungo's case. They all had.

Accepting the commiseration of his fellow officers had not been easy. It had been even harder to persuade them to transfer their loyalty to this new man whom so few of them knew. Lorimer had met him on various courses and at George Phillips' retiral dinner. He was a smooth, good-looking individual who curried favour with the Press boys. Anyway, it was done now, the man had been in the post for almost six months and if Maggie was disappointed by

Lorimer's failure that was just too bad.

A knock on the door banished all these thoughts from his mind and he looked up to see the dark head of DC Cameron appear.

"A call from on high, sir," Cameron grinned. It was his oblique way of telling him that Mitchison required his presence. Why the blighter didn't simply phone through to his extension baffled the DCI. It was yet another of the man's annoying traits, using an officer to summon him to his office.

"Sit down, Lorimer," the Superintendent waved his hand in a sweeping gesture. Mitchison was full of this sort of little thing: mannerisms that only irritated. You'd think you were being invited into a Papal audience, Lorimer had remarked to Alistair Wilson the first time Mitchison had summoned them into what had been George's old room. Now, as he looked around him, Lorimer realised there was no trace of his old colleague whatsoever. The walls had been painted beige and there were mementoes from Mitchison's career hanging everywhere. Lorimer glanced at them. There was plenty to show that the Superintendent had been busy in various parts of the globe. It was, reflected Lorimer, like a kid's bedroom full of football pennants.

"I really don't know how to begin, Chief Inspector," Michison's frigid smile was directed at Lorimer.

"I understand that you have been contemplating a move to Tulliallan." The nasal voice was not asking a question. Lorimer clenched his teeth. Someone at the training school had been gossiping. He cursed inwardly. It was becoming like the bloody Secret Service the way this man kept tabs on them all. Lorimer shot him a look but said nothing.

"Hm. Not too happy with detective work these days, perhaps. Too many cold cases?"

"On the contrary, sir," Lorimer forced himself to be icily polite. "Just keeping my options open."

"In that case you'll be pleased to increase your present

knowledge of investigative procedures." Mitchison's smile never faltered and Lorimer had a sudden longing to wipe it off the man's face.

"Part of the Chief Constable's strategy for effective urban policing is to encourage you all to study methods used by police officers from overseas. This division is one hundred per cent behind him on this, naturally." The Superintendent rolled back and forth in his chair while Lorimer tried hard not to grit his teeth. Maggie was complaining that he even did it in his sleep these days. Mitchison's nasal voice expounded the virtues of his latest ploy.

"You may be interested to know that we have been chosen to play host to a most experienced officer from the State of Florida." Mitchison's smile became almost beatific but if he expected Lorimer to grin inanely he was much mistaken. This DCI wasn't giving the Chief Constable many brownie points for originality. It was only a few years back that there had been similar interest in comparative policing methods during the highly acclaimed *Operation Spotlight* campaign, when New York had supplied some specially trained officers to liaise with Strathclyde.

"Officer Lipinski will be arriving at Glasgow Airport at 10.30 a.m. next Thursday. I want you to be there to do the usual welcome-to-Glasgow on our behalf. Here's the dossier. I think you'll find it makes fascinating reading." Mitchison handed over a slim black file then raised his hand in another imperious gesture to show that the meeting was over. Lorimer stood up and dragged his chair over the thick new carpet pile.

"Sir," he gave a swift nod before turning away. It was all he could do to stop himself clicking his heels and saluting the man. Once out in the corridor Lorimer strode towards his own room then halted abruptly. He needed some fresh air after that. In a few minutes Lorimer was down the stairs and out of the building. He took a turn away from the main part of the city, out of reach of any close circuit television cameras that would show his whereabouts, and headed for the nearest park.

Glasgow wasn't short of wide green spaces. That was one of the things most visitors marvelled at. There were parks and gardens within walking distance of most parts of the city. And it wasn't just the tourists who wandered among the flowerbeds and fountains. Summer brought out the mini-skirted office girls clutching their lunches in paper bags. The first blink of sun and there they would be, basking in the warmth as if it were Lanzarote instead of the west coast of Scotland. They were as predictable a phenomenon as learner drivers in the spring.

Lorimer slowed his pace as a flurry of birds flew in front of him. The pigeons thrived on lunchtime crumbs. Lorimer screwed his eyes up against the sunshine, taking in the figures seated along the pathway. There were always some derelicts sunk over in the benches, biding their time to rake in the bins for scraps of their own. Lorimer knew them all by sight. Since some of them included his own touts, he liked to roll by the park when he could. However nobody was paying the detective any attention today and he came to a halt in front of an empty bench beneath a flowering cherry tree. Pink blossoms lay scattered on the newly cut grass and Lorimer flicked his hand over the seat where more of them had fallen.

If he closed his eyes for a moment he could pretend that he was back on holiday in Portugal. The heat gave that momentary illusion of continental sun. Even the noise of traffic didn't diminish the feeling. Lagos hadn't been far away from civilisation. For a few moments Lorimer indulged in the sights and sounds of Portugal in his imagination until the file slipped off his knee to the ground. As he bent to pick it up with a grunt he wondered briefly about the man he was about to meet. He'd be on his way pretty soon. Curious now, in spite of himself, Lorimer crossed one foot over his knee to balance the file and opened it. The officer's face looked up at him from the colour photograph. Lorimer grinned back. So this was Officer Lipinski, was it? Well, well. Maybe the Chief Constable's ideas about sharing policing methods wouldn't be too bad after all.

4

The Grange was perched on a windy hill overlooking the terraces of Mount Florida and Cathcart. Like many of the old Victorian properties that had survived conversion into service flats after the war, it now served as a medical clinic. A wide strip of lawn curved around the chipped driveway then fell sharply away to a steep bank, ending at the path below in a mass of shrubbery. Tom Coutts noticed the huge buds of the rhododendrons tipped with scarlet. A few more weeks of sunshine and the whole lot would be a blaze of colour. As he approached the massive front door his eye rested on the ancient brass bell that pulled straight out of the stonework. There were still so many original features in this rambling place and Tom had sometimes wondered why they hadn't been swept away with all the other alterations to the old house. He heard the jangle of the bell and almost immediately footsteps came hurrying towards the frosted glass door.

Her smoky blue uniform appeared as an Impressionistic blob then the door was flung open and a young nurse stood there staring at him. Tom frowned at her then his brow cleared in recognition.

"Kirsty? Kirsty MacLeod?"

"Dr Coutts. Gosh. It's a while since I saw you. What brings you here?" The nurse ushered Tom into the darkened hallway where light from outside filtered through lozenges of stained glass flanking the main door, casting streaks of green and yellow across the pale emulsioned walls.

"I'm a patient," Tom grimaced but saw that his half-smile had brought a look of curiosity to the young woman's eyes.

"Depression. Like most of the cases in here." Tom shrugged. "Just never got over her death, I suppose."

"Oh," the girl suddenly seemed embarrassed. "I'm sorry. Are you in for a therapy session, then?"

"Yes. I've been coming for a while now," Tom answered, directing his gaze at a spot on the floor. "Anyway, I didn't expect to see you here." He looked up then put out a hand, touching her sleeve.

"Community nursing wasn't ..." she broke off as if stuck for an answer.

"Satisfying enough?" Tom suggested.

"Something like that. There was a post going here and I grabbed it. Not too many private clinics for nurses specialising in neural diseases, you know. I was lucky to get it."

"Nonsense," Tom chided. "Nan always said you were the best." He hesitated as if trying to find the right words. "We couldn't have survived without you, you know."

Kirsty looked away from him and he tried in vain to see her expression.

"Funny I've not seen you here before."

"I'm normally on nights. Just covering for someone today," she replied. Kirsty turned back towards Tom but did not meet his eyes. "Your appointment," she reminded him, stepping towards the corridor that led to the therapy rooms.

Tom followed her, his heart thumping. It was the same every time. He had come to banish his demons but now the very act of entering this place had added to them. What tricks would they have in store for him today, he wondered, giving Kirsty MacLeod a little nod as he turned the door handle of a room marked "Patients' Lounge".

Inside there were several people seated in a circle. One metal chair was empty and as Tom entered all eyes turned towards the latecomer. His mind shifted briefly to the comforting familiarity of the lecture theatre where his students would meet his arrival with friendly enthusiasm. Now, as he faced this room full of people who were still strangers, all he could feel was a clutch of fear deep in his stomach.

"Tom, come on in," the psychotherapist beckoned him over to the only remaining chair set in the circle. On either side of the empty seat were the two men he least liked in the group. One was a young man whose shaved head bore strange Celtic tattoos. His faded black t-shirt was torn at the shoulders with another twisted design circling each pale, muscular upper arm. Bron had been in hospital for his depression, a fact that he flaunted to mere day patients like Tom.

On Tom's other side was Sam, a former shipyard worker who had been redundant for years. In the beginning they had told one another of their occupations and Sam had been openly contemptuous about Tom's profession.

"Psychologist, eh?" he had sneered. "How come ye cannae sort yourself out, then?"

Now as Tom sat down, he glared at the University lecturer as if he had no right to be there at all. Even the therapist came in for some verbal abuse but Tom knew this was part of his job. He probably expected it. How about the nurses, though? Were they trained to take that sort of crap, too?

As the therapist began his session Tom tried to concentrate on his words, using them as a mantra to focus on the topic. Anxiety. It was ironic that the very act of coming into this group situation should create anxieties for him, he thought. Being a psychologist didn't help in the least, in fact it had made him even more self-critical. Nan's death had been the trigger. But now he must move forward, he'd been told. Be positive. Affirmation was the key.

He would heal. He would be well again. Then there would be no need for him to sit with these patients whose anger reached out at him with invisible tentacles.

5

Divine unclipped the belt that had pinioned her to the airline seat for considerably more hours than the scheduled flight should have taken. Her fellow passengers were rising now and pulling travel bags from the overhead bins. Divine waited. She was in the unenviable middle of the row of five that DC10 passengers strive to avoid, so she wasn't going anywhere fast. Besides, she was in no hurry now that they'd landed. The shuttle was leaving Heathrow in just under two hours. Plenty of time to ease herself out of this pigeon coop and find her connection.

The flight attendant smiled at her sympathetically. Not a hair of the young girl's head was out of place. It prompted Divine to return the smile and comment, "How come you girls look so fresh after a night like that?"

In an Irish accent that had charmed her American passengers the girl announced, "Oh, I'm bionic, me!" As if to prove her point she hopped up onto an armrest, revealing a tiny waist and a slim pair of legs as she reached towards another bin. Stretching her own long legs was something Divine was longing to do. Her sigh turned into a yawn.

At last the trail of passengers disappeared down the aisle and Divine ducked out of the seat and made her way onto British territory for the first time.

The flight to Glasgow was uneventful and a lot more comfortable than the larger aircraft that had ferried Divine across the Atlantic. She recognised several of her fellow travellers from the earlier flight. Some were obviously families and couples returning home to Scotland after their trip to the sun. There was a tall man with greying hair who had spent the entire journey deeply ensconced in paperwork. Divine glanced at his hawk-like profile several times. He was worth looking at and he intrigued her. Divine was a people person, her old mother used to say of her youngest daughter. If she couldn't work out what a person's occupation was, then she'd simply make it up. Like Paul Simon, she had always loved "playing games with the faces" of people she travelled with. Who was the guy? Expensive suit, thin tweedy coat folded on the spare seat beside him. (Another good thing about this flight were the empty spaces where folks could spread out.) A scientist, maybe? Looked the scholarly type.

Her gaze swept over the other travellers. There was that boy with the ponytail. He'd come across with them too. American down to the toes of his sneakers. But not such a boy either. His ponytail was thin and the sideburns showed grey curls. He could be anybody. Divine knew these things now. Anonymous looking guys might be bums or millionaires. She used her powers of observation these days instead of her imagination. After all, that's what had brought her so far in her varied career.

Lorimer looked at his watch then scanned the arrivals screen. Where the hell was Lipinski? At last the information on the screen rolled over and proclaimed that flight BA2964 had landed. Lipinski would have gone through customs at London so there wouldn't be too much longer to wait.

At last the figures of travellers began to emerge and Lorimer's blue eyes bore down the corridor. A thin fellow carrying a worn leather document case under one arm strode past the policeman without a glance, his long tweed coat flapping around his legs. There were several family groups, one of whom was an Asian couple and their little daughters. The two children were obviously exhausted, clinging to their parents' sides like colourful small limpets.

The stream of passengers dwindled and Lorimer began to look at his watch again with impatience. A tall figure strode into view, wheeling an enormous carry-on bag behind him. As the figure drew closer, Lorimer could see that it wasn't a man at all but a black woman, her shiny hair drawn back into a tight knot. There was something commanding about her that made Lorimer stare; that loping stride and the head held high. For a brief moment the woman's eyes flickered in his direction and he looked away. It was rude to stare, his mum used to scold him. From the corner of his eye Lorimer noticed the woman pausing to change the hand that dragged her baggage. But then he was aware that she had not moved on and was standing right beside him. For a moment Lorimer was confused as he cast a look over a face that was on a level with his own. Then she smiled that smile he'd seen in the photograph and Lorimer recognised her.

Divine thrust out her hand at the rugged-looking man before her. "Officer Lipinski. How are you?"

The introductions at Divisional HQ were over and Divine Lipinski from Florida State Police Department was ready to go. She'd made an immediate impression on the team, though at six feet-two that wouldn't be hard, Lorimer thought. A commanding figure she might be, but the woman was yawning now and Lorimer was suddenly glad that Maggie had insisted on him bringing the American home for her first evening in Scotland.

"Okay, you'll meet them again tomorrow." Lorimer was about to turn and escort Divine out to his waiting car when he noticed DC Cameron stiffen and look beyond them. He sensed rather than saw the Superintendent enter the room and there was an almost tangible shift in the atmosphere. Even Divine noticed that, he saw. She straightened up, feet together, and folded her large hands behind her back.

"Ms Lipinski, Superintendent Mitchison," Lorimer

heard his own voice make the necessary introductions as the Superintendent came forward, a smile fixed to his thin face. Again Lorimer found himself irritated by Mitchison's body language; the fingers circling the air, that condescending head to one side. He watched Divine's face to see if she would succumb to the good-looking senior officer's overtures. Detached, Lorimer heard the small talk as Divine politely described her flight.

"I'm sure Chief Inspector Lorimer will take good care of you. We'll see you in the morning," and he swept a gracious hand in their direction. Lorimer glanced at Divine and was gratified to see her narrow her eyes at Mitchison's back as he left the muster room.

"Okay. Home-time. You're bound to be pretty tired, right?"

"Yeah. I could do with a nap." She waved briefly at the other officers who were beginning to drift back to their various duties, then followed Lorimer. He took her the quick way down the back stairs to the car park and opened the door of his ageing Lexus. Divine seemed to notice the car for the first time.

"Hm. Nice wheels. What kind of salary are you guys on?" she asked.

It was meant as a joke but somehow the question got under his skin. It was as if Divine Lipinski were suggesting that the Lexus was the fruit of some illicit backhanders. Lorimer shrugged and gave her his standard reply, "No kids." Even in its perennially unwashed state the car raised a few eyebrows.

He'd given his passenger plenty of legroom on the return from the airport and now she sank gratefully into the worn leather seats.

"A short guided tour on the way home?"

"Sure."

Lorimer took the car right into the heart of the city, drove slowly around George Square, pointing out the City Chambers, before heading for the new High Court building.

"That's the city mortuary, right there," he nodded, then glanced across at his companion. She was fast asleep. For a moment Lorimer took his eyes off the road and contemplated the woman beside him. In sleep her features had relaxed and she looked older and more vulnerable. Suddenly he was glad that Maggie would be at home waiting for them.

6

Kirsty MacLeod stretched her arms above her head and yawned. God, she was weary. Never again, she chided herself. That extra shift three days ago had totally wiped her out. Never mind, it would soon be the weekend and she had the prospect of two whole days when she could lie in bed if she felt like it.

All the patients had settled down for the night. The ones on suicide watch were usually the last to drop off, despite their sleeping pills. Peter and the others were all in place, sitting near the opened doors of the winding corridor so she wouldn't have to worry about that part of the clinic. Upstairs the girls and women with eating disorders had long since turned in. Kirsty had checked on each patient, adjusting drips and turning the heaters up. It was a cold night and these poor souls really felt every draught in the old building. She only had to see to Phyllis and that would be that. Then she'd have supper with Brenda and a bit of a blether before writing up the evening's notes.

It had been hard working here at first after having been out and about in the community. She'd been accustomed to her housebound patients but that could have become a problem too. Kirsty wasn't the sentimental type but she had become close to a few terminally ill patients, and their deaths had been hard to take. Nan Coutts, for instance.

The woman's multiple sclerosis had worsened so

rapidly that the pneumonia hadn't been too much of a surprise. And poor Dr Coutts. Now he was here as a day patient, suffering the aftermath of all that strain. Kirsty gave herself a shake. It didn't do to dwell on the past. She'd made her choice now and the clinic was a really interesting place to work, full of challenging patients. Her training in neural disorders had made Kirsty an ideal candidate for the post here, she thought with satisfaction. Not only was she experienced with MS patients but she had nursed psychiatric cases in the community too.

The Grange only housed one patient with multiple sclerosis, however, and that was Phyllis Logan. She was in a specially designed room near the back of the house, overlooking the gardens, away from the busyness of the clinic's everyday appointments and therapy sessions. It was peace and quiet that the woman needed now for the remainder of her days.

Kirsty closed the door to the nurses' rest room and made her way quietly down the back stairs. Dim light shone from the uplighters cupped against the wall as she descended into the gloom. Odd, she thought. Someone's put the downstairs light off. Kirsty fiddled with the switch at the bottom of the stair, hearing it click back and forwards. The corridor stretched into blackness and no light was visible from Phyllis's room. It must be a fuse. She felt her way along the wall slowly, hoping her eyes would become accustomed to the inky darkness before she reached the patient's bedroom.

Suddenly there was the noise of feet coming towards her and Kirsty felt herself relax.

"Thank goodness," she began, then her eyes widened as she saw the figure loom up out of the dark.

Her cry was stifled as gloved hands seized her throat, pressing into the jugular vein. Her heels slipped on the polished surface of the floor as she struggled. Then she felt herself falling backwards into a deeper darkness than she'd ever known.

Phyllis stared at the doorway. In the darkness she could make out a shape coming towards her. The figure moved closer and closer until she could see the eyes boring into her own. Then there was a smile that chilled her bones and a slight shake of the head that she couldn't understand. The figure leaned over her and she closed her eyes in terror, feeling the weight of this intruder across her bed. A cold wet drop of something fell against her hand as the pressure on the bed was released. When she opened her eyes she could see the figure looking back at her from the door. He put one finger to his lips and tiptoed out again.

Phyllis shuddered under the thick covers, wondering why he'd come in the dead of night to steal one of her flowers.

7

Maggie had surpassed herself. Lorimer wiped his lips on the pink damask napkin, thinking about why he'd never seen this table linen before. A wedding present unearthed for the occasion after all these years, perhaps? Their best crystal shone in the candlelight and it reminded Lorimer of Christmases long ago when they'd been to Maggie's parents for dinner. Then all the family silver had been specially polished for the celebratory meal. He could still remember the agony of trying to hold those tiny porcelain coffee cups without breaking off their handles. Maggie had understood his discomfiture and had never made that sort of fuss at home. Still, tonight he was impressed with her efforts for their visitor. Divine had slept the rest of the afternoon and into the evening.

"Great dinner, Maggie!" she enthused.

"Makes a change to have company," Maggie replied acidly, "and to have my husband at the table."

"Ouch!" Lorimer made a face at her but he knew fine she was right. He was hardly ever home to eat with her and as for guests, well, who'd accept an invitation when he was never there?

"How d'you put up with it? If it's anything like back home, the hours are hell," Divine remarked.

"Well, there are *supposed* to be working time regulations but..."

"But I don't keep to them," finished Lorimer. "We're meant to work no longer than an average of forty-eight hours but you know how it is," he shrugged, spearing a piece of asparagus with his fork.

"Sure do. But how about you, Maggie? Doesn't it bother you?"

Maggie gave a half-smile and Lorimer could see the struggle on her face to appear nonchalant.

"Oh, I have my own work to keep me busy. And we do *sometimes* see each other."

"You teach school, right?"

"Yes. What you call high school."

"You were an English major, yeah?"

Maggie's eyes widened. "How did you know that?"

Divine gave a smile and raised one eyebrow knowingly. "They don't call me Sherlock Lipinski for nothing!" She took a sip from her wine glass and Lorimer gazed at the two women, fascinated to see their faces in the flickering candlelight. Divine's skin shone and her huge brown eyes glowed. Maggie's pallor was in sharp contrast. Lorimer felt a pang as he noticed the dark shadows under her eyes. Just how much did his job take its toll on her? He watched as she tilted her head back to drain her glass. That oval face and those high cheekbones still moved him. He knew her body so well. The slim tapering fingers that twirled the stem of her glass, the halo of dark curls caught in the light. He shifted his gaze and saw Divine staring straight at him. She wasn't smiling, and her expression was one of pity. For whom?

"Tell us all about Florida," Lorimer's tone was an affected heartiness, breaking the mood that threatened to make him poor company.

"Well. Tall order, Chief Inspector! Where do I start?" But once she'd started, Divine had no difficulty in talking. About Florida, about her home in the Everglades and the move she'd made to the Gulf Coast.

"Did you ever have any problems about being a woman

49

in the police force?" Maggie wanted to know. Divine looked thoughtful for a moment then a hint of a smile animated her face as she recalled an incident.

"One time, not long after I joined the force, there was a woman who took exception to being arrested by a female officer. She was a kind of hippy type, you know, long-haired and dirty. But not the peaceful sort. Bit of a redneck, we thought. And my, was she feisty! My partner was a male officer, Rod Douglas. Biggish guy, almost my height," Divine smiled. "Well, this female, she keeps insisting in this little bitty voice that she wants a man to arrest her. Big Rod just shook his head and walked away. But she keeps on all the way down town that she *don't want to be handled by no woman cop.*"

Maggie and Lorimer laughed together at the woman's exaggerated accent.

"Anyhow, when we finally brought her in she gets the once over in the cells and it turns out that she's not a female at all." Divine paused for dramatic effect. "She's a he!"

"Who got the biggest surprise?" Lorimer wanted to know.

Divine shook her head at the memory. "That guy was such a misogynist and there he was all dressed up fine and dandy in women's clothing!"

Lorimer looked across at Maggie, who was still laughing. It was nice of the American woman to have chosen an innocuous story like that. The night wore on with Divine recalling things from her past. She had them alternately laughing about the crazy things she'd encountered in some police cases and sobered by others that touched on the more bizarre side of human nature. She didn't elaborate, for Maggie's sake, he thought, but Lorimer found himself more and more intrigued by the way certain homicides were dealt with. The physical side to apprehensions wouldn't go down well on this side of the Atlantic, he knew, given the current legislation about human rights. But Divine seemed to relish that part of law enforcement. There was a lot more emphasis on getting results, too, he realised, remembering an item in the officer's file; Divine Lipinski held the highest total of successful cases in her own head-quarters.

"The punishments meted out by your courts are a lot harsher than ours, aren't they?" Maggie observed.

Divine nodded her head but Lorimer couldn't tell if she was agreeing with his wife or with the severity of Florida's penal system.

The black woman raised her glass and looked at them both. "You guys let them off with murder, don't you?" The question was spoken softly and it made Lorimer feel distinctly uncomfortable. He wanted to defend his country's legal system but at the same time a number of his past cases screamed out at him. For a moment he looked at Divine in a new light. Just why was she here? Was it really just about comparative policing methods? Or was there a political agenda somewhere that he couldn't yet see? Lorimer wasn't ready to be drawn into an argument about the merits or demerits of their differing legal systems. Just how much might filter back to Mitchison, for a start?

He felt Maggie's bare toe against his ankle as if to warn him off. She needn't have worried. Divine was good company but she was still a stranger in their midst.

"Tell me a bit about your education system," Maggie's change of subject was welcome, if rather obvious.

"You mean our high schools?"

"Yes." Maggie leaned forward on her elbows and Divine began a discourse on the state school system she'd experienced.

Lorimer let his mind wander as the two women discussed schools and students. It was really late now, well after one o'clock, and he had to have Divine back at HQ before nine this morning. Her body clock was probably all awry. He stifled a yawn as he let their conversation wash over him. He was vaguely aware that they were discussing scholarships of some kind when the phone rang in the hall.

"I'll get it," he was out of his seat and into the hall in three strides.

"Lorimer," his voice was crisp and formal.

"DC Cameron speaking, sir. We've got a big problem. I'm at the Grange near Mount Florida. It's a clinic of some kind. There's been an incident."

"One of the patients?"

"No, sir. Nothing like that. It's one of the nurses." Cameron paused. "Sir. It looks like she's been murdered."

Divine had made a move to join him but one look from Lorimer stopped her in her tracks. Besides, there was her hostess to consider.

For a moment Divine's expression showed her sympathy for anyone fool enough to take up with a cop. Lorimer was heaving on a dark jacket as he kissed the top of his wife's head.

"Don't wait up," he joked. Then he was gone, the pretty table and the candlelight forgotten as he closed the front door behind him.

The two women eyed each other in silence for a moment then Maggie reached for the Chardonnay. It was empty.

"Coffee?" she asked doubtfully, "or would you prefer something stronger?"

Divine flashed her a sudden conspiratorial smile. "Every time," she answered.

8

The big car leapt into the night and soon Lorimer was in the outside lane of the motorway. It should have taken him at least ten minutes to reach the Grange but the clinic came into view a whole lot sooner. As he walked up the drive, he wondered whether Cameron had alerted Mitchison. He would soon find out if the Superintendent had decided to make his presence felt.

"Okay, who's here?" Lorimer demanded as Cameron's rangy figure came up at him out of the dark.

"Dr Fergusson, Mr Boyd with the scene of crime officers and some local uniforms, sir."

"The Super?"

Cameron shook his head.

"Right, let's get on with it."

"Round the back, sir. The body's under the house in the basement. It's a sort of boiler room."

Lorimer was matching the Lewisman's long stride as he led the way round the side of the building. There were lights on upstairs, he noticed, and wondered which patients had been disturbed. He'd talk to them later. Find out if anyone had heard anything.

"A Mrs Duncan found the body. She's one of the ancillary nursing staff. Telephoned the local station and they contacted us." Cameron held up his hand in a warning. "Just watch the railing, sir, it's pretty shaky."

He wasn't joking. Lorimer felt flakes of rust come away on his bare hands as the railing sagged against the stone steps that led to the basement. It was obvious that this entrance wasn't used much. Why come in this way, then? Lorimer soon found out. The scene of crime boys had cordoned off the interior stairs of the basement. Lorimer stood at the back entrance of the Grange seeing the fluorescent lights that beamed down on the figures below. Rosie Fergusson was bent over the nurse's body. He could only see Rosie's back and the lower half of the corpse from this angle. Above them, on the other side of the grey room, Boyd's men were going about their painstaking work.

Lorimer moved towards the body, careful to avoid the area Boyd had sectioned off. Rosie glanced up at him quickly, gave a nod then shifted aside to let him see.

The nurse lay on her back, legs spread out under her uniform. Her arms had been pulled together, though, hands flat against one another, the tell tale carnation stuck between their stiffening fingers. Lorimer looked at her face. The soft dark hair had come loose from its hairband, he noticed, and was spilling over her cheeks. Hunkering down beside Rosie, Lorimer lifted a lock gently and then let it fall away from her pale skin. Her eyes were still wide open with fright. So was her mouth. Had she begun to cry out before he'd strangled her, he wondered? There was an expression of agonised disbelief that Lorimer had seen before on the faces of murder victims. He looked the length of her lifeless body. The pale blue uniform was crushed and there were rips in her black tights. That must have happened when someone dragged her down here, Lorimer surmised.

"From what I can see she's been attacked before entering the boiler room," Rosie told him. The footsteps of the scene of crime officers echoed against the concrete walls.

"And then given her flower," Lorimer muttered. The parallel was obvious. But would they find something here that would lead them to the killer of Deirdre McCann?

"Oh, no!"

Lorimer whirled round in time to see Cameron's white face, then the young detective was off up the stairs like a shot. Rosie shot Lorimer a look as they heard a sound of retching coming from the garden outside.

"Didn't put your man down as the squeamish sort," she commented. Lorimer frowned. She was right, but this was not the time to inquire about Niall Cameron's delicate disposition.

"Okay. Cause of death?"

"Manual strangulation," Rosie replied, tracing the curve of neck directly below the nurse's chin. "He came at her from in front, grabbed her with both hands, then did it." She looked across at Lorimer, eyebrows raised. "I think you'll find the compression was strong and swift. She died pretty quickly."

"But you'll know more in the morning," Lorimer added.

Rosie gave him a weak grin. "Yeah." She cradled the girl's head in both hands, shifting it gently to one side. "Hope you will, too."

"Don't bank on it. He hasn't even left a scarf this time."

Lorimer looked towards the girl's fingers, flattened in a gesture of prayer. The red carnation pointed downwards towards her thighs. "Just his calling card."

He stood up, still staring at the young nurse. Kirsty MacLeod. Now who would break into this place and kill a nurse? Only a madman, a voice answered him. Lorimer gritted his teeth. He stepped away from the body and sidled around the area being dusted down before heading for the stairs to the clinic.

"May I?" he asked the nearest boilersuited officer.

"Just keep right against the wall, sir, would you?"

Lorimer made his way gingerly up the steps. There could be all sorts of traces here where she'd been dragged down. There was a handrail to one side. This one was painted with black Hammerite, unlike the one rusting outside. He hoped to hell there would be some fingerprints on it. The metal door at the top had been tied open with the orange binder twine that Boyd always used. Lorimer kept to the edge of the steps as he turned into the ground floor corridor. The floor was covered in grey-green vinyl, another good source for forensics to examine.

Was this where she'd been killed? The lights had been put out deliberately so it looked as though the killer had meant to waylay Kirsty MacLeod in this very corridor. Lorimer frowned; another suggestion that this was a crime committed by someone in the clinic. His eyes lit up. Could there be a patient here who'd been in Queen Street station three months ago? First thing in the morning he'd be back asking lots of questions. That was for sure.

There were swing-doors at the end of the corridor, hooked back against the walls on either side, and Lorimer could see that the main part of the building lay beyond this area. Large cupboard doors lined one side of the corridor walls. Lorimer opened them, only to discover shelves and shelves of hospital linen.

There were two doors opposite and Lorimer saw that one was ajar. He left it for the time being and tried the other. It was locked. Frowning, he pushed the other door, hearing it creak. Then he stood in the doorway.

Here was a patient and a very ill one at that. There were tubes protruding from the body and a machine that seemed to be pumping her mattress up and down. Was this where they nursed the terminally ill patients, perhaps? Lorimer had never seen anything like it. He was about to tiptoe away when a tiny movement caught his eye. The patient's head had moved the slightest bit and Lorimer found himself staring into a pair of bright eyes that were very much alive.

Phyllis had heard it all. The clang of a door in the distance, then nothing until the swing-doors had been swept open and that awful screaming had rent the air. During all the commotion, unseen hands had quietly closed Phyllis's door. The sounds were muffled after that but she'd been aware of voices and had heard enough to let her know something of what had taken place. Did they imagine she wouldn't hear them behind her closed door? They were wrong. This disease had robbed her of much, but her sense of hearing was heightened as never before. She knew when the police had arrived. She also knew that some unspeakable horror had taken place not far from her own room.

As she lay listening intently, she recalled the terror of that footfall. Her eyes had shut against the shadow entering her room. She didn't want to think about it any more. But now she found herself staring into a different pair of pale eyes. Were they blue? She couldn't make them out in this light. The man was staring back at her.

He was taller than average, built like a sportsman. Even though he stood quite still, Phyllis sensed a restless energy about him. His hair was dark against the outline of light from the corridor. She could see that much. He was the sort of man she'd once desired, she suddenly realised. Strong. Not the type to be indoors for long; always on the move. She'd always liked that in a man.

"I'm sorry. Didn't mean to disturb you," he said at last.

Phyllis liked the voice. It was a recognisable Glasgow accent but he spoke clearly and didn't mumble. How she wished she could reply. Carry on a conversation. A peculiar moan broke from her lips and she tried to move her head again. There was nothing she could do except widen her eyes to communicate her fear, her desperation. He looked at her harder and for a moment Phyllis thought he was going to step towards the bed. Just when she thought he was coming towards her, he seemed to change his mind and stepped back into the shadows once more.

"I'm sorry," he said again, but whether he meant he was sorry to disturb her in the middle of the night or that he was sorry for her, Phyllis couldn't tell. Then, as suddenly as he had appeared, he was gone.

9

Phyllis woke early every day. The night nurses always came to the laundry cupboard outside her room, pulling out the sheets, clattering the stiff doors and gossiping in their loud voices. Bored and wanting their shift to end so they could go home, they didn't give a thought to who might hear their raucous laughter. They always reminded Phyllis of the magpies outside her window, loud and rude. The cupboard door was banged shut at last and the voices disappeared down the corridor. Her door was deliberately left ajar and the wedge of light from the corridor shone dingy yellow through the gap. The venetian blinds shut out the daylight until other hands came to pull on the cord. Until then, Phyllis had to content herself with this half of her world. She thought of it as Inside now. Never as home any more. Inside was normally boring and predictable.

Her room lay swathed in darkness, only the corridor light picking out familiar shapes. The high bed dominated the room with its special mattress that moved in constant undulations to prevent bedsores. A hissing sigh from the pump mechanism below the bed repeated itself over and over, a sleepy rhythmic sound that Phyllis didn't notice any more. On her left was a chrome stand holding a plastic bottle that dripped fluids into her unresisting body.

The tubes disappeared below the white sheets. Other tubes led outwards and away, discreetly hidden by the folds of bedding. To the right of the bed a grey plastic chair gathered dust. It was for any visitors who might come at the appointed times. Phyllis no longer expected visitors from the outside world. Only the nursing staff attended her needs with monotonous regularity.

The window was on Phyllis's right. In the daytime she could see her lawns and flowerbeds, some shrubbery and the sky. Birds came pecking around the borders, friendly chaffinches or the robber magpies. Sometimes a robin trilled its distinctive note, and Phyllis tried to remember what cold, frosty days were like. The birds were highly satisfactory, but she liked the sky best of all. For hours she watched the cloud shapes slither and change; her imagination creating Gods and chariots, characters from mythology, maenads with streaming hair. She rarely saw the stars except in winter when Venus rose in late afternoon on a velvety blue sky. Then hands pulled the blind cord, shutting off her Outside with a sharp metallic snap. For now the sky was dark and shuttered from her sight.

In a corner of the room a small wardrobe held Phyllis's few clothes. They were all cotton for she never left the heat of this room any more. In earlier days when she could still move her arms and turn her head the nurses would heave her into a wheelchair and push her down the corridor to what they now called the day room. There she had been parked in her old lounge with its egg and dart plaster coving around the ceiling. The other residents had upset her with their staring or feeble attempts at one-sided conversation and she'd always preferred the relative peace and quiet of her own room.

Nowadays there were directives about lifting patients. It took two nurses to sit her upright. And they were always short of staff. So Phyllis was left with the television for company. She rarely permitted the staff to switch it on these days. They always asked first, thank God, and her tiny shake of the head allowed her room to stay silent. Once, long ago, she had watched the quiz shows, but nobody came to switch the thing off and she had tired of the interminable soaps that followed, invading her space. The programmes had been punctuated by advertisements reminding Phyllis of so many things she would never need again.

The yellow light flooded across the linoleum floor as the nurse pushed open the door. It wasn't Kirsty, her designated nurse, but one of the others whom she rarely saw.

"Morning, Phyllis. Time for your pills." The nurse barely made eye contact with Phyllis, turning her attention instead to the glass of yellow goo and the plastic phial of assorted tablets. Phyllis watched her face as the woman concentrated on tumbling all the pills onto a spoonful of the thickened liquid. The nurse's eyes never left the outstretched spoon on its journey to Phyllis's open mouth. She felt the metal spoon then the saliva began to ooze from beneath her tongue. One swallow and it was over.

"Right, then." The nurse flicked the residue from Phyllis's lips, leaving a smear behind that would feel sticky and uncomfortable until someone else came to wash her face. It was strange, she reflected, that she could still swallow a mouthful of medication like that in one gulp when a few drops of water would have set her choking. This disease had taken its toll on her throat muscles as well as so much of the rest. Speech was impossible now, and she rarely tried to communicate beyond a shake or nod of the head.

With a clack, the blinds were opened and weak daylight fell onto the objects in the room. Now the daily routine began. The first nurse was joined by a small, stout auxiliary with dark hair.

"Morning, Phyllis," she swept a practised eye over the bedclothes, resting for a moment on the patient's face. Phyllis was heaved into a sitting position to participate in the ritual of blood pressure, temperature and removal of her bodily wastes. She watched, detached, as if it was happening to someone else. She endured the harsh wet flannel on her face and body while the two women carried on an earlier conversation as if she wasn't there.

"Did you see her being carried away?"

"Sh!" the nurse frowned at her, nodding her head towards Phyllis, belatedly acknowledging her presence.

"Oh. Right. Och, she'll never know. Will you, darling?" she smiled a pasted-on smile in Phyllis's direction.

Phyllis closed her eyes as the hook pulled up the sling and raised her off the bed. Below her the two women pulled at the sheets, dashing the soiled linen onto the floor then smoothing on the fresh bedding with an expertise born of much practise. At last she was lowered back onto the cool sheet and the perpetually moving mattress. The ritual was completed by the auxiliary spraying the air with the scent of roses. For a while this would serve to mask the unpleasant smell of human urine. Left alone, Phyllis watched the spray, like mist catching the light as it fell. Her day could now begin. The sky with its ever-shifting shapes was there to see; and imagination, if not memory, would people her hours.

Now she could banish the memory of that nightmare in the dark. She closed her eyes but heard again the cry that had left her shivering. Had she really seen that shadow of malice falling against the cupboards outside her room? And those hands reaching to pluck a flower from her vase? No one would ever know what she had seen.

10

Lorimer stood outside the front entrance to the Grange, watching as Niall Cameron approached, recalling their conversation of the night before. He had found the detective constable leaning against the side of the building, head pressed against his arms. Lorimer had wondered at the sound in the dark until he realised the young man was sobbing quietly.

"I knew her, sir. She's a girl from back home," Cameron had told him, his face streaked with tears. "She's Kirsty MacLeod. We grew up together. She was in my wee sister's year at the Nicholson."

Lorimer had guided him towards the car where he'd heard the rest of the story. How Niall Cameron had left Lewis to join the police force against his family's wishes. How they'd wanted him to take over his late father's fishing boat but Niall hadn't seen a future there anymore. Now there was only his mother at home with the youngest one. All the others had left. Kirsty had come to the city too, but he'd never seen her. Until now.

"Should I come off the case, sir?" Cameron had wanted to know. But Lorimer had shaken his head. Some background knowledge would be useful.

Now the DC was closer Lorimer could see his bloodshot eyes, signs of a sleepless night. Well, it happened to them all in this profession. Young Niall Cameron had better get used to it.

"Okay?"

"Yes, sir."

"Talk to anyone from home yet?"

Cameron nodded. "There's only one next of kin, the old auntie who lives in Harris. Kirsty's mother died of cancer when the lassie was twelve. Her dad was drowned some time back."

"Right. We'll probably find out more now from the director, Mrs Baillie. She lives on the premises. We only took a preliminary statement last night but there'll have to be proper interviews this morning. Alistair's here already, setting up an incident room."

Some things were better done in daylight, thought Lorimer. There was a team of uniformed officers doing a house-to-house inquiry along the road. It was a residential district with not a close circuit television camera in sight. They'd have to rely on the local insomniacs for any sighting of the killer. Last night had been thoroughly unpleasant. None of the staff had known much about the nurse's background or else they weren't letting on. The auxiliary who'd found her, Mrs Duncan, had been in a state of shock and could barely verbalise. Lorimer had been given a full list of all members of staff. It was a long list, given the staffing requirements for a twenty-four hour day to care for a number of vulnerable people. Still, records would be cross-checked on the computer and that might throw something up.

Those patients who'd emerged from their rooms last night had been surprisingly calm. Though perhaps some of them were sedated at night, anyway. They would all be interviewed at greater length this morning. Lorimer hadn't forgotten all those lights switched on upstairs.

Now, in the spring morning, it was hard to imagine that a murder had taken place in such a pleasant spot. The sky was clear and blue although there was still a chill in the air. Above him a blackbird was whistling unseen in the trees.

Lorimer stepped back out onto the front lawn and walked as far as a curve of rhododendron bushes. Turning, he looked back at the house. It had a pleasing aspect from the front. Two enormous bay windows flanked the front entrance. The huge storm doors were fastened back and Lorimer could see shadowy shapes moving beyond the frosted glass. The clinic's employees were already having to go about the business of caring for their patients, after all. Some of the upstairs windows showed drawn curtains still, though it was past nine o' clock. Whose sleep had been disturbed during the night, he wondered?

Lorimer looked around him. The drive looped all round the grounds. To the rear were trees, more shrubbery and a high, stone wall. Beyond that was farmland. Could anyone have vaulted that wall and made off over the fields in darkness? Or, indeed, arrived from that very direction. An outsider. A nutter. That was the theory he was working on, anyway. Some creep who had a fetish about dead women and flowers. Brightman would surely have an opinion to offer. It was time he called him up.

The front drive gave on to an avenue of Victorian villas then a row of solid tenement houses on each side. There was a main road at right angles to the avenue, a mere hundred yards away.

One thing Lorimer had noticed as he'd turned the car into this narrow avenue: there was barely room to swing a cat because of the double-parking by residents. Maybe someone might have noticed a car in a hurry last night? That was just one of the questions his team of officers would be asking. Over the hill beyond the Langside Monument lay the Victoria Infirmary. Queen's Park stretched out the whole length of the main road right up to Shawlands. Another possible escape route for a killer. Lorimer grinned to himself, realising that he was already tuning into Solly's way of thinking. The psychologist liked to pore over maps relating to the locus of a crime as he began his search into the criminal mind.

Lorimer thought back to the long drawn-out investigation into the Saint Mungo's murders. That Glasgow park had been scoured from end to end. *The Dear Green Place*, folk liked to call their city. And so it was. He'd read somewhere that they had more parks than any other city in Europe. A source of pride to some, maybe, but a right bugger when you were trying to track a killer.

"Sir."

Lorimer's mind came back to the present. Detective Constable Cameron was standing in the porch and with him was the very lady that Lorimer wanted most to see. Mrs Baillie was the woman in charge here, her official designation being director of the Grange, a clinic that specialised in neural disorders.

As he walked towards the steps, he could see a tall, angular woman dressed in black shading her eyes from the morning sun.

"Good morning Mrs Baillie," Lorimer shook a hand that was damp with sweat.

As they turned away from the dazzle of light that bounced off the open glass door, Lorimer could see the director's face more clearly. Mrs Baillie would be somewhere in her early fifties, he surmised, though she'd looked a lot older last night.

Her dark hair showed not a hint of grey but this was belied by the network of tiny lines around her eyes and mouth, a mouth that was turned down as if in an expression of permanent disapproval.

"Come through to my office, please, gentlemen," she said and immediately turned right, opening a door set into the wood panelling. At once Lorimer noticed how the old house had been altered to form the present day clinic as vinyl floors gave way to thick patterned carpet. Light filtered from a landing window where a broad staircase swept upwards. An open door to the front showed them a huge bay-windowed lounge where uniformed officers were already setting out tables and chairs. Across the hall a curved desk wrapped itself around two angles of the walls, segmenting the corner into a reception area. A young woman in a dark suit and white shirt glanced up at them unsmilingly then continued with whatever she had been doing behind the desk, out of sight behind her computer screen.

"That's Cathy. You'll want to talk to her later, I suppose."

"We'll be talking to all the staff, ma'am," Cameron replied, glancing at Lorimer who had wandered towards the stair and was peering upwards.

"There are private rooms on that floor," Mrs Baillie snapped, making Lorimer turn back suddenly. "The patients are restricted to the west and south wing and use both upstairs and down. We have the administration down here." She strode ahead of them, ignoring the girl at the desk, and opened a door leading to the back of the building.

Lorimer and Cameron followed her down a set of four stairs that led into another corridor. Here windows to one side gave a view of shrubbery and an expanse of kitchen garden where a man in brown overalls was digging with a spade, his back to the house. A patient, Lorimer wondered, or one of the staff? Shadows thrown onto the garden made him press his head against the glass and look along the side, seeing angles of pebble-dashed walls masking the original contours of the house. A modern extension had been built onto this part of the Grange, he realised. Lorimer ran his hand along a grey painted radiator as Mrs Baillie unlocked a door opposite the window. It was cold to his touch.

"This is my office. Please sit down," Mrs Baillie had already taken her place behind an antique desk. Two upright chairs with carved backs sat at angles in front of her. The wood panelled ceiling of the office sloped into a deep coomb showing that the room was positioned immediately under the main stairs. There were no windows and so Lorimer left the door deliberately ajar. Claustrophobic at the best of times, he wasn't going to let his discomfort show in front of this woman.

"Who has access to this part of the house?" Lorimer asked.

"Oh, it's not kept locked, Chief Inspector, except my private office, of course. But only the staff would come through here. The patients have their own rooms."

"And is there any other way to reach this part of the building?"

"We have a back door that leads into the garden. It can only be accessed from this side of the house."

"Not from the clinic?"

"No."

"And it's kept locked at night?"

"I do the lock-up myself. It's my home too, you know," Mrs Baillie gave a twisted smile and Lorimer found himself suddenly curious about the director. He inclined his head questioningly.

"My flat is upstairs. Part of my remit here is to act as a nursing director. Yes, I'm a fully qualified psychiatric nurse," she said, lifting her chin. "I run the clinic but I also have a say in the overall medical policy."

"I'm afraid we will have to interview the patients who were here last night," Lorimer told her.

Mrs Baillie hesitated then shuffled at some papers on her desk. Then she raised her head and regarded Lorimer steadily. "I'm afraid that won't be possible."

"This is a murder inquiry. The feelings of your patients simply don't come into the question."

"I hope you will respect their feelings, Chief Inspector. Many of our patients are seriously ill people and interrogation could do some of them untold damage.

"We quite understand."

"No, Chief Inspector, you don't. When I said it would be impossible to interview everybody, I meant just that," Mrs Baillie answered him defiantly. "You see, two of our patients left for respite care early this morning."

"But that's preposterous! You can't just let them walk out of here like that!"

"I didn't. In fact I took them to the airport myself."

"Where were they going?" Cameron asked.

The woman tilted her head and gave him the ghost of a smile. "Your part of the world, by the sound of it. A little place called Shawbost. It's on the Island of Lewis."

"But why on earth couldn't they stay here? And who are they anyway?" Lorimer protested.

"Sister Angelica and Samuel Fulton. Their plane tickets were paid for. And they were ready to go. I couldn't see any point in keeping them here."

For a moment Lorimer was speechless at the woman's audacity. And Lewis? Could there be some link between the victim and this respite centre?

"Give me the details of this place, please," he asked.

"Certainly," She pulled a card from a file on her desk and handed it to him.

"And, Mrs Baillie, no further patients will leave here without our knowledge. Do I make myself clear?"

"Perfectly, Chief Inspector," the woman folded her hands together meeting his angry glare with a cool gaze of her own.

Lorimer gave the card a perfunctory glance and pock-eted it. It would be counter-productive to alienate Mrs Baillie, no matter what police time she had wasted. There was Kirsty's murder to solve and she was in a position to help them.

"Kirsty MacLeod. She was a psychiatric nurse, wasn't she?"

Mrs Baillie shook her head. "Kirsty had specialised in neural disorders, Chief Inspector. Her background was Care in the Community so she had worked with many patients who had illnesses of a psychiatric nature. However, the main reason for employing her was her expe-rience with multiple sclerosis patients."

"Do you have many of those sorts of patients here?" Cameron asked.

"No, just the one. Phyllis Logan."

Lorimer nodded. Of course. That explained the woman down in that back room away from all the other patients. He recalled those bright eyes and that sepulchral moan. That was one resident who wouldn't be answering any questions.

"Isn't that rather unusual," Cameron persisted. "After all, this is a clinic specialising in psychiatric cases."

"We prefer to call them neural disorders. And MS is a neural disease," Mrs Baillie chided him. "But it's not unusual for Phyllis to be here. Not at all." She paused, glancing from one man to the other, a sudden twinkle in her eye. "You see, Phyllis Logan is the owner of the Grange. It really is her home."

11

Lorimer had to hand it to them. They'd organised the interview schedule perfectly. Alistair Wilson had taken possession of the large lounge to the front of the house that was now their incident room. The minimum disruption to patients had been Mrs Baillie's priority. He wondered about that lady: a cool customer, but there had been something in her manner that the Chief Inspector had found disquieting. Maybe she'd been in denial, but he'd found the woman's detached, clinical manner rather off-putting. He thought over their recent conversation.

"She was a capable nurse. No problem to us at all." That was how she'd answered when Lorimer had tried to elicit information about the murder victim. Not "Poor girl" or, "I can't believe this is happening" which would have been understandable under the grim circumstances. Why might Nurse Kirsty MacLeod have been a problem to the clinic anyway? Or had there been staffing problems in the past? Lorimer picked up such nuances with his policeman's ear for detail. It wouldn't be a bad idea to investigate the staffing over the past twelve months. "All of our residential patients had retired for the night. Only the night staff were on duty. I was in bed myself."

In bed, mused Lorimer, but had she been asleep? And who else might have been lying awake staring at the ceiling, counting the hours till an uncertain dawn? He'd know soon enough.

The residents were to be made available to them after breakfast. That was exactly how Mrs Baillie had put it. And this morning she had shown no trace of sorrow for the sudden death of one of her staff. Her starched white collar and black jacket bore testimony to a careful toilette. There was nothing hasty or flung together about this lady. Lorimer had stared at her earlier, mentally contrasting her with the image of his wife flying out of the house that morning, hair tousled and jacket pushed anyhow into her bulging haversack.

Dark circles showed under Maggie's lovely eyes but Lorimer wasn't about to waste too much sympathy on a self-inflicted hangover.

He'd dropped officer Lipinski at HQ for her scheduled lecture before setting off for the Grange. That was one talk he'd be missing. He grinned to himself. What a pity! The squad at Pitt Street would just have to get on with it without him. All in all, Lorimer doubted if he'd had three full hours sleep himself. Mitchison would be banging on about Working Time Regulations before he was much older.

Lorimer was sitting at a table that had been pushed up near the huge bay window that overlooked the gardens. The morning light streaming in would show Lorimer and DS Wilson the full face of whoever came to sit on the other side of that table. Each person was going to be confronted by a pair of steely blue eyes that brooked no nonsense. It was just as well that Alistair Wilson was on duty. His sergeant's knack of showing deferential politeness would be especially soothing to the damaged souls in this place.

"Ready, sir?" Wilson had brought in the file of current residents' names.

"If they've all had their breakfasts," Lorimer growled.

He hadn't even had a cup of coffee and no one seemed to be interested in offering him one. He looked at the annotated list. There were red asterisks against certain names. These belonged to residents whose rooms looked out to the front of the house. Mrs Baillie's was amongst them. Her bedroom was right above this lounge.

"Eric Fraser?" Lorimer read aloud, "Let's have him in first." The uniformed officer by the door disappeared.

"D'you want to start, Alistair?" Lorimer turned to his colleague. Wilson just smiled and shrugged. "Butter him up, you mean?" Detective Sergeant Alistair Wilson was no stranger to his superior's strategies.

The uniform returned. "Mr Fraser," he said, retreating immediately to his post by the lounge door.

Eric Fraser was a young man of medium height dressed in navy jogging pants and a matching hooded sweatshirt. As he approached, he ran one hand over his cropped bullet head and stared right at Lorimer with small, intense eyes. He hadn't shaved for days, by the look of him, and his clothes hung loosely over a thin frame.

"Mr Fraser, I'm Sergeant Wilson, and this is Chief Inspector Lorimer," Wilson had risen to his feet, come around the table and was shaking Fraser's hand. "Thank you for coming in to talk to us. Please sit down." Wilson's voice was all solicitousness. They didn't yet know the nature of these patients' illnesses. That was confidential, Mrs Baillie had insisted. "Meantime," had been Lorimer's terse reply.

"They told me about Kirsty," the young man began without any preamble. "She was nice. She listened to me. Not all of them take the time to listen," his voice held a querulous note and he looked accusingly at Lorimer although it was Wilson who'd begun the interview.

"We'd like to know if you heard anything unusual last night, Mr Fraser," Wilson spoke firmly, trying to draw the man's attention back.

Fraser made a derisory noise. "You mean all that screeching and carrying on?"

"What screeching was that, Mr Fraser?" Wilson put in. Lorimer pretended to scribble something on a pad in front of him, avoiding eye-contact.

If Wilson could capture his attention then he'd be free to observe the patient's body language. Right now he was sitting, hands clasped between his knees as if, despite the sun's heat through the glass, he was feeling cold.

"Mrs Duncan. She raised the roof with her racket. Came right up the stairs to fetch Mrs Baillie. I think anyone would've heard it through the partition walls. I certainly could."

"You don't have any sleeping medication, then, Mr Fraser?"

"Not at the moment," he replied, sitting up a bit straighter as he spoke.

Lorimer nodded to himself. A patient on his way to recovery, perhaps?

"How well did you know Nurse MacLeod?"

Fraser shrugged, crossing one leg over the other. "Not that well. She was nice. Nice-looking too. She always made sure we were comfortable at bedtime. She'd go to the bother of bringing me up a hot water bottle. That sort of thing."

"Did she ever talk about herself?"

"No. Not really. I'd asked where she was from. The accent made me curious. But she didn't really tell me much about herself." Fraser looked hard at Alistair Wilson. "We're a pretty self-absorbed lot in here, you know. Fragile psyches and all that," he sneered. Lorimer watched as his foot began to tap rapidly up and down, an involuntary movement, agitated. He wondered what the man's blood pressure would be if he had it taken right now. A worm-coloured vein on Fraser's temple stood out and Lorimer could imagine the beat of a pulse.

"Where were you last night, Mr Fraser, from midnight onwards?"

The foot tapping stopped abruptly and the man uncrossed his leg, looking towards Lorimer who had suddenly asked the question. For a moment he said nothing, simply stared at the Chief Inspector as if he had temporarily forgotten his presence.

"In bed. In my bed in my room. All night."

"And can anybody verify this?"

Fraser looked from one man to the other, bewildered at this sudden change of tack.

"I don't know. Kirsty and Mrs Duncan were the only two who would have been able to say I was in my room. They were the night staff on duty." He twisted his face into a frown. "But that's going to be the same for all of us. Except..."

He stopped, rubbing his hands up and down the thighs of his joggers.

"Except?" Lorimer prompted.

"Some patients are on suicide watch. They have nurses posted along the corridor who sit there all night."

"And you'd have had to pass them to reach the back of the clinic, I take it?"

"Yes," Fraser replied, something like relief in his face. "Yes. Any of them would have seen me if I'd passed that way."

"Mr Fraser, you've been very helpful. I'm sorry we've had to disturb you but it is important that we have some sort of input from all the people who were here last night. Do you remember anything else, perhaps? A strange sound from outside?" Wilson asked.

"No. Nothing I can remember."

"Well, if there is anything at all, please get in touch with us. We'd be most grateful for anything you might recall later," DS Wilson rose to his feet and slid a card across the table.

"That's the number to ring. We'll be issuing this to all of the staff and patients," he smiled warmly and Fraser nodded, glancing warily at Lorimer before standing up again.

"I can go now?"

"Of course, sir, and thank you once more for your co-operation," Wilson's smile was positively beatific.

"Constable, would you ask Jennifer Townslie to come in,

please?"

At last Lorimer was downing a cup of coffee. The morning had been reasonably productive. They had been able to eliminate most of the residents from their inquiries. Some, as Lorimer had suspected, had been dead to the world having been given sleeping pills. These included a few women with eating disorders who were on the upper floor. None of them were currently on suicide watch. Some of the residents were pretty frail and Lorimer knew it would have taken someone of considerable strength to attack and strangle the young nurse.

What most of them had heard amounted to very little other than the furore caused by the auxiliary, Mrs Duncan. It was time to wheel her in.

Lorimer wiped his mouth with the back of his hand. "Okay?"

Alistair Wilson gave a brief nod. They'd discussed this at some length. This was one witness whose statement would be crucial to the investigation. He just hoped she was in a better state than she'd been the previous night.

Brenda Duncan was a portly woman in her fifties. She rolled slightly as she entered the room, a thick winter coat folded clumsily over one arm, her handbag clutched in two ungloved fists. As she sank into the chair in front of him, Lorimer could see that her eyes were heavy. It didn't take much to guess that she'd been given some kind of medication after her trauma. She was smiling uncertainly and he wondered if she'd ever had to encounter the police before.

"Mrs Duncan," Wilson's voice was all concern, "thank you so much for coming back in. We realise how bad this has been for you." He gave his most encouraging smile as if to say there was nothing to worry about, they'd take care of it all. Lorimer could see the woman's shoulders visibly relax.

"Just take your time and tell us everything that happened yesterday evening."

"Well, when I found poor Kirsty…"

"No," Lorimer broke in, "before that, please. We'd like you to tell us everything that happened from the time you arrived for your shift."

"Oh." The woman looked from one of them to the other. Her mouth was open and her eyes looked vacant for a moment. Lorimer wondered just how much medication she'd been given. And by whom? a little voice asked.

The mouth closed and the jaw became firmer. Her bosom heaved in a long sigh. "I start at ten so I was here at about twenty-to. The bus drops me off at the Monument and I walk the rest of the way. It only takes about five minutes or so. The patients are usually ready for their beds although there's no strict rule. We don't put out lights or anything like that. They can sit up and watch telly if they like. Some of them don't sleep too well, either. But most of them are early bedders.

"And which ones aren't, Mrs Duncan?" Lorimer wanted to know.

"Oh," the woman looked confused as if unsure whether by imparting this information she might be implicating a patient.

"Sometimes Leigh sits up late. He likes to watch the creepy programmes." She leaned forward, speaking in a whisper of confidentiality, "I don't think he should, mind you, but that kind of thing's not my decision."

"Leigh?" Lorimer was looking down the list of patients' names.

"Leigh Quinn," Mrs Duncan supplied.

"The Irishman," Wilson added.

Lorimer nodded. Leigh Quinn had been practically non-verbal during his interview, staring out of the window mostly. Afterwards they'd decided that a good look at his casenotes would be required. The man didn't seem quite on the same planet as the other patients.

"Did you notice anything unusual during the earlier part of your shift, Mrs, Duncan?" asked Wilson.

Brenda Duncan chewed her bottom lip for a moment or

two, her eyes fixed on the bag on her lap. Then she shook her head, still gazing down as if struggling to see the events of the previous night in her mind.

"Nothing untoward, then. Just a normal night?"

The woman nodded her head.

"Where were you before you found Nurse MacLeod's body?" Wilson spoke in a matter-of-fact voice.

"Where was I?" Brenda Duncan looked flustered. "I, em, I would be…" her voice trailed off as she looked at the detective sergeant.

"Just take your time," he told her. "Try to remember your movements. What you were doing on the normal night shift."

"I suppose I'd been round the doors. They leave some doors open for the patients. The ones that need a bit of watching, you know," she whispered again. "I chatted with Peter, he's one of the nurses who sit with their patients at night. They all have designated nurses, you see," she explained, nodding to emphasise her point.

"Can you remember what you chatted about?" Wilson asked, an encouraging smile on his face.

"He was telling me about his holidays. He's just booked up a fortnight in Mallorca for himself and the family. I remember because it was such a windy night and I told him he was lucky to be getting away from all this horrible weather."

"And then?" Alistair Wilson let the question dangle in front of the woman like bait. Lorimer had been watching her face with interest. It had become more and more animated as she'd continued, almost as if she was relishing the build-up to her discovery of Kirsty's body. A dramatic event in a humdrum existence, perhaps? Sure enough there was a pause for effect and Brenda Duncan cast her eyes down. Lorimer watched her fumble in her handbag for a handkerchief. There was a loud blowing of her nose before the woman took up her story again.

"I went to make cocoa for Kirsty and me. There's a wee

kitchen through the doors from where the patients' rooms are. I was surprised when I saw Kirsty wasn't there. She should've been down from checking the upstairs rooms by then. I thought maybe she'd gone to the bathroom, but I'd have seen her going past."

"It struck you as odd?" Lorimer asked quietly, confirming the tone in the woman's voice.

She nodded, "Aye. Odd. You could say that. Anyway she didn't come back and the cocoa was getting cold so I thought I'd better go and find her. She wasn't in the loo and she wasn't in either of the residents' lounges." Brenda Duncan bit her lip. "I don't know what made me go along the back corridor. Maybe it was when the light came on."

"What light?" Lorimer demanded.

Brenda Duncan frowned. "It was funny, now I come to think of it. The back corridor light just came on. I hadn't noticed it was off until I was through the swing-doors then it just came on."

Wilson scribbled something on his notepad.

"Go on, please," Lorimer pressed her.

"I didn't see anything at first. I just walked along the corridor. It was that quiet. Then I heard a noise. A kind of scraping sound. It was the door down to the basement. Someone had left it open and it was creaking in the wind. I pushed it open and switched on the light. And then I saw her."

This time the pause was for real. Lorimer could see fear loom large in the woman's widening eyes and he could easily imagine her screams. But now her voice sank to a whisper as she stared past them.

"She was lying on her back. I thought at first she'd fallen, so I hurried down the stairs." She swallowed hard. "Then I saw it. That flower. I knew then. I just knew she was dead."

"Did you feel for a pulse?" Wilson asked.

She shook her head and Lorimer saw her eyes staring into space, mesmerised by that image fixed in her brain.

"Kirsty was dead and all I could think of was that she hadn't had her cocoa!" Brenda Duncan suddenly burst into tears. The woman PC who had accompanied her into the lounge was by her side now and looking quizzically at Lorimer for instructions. No doubt she was expecting him to terminate the interview. Spare the poor woman any further suffering. Well, that wasn't always Lorimer's way. There were still things he needed to know.

"How long was it between the time you saw Nurse MacLeod alive and the discovery of the body?" The question brought a halt to the flow of tears. There was a wiping of eyes and the WPC retreated to her post by the lounge door. Brenda Duncan looked distractedly around her for a moment.

"I'm not sure, really. I remember it was after midnight on the alarm clock in one of the rooms. I'd seen Kirsty about quarter-past eleven, maybe. She'd been writing up some paperwork before she went upstairs. I went through the front to check the rooms. I put fresh loo rolls in, give the basins a wipe, that sort of thing." She looked nervously at Lorimer. "I don't know what time it was when I made the cocoa. Not long after."

"So that was the last time you saw her alive. At approximately eleven-fifteen?"

The woman's lip trembled. "I just made her cocoa. We'd always have a blether. But she never came. She never came." Brenda Duncan clutched herself with both arms rocking back and forwards, whimpering softly.

"Thank you, Mrs Duncan." Lorimer was finished with her for the moment. He nodded to Wilson who rose and helped the woman to her feet. "If you would just follow the officer out. We have a car to take you home," Lorimer's detective sergeant reassured her. "There will be a statement to sign later on but we'll let you know about that."

"Oh, just one more thing," Lorimer's voice stopped them in their tracks. "What about the patient whose room is at the back of the nursing home?"

Brenda Duncan looked nonplussed. Then she gave a small shake of the head. "Oh. You mean Phyllis? She's an MS patient. Totally paralysed. Can't speak. Poor thing. Mrs Baillie can tell you more, I'm sure." She looked uncertainly at Lorimer then added, "Can I go now?"

"Of course. Thank you for your help."

Lorimer stood looking out as the police car drove off. She hadn't mentioned seeing to Phyllis Logan that night. Had anybody spoken to the owner of the Grange? Was she even aware that a murder had taken place under her own roof?

12

Sometimes he let his mind wander back to the time when he'd been happiest. In his memory the days were always sunny, the cloisters full of friendly shadows. The work had been hard, especially all the studying, but the compensations of having his own vocation made up for everything. There were days like today when the wind blowing from the west reminded him of the gardens with their high walls clad with espaliers and creeping vines. If he closed his eyes he was back there once more, the mumbling sound of bees as they staggered from one lavender bush to the next making his head feel drowsy. The soil had been fine and black beneath his fingernails, a joy to cultivate. And they'd been so pleased with him, hadn't they?

A cold shadow crossed his face, making him look up as the sun disappeared for some moments. The nights, too, had been his. He'd plundered the hours of darkness, his footfall a bright echo on the stones of the chapel. A candle. He remembered there had been a candle, tall, the colour of honey, its flame bent sideways by the draught of his passing. The candle had stood for a sentinel on these special nights between midnight and dawn, flickering its pinpoint lights against the metal cross that lay within the coffin.

The bodies were always carefully dressed in white robes, the faces of the deceased facing skywards. Sometimes, watching them for long hours at a time, he wondered if their eyes would open and see him staring. In dreams he saw their dead eyes glaze like pale gobs of jelly, their heads turn accusingly in his direction. Perhaps that's why he had given them the flower, to appease them, stop their looks of disdain. They seemed to know everything, to understand his innermost thoughts. He'd decided that they were dangerous, these dead people, especially the very old ones with their wrinkled flesh hanging in folds, the candle-light magnifying each crease on the tallow skin.

The first time he had placed a red flower between the praying hands the wind had sighed outside the chapel door like a benediction. Then he knew it was all right. He had a blessing. The priests had sounded their delight. Bells had rung in his honour and the clever boys had lifted him shoulder-high through the college gates. He'd been feather-light, a wisp on the air, able to float down into the coffin and embrace the cold figures lying there so stiff, so stately. Death was sweet. Couldn't they understand that? Death released them all. He released them now, these women, from their hateful lives. Better to be dead and in a clean white coffin. Clean and cool with the flicker of candle-flame.

He groaned as the pain filled his thighs. Would they never leave him alone, these waking dead? Was he burdened with this task for all eternity?

13

Number twenty-eight Murray Street was one in a row of faded red sandstone tenements, once the glory of the tobacco merchants who had helped the city to prosper, but now split into a mismatch of bedsits and small flats. Kirsty MacLeod had rented one of the basement rooms.

Lorimer had spoken to the landlady briefly on the telephone. Now their feet thudded on the uncarpeted wooden stairs that led them in a spiral down to the lower level. Lorimer took in the landlady's scuffed leather shoes and much-washed cardigan as she turned the stairs below him. Her clothes were covered in an old-fashioned overall, the kind his granny had worn to the steamie to wash the household linen, but he noticed the hem of her skirt was unravelling at the edge. Whatever rent her tenants were paying, it didn't seem to make a fortune for the woman.

"How long had Miss MacLeod been renting from you?"

"Well, let me see," the woman turned her head towards Lorimer. "She's been here about eighteen months." Lorimer caught a glimpse of tears start in her eyes. They had reached the bottom of the stairs and stopped outside a door marked 3B.

"I can't believe she's dead," her words fell in a whisper and she looked away, suddenly embarrassed at her own emotion. She fiddled with the key in the lock. Lorimer cast his eyes over the green painted walls. The place reminded him of an institution rather than a warren of bedsits, although the faint smell of joss sticks lingering in the corridor spoke of a student life he remembered well. Lorimer stood on the threshold of the room. The dark green curtains were still drawn and his eyes took a few blinks to adjust to the dim light.

"Have you been into this room since Miss MacLeod left for work on Thursday?

The landlady looked fearfully at him, shaking her frizzed grey hair.

"Oh, no, Chief Inspector. I didn't like... Well. You know. It didn't seem decent," she trailed off, her hands wringing the flowered cotton overall. She hovered in the doorway, uncertain.

"You don't need to stay if you have other things to get on with. I'll bring the keys when I'm done. All right?" His face creased into the reassuring smile that he brought out of his stock expressions for the old and vulnerable. The woman nodded and disappeared along the corridor. He waited a moment until he could hear the sound of doors banging and pots being clattered before turning into the room once more.

Kirsty MacLeod would have kept the curtains shut whenever she'd had a night shift, he told himself. Security-conscious. Even when the windows looked out onto a brick wall, he mused, leaning over a wide desk and drawing the heavy folds aside to let in the daylight. He stood with his back to the desk taking in the contents of her room.

The neatly made up bed was up against one wall, a scattering of soft toys over the pillow. Lorimer recognised a rabbit with floppy ears and a stupid grin embroidered onto its face. It was a Disney character but he couldn't remember which one. There was the usual tired-looking furniture that every city bedsit seemed to afford: dark varnished wardrobe, chest of drawers, bedside cabinet. At least they matched, he thought. A stereo system had been rigged up in one corner on top of a steel cabin trunk. Lorimer looked at the walls, expecting to see the usual wallpapering of pop posters but there was only one of a Runrig concert dating from several years back and a travel poster depicting the standing stones of Callanish.

Lorimer flicked on an angle-poise lamp that stood on the desk and gazed at the picture. The stones seemed to heave out of the Lewis earth as if they'd grown there from ancient roots. So, Kirsty had reminders of home. That was hardly surprising. Lorimer's gaze continued along the line of photo frames on the mantelpiece. There was one of a laughing girl with her arms around an older, white-haired woman. It took him a moment to realise that it was Kirsty. Images of her body sprawled across that concrete floor flicked through his brain. He'd only seen her once, dead at the Grange. This was a younger, carefree teenager and the old lady might be a relative, the aunt, he thought, taking in the background of hills and sea. The other photos included one of her graduation, a close up of a collie dog, its tongue lolling, and an old black and white photograph of a man and woman outside a cottage. Her parents, probably. No young men were included in the line-up. A surprise, really, given that she'd been such a pretty girl.

An empty coat hanger swung from a discoloured brass hook on the back of the door. Her personal clothing had been taken from the nursing home to forensics for examination. Lorimer turned suddenly at the noise of a bluebottle buzzing at the closed window. It heightened his awareness of the silence in the room. No hands would come to switch on the stereo. Nobody would sing a Gaelic song as they tidied or made up the single bed. There was a feeling of utter emptiness, as if the room itself knew that Kirsty was never coming back. Remembering the landlady, Lorimer supposed that another tenant would eventually move in. He sighed, shoving his hands into his pockets. Life went on. It had to. Someone would come to take the girl's personal effects away later in the day. More forensics. More grief for the relatives, wherever they were. For now

Lorimer had to gauge the sort of girl Kirsty had been and hopefully find some helpful documentation. A neat, tidy person; from the look of the room, she would have her paperwork somewhere to hand, collated and sorted.

The desk drawer was the obvious place and Lorimer was not disappointed. A red leather five-year diary sat on top of a sheaf of papers. He rustled through them. Payslips were clipped together, a plastic bag contained a pile of receipts and a guarantee for the stereo. Bank statements lay in order in a blue ring binder. Lorimer flicked through them. Nothing obviously wrong there. A floral paper file held letters with a Lewis postmark. It would all have to be taken away for close perusal. Suddenly it all seemed so intrusive to Lorimer. It didn't stop with the killing. Even after death, the girl's private life had to be dissected as thoroughly as her cold corpse.

His fingertips brushed against a small, metal object in a corner of the drawer and Lorimer pushed it into sight. It was a tiny key. Lorimer picked it up. Her key to the diary, surely? He fitted it into the lock and turned. The red book sprung open as if someone had breathed life into its pages. Flicking from the back, Lorimer noticed that the diary had spanned all of the last five years, its tightly written pages giving details of Kirsty's life.

The final entry had been 31 December last year. Starting at the top of that page he read of five different sorts of Hogmanays.

1999 Ceilidh at the Halls. Didn't get in till after two. What a night!!!!

2000 Working tonight. Watched the Rev. I. M. Jolly on TV. A good laugh. Wish Aunty Mhairi had the phone.

2001 George Square for the bells. Millions of mad folk but it was great fun. Bitter cold. Went to someone's party in Hyndland afterwards.

2002 Great to be home. Chrissie and I stayed in with Mhairi as she had a bad cold.Loads ofneighbours came in after the bells. Malcolm's black bun went down a treat.

2003 Last New Year in Glasgow. Hope next year brings better luck.

Lorimer gritted his teeth. What bloody irony. All this year had brought her was a grisly death at the hands of some lunatic. He glanced over the five entries again, turning back to confirm his first impressions. Yes, she'd been back to Harris twice in those five years. Had she intended to go back for good? *Last year in Glasgow.* What had her plans been for the future? And with whom? Who was Malcolm?

He flicked back through the pages until the diary fell open of its own accord. Lorimer frowned. Cut neatly out of the centre of the little book were several pages, the remaining thatch of paper left to prevent the diary falling apart at its stitched seam. What had taken place to make Kirsty MacLeod obliterate several weeks out of a record of her life? And in which year had this event happened? A love affair gone wrong? Something so embarrassing that she couldn't bear to re-read it in the following years? Lorimer closed the diary, weighing it in his hand. He'd have to read the whole thing. Then ask even more questions. Slipping the diary into his pocket, Lorimer let his eyes rove around the room once more.

He'd had enough. The place gave him an impression of girlish innocence, of a Kirsty MacLeod who was doing her best to survive in this alien environment. As he looked again at the picture of the standing stones, Lorimer couldn't help feeling that the nurse would have gone back to the islands eventually.

He turned on his heel. The boys would be back later to strip the place. For now, all Lorimer wanted was to leave the airless room to the fly trapped against the dusty windowpane.

14

Glasgow University sat high above the west end of the city on Gilmour Hill, its spiked spire a landmark for miles around. To the south it overlooked the Art Galleries and the river Clyde beyond. That particular morning Tom Coutts felt real pleasure in the view.

"Makes you feel good, doesn't it?" he smiled at Solomon. They were sitting on a wooden bench by a strip of grass, warmed by unexpected sunshine.

Solly smiled back. Tom hadn't looked as relaxed as this for a long time. He nodded at his companion.

"Coming back into work soon, then?"

Tom sighed. "I hope so. They tell me I've done well, whatever that means. Thought I knew all the psychobabble but it's different when you're on the receiving end," he grinned wryly. "But I can't fault them. Okay, it's taken a while and you must be fed up with all the extra marking. Sorry about that," he added. "Still, I feel better than I've felt in ages. And this helps," he spread a hand over the banks of primulas spreading down towards Kelvin Way.

"I wanted to ask you something, Tom. About the clinic."

"They using you as their profiler, are they? Good. I'm glad," Tom Coutts nodded approvingly.

"I know DCI Lorimer's spoken to you about the victim. Must have been hard when she was Nan's nurse."

"One of Nan's nurses," Tom corrected him gently. "Yes.

It was a shock. I'd only seen her a few days before the murder. Hadn't even realised she worked there. But then I didn't keep in touch with any of them after the funeral."

"I wondered if you would help me. Give me some information about the clinic. From an insider's viewpoint, as it were."

"Listen, I'd be glad to. You've no idea how grateful I've been for all your help, Solly. Anything I can tell you, anything at all that might help build up a decent picture for you." Tom laid a hand on Solly's arm as he spoke. "Mind you, I can't fault the clinic. The therapists were very professional. I thought the place seemed well run."

"How about the other patients?"

Tom grinned. "Aha! Run into a problem over patient confidentiality, have you?"

"Something like that," Solly replied blandly. Mrs Baillie had not been pleased at having to give her patient files to the police. She would be even less inclined to co-operate with a civilian, he thought.

"Want to give me a grilling before I go up to Lewis?"

"Lewis?"

Tom inclined his head. "Didn't you know? They've got a respite centre on the island. Most of the longer term patients have a chance to go up there for a break at the end of their treatment. I was offered the chance and I thought, well, why not. A few days with some clean air can only help. Then I'll be ready for work again."

Solomon shook his head. A respite centre. On Lewis? He wondered if Lorimer had any inkling of this. Kirsty MacLeod came from Lewis. This was an element that kept coming into the equation. A coincidence? Or was there something more sinister going on that they'd all missed?

"Tell me a bit about the patients you met during your therapy sessions."

"What's there to tell? These are folk who are part of a system, Solly. They're more a danger to themselves than to anyone else. It's the loose cannon you're looking for. The one who's never seen his G.P. The one everyone sees as normal. *You* know that." Tom drew him a disapproving look.

Solly nodded and shrugged. "Perhaps. But just indulge me for a little. Tell me about the patients who were in your group."

Tom took a deep breath. "Well. They weren't the same for a start. I can remember one or two who came after I started, but to be honest I don't have a lot of memory about who was there at the beginning of my treatment. Except the long termers, the residents."

Solomon crossed one leg over the other, listening but not interrupting.

"The Irish chap, Leigh, he's been there all along. Eric came a couple of months back. Then there was an older man called Sam something. He'd been a shipyard worker. And the nun, of course. She's been there for ages. How she can afford it, goodness knows. I thought they took a vow of poverty and that place doesn't come cheap. Even with medical insurance."

"The nun. What was her name?"

"Sister Angelica. Poor soul. She'd been displaced from her last convent when it was closed down. Had lived there all her professional life, I believe. She simply couldn't come to terms with any change." Tom turned to Solly, his eyes suddenly hard. "Bereaved, really. Like me," he added. "People tell you to pull yourself together, you know. Think time will help, as if grieving should be contained in a respectable amount of time: so many months and no longer. It's not like that, though. Not for some of us. Sister Angelica suffered from manic depression. She'd come into the Grange after an attempted suicide."

"When was this?"

Tom shrugged. "Don't know. She was there when I started the sessions and she's still there, as far as I know."

"Do you remember any of the patients who were given the chance to go to Lewis?"

"No. You see, the make-up of the group changes so much from week to week. There were the ones, like me, who came in as out-patients and then there were the residents."

"But some of the residents would continue as out-patients for a while, surely?"

Tom frowned. "Yes, I suppose so, but you'd really need to check with the Baillie woman. She'll have all that sort of thing in her files. Cathy, the girl on reception might be a better bet, mind you," he grinned conspiratorially at Solly.

"Thanks, Tom. Would you do me another favour?"

"Surely. Anything I can."

"Would you mind writing down everything you can remember about the residents in your therapy group? It might help me."

"Of course," Tom patted his arm. "In fact I'll get on with that right away." He rose from the bench and flexed his shoulders. "Getting too old for sitting on park benches," he laughed. "Good hunting, Solly."

Solomon stood on the platform of the bus, gripping the rail as it braked to a halt. The bus had taken him from University Avenue all the way over to the south side of the city. Now, according to his A to Z, there was only a short walk to the Grange. His mind was still buzzing with last night's marking load. Final year exams were a headache for all the staff at this time of year and Solly found it one of the few times when he had to struggle to clear his mind and focus on other things. They were such a vulnerable lot, his students, under their guise of bravado. One girl in particular, bright, feisty and chasing a First for all her worth, seemed to have cracked under the strain. The psychologist had been saddened to read her scripts full of generalisations and glossed-over statistics. Hannah was so much better than her results would suggest. The girl was one of a group who had failed to come to his exam preparation classes earlier in their course, he remembered now. Solly always made it his duty to give every student a chance to find out about the psychology of exam preparation. It had so much more to do with strategies and mental attitude than sitting up burning the midnight oil. Still, there were some kids, like Hannah, who would never be convinced.

Dismissing students from his mind, Solomon recalled the file on Kirsty MacLeod. His present remit was to the dead rather than to the living.

The road to the clinic ran slightly uphill and the pavements were narrow on either side of the road where, as Lorimer had told him, there was extensive double parking. Even during the day, thought Solly. Perhaps a fair proportion of the residents were retired? An interesting thought. Would there be more eyes to see during the daytime? The psychologist had a list of local people who had been interviewed in the house-to-house enquiries following Kirsty MacLeod's murder. These were so time-consuming for the police whose resources were often stretched to breaking point anyway.

Solomon stopped at the brow of the hill. The red sandstone tenements petered out here, giving way to a few solid Victorian villas at the end of the cul-de-sac. The Grange was just one of those that had undergone extensive renovation. Most had been divided into residential flats, a more marketable proposition these days, and certainly a saving on Community Charges. Opposite the Grange two houses had been given quite different makeovers, however. What at first appeared to be a large family home was in fact a dental surgery. Next door to that was a pub, the sort that could be found in any town the length and breadth of Britain. There was a poster outside advertising the weekly events along with its chips-with-everything bar menu. The psychologist crossed the road towards the surgery, noting the house name, Palmyra, still engraved in faded gold over the glass lintel. Standing back, he could see several cars nosing around the back of the building. The front gateway was only wide enough to admit pedestrians so there must be another entrance to the driveway, Solly thought, his feet taking him round the side of the old house.

There were four cars parked: two were BMWs with this year's registration and one was a classic Jaguar, its racing green bodywork sleek and polished. Dentistry was paying well in this part of the world, if appearances were to be believed, Solly smiled to himself. The fourth car was a Vauxhall, K656 BLS. He made a note of all their numbers, telling himself that Lorimer's team had probably covered just such details already. He was aware of the need to tread carefully. There was no reason to fracture the relationship between the DCI and himself. What really interested him, though, was how the cars had come into the parking area. Sure enough there was a double wooden gate that had been fixed into the high stone walls. No moss was clinging to the stone posts either side of the gate, unlike the furred surface along the older section of the wall, suggesting that the entrance had been constructed in recent years. On closer inspection Solly could see trails of purple toadflax growing out of the crevices between the pitted stonework. The gate itself was a solid affair of thick timber, dark with creosote that had not yet weathered. He gave the latch a push and found himself in a cobbled lane running down the length of the street.

Solly shut the gate behind him. There was no sign of a padlock although there was a hasp attached to the left gate. He fingered the metal loop, checking for fresh scratches that might show if a padlock had been taken off recently. There were none that he could see. Did that suggest a laxity in the dentists' security? Or was this a fairly low risk area? Solomon decided to walk back down the lane rather than retrace his steps through the grounds of the surgery.

Looking up and down he could see the black shapes of wheelie bins all along one side of the lane. A bin lorry could manoeuvre its way up here, then. The lane wasn't as narrow as it seemed. Solomon looked again at the wooden gates. Had the killer opened them and simply parked his car in the empty driveway, leaving quietly from the back lane? Was that a possibility Lorimer had considered? The wall ran all the way back down to the main road so Solomon headed towards the last building on the street.

At one time it may have resembled its neighbour but now several ramshackle extensions had transformed the house into a mock Tudor pub. The roof still had the same grey Welsh slate but there the similarity ended, the building having spawned a series of flat-topped, concrete extensions that almost reached the perimeter wall. Here, too, there was a back entrance, but this was a high narrow green door. Solomon tried turning the round handle but it was locked fast. There was no other exit that he could see. With a small sigh, he headed back to the surgery gate and slipped into the grounds. There was nothing to be gained from walking all the way back down the lane and up the road again.

As he made for the front gate, the door to the surgery opened and a woman appeared, buttoning her raincoat as she emerged. Solomon gave her his usual benign smile but she merely stared for a moment at him before crossing the road to the Grange. He watched her walk up the driveway until she was hidden from sight by the rhododendron bushes.

Solomon stood for a few minutes just outside the gate. From here the upper windows of the clinic were visible. Anyone standing at those windows could see into the grounds of the dental surgery, Solomon's logical voice reasoned. It was time to have a look around the Grange itself. He rubbed his hands together. The residents might prove to be quite fascinating.

Rosie washed her hands, noting where the sweat from her surgical gloves had left pink tinges along the palms. She dried them thoroughly on the paper towel then pressed the lever on the industrial-sized hand cream dispenser that sat over the basin. It was a routine she followed religiously after a PM. Your hands are your primary tools, she often told her students. The girls were the ones who usually followed her advice. It wasn't a very macho thing for the boys to rub hand cream into their fingers. Body-piercing, dreadlocks, they were quite the thing, but hand cream?

Rosie smiled as she thought of her conversation with Solly on the subject. He'd made her laugh with his acute perception of their attention-grabbing strategies, showing her, even as he gently mocked their outward appearances, how sensitive he was to the students' underlying vulnerability. At the time Rosie had found herself thinking what a great father Solomon Brightman would make. She had been immediately appalled at herself for the thought. Was she becoming broody or what?

Solomon was going to see the people at the Grange today, he'd told her. She'd likely see him in the staff club just around teatime. Sometimes she'd have a quick orange juice as she scanned the room for her dark, bearded friend. Other times he'd be there ahead of her reading the papers in what had become their favourite corner. Funny how he was a creature of habit in some ways when he was so unpredictable most of the time. They'd discussed the two murders, Rosie offering her professional opinion but sparing him the grislier pathological details when she remembered. Solly had a delicate stomach for such things. The pathologist usually delighted in tormenting lay people with the finer points of her post mortems but she'd made an exception with Solly.

Lorimer had teased her about their relationship. She was fairly sure Solly found her attractive. He had invited her down to London for his sister's wedding, hadn't he? They'd had a great time. He'd been so attentive, showing her all the traditions surrounding a Jewish wedding to make her feel at ease. And afterwards they'd danced and laughed all night. Lorimer was no fool. She fancied Solly like crazy. It had taken all her powers of concentration to keep her hands on the steering wheel as they'd driven back up north. But Solly? Just how did he really feel about her?

Rosie looked in the mirror above the basin. She pushed

her fingers through her blonde hair. There were a few wee laughter lines around the eyes but it wasn't a bad face, she told herself. No need for the Botox just yet. Maggie Lorimer always joked that Rosie was the other woman in her husband's life. That was just Maggie's way, though. The older woman was given to flattery. Rosie stuck out her tongue at the face in the mirror and turned away. Poor Maggie. She didn't have much fun with Lorimer working all the hours that his job demanded. Maybe she could suggest a night out. A foursome. Cheered by the idea, Rosie whistled to herself as she came out into the corridor of the mortuary. A shelf full of white skulls grinned down from above as if sharing in her good humour.

Alice paused from cleaning the bathroom windows as she looked down on the figure below. From her vantage point high above the grounds of the clinic she could see him wandering slowly towards the back of the building as if he was looking for something. She gave the window a push outwards so that her cloth could reach the fixed pane in the middle. But she couldn't take her eyes off the stranger.

"Hey, Nellie," she called back into the room. "C'mere an' see this. This one doesnae look like polis, does he?" she asked as a thickset woman in green overalls pushed her way towards the open bathroom window. Together they stared at the figure below them. As if sensing he was being watched, the man turned and looked up at the two cleaners.

"Naw, he isnae polis," Nellie decided. "Looks mair like a foreigner tae me, hen."

"Whit's he doin' moochin aroon' here, well?"

Nellie shrugged. It was none of her business. She hadn't liked being questioned by that wee slip of a polis wumman. But still an' all, there wis a murderer on the loose.

"Ach, I suppose we'd better tell Mrs Baillie," she decided.

Alice screwed her face up. "Gonnae you go, eh, Nellie? Ah don't like."

Nellie grinned. "Feart of her are ye?" Seeing Alice's weak grin, the older cleaner stuffed her cloth into the pocket of her overalls and turned to leave."Ach, a'right. But keep an eye on whatshisface, okay?"

"Aye. Thanks, Nellie. Yer a pal."

Down below, aware of the slight interest he had created, Solomon turned back towards the front door. He would have to request permission now to walk about the grounds. A pity. He'd liked to have wandered around the back of the building free from any prying eyes. He looked up at the name carved out of the keystone above the main door. *The Grange* were the only visible words, there was no brass plate to intimidate the patients with the idea of a clinic for neural disorders. In fact, it was more like coming to a private residence. That was probably the whole idea, he told himself.

Solomon stood on a tiled porch beyond the open storm doors trying to peer through the frosted glass. The security panel to the right of the door showed five buttons. Five numbers to be memorised. Solomon wondered how often they were altered, how they were chosen and by whom. He heard the sound of feet approaching, then a blurred shadow opened the door to him.

"Dr Brightman? We were expecting you. I'm Mrs Baillie. Won't you come in." As the director of the clinic held open the door, Solomon's first impression was of a woman who'd had too little sleep for too long. She looked as if she were holding herself together by sheer strength of will.

"Actually I'd like to look around the grounds. Especially at the back of the building," Solly explained in his gentlest voice. "Would that be all right, Mrs Baillie?" He could see the relief in the woman's body as she nodded.

"Will you need me after that, Dr Brightman?" she asked, then seemed to hesitate before adding, "I have an appointment in town."

"If I might just have your permission to stroll around? It helps to form an impression of what may have happened that night."

"Of course. Ellie Pearson will be here to show you the layout of the Grange. She's our most senior member of staff."

The woman's voice had become more brisk, as if she resented Solly's deference. As the door closed behind her Solly wondered what sort of a strain it must be to run a clinic of this sort where one of your staff had been murdered.

At the back of the building a high wall ran the length of the grounds. Thick rhododendrons divided the Grange's gardens from those properties on either side. Solomon imagined the closed-in aspect of the grounds had been simply to maintain privacy whenever the house had been a private dwelling. Now it took on another aspect. As he gazed around he could see that there was little chance of escape for anyone who wanted to make a secret getaway. And that included the residential patients themselves. They had to have a certain amount of security, Solly told himself, remembering the panel on the front door. There was a responsibility to care for fragile people here, some of whom were being protected from themselves. How, then, had the killer made his way in and out of the house when there were such watchful eyes among the staff? The only conclusion he could come to was that the killer had been inside the clinic from the start. That's what Lorimer had suggested. One of the patients might be the self-same killer that had strangled Deirdre McCann. They were trying to obtain permission to take forensic samples right now. Adhering to Human Rights legislation held up the process considerably, he knew, making officers like DCI Lorimer champ at the bit.

So far medical staff, auxiliaries, cleaners and odd-job men had all been questioned along with the more lucid patients. Even their friends and families were coming under Lorimer's scrutiny. There was nothing to indicate an escape route for a killer coming out of this area unless he had been a pole-vaulter. The wall behind him was easily twelve feet high and the bushes seemed quite impenetrable. No, the killer must have taken the route across the road, possibly through the dentists' car park and out into that back lane. Or, a little voice reasoned, he'd simply stayed inside the clinic, going about his normal night-time activities. His or hers.

Nothing was even clear about that, although Rosie had voiced her opinion that it probably had been a man who'd taken the lives of the two women. Strangulation had been exacted with considerable force. But, Solly had argued, many of the nursing staff were females used to hard manual work. Nursing was a pretty physical occupation after all, even in a private clinic like this one.

As he stood looking at the basement door he knew there would have to be much more data before he could create any sort of profile. The signature of the praying hands with the flower conjured up a picture of a person who had remorse for his actions. Was the killing a compulsion motivated by some deep-seated problem in his past? Something that therapy had failed to resolve? Solly looked from the basement door back towards the street. Opportunity might be a starting point but it only led him back to the clinic itself. Clasping his hands behind his back, Solomon walked thoughtfully round the far side of the building. His shoes crunched on the pale golden gravel that served as a pathway. Was that another form of security? Did the staff listen for wayward feet outside the walls of the clinic? The killer had opened the basement door and left it swinging in the wind that night. But where had he gone afterwards? That was a puzzle indeed.

"Dr Brightman? Mrs Baillie's gone out but she said you could stay as long as you needed," Ellie Pearson told him.

She looked at him uncertainly as if this exotic-looking man were not to be trusted and that the director was slightly crazy in letting him loose among their patients. Her white slacks and short-sleeved tunic gave the woman an extra air of briskness. Round her neck dangled a pair of half-moon spectacles. The woman was probably about his own age, Solly guessed.

There was something intimidating about medical personnel in uniform, Solly mused. Not that he could be easily intimidated. Such observations impinged on his consciousness without making him react to them in the slightest.

"Thank you. I have a note of the clinic's layout somewhere." He searched in several pockets before drawing out a much-folded piece of paper.

"Here we are. So I won't need to keep you from your duties, Sister," he added, nodding wisely at the name badge on the woman's chest. He turned slightly away from her and opened the makeshift map. There were red highlights showing the basement and related areas. To reach these he would have to pass the residents' main lounge and the long corridor where their downstairs rooms were located. Through an open door to his right he saw Sister Pearson making for a staircase. He looked back at the plan. That led to Mrs Baillie's own apartment. What else might be up there? Anyhow, she seemed to be satisfied that the psychologist could be left to his own devices. Perhaps they'd become inured to strangers crawling all over the place since Kirsty MacLeod's murder. Just as the thought came to him, Solomon was aware of an emaciated figure shuffling out of a nearby room on his left, pushing a zimmer frame in front of her. His heart sank as he took in the woman's face with its cadaverous hollows. She wasn't old at all, but wracked with whatever eating disorder had ruined her body. She stopped and looked up at him as Solomon drew level with her.

"Good morning," he smiled politely, giving a nod in her direction. The woman smiled back at him showing red exposed gums. At least her hair showed some signs of care, a shiny grip held its wispy strands back tidily from her brow. China blue eyes regarded him hopefully for a moment then looked away as if failing to find the face that they sought.

As Solomon passed her by, he noticed her hands clutching the zimmer's metal rail. Despite the blue veins standing up on her hands, the fingernails were trimmed and polished. There were some signs of care here, at any rate, thought Solly. Some attractive prints on the wall, bright pastel scenes of Tuscany depicting gardens and arbours. Restful, he mused, good choices for a place like this. Somebody had put plenty of thought into the details and Solomon was impressed.

The corridor came to an end with double doors that swung away from him automatically and Solomon stepped into an area that had the unmistakeable smell of a hospital. His map wasn't needed here. There were signs on the walls indicating an upper level of residents' accommodation and another door marked Staff Only. There was no window on either side of the corridor, the only light coming from overhead strips that glared down on the pale linoleum flooring. A door to one side was slightly ajar. Remembering Lorimer's description of the multiple sclerosis patient, Solly paused. Whoever had killed Kirsty MacLeod had passed by just here. There was a faint mechanical sound from within but nothing more. Not wishing to disturb the patient, Solly crept past quietly. Beyond the stairs was the door leading to the basement. He pushed it open.

Rosie had described exactly where the murder had taken place. The floor was clean now, but there was a red cross on the paper that showed the spot where they thought Kirsty MacLeod had been killed. Solomon stood looking back down the corridor. The swing doors would have muffled any sound the girl might have made. Only one person could have heard her had she cried out. Once more he looked towards the room where a woman lay wasting away with that awful disease. She was completely paralysed, Lorimer had told him, and had no power of speech. No threat to a killer, then.

The basement door creaked as Solly turned the handle. Darkness met his gaze and he fumbled for the light switch as his eyes adjusted to the gloom. Only the first few steps were visible. His hand felt the switch yet he resisted the instinct to flood the place with light, trying instead to see through the shadows; trying indeed to imagine what the killer would have seen. Had he thrust the young nurse's body down the steep flight of steps? There would have been a thud as her corpse hit the concrete floor below. Or had he dragged her step by painstaking step into the boiler room?

Solomon tried each idea on for size. The victim's tights had been ripped, suggesting she'd been pulled rather than pushed. But if she'd been dead, the weight would have been considerable even to drag downwards. As his eyes became accustomed to the dark, Solly counted the seventeen metal steps that separated the boiler room from the upper floors of the Grange. Perhaps he'd pulled her down the first few steps where definite traces of fabric had been found. The door opened outwards so there would not have been so much effort needed to manoeuvre a body through in the first place. Had he given up after the first few steps before sending her corpse tumbling down? Had something panicked him? He must have made sure she was dead.

Forensics found nothing to suggest that he had interfered with the body. His only need had been to pull her hands flat together and then add his final touch, the red carnation.

Solly switched on the light and the room below was suddenly visible. It was smaller than he had thought it would be with its fluorescent strip hanging on a long wire suspended from a fitting on the ceiling. The wire had been looped and fastened to one side, presumably as an aid to changing the light fitting.

"How many psychologists does it take to change a light-bulb?" Rosie had teased him. Her voice came unbidden into his mind. He was suddenly very aware of her presence there in that basement room where she had examined the young nurse's body. Solly had seen her at scenes of crime before and marvelled at her clinical, detached manner. He stared down into the basement room. Had the killer walked calmly out of the back door, stepping over the girl's dead body? Had there been a quickening of his pulse as he'd climbed the stairs out into the back gardens, escaping from the sight behind him? Or was there another explanation altogether that involved someone staying behind in the Grange? And Brenda Duncan had come on the scene so soon after that, hadn't she?

Solly stroked his beard thoughtfully. Whatever scenario he came up with, one thing stood out clearly: it had taken a very cool and determined person to carry out this attack. Whoever had planned this had expected to get away with it. They'd known the layout of the clinic and had knowledge of where the nurses would be on duty. Or had they? Was this just a random stranger killing after all? Solomon closed his eyes. Had the killer known about the MS patient, too? Try as he might his vision of this killer was of a figure that had disappeared back into the labyrinth of doors and corridors, a killer who had brought a red carnation for a pretty lady.

He would have to seek plenty more information before the vision took on flesh and bones but for now he had the sense that creating this profile was going to take all his time and energy.

15

The boat from Uig was always on time, the man at the pier assured them. Lorimer, wrapped in his winter jacket, hoped fervently that he was right. Solly stood near the edge of the metal ramp looking out over the choppy grey water, his long black coat flapping round his legs. Even his beard had lifted in the wind, making the psychologist look like one of the ancient patriarchs.

They had travelled up early that morning, Lorimer doing all the driving. Solly didn't drive, never had and claimed it was something he could happily do without. He'd certainly enjoyed the trip though, gazing out of the window and commenting on all that he saw on the way up. It had been Lorimer's idea for them to make the journey together. Almost a week had passed since Kirsty MacLeod's body had been found in that dingy basement. Forensic reports showed that strangulation had probably taken place in the clinic's corridor. The body had been dragged through the clinic to the basement door then halfway down the stairs. It appeared that the killer had then flung Kirsty away from him, making her land flat on her back on the cold concrete. That much they did know. What had happened next was a matter of conjecture, though Solomon had been inclined to think the killer might have remained inside, despite the open door.

A huge file of statements from staff, residents and

anyone who had known the young nurse had accumulated back at the Division. Yet Lorimer was troubled by how few people there seemed to be who had known the girl intimately. It was almost as if she'd deliberately kept a low profile. Or perhaps her friends just weren't willing to talk for some reason.

The landlady hadn't had much to offer apart from the fact that the rent was always paid on time and she'd been a quiet girl. No one in the neighbouring bedsits had offered more than that. It was Dr Tom Coutts who had been most helpful. He'd seen Kirsty MacLeod a few days prior to the killing and gave the police a fair amount of background information. She'd been one of the community nurses who'd cared for his wife up until her death last year and Tom had only charitable things to say about the young woman from Harris. She'd been a caring, compassionate person, he'd told them. Had the knack of making Nan feel better just by being there beside her. They'd followed this up with visits to the other community nurses and heard the same story of a nurse who'd had a proper vocation. All the residents at the Grange had liked her. She'd been a good listener, Eric Fraser had told them.

There was an old aunt, Kirsty's only living relative, whom they would interview, but the main spur behind this journey was the revelation about the respite centre, Failte. Mrs Baillie had been strangely reticent about its existence and quite unrepentant about letting her two patients be transferred there the day after Kirsty's death. One was Sister Angelica, the nun, and the other was a man called Sam Fulton. Both patients had been in Tom Coutts' cognitive therapy classes. DC Cameron had raised an eyebrow when he'd been told that the DCI was heading for Lewis and Harris.

He could have dispatched one of his junior officers but there was something that he wanted to see for himself up here. This respite home was a sanctuary of sorts. And right now it was sheltering two people who had suddenly disappeared following Kirsty's murder. Samuel Fulton's name had come up on the police computer. His record showed an involvement in two domestic incidents. There had been more, according to the file but previous charges had been dropped until he'd broken his wife's arm. A man with a record of violence being quietly shipped up to the Hebrides at the outset of a murder inquiry did not rest easily with Lorimer. The significance of the other patient being a nun was not lost on him either. Those praying hands on each of the two victims might have emanated from some twisted religious brain. And Harris and Lewis were famous for religious piety. Looking into the water, Lorimer wondered what these islands were like. He would be there soon enough.

The journey up from Glasgow had taken more than six hours. Lorimer had pushed on through Rannoch Moor, a strange, bleak landscape that never failed to conjure up the blasted heath of *Macbeth*'s three witches, he told Solly, who'd nodded wisely. Glencoe had shown its usual dark brooding shadows but the sun had appeared briefly on the Commando Memorial at Spean Bridge as Ben Nevis lowered through a covering of cloud, snow still visible on its higher slopes.

"I'm ashamed to say I've never been further north than Loch Lomond," Solly had told him as they drove past loch after loch on the way to Skye. Lorimer had slowed down at Eilean Donan, letting Solly have an eyeful of the well-photographed castle out on its peninsula. Lorimer had been polite about it but that was all. There were some tourist spots for which he couldn't muster up much enthusiasm. The quiet and lonesome places like Rannoch and Glencoe held more real magic for him. He'd hoped to show Solly the Cuillin but the journey from the Skye bridge north to Uig was a disappointment. Mist had covered the mountains and there was hardly anything to see save the hunched, damp shapes of sheep at the roadside.

They'd driven through Broadford on the road north and

now here they were at Uig, waiting for the boat that would take them across to Harris. At least the rain was off, thought Lorimer, clapping his hands against the arms of his jacket to keep warm.

Solly had given up his post by the water's edge and was slowly walking towards him.

"Any sign of it yet?" Lorimer asked him.

"Just coming in, now."

Lorimer walked further down the pier, glancing over the concrete wall. There it was, Caledonia MacBrayne's ferry. *The Hebrides*, the man at the ticket office had told them. The car ferry cut a swathe of white foam from her bows as she neared them. She was making good speed and Lorimer wondered if she'd overshoot the pier. Solly and he quickened their pace as they walked the length of the pier back towards the parked cars. In a matter of minutes the boat had moored, disgorged its passengers and Lorimer was driving into the bowels of the car deck. By the time they'd collected jackets and locked the vehicle, *The Hebrides* was sliding through the waves once more.

"Look, I know it's cold, but how about coming up on deck?" Lorimer asked. Solly nodded cheerfully enough but pulled up his collar as they ascended the narrow metal staircase. The wind hit them full on the face as Lorimer opened the door to the upper deck. But the DCI didn't care. There was an hour and a half of sailing before they reached their destination and he wasn't about to spend it sitting in a smoke-filled bar.

"Is that your famous Cuillin, then?" Solly asked, pointing to the flat-topped hills rising above the mist.

"No. They're MacLeod's Tables. We couldn't see the Cuillin from here anyway, even if the weather had been any good," Lorimer told him, watching as the huge hills reared their heads above Skye, as if mocking their departure.

"Still, you've seen some of Skye's mountains."

"They're amazing!" Solly stared as the hills receded

from them.

Lorimer was gratified as Solly exclaimed his delight. There was something childlike about his enthusiasm. They stood huddled together on the top deck, the sea breeze whipping across their faces, watching as Skye faded into the distance, a tumble of clouds obscuring its contours.

For a while there was only a large expanse of moving water, then a group of islands came into view.

"What are they?" Solomon wanted to know.

"Think that's the Sheant Isles," Lorimer replied, trying to recall the OS map he'd pored over the previous night.

A smoky green horizon unfolded as the light played over the contours and curves of the landscape. Then the shadows deepened and became the hills of South Harris.

A lighthouse stood bravely amongst a cluster of black rocks, dazzling in the spring sunlight. Somewhere, Lorimer had read, these southerly shores boasted miles of deserted, white sandy beaches. Now he could make out a rocky shore with dots of white here and there along the coastline. As they drew nearer the dots became small houses.

"What's that?" Solly asked, pointing into the waters ahead. Lorimer followed his gaze. Orange marker buoys bobbed up and down quite far from the shore; too far for an anchorage.

"Creels, I think," Lorimer answered. "They're probably floats to show where the lobster creels are kept."

The boat rounded the rocks and suddenly they were coming inshore to what appeared to be a tiny hamlet. This couldn't be Tarbert, the largest town in Harris, surely? Lorimer looked over the harbour. The colours seemed to have been washed with a different sort of rain from the slate grey stuff that fell on his city. Or was it the light? It was as though everything was being magnified. Details were sharper, like the cluster of men in orange jackets who were working on the pier; uncoiling the thick mooring ropes, pulling the gangway into position, standing by the few motorists who were about to leave those shores. A knot of people stood around the edge of the pier waiting for the boat, but not passengers. He could see that. Waiting for the mail, perhaps?

There were women whose heads were wrapped in scarves and men in flat tweed caps. Bunnets. His dad had worn a bunnet, Lorimer remembered. He had a sudden vision of that tall, spare figure doffing his tweed cap to any ladies passing by; a gesture from a bygone age. Would Harris have retained any of the dignity of yesteryear or would it be just like everywhere else, in pursuit of the latest trends?

Lorimer's reminiscing came to an abrupt halt as a voice called over the loudspeaker system.

"We are approaching Tarbert. Would all drivers please return to their vehicles. Thank you." The voice was taped, of that Lorimer had no doubt, but it had a soft melodious quality that he recognised. It sounded just like Niall Cameron.

They made their way down the very steep staircase leading to the car deck and located the Lexus wedged between a British telecom van and an ancient Ford Transit. Two men in overalls and thicksoled boots were squeezing their way amongst the vehicles.

As they passed, one of them nodded briefly, saying, "Aye, aye. Grand day," as if he were exchanging pleasantries with old friends, instead of total strangers. Solomon gave Lorimer a meaningful look. This was certainly a world away from their city streets.

Then they were inside the car and all around them engines were roaring into life in the bowels of *The Hebrides*. There was the unmistakeable sound of wood against steel as the boat docked and Lorimer waited impatiently for the moment when he could surface again. If there was one thing that made him uneasy it was being locked in below water level like this. Maggie even teased him for his dislike of war films depicting life in a sub.

At last it was his turn. As Lorimer accelerated off the

metal ramp and onto the safety of the Tarbert streets he glanced at Solly and smiled indulgently, noticing how he twisted around to catch a glimpse of the tiny shops and houses as they passed out of town. The gesture reminded him of his wife and her zest for anything new and unfamiliar. Suddenly Lorimer wished that he, too, could recapture Maggie's vast capacity to enjoy life. He'd lost that feeling long ago, somewhere between the back streets and the City Mortuary.

Kirsty MacLeod's last known Harris address was c/o Mhairi MacLeod at Borve Cottage in Rodel. There had been no telephone number. Rodel was not so far away in terms of mileage but it took Lorimer the best part of an hour before the road sign proclaimed that they had reached the village. Several times he'd had to swing into the curve of a lay-by to let another car pass. Lorimer hadn't minded. They weren't running to a time schedule after all, and had booked into the Rodel Hotel for one night, so all the stopping and starting had given him the opportunity to look over the coastline. The day was still fine, although he'd noticed more clouds gathering overhead. The blues and greys of sky were reflected in the water but it was the green that really struck him; everything from a dark bottle green where rocks undoubtedly lurked, to a dazzling emerald reflecting light above the white shores. The brochures hadn't exaggerated.

These beaches were endless swathes of white sand licked by curling waves; and not a soul to be seen.

"We could be on another planet," Solly had murmured, gazing round from the shore to the hills crouching around them. He'd been pretty impressed by this Hebridean island and Lorimer was gratified. Okay, so it was his first visit to these parts too, but he still felt proprietorial. Scotland was *his* country.

Rodel, or *Roghadal* as the Gaelic sign proclaimed, appeared to them suddenly around yet another winding corner between the hills. A quick glance told Lorimer that he was below the infamous site of the quarry that had caused so much public dissension amongst the islanders. As they drove past a lone cottage a man rounded the side of his shed, stopped and caught their eye. Suddenly he waved and smiled. Lorimer was struck by the expression of open friendliness on the man's face. It was as if he were welcoming them home rather than saluting a pair of strangers to his island.

Lorimer had only moments to absorb the man's working dungarees and shock of weather-bleached hair as they drove by. Looking in the rear view mirror, he could see the man leaning on the cottage gate, following them with his eyes. It was a small thing, maybe, but it impressed itself on Lorimer. Suddenly the city seemed light years away.

"The natives are friendly," quipped Solly, nodding into his beard as if the incident were being filed away for future reference.

"Looks like we've arrived," Lorimer replied, indicating a sign for the Rodel Hotel.

"Not exactly a metropolis, is it?" Solly joked. There had been very few houses along the road and now they were passing an old church.

"That looks interesting."

"It is," replied Lorimer. "That's not just any old church. What you have here is the ancient cathedral of Saint Clements. I fancy having a look around it while we're here," he added to himself. But business would have to come first.

The road took them on a loop and soon he was driving through a courtyard to a large edifice whose grey stones rubbed shoulders with the harbour walls. So this was Rodel; one hotel and a scattering of houses strung out along a windswept stretch of land.

"Hardly surprising that Kirsty came away to the city," he told Solly.

"Interesting, though," replied the psychologist. "I expect it's a close-knit community. The sort of place where it's well nigh impossible to keep things to yourself." Solly gazed over the harbour wall at the stretch of ocean.

"This is the sort of place where people would know each others' secrets," he added, turning to raise his eyebrows at Lorimer.

"See you in the bar," Lorimer gave Solomon a nod and made his way up the narrow stairway. He pushed open the unlocked door of his bedroom and shivered as an icy blast came from the open window. They were a hardy lot up here, then. Telling himself that he'd had enough fresh air during the crossing to last a good while, Lorimer pulled down the sash window. For a moment he looked out at the waves beating against the harbour wall. Had Kirsty MacLeod stood on that very pier watching for a boat that never came home, he wondered. He'd ask a few questions downstairs. Bars the world over were a perennial source of information.

There was no one behind the bar although the brass clock on the wall made it after five. A faint rolling sound came from the floor beneath his feet and Lorimer guessed that a new beer cask was being brought up from the cellar. The noise grew louder and then a slim figure appeared from a door behind the bar. He was about nineteen with that fresh complexion and shock of dark hair that defines the Celt. The green t-shirt sporting a brewer's logo showed that he was one of the staff.

"Oh, hallo there. Didn't realise there was anyone in yet. What'll it be?" The words came out in a breathless rush.

"Vodka and tonic, please." Lorimer had already considered the possibility of an interview with an old Hebridean lady and he didn't want to be smelling of drink.

"Just come in, have you?" the young barman inquired.

"That's right."

"Holiday?"

"Not exactly though I'd like to do a bit of sight-seeing," Lorimer fenced the question.

"Oh, you'll see some grand sights over here. Never seen

beaches like ours, I'll bet!" The pride in the lad's tone was unmistakeable. "Or the standing stones."

"You mean the ones at Callanish?" Lorimer knew a bit about these ancient rivals to Stonehenge.

"Och, no. Not just those. We've our own down here. There's MacLeod's stone just along the road. You'll have passed it by, no doubt, not knowing what to look for." The boy smiled and Lorimer had the sense that he was indulging this visitor from Glasgow. He'd have cultivated a pleasant manner for the tourists, no doubt.

"Is this your first time on the island?"

"Yes, it is, but I was hoping to look someone up while I'm here," Lorimer fixed his gaze on the barman. "A Miss MacLeod."

The boy gave a short laugh. "Oh, there are lots of MacLeods in these parts. Which one would it be that you're after, now?"

"Mhairi. A Miss Mhairi MacLeod. An elderly lady."

The boy's smile dropped like a stone. He narrowed his eyes at Lorimer, trying to sum up his visitor. "You mean Kirsty's Aunty Mhairi?"

"That's the one," Lorimer said cheerfully, taking a swig of vodka. His expression never betrayed the vision inside his head, of that lonely little figure in blue dumped in the basement of a Glasgow clinic.

"You Press, or what?" The lad's voice was devoid of any semblance of courtesy now and he placed both hands on the edge of the bar defiantly.

"Or what, I'm afraid," Lorimer replied, taking out his warrant card and laying it open on the polished surface of the bar. He watched the boy's face relax a fraction.

"Chief Inspector Lorimer," he read aloud.

Lorimer pocketed the card again. "Miss Mhairi MacLeod?" He let the name hang in the air.

"Aye, she's at home, just along the road past the cathedral. The two white houses joined together. Miss MacLeod's is the first one. You can't miss it."

16

Borve Cottage was a five-minute walk from the hotel. They must have passed it on their way into the village, thought Lorimer as he and Solly reached the long white house. It might have been a single dwelling house in days gone by but was now split into two semi-detached cottages. Deep-set windows told of thick walls that had withstood centuries of Atlantic gales but, despite its age, the stone seemed freshly painted and both gardens to the front showed signs of recent care. As Lorimer reached out a hand to the brass knocker, his sleeve caught on a tendril of clematis trailing down beside the door. He looked up to see fat buds along the new shoots, promising a froth of pink to come.

Solly stood to one side, whether out of deference to the DCI or simply to see how the old lady would react, Lorimer couldn't tell.

When the door opened a diminutive, grey-haired woman stood before them. Her lilac twin-set topped a heathery coloured tweed skirt and her leather lacing shoes looked as if they'd walked for miles over the rough island terrain.

"Miss MacLeod?"

"No. She's through the house. Who shall I say is calling?"

"Detective Chief Inspector Lorimer, Strathclyde CID

and Dr Solomon Brightman," Lorimer held out his warrant card and the woman peered short-sightedly at it.

"You'll be here about Kirsty, I suppose?" her tone was disapproving but she opened the door wider to let them in.

"That's right," Lorimer answered and was on the point of asking the woman's name when she fixed them with a gimlet stare and said, "Follow me, please."

The woman closed the door behind them and stepped into a darkened hallway.

"She's through here." Lorimer and Solly followed her into a light, airy room facing the water. An old lady was sitting with her back to them in a huge wing chair that faced the bay window.

"Mhairi, it's folk from Glasgow to see you. A Mr Lorimer from the police and his Doctor friend." Lorimer was struck by the change in the woman's voice. It was the tone one would use with a child, soothing and whispery. He stepped forward just as the old woman turned her head towards the voice. For a moment he was speechless. Mhairi MacLeod might be over eighty, but she was one of the most beautiful women he'd ever seen. Her face was smooth and brown with not a sign of a wrinkle except where fine spider's web laughter lines spread from her mouth and eyes. The snow-white hair was wispy and caught back in a net but he could see its abundance of plaited coils and wondered if it had ever been cut. The eyes regarding him were blue, but faded.

"Mr Lorimer, Dr...?" she turned to Solomon and gave him a sweet smile.

"Brightman. How do you do, Miss MacLeod," Solly came forward, gave a stiff little bow then took the old woman's hand.

"Would you like a cup of tea, gentlemen?"

"Thank you. That would be most welcome," Solomon replied before Lorimer had time to think.

"Make us all a pot of tea, would you, Chrissie. And could we have some of those lovely scones you brought in?

Thank you, dear."

Mhairi MacLeod waved her hand at the two men. "Bring a couple of chairs over and sit beside me. The view's too good to miss." There was a twinkle in her eye as she addressed Lorimer. He looked around, found two small wooden chairs, each with plump embroidered cushions, then lifted them over and set them down on either side of the wing chair.

"I don't know what I'd do without Chrissie. She's been so good to me since Kirsty's passing."

"She's your home help?" asked Lorimer.

"Oh, don't let her hear you say that! No, no. Chrissie's my next-door neighbour, which makes life easier for us both. Home help? Dear me, we don't have such luxuries in this part of the world unless we're really poor old souls with nobody to care for us." She glanced as Lorimer turned his chair slightly inwards. "Did you have a good journey up?"

"Yes, indeed," Solomon answered.

"You're not with Strathclyde Police, are you, my dear?" Mhairi MacLeod looked at Solomon with interest.

The psychologist shook his head and turned his large brown eyes upon the old lady. "No, I'm helping the police with their case. I may be able to construct a profile of Kirsty's killer which would assist the investigation," he explained.

"Ah, like *Cracker* on the TV?" she smiled at them. "Oh, we're not entirely in the backwoods here, we do have the television. Don't know what Chrissie would do without *Coronation Street*," she added. "You're not from this part of the country, then Dr Brightman?"

"No. I was born in London, but Glasgow's my home now," Solly replied.

She nodded. "Aye. And it was poor wee Kirsty's home for a while." Lorimer noticed her lip tremble for a second but then Chrissie came bustling into the room bearing a tray laden with what looked like the best china and a huge plate of buttered scones. She set it down on the table in front of the old lady.

"Right, I'm away ben. Just give me a knock when you want me through," Chrissie told her and marched out of the room. They heard the front door close behind her.

"She said to give her a knock?" Solomon asked, puzzled.

Mhairi MacLeod smiled at him. "Aye, with my stick." She picked up a walking stick that lay at her feet and motioned with it towards the partition wall. "I don't have the telephone, you see. A couple of raps and Chrissie knows I need her."

The old woman leaned forward and grasped the teapot with both hands then concentrated on pouring out three cups of tea. Lorimer's instinct was to offer to do it for her but a glance from Solly warned him off. Mhairi MacLeod might be old and infirm but she was still the hostess in her own home. Lormer watched her frail hand shaking as she passed him a cup. She saw his expression and pursed her lips together in a gesture of determination. Chrissie might have to make the tea but she was the one who would serve her guests.

She took a few sips of tea then placed her cup back on the tray, rattling the saucer. Her shoulders sagged as she leaned back into the deep armchair and patiently folded her hands.

Mhairi MacLeod gave a short sigh. "Right, now. You've come to see me about Kirsty, haven't you?"

Lorimer looked straight at her, returning her directness. He nodded. "I'm afraid so."

"Don't be afraid, Chief Inspector." Her hand was suddenly covering his own and he felt the warmth of its light touch. "May I ask you something first?"

"Go ahead."

"Kirsty," she paused to let the name roll off her tongue as if she'd become unused to saying it. "Did she suffer much? I never asked before."

Lorimer saw her bite her lip to stop it trembling. "No.

Not at all. She'd hardly have known what was happening. The Doctor said it was over very quickly. There were no signs of a struggle," he added gently.

For a moment Mhairi MacLeod stared at him, those faded eyes trying to outmatch his own blue gaze. Then she nodded, apparently satisfied that Lorimer was telling her the truth.

"There are several things we'd like to ask you about Kirsty, your niece."

"Great-niece, Mister Lorimer." There was a faint smile around her mouth as she corrected him. He smiled back.

"Did you know of any men friends that she'd made in Glasgow, anybody she might have written to you about? A particular boyfriend perhaps?"

"No. Nobody special. She used to say she was waiting for Mr Right. But I don't think he ever came into Kirsty's life." She gave a sigh. "She wrote regularly and would have told me if she'd met a young man. Always started her letters, *Dear Aunty Mhairi, I'm fine, how are you?*" Suddenly the old woman's face crumpled and she groped into the depth of a cushion behind her back for a handkerchief.

"Here," Solomon was immediately hunkering down by her side, offering a large white linen hanky. There was silence except for the blowing of her nose and a muffled sobbing from the folds of the handkerchief until Mhairi MacLeod shook her head at them. "So sorry. I'm just a silly old woman."

"No, you're not." Solomon was holding her hand now and stroking it with some concern, his eyes fixed on the old lady's face. She straightened up again and wiped her eyes.

"What was I saying? Yes. Kirsty had nobody special down in Glasgow. She'd had a nice boyfriend up here, Calum, but he went away down to university and they only kept in touch occasionally; birthdays, Christmas cards, that sort of thing."

"Did she ever mention anything about her work in the letters?"

"What sort of thing?" The faded eyes were alert again.

"Did she say if she was happy? Did she like the staff? Was she was coping with the patients, that sort of thing."

Mhairi MacLeod frowned. Was she remembering something? Lorimer asked himself.

"I sometimes wondered if Kirsty was suited to the nursing," she began slowly. "She took everything so much to heart. Became involved with her patients. Grieved terribly whenever one of them passed over. Oh, I know it's a grand thing to be concerned about those who are sick, whether in mind or body," she said, waving a hand at them. "But you need to be a bit hard to be a good nurse, don't you think? It's the same in the police, I suppose," she directed her question to Lorimer who nodded silently. Her voice was quiet when she added, "Kirsty wasn't hard enough, I'm thinking."

They waited for the old lady to elaborate on that statement but apparently that was all she had to offer on the subject.

"Did Kirsty ever talk to you about anything that was worrying her?" Solomon asked.

The old lady looked at him, troubled, as if such questions had never occurred to her before. Her eyes drifted away from them and looked out over the view of the water beyond the shore. Solomon and Lorimer watched her intently. Was there something she recalled? They waited.

"I don't know. Maybe there was something. I felt a sort of sadness in her a while back. I thought maybe she was homesick. She was so good to me, you know. Always wrote cheery letters. Kirsty wouldn't have wanted to burden me with her troubles."

"She kept a diary," Lorimer began.

"Ah, yes. Her five-year diary. I gave it to her one Christmas." Mhairi MacLeod narrowed her eyes."You've been reading Kirsty's diary?" she asked, affronted.

"This is a murder inquiry," Lorimer reminded her quietly.

"Of course. It's just…" she bit her lip.

"Just that we seem to be invading your great-niece's privacy," Lorimer finished for her.

Mhairi MacLeod nodded. "Just that, Chief Inspector."

Lorimer drew the red diary from his pocket. He'd read and re-read the entries till the wee small hours but had found nothing enlightening in its pages.

"She mentions someone named Malcolm. On the Hogmanay before last," Lorimer suggested.

"Aye, she would. That'll be Malcolm Munro from the store. He always brings the black bun. They were all here then, all the folks from Rodel."

"This Malcolm, he's not an old boyfriend, then?"

Mhairi MacLeod's eyes twinkled for a moment. "He's sixty if he's a day, Chief Inspector. Kirsty's known Malcolm-at-the-store since she was a wee girl spending her pennies on sherbet dabs."

Solomon smiled and caught Lorimer's eye. The picture of Kirsty MacLeod was beginning to take shape. Solly warmed to this island girl who had become a victim for no apparent reason.

"There are several weeks missing," Lorimer opened the diary and showed her. "From May to late June."

The old woman took the book from his hands and turned its thin pages, her gnarled fingers tracing the dead girl's writing.

"Why would she do that?" Mhairi MacLeod asked, her eyes troubled.

"I was hoping you might be able to tell us," he replied. "I thought something might have happened that she didn't want to remember."

"Or let anybody else see," Solly put in.

"Kirsty never did anything she'd be ashamed of," she said firmly. "And there were no affairs of the heart," she added, looking down at the diary. Solomon watched her stroke the pages as if she were giving comfort to a troubled mind. She wasn't so certain of that, though, was she? What young woman was going to confide her most intimate secrets to an old lady? One she loved too much to burden with her own troubles, he thought, echoing the old woman's words.

"So there's nothing you know that would have upset Kirsty to the extent of cutting up her diary?" Lorimer asked.

Mhairi MacLeod shook her head slowly.

"We think we know so much, don't we? And all the time we really know nothing at all." She spoke softly to herself as if she'd forgotten their presence in the room. Then she turned and Lorimer could see tears in her eyes. "It's not right, is it?" she whispered. "Her mammy and daddy and now wee Kirsty. I should have been away long before them all." She lifted her hand as if in protest. "And here I am. An old, done woman taking up space."

Lorimer didn't reply. For how could he be expected to comment on the unfairness of life? That was what his job was about most of the time. Solomon's eye caught his as Lorimer looked up and the psychologist inclined his head towards the door. Lorimer gave a brief nod in reply. It was time to go.

The early evening sun was glowing against the hillside as they stepped out of Borve Cottage.

"Do you mind if we pay a short visit?" Lorimer asked, indicating Saint Clement's Church.

"Why not," agreed Solly. The two men made their way over to the entrance, Lorimer stooping slightly as he ducked through the doorway. It was the smallest cathedral he'd ever seen, Lorimer thought, blinking as the gloom enfolded them. The stone flags that were polished from centuries of use gave a dull echo as they walked out of the light and into the shadows.

Neither of them spoke a word. It was as if these grey walls hadn't noticed the passing of time. Lorimer had felt like this before. Sometimes standing by a mortuary slab he had that sense of being a tiny speck of dust in a swirling, meaningless universe.

Now here, as his footfall sounded on the worn stones, the Chief Inspector wondered at those Saints who had risked everything to try to bring their beliefs to these parts. What had it all been for? Was the so-called Christian West more law-abiding than in those far off pagan times? Perhaps, just perhaps. He looked over to where Solomon stood poring over a leaflet that he'd picked up from a small wooden table. Did Solly have any religious beliefs? Judaism was so old and venerable. In all his dealings with human behaviour had Solomon retained something extra to sustain him against cynicism? Somehow Lorimer knew that was a question he'd be unable to ask.

As if aware of his companion's scrutiny, Solly turned around, waving the leaflet in his hand.

Lorimer joined him, noticing that there were postcards for sale. An honesty box lay beyond them, fixed to the wall.

"Listen to this," said Solly. "Tradition has it that Saint Clement of Rome was banished to the Crimea where he was put to death by being thrown into the sea with an anchor around his neck. The Church was built by MacLeod of Harris in the thirteenth century as Saint Clement was the patron saint of the MacLeods. Within the church is the tomb of Alexander Macclod, domino de Dunvegan 1528."

As Solly picked up a few postcards and rattled in his pocket for change, Lorimer took a lingering look at the interior of the tiny, ancient cathedral. He tried to imagine all the folk who had come to worship here over the years. Then another thought came to him. Kirsty would have come here. And her old Aunty Mhairi. Lorimer chewed on a raggled nail. The MacLeods had been here for centuries. That meant that there would be a whole load of them outside. In the graveyard.

For a moment Lorimer stood with his face up to the last warmth of the setting sun. Heedless of his presence, a sheep cropped at the grass. Overhead a gull mewed. He took a deep breath and smelled something fragrant in the soft air. All his weariness seemed to fall away like a cloak being shed. He could so easily forget everything in this quiet corner away from the world. The sky and sea merged into one blur of blue. Somewhere beyond lay a world of offices, streets, computers, files, telephones…all the paraphernalia of his working life.

Lorimer gave himself a shake. He was in danger of being beguiled by the quiet of this island. It was a place like any other, he persuaded himself, inhabited by people as culpable as any in the city.

He stepped in among the lichened gravestones, looking at the names. He was right. There were lots of MacLeods. Some were so old that their inscriptions had faded into decay. He moved among them, shaking his head at all the infant deaths centuries before. Lorimer bent to read the carving on a stone that had leaned over with years of westerly gales. The words were still clearly marked:

> Be Ye Also Ready
> The Small & Great Are Here

Lorimer gave a rueful nod of acknowledgement and passed on down the line.

There was another MacLeod, a Donald MacLeod who had fought in the '45 rebellion. Several lines of inscription told any passer-by that here lay a man who'd been preceded by three wives, who had borne him nine children. Lorimer gave a twisted smile. He was barely in his forties himself, but he'd long ago given up any hope of producing any kids to carry on his own name. He read on. The old man had died in his ninetieth year, it said.

"Incredible, isn't it?" Solly was suddenly by his side. "What accounted for their longevity, do you think?"

"The whisky?" Lorimer joked.

"I wonder. Did they have a healthier way of life, perhaps?"

Lorimer shrugged. The world that he and Solly came from wasn't particularly healthy any more. The Sunday supplements were forever carrying a story about someone who had changed their city life for one in a remote part of Scotland. Taking another lungful of Hebridean air, Lorimer could understand why.

There were more modern headstones on the far side of the graveyard. The detective's feet left soft imprints on the springy turf as he walked amongst them.

At last Lorimer found the one he'd expected to see. It was inscribed to another Donald MacLeod. Lost at Sea, told the deeply cut words. The wife's name had been added not long after. Kirsty Grace. There was space below for another inscription. When would this grave be opened to lay their daughter to rest? That was the question emanating from the blank grey patch of marble.

"When I find her killer," Lorimer spoke softly to the gravestone.

17

"Okay, be with you in half an hour."

Maggie put the phone down. She was really far too busy with marking these junior exams to go out for the evening but maybe she could catch up in her spare periods tomorrow. The seniors were off on exam leave, after all, she argued with herself, and it was Divine Lipinski's last evening in Scotland.

The papers were neatly piled up by her armchair, red marking pen on top, ås Maggie glanced guiltily at them. Someone had once teased her that all teachers were programmed to serve. It was true. She found it hard to switch off from work. There was always pressure, always new demands, new directives. In recent years she and her colleagues had hardly time to learn one set of assessment techniques when some wise guy supplanted them with something different. The wise guys had never been teachers, or if they had, they'd long forgotten what the inside of a classroom looked like or, more to the point, what kids really needed for the big, bad world after school was out for good.

Maggie suddenly found herself longing for a change. Surely other countries' systems couldn't be as restrictive as the current Scottish curriculum? She day-dreamed her way to the bathroom and started to wipe away the day's make-up.

She'd dress up tonight. It was a lot warmer and it was staying lighter for longer now. The face in the oval mirror stared back at her, pale skin with fine lines etched around a discontented mouth. She faked a smile then made a face at her reflection. Time for war paint, she told herself.

Thirty minutes later Maggie alighted from a taxi outside the Corinthian. The effort of dressing up in a shorter skirt and slim-heeled shoes was well rewarded when she caught sight of all the lovely young things parading their designer gear at the bar. As usual, Maggie's eyes were drawn towards the gorgeous gold painted ornamentation that gave The Corinthian its name. Her gaze lingered on the fabulous dome with its subtly shifting colours, then she looked around and saw Divine sitting by the hearth. The fire wasn't lit tonight but it still looked the cosiest part of the enormous room.

"Well, what d'you know. Mrs Lorimer. Fashion statement herself!"

Maggie stuck her tongue out and both women laughed.

"What're you drinking tonight, ma'am?" Divine asked in mock flattering tones.

Maggie rolled her eyes to heaven, "I don't mind so long as there's lots of it. I came by taxi and I intend to go home that way. *Happy.*" She emphasised the word. But when the waiter came for their order she found herself about to ask for the usual white wine spritzer.

"Two Harvey Wallbangers," Divine drawled before Maggie had time to speak and suddenly that was exactly what she wanted. Something different that fitted her mood of rebelliousness. She leaned back, crossing her legs over silky stockings, not caring if she showed a bit too much thigh.

"Well, Divine. This suit you for your last night in Glasgow?"

"It's neat. Pretty. Reminds me of some of our old buildings back home. What did it used to be before?"

"Oh, it's an old building all right. I can remember when

it was the High Court but before that it was the Union Bank of Scotland. Long before my time. I think I read somewhere that it was originally a family house." Maggie scanned the Classical mouldings around the ceiling. "The present owner made sure that all the original architectural features were kept."

"Wish more people were like him," replied Divine. "If you ever come over to Florida I'll show you something. It's called the Ca'de Zan. Built right on the water to look like an Italian Palace. You'd like it."

Maggie bent over her drink, considering. Should she confide in this woman?

"You might be able to show me round sooner than you think," she replied.

"Oh? Why's that?"

"Listen, I know you'll not be here after tomorrow, but I'd still like you to keep this confidential," Maggie began.

Divine nodded, her dark eyes solemn.

"I've applied for a transfer to America. Just for a year. It's an exchange programme that's run between Scottish and American schools."

"And how does the Chief Inspector feel about that?"

Maggie didn't answer and in the silence that followed Divine's eyebrows rose in surprise. "You mean you haven't told him?"

"No. Not yet. I wanted time to think about it."

"So why tell me?"

"Oh, I don't know. Maybe because you're a policewoman. You travel." Maggie hesitated. "I just thought you might understand."

Divine gave a sigh. "Honey, I do, believe me. Being in the police force takes over your whole life, whether it's here or back home. I've seen lots of folks split up because of the pressure."

"Oh, but we're not, I mean…" she tailed off, confused.

"Just need a bit of time out?"

"Something like that. I've always wanted to travel but

the years just seem to have slipped by and I've got into this rut. We both have. Then I saw the poster about the exchange." She shrugged her shoulders. "It was like something telling me to grab the chance with both hands."

"And how d'you think your husband will react?"

Maggie looked away. "I'm not sure. I really don't want to hurt him. But lately I wonder if he even thinks about what my life is like."

"Hey. Want my advice? Go for it. It's only a year and if you hate it you can always come back. I mean," she grinned at Maggie encouragingly, "nothing's set in stone, is it?"

"No. I suppose you're right."

"Of course I am. Now let's drink to the future."

Divine raised the tall glass and gave a wink.

Suddenly Maggie felt a lot better. Was it such a big deal after all? Surely people went abroad all the time with their work and without their partners?

"The future," she agreed and took a long cool drink. The cocktail tasted sweet and different, a portent of good things to come.

18

Lorimer's mouth felt like someone had made him chew on sandpaper. He groaned and rolled over, reaching out for Maggie's warm body. He came to, feeling the sudden edge of the bed. Maggie? Then he remembered where he was. He opened his eyes to the light. Someone had drawn the curtains closed and the room was flooded with deep pink reflected light. Lorimer closed his eyes again. What was it that was flickering at the edge of his mind?

Dougie, the youngster behind the bar. He'd sat there drinking malts and quizzing the boy for hours. Solomon had listened to their questions and answers, sipping his orange squash and nodding as he absorbed the information. Had Dougie known Kirsty? That was what Lorimer had really been after. At first he thought he'd hit pay dirt. Everyone had known her and her business, it seemed. From birth to death there didn't seem to be a way of keeping secrets on this island. What was it the lad had said? *It's not gossip. Folks just share their lives with one another. That's the way it is.* And Kirsty MacLeod's life had seemed just the same as any other young islander's. She'd left home to board in Stornoway and attend the Nicholson Institute, like all the teenagers from these parts. And, like many of them, she'd made her way to the big city. For what was to keep her here? Unemployment was just as bad up here as anywhere else, Dougie had pointed out. That was why so many folk had wanted the quarry to go ahead. He'd been okay, his dad owned the hotel. That's what he wanted, to stay here and live in Rodel. Kirsty had been no different from the young folk who had left the islands to work in Glasgow, Lorimer conceded. It was her death that made her stand apart from them. But there was still too much missing from what Dougie could tell him. There were no hidden depths, nothing to distinguish Kirsty from any other young island girl leaving home to train as a nurse.

He heaved himself out of the narrow bed and felt the floor cold beneath his feet. Today would bring him into contact with other nurses who cared for the Grange's patients, and, of course, the patients themselves. Lorimer found himself speculating about the two who had been in Glasgow at the time of Kirsty's murder; Sister Angelica and Samuel Fulton. They'd caught an early morning flight from Glasow to Stornoway. Mrs Baillie had not been prepared to make any cancellations. The clinic would have lost money, she had claimed. Lorimer shook his head. Call him a suspicious beggar, but there was more to all this than met the eye.

"This came for you, sir." Lorimer looked up from his bacon and eggs to see young Dougie holding out a long white envelope. He waited until the boy had gone then ripped it open. Solly glanced up inquiringly as Lorimer studied the message. It was a fax from Alistair Wilson. Suddenly South Harris was back in the twenty-first century, mused Lorimer. He scanned the opening paragraph quickly.

The Grange was trying to forge links with another expanding group of clinics, he read, and there had been a report ordered by their bankers into this group's financial stability. Lorimer's eyes travelled down the rows of facts and figures. There were sections on the group's business profile, accounting systems, profit and loss forecasts and future strategies, one of which included the absorption of the Grange. The directors had borrowed heavily in order to expand and modernise their existing clinics. The report's advice was that the bank would continue its level of lending meantime but wanted to know a definite date for the acquisition of the Grange. But how could that be? Phyllis Logan was the legal owner. Had the paralysed woman some legal representative who would advise her on such matters?

Lorimer frowned, remembering the woman's argument that the clinic could not afford to waste her patients' plane tickets. Mrs Baillie seemed to be more concerned with saving money than an investigation into the death of one of her staff. She'd not even told them about the existence of the respite home until then, this other part of the MS patient's estate. Failte, it was called. The word was Gaelic for welcome, Lorimer knew. What sort of welcome would they have for a Glasgow policeman and a criminal profiler?

His car wasn't built for roads like these, Lorimer realised as he pulled into a lay-by for the sixth time in five minutes. They had obviously met the ferry traffic coming from Tarbert. He paused to look out over the wide sweep of sands below them, then his eye travelled inland. The road was clear again and he turned back onto the grey strip that wound down towards sea level, glancing every now and then at the changing colours of the water.

"Look out!" Solly's shout made Lorimer yank the wheel sideways as something white bounded towards them. There was a thud as the car hit the verge. He pressed the window button, cursing the object of their sudden stop.

"Bloody sheep!" Lorimer looked down at the offending beast that was now grazing frantically on the other side of the narrow road. He glanced across at Solly, who was trying to hide a grin, then he eased the big car off the grass verge and back onto the road. He'd have to be more attentive to these sheep meandering across his path.

The rest of the journey passed without incident though Lorimer had to keep his wits about him negotiating the twists and turns, especially among the rocky landscapes as they climbed into the hills north of Tarbert. The treeless wastes were bleaker to Lorimer's eyes than even Rannoch Moor. No wonder so much of the population had left over the decades. Yet there would always be a core of islanders who stayed at home. There were signs of recent resurfacing to the road and Lorimer reminded himself that tourism kept many local folk in employment. He had to admit that there was a wild beauty about the coastline. And these slabs of black rock striped with silver crystals were amongst the oldest known rocks on earth. Lorimer passed a sign for Callanish. He'd love to bring Maggie here to see these legendary standing stones.

"Who exactly runs this respite centre?" Solomon asked suddenly.

"A couple by the name of Evans. He's a psychiatric nurse and she does the housekeeping and suchlike, I believe. They're not locals. Came up in answer to an advert, in fact."

"What do you know about them?"

"Not a lot. But I think we'll soon find out," replied Lorimer. Roadside cottages were no longer solitary dots on the landscape but were now like joined up writing. "Civilisation," he muttered under his breath as he read the sign, *Steornabhagh*, though he wasn't at all sure that he meant it.

"Do you mind if we don't go straight to the clinic? I'd like to pay a courtesy call to the local nick," Lorimer asked. "I feel the need to rally the troops, if you know what I mean."

"Do you think the troops will be on our side?"

Lorimer grunted. Solly had a point. Nobody liked officers from another division, let alone another region, encroaching on their patch. He'd just have to hope the natives were as friendly here as they'd been in Harris.

Stornoway came as a surprise. Fishing boats swung gently on their moorings along the harbour's edge as Lorimer drove slowly towards the centre of town. He rolled down the window and breathed in the salty, fishy tang.

"Fancy a walk?" Solomon asked.

"Okay. I could do with stretching my legs," Lorimer replied. He parked away from the harbour in a designated area. For a small place there were plenty of double yellow lines and he wasn't about to get on the wrong side of the local lads.

"This is where she came to school," Solomon spoke half to himself as Lorimer locked the car.

"Yes. The Nicholson Institute. One of Maggie's friends came up here to teach languages years ago."

He tried to visualise Kirsty as a teenager, giggling on her way from the hostel to the famous high school, then breathed a long sigh. The Stornoway air stinging his eyes had a purity that was suddenly at odds with his vision of the nurse, her hair scattered over that lifeless young face.

The local police station was in Church Street. From the pavement in front of it Lorimer spotted three steeples close by, a reminder that these parts were supposed to be full of God-fearing folks. Well, that remained to be seen.

"Chief Inspector Lorimer, Strathclyde CID," Lorimer held out his warrant card carefully for the duty sergeant to see. The officer, a huge bear of a man whose grizzled hair still held a hint of red, raised his eyebrows but looked past Lorimer to the Jewish psychologist, who stood smiling his knowing little smile. Following the man's questioning gaze, Lorimer stepped aside.

"This is Dr Brightman from Glasgow University."

Solly held out his hand to the sergeant who gave it an abrupt once up-and-down.

"Dr Brightman is assisting Strathclyde with our double murder inquiry," Lorimer explained.

"Aye, the MacLeod girl. Terrible thing, that," replied the sergeant. "How can we help you, sir?" he said to Lorimer.

"We're here to visit a place called Failte. It's some sort of respite home for recovered mental patients." Beside him Lorimer could feel Solly wince at the description.

"Isn't it for patients who have suffered some sort of

neural disorder?" the sergeant replied, frowning. "That's what we were told." He sidled along behind the desk and tapped at the keyboard of his computer.

"There, see." He swivelled the screen around for the two men to read.

Failte: Centre for holistic care and recuperation. Specialising in the after care of patients who are recovering from neural disorders. Patients are often disorientated when they arrive and may take some time to integrate with staff and nearby residents. It is hoped that the local police officers will do their best to be discreet and understanding while those patients are part of the community.

"That's community policing for you," the big policeman said proudly. "We take care of people up here, respect their needs, you know."

"There isn't a big crime scene here, then," Lorimer joked.

The sergeant bristled, obviously disliking Lorimer's flippancy. "We may not have the kind of crimes you boys have down in Glasgow, but there are still law breaking elements about. Especially with drugs," he shook his head wearily.

"But there's been no trouble of that sort at Failte?" Solomon inquired politely.

"Oh, no. They keep themselves pretty much to themselves. We see them wandering along the roads, out for fresh air, poor souls. No, we've never had any bother with them at all," he replied, adding, "Are you staying long, Chief Inspector?"

"I shouldn't think so," Lorimer told him. "Though I'd like to see it from a visitor's point of view some day."

"Aye, there's nowhere like it. They can say what they like about their fancy Benidorms and Lanzarotes but we've a better place than any of them," the sergeant stated emphatically.

"Well, maybe I'll manage to come up here again. Thanks for your time." Lorimer shook the sergeant's hand and turned to go.

"Do you know where this place is?" Solomon asked as they walked back along the street.

"Yes. According to my AA map it's further out along the north coast," Lorimer replied. "Near a place called Shawbost. Shouldn't take us too long to find it. And we certainly won't get lost. There is only one road from Stornoway."

Lorimer was right, the road from the main town in Lewis cut directly across the land towards the further coast. Apart from the ubiquitous sheep, there were few signs of habitation along their route. Gazing out of the window, Solomon marvelled at the landscape of windswept grasses and gently sloping hills. Small birds swooped past the windscreen and away, their identities a mystery. Despite a lack of trees the landscape was pleasing and, as the clouds raced across the sky, the psychologist smiled to himself, enjoying the shifting scenery as if it were a gift.

19

The sign for Shawbost was accompanied by another giving the mileage to Callanish, Carloway and Stornoway. There was nothing to indicate the whereabouts of Failte. Lorimer drove slowly along past the houses scattered on either side of the road until even those petered out.

"Maybe it's further on?" suggested Solly.

"We'll see."

Turning a bend on the road, Lorimer saw a long driveway that ended slightly uphill at a large, grey two-storey house. There was no sign at the road end.

"Bet you that's it," he said and swung the car along the rutted path that led to the house.

To one side of the old house was a pebbled area with a red pick-up truck, so Lorimer parked nearby and signalled to Solomon to come with him.

"You're right," said Solly, pointing to the word cut into grey slate by the doorway. Failte.

"My great detecting skills," Lorimer smiled, raising his eyebrows. So far, so good, he thought, but what would their reception be now that they had arrived?

They hadn't long to find out. In answer to the shrill bell, footsteps came thudding downstairs towards the door. It swung open to reveal a young woman dressed in jeans and sweater.

"Hallo. Can I help you?" she looked curiously at Lorimer then shifted her gaze to Solomon. Lorimer saw the smile spread across her face and watched as she flicked back her long fair hair. He made a mental note to tease the psychologist about his fatal attraction to blondes.

As always, Lorimer held out his warrant card. "I understood Mr and Mrs Evans were in charge here," he ventured.

"Yeah, that's right," she turned and yelled up the stairs. "Mu-um! There's a policeman to see you."

The sound of a door slamming and a toilet flushing was followed by a voice calling out, "Just coming!" then a woman appeared at the top of the stairs, wiping her hands on the apron tied around her waist.

"Frances Evans. You must be the men who phoned me from Glasgow, right?" she spoke breathlessly taking Lorimer's hand in a damp grasp. "This is my daughter, Rowena," she added, indicating the girl who still continued to smirk in Solly's direction. "Finish off those bedrooms for me, will you, lass?" she said, giving the girl a friendly pat on the shoulder.

"See you later, maybe," Rowena grinned then raced up the stairs and out of sight.

"Come on into the lounge, will you. Would you like a cup of tea or coffee? Or can I offer you both a spot of lunch? We're just having soup and sandwiches, but you're welcome to join us."

Frances Evans spoke in a rush, making Lorimer wonder if she were always so garrulous. Or was it the presence of a police officer that provoked this nervous chatter? Lorimer had witnessed this effect countless times. It didn't mean a person had anything to hide; sometimes it was simply the awkwardness of unfamiliarity.

"Thank you, but no. We'd really like to speak to your two residents as soon as possible."

"Ah," the woman dropped her hands by her sides. "Of course. That's why you're here, isn't it, to see Sam and

Angelica. Well, Sam's out with my husband at the moment and Angelica's gone for a walk. Oh, Just a minute," she broke off and crossed to a window that overlooked the road. "That's them now," she said, turning back to Lorimer.

"They had to go into Stornoway to the chemist's. Sam's on special medication, you know," she confided, stepping past them and bustling out into the hall once more. The rattle of a car braking against the stony drive set off a dog barking.

Following the woman out of the front door, Lorimer saw a black and white collie racing towards the car, a distant figure following.

Standing in the doorway, Lorimer saw two men emerge from the car. One was stockily built with thinning hair, the other a tall spare man wearing well-worn tweeds. As they approached, Lorimer saw them exchange glances. They'd have seen his car in the driveway and put two and two together.

"Detective Chief Inspector Lorimer, I take it?" the tall man took the front steps two at a time and Lorimer found his hand grasped firmly. "I'm John Evans. And this is our guest, Sam Fulton," Evans turned to the man behind him who had bent down to fondle the collie by his side.

As Sam Fulton straightened up, Lorimer knew instinctively that the two men had discussed a strategy between them. He looked back at Evans for a moment, aware of the frank, hazel eyes regarding him with interest.

"Mr Fulton, hallo," Lorimer smiled and raised a hand in greeting. "I believe we've arrived at an awkward time. Mrs Evans here tells me your lunch is ready. Please don't let us keep you back." He turned and met the Welshman's eyes again. "We can talk while Mr Fulton is at lunch," he said. Evans nodded. His expression showed that he knew it wasn't so much a request but a demand from this Glasgow policeman.

"Aye, okay. I'll see youse later," Sam Fulton licked his lips nervously and slunk past them into the house, followed by Frances Evans who ushered him along the corridor like a recalcitrant child.

"This is my colleague Dr Brightman," Lorimer said, watching as Solly shook hands solemnly with the tall Welshman.

"Pleased to meet you, Dr Brightman," Evans had stooped slightly to meet the psychologist's eyes but was now looking over his shoulder. "I think we could talk in the lounge, but first, there's someone else you should meet."

Both men turned to follow his gaze. The figure that had been following the collie was heading up the path. Close to, Lorimer could see her raincoat flapping against a pair of stout legs clad in thick socks and heavy walking boots. The headscarf knotted under her chin made the woman's face appear like a pale, round moon. In one hand she carried a staff and each step she took was defined by a thump as she lumbered forwards.

"Sister Angelica?" Solomon looked enquiringly at John Evans.

"Yes."

"Wretched dog. Never comes back when I tell him to. You have to train your animals better than that, John." The woman puffed to a halt before them. "This the policemen, then?" she asked, indicating Lorimer and Solly with her stick.

"DCI Lorimer and Dr Brightman," Evans stated, standing aside for the woman to shake the outstretched hands.

"I'm Sister Angelica. How are you? Don't answer that. I don't really want to know. Had enough of hearing how everybody is back in the Grange," she cackled.

"Frances is doing lunch then these gentlemen will want to speak to you," John Evans told her. Lorimer saw her hesitate for a moment. The psychiatric nurse had a firm manner that brooked no nonsense yet there was a reassuring gentleness in that Welsh accent.

"Suits me. Sam in already?" Without waiting for a reply the woman strode into the house, the collie wagging its tail at her heels.

"Please go into the lounge. I'll ask Frances to do some tea for us," Evans said and disappeared in the wake of Sister Angelica.

"What d'you make of them?" Lorimer sat down and whispered to Solly.

"Sister Angelica seems pretty well adjusted, don't you think? No sign of weakness in her personality at first sight. She's getting on with things, I'd say. Out with the dog in the fresh air. And she had no problem about facing us, did she?"

"What about the man? Fulton?"

"Didn't want to make eye-contact, did he?"

"You noticed that too?"

"And…" Solly broke off as John Evans pushed open the lounge door with a tray. He set it down on the table between the two men and began offering sugar for the steaming mugs.

"We found it rather strange that two patients who were in the Grange during a murder should be allowed to disappear up here the very next day," Lorimer began. "Mrs Baillie said the reasons were financial," he added, raising his eyebrows to show John Evans just how sceptical he was of this excuse.

"Did she?" Evans looked surprised. "I would have thought she might have explained about Sam and Angelica."

"What about them?"

"Well. Both patients had completed their course of treatment. They really needed the respite care we offer at Failte. You have to understand, Chief Inspector. They'd been through a very difficult time and for them to become embroiled in a police investigation might have seriously set either of them back."

"What about now? Will we damage their recovery?" Lorimer asked, sarcastically.

"Maybe. But they've had a while to rest and take stock

of all their therapy. I think you can safely interview each of them without too much upset."

Evans crossed his legs as he spoke and leaned back into the armchair. He regarded Lorimer thoughtfully over the rim of his mug.

"Neither of your patients were in the Grange in January when the first murder took place," Solly pointed out. "Chief Inspector Lorimer will have to know their where-abouts for that particular date."

"You're not seriously suggesting that Sam or Angelica might be suspects?" Evans sat up suddenly. Neither man replied, letting the silence answer his question.

"But why? Just because they've been ill doesn't mean they'd be capable of carrying out something like that!"

"The perpetrator of those killings appears to be some-one who may very well be ill," Solly answered slowly. "In building up a profile I have to consider the extent to which any risk of discovery was considered. Whoever did these killings was either very cunning or totally disregarded the thought that they might be caught. Someone whose behav-iour was prompted by an uncontrollable urge might even have wanted to be discovered."

"And how do you come to that conclusion, Dr Brightman?"

Solly shook his head. "I'm sorry. I'm not at liberty to divulge that kind of information."

John Evans looked at each of them in turn, his mouth a thin line of disapproval.

"Well," he said at last, "I suppose we must be as co-operative as we can. Still, I do hope you can see our side of things. Mrs Baillie would not have seen her actions as obstructing the course of a murder inquiry. She would sim-ply have put her patients as a higher priority."

Lorimer listened to the man's measured tones. There was no sense of outrage nor was there any attempt to thwart this stage of the investigation. Evans was a man of some sense.

"Were you always a psychiatric nurse?" he asked, curious suddenly about the Welshman's background.

Evans smiled and shook his head. "No. I retrained some years ago."

"I'd have hazarded a guess that you were an academic of some sort," Solly stroked his beard thoughtfully.

"Well done, Doctor. Spot on," Evans replied, putting his empty mug back onto the tray. "I was at Cambridge for many years. Lectured in philosophy." He smiled again, looking straight at Lorimer. "You can check it all up if you like."

"So why did you change careers?" Lorimer wanted to know.

"Perhaps I saw that nursing had a greater value than teaching philosophy," Evans replied, his eyes suddenly grave. "You will take care not to put Sam under too much stress, won't you?" he added.

Lorimer and Solly waited in the lounge while Evans brought his patient to them. Sam Fulton shambled into the room ahead of the nurse, who placed an encouraging hand on his shoulder before stepping out and closing the door behind him.

"Mr Fulton, please come and sit down," Lorimer stood and indicated the chair recently vacated by John Evans.

Eying them suspiciously, Sam Fulton sat on the edge of the armchair, clasping his hands together as if to warm them.

"You know we are investigating the murder of Kirsty MacLeod, a nurse from the Grange?"

Fulton nodded.

"She was killed during the night before you left to come up here."

"Aye. Ah know. Me an' Angelica thought it wis mad comin' here when a' that wis goin' on."

"You didn't think it was wise to leave, then?"

"Wise? You kiddin'? It wis pure mental. That Baillie woman's aff her trolley. We should've bin ther wi' a' they others, shouldn't we?"

Lorimer nodded. "We think so. Still, now that we have the chance to talk to you, Mr Fulton, perhaps you can help us."

"Aye," Fulton replied then screwed his face up. "How?"

"Can you describe what took place on the night of Nurse MacLeod's death? Just talk us through everything you did and can remember."

"Aye. Well," Fulton scratched his head and hefted his bottom more comfortably into the chair. "Ah did ma packin' fur comin' up here. Not that ah've goat much. Then went tae bed. Ah'm oan medication so ah went straight oot like a light. Didnae hear a thing until the screechin' began."

"What time was that?"

"Whit time? Jesus! Ah don't know. Ah wis that bleary wi' sleep. Ah came oot intae the corridor and Peter telt me there had bin an accident."

"Peter? That was one of the other nurses?"

"Aye. He telt us tae get back tae wur beds."

"Who else was out in the corridor with you?"

Fulton gave a sigh, "Ah cannae remember. There wis that much goin' on. Ah jist went back tae ma bed."

"When did you find out about Kirsty MacLeod's murder?" Solomon asked.

Sam Fulton turned as if he had forgotten the psychologist's presence. "The next morning. Mrs Baillie telt us on our way to Glasgow Airport."

"So you knew nothing about it before then?"

"Naw." Fulton's chin came up defiantly as he looked Solly in the eye.

"Where were you on the night of January 12 this year?" Lorimer asked suddenly.

Fulton frowned. "How the hell should ah know that? Ah've no been well. Ah cannae remember dates an' things," he added with a hint of a smirk across his face.

"Is there anybody who could help you remember?" Lorimer asked. "A friend or family member who could verify your whereabouts?"

Fulton licked his lips nervously. "Here. Whit is a' this? You sayin' ah done something? Is that it?" he leaned forward on the seat once more, his shoulders bunching around his ears.

"We have to eliminate as many people as possible from our inquiries, Mr Fulton. We are looking into the possibility that Nurse MacLeod was killed by the same person who carried out the murder in Queen Street station in January."

"Aw," Fulton's face showed some relief. "That one. Aye. Ah read aboot that in the papers. Naw. Ah wisnae there. Ah wis up the hoose maist o' that time," he turned to Solomon. "Wi' my *problem*," he said.

"According to our notes you became an in-patient at the Grange on January 25," Lorimer told him.

"Aye. Burns night. They had tae haud me doon," Fulton smirked again.

"Mr Fulton, forgive me, but wasn't it rather an expense for you to enter a private clinic for such a prolonged stay?"

"Oh, aye. It's a hell of an expense. But ah've goat kinda special terms, see?"

Lorimer nodded. He'd let that one pass. How a former shipyard worker who had been unemployed for as long as Fulton could have obtained private medical insurance, if that's what he meant by *special terms*, was something of a mystery, though. There were things about this man that didn't add up.

"So could you find anybody who would verify that you were housebound on the night of January 12?" Lorimer insisted.

"Aye. Nae bother. Ah'll speak tae wan o' the boys."

"Boys?"

"Aye. Ma lads. Gerry and Stephen. They'll tell ye ah wis hame a' the time."

"Thank you."

"When do you expect to return to Glasgow?" Solomon asked.

Fulton shrugged. "Don't know. Sometime. It's an open

ticket we've goat. Maybe in a week or so. How?"

"We need to know your whereabouts, Mr Fulton. It's routine, that's all," Lorimer answered for him. "Anyway, thank you for your time. If Sister Angelica is ready, we'd like to speak to her now."

"That it?" Fulton asked, rising to his feet. "Right. Okay, well. I'll see if she's there," he raised his hand in a short salute of farewell and headed for the door. As he left, he turned and glowered at the two men sitting by the window. Solly, seeing his expression merely smiled and nodded in return.

The woman came into the room immediately. She was, they saw, dressed for the outdoors, her wax coat already buttoned up.

"Not a day for sitting inside. You can talk to me all you want but don't expect me to sit in here."

She paused for a moment, regarding Solomon and Lorimer who had risen to their feet. "Got any warm jackets? That's a north easterly wind, you know." Looking them up and down, she went back into the hallway calling, "Sula! Here, lass!" There was the sound of claws scrabbling along the polished wooden floor then a dog whining excitedly. "Come on, then," Sister Angelica flung over her shoulder, "What are you waiting for?"

Lorimer handed over the car keys to Solly. "Jackets?"

"If she says so," Solly raised his eyebrows.

The road from the house flowed over a rise and down towards the sea. Sister Angelica strode ahead, the collie barking at her heels. Overhead a gull squawked. Catching her up, Lorimer signalled the woman to slow down. Behind him, Solly walked, just within earshot.

"Right-oh. What d'you want to ask a mad old nun, then?" she grinned, turning to meet Lorimer's eye.

Lorimer smiled back. "Not so old and not so mad, I think."

Sister Angelica flung back her head and gave a hoot of laughter. "Well, maybe not so mad any more. Whatever they hoped to achieve seems to have worked. I'll grant them that. Still, you can't turn the clock back and I'm not going to see the right side of fifty again. There's no known cure for the ageing process."

"We need to ask you about Kirsty MacLeod."

The nun slowed her stride but kept on walking. "She's dead. Someone killed her and it happened in the Grange while I was there." She looked at Lorimer, a thoughtful expression on her face. "That's all there is to know. She was a thoroughly nice young woman and nobody had any right to take her life away."

Lorimer nodded. "That's how I feel. That's why we're here. To try to find out as much as we can about the people who were there in the Grange that night."

"Chief Inspector. I really don't see how I can help you. Some intruder obviously broke in and killed the girl. The back door of the basement was open, after all."

"How do you know that? You left early the next morning."

"Mrs Baillie told us. She said someone had broken in and attacked Kirsty. She said we'd be questioned by the police eventually. Sam thought it was a bit daft to go, just like that."

"So why did you leave?"

Sister Angelica gazed at the ground as if the windblown grasses could supply her answer then she looked up at Lorimer.

"Cowardice, I suppose. We just wanted to be away from the place. Even though I knew it was our duty to talk to the police we let Mrs Baillie persuade us. I'm ashamed to say we didn't take much persuading."

"Can you remember the events of that night?"

"Oh, yes. I remember them all right. I was sitting up in bed when Mrs Duncan began screaming at the top of her voice. We all began to drift into the corridor to see what had happened."

"What did you think had happened?"

146

"I thought someone had topped themselves. Peter said there had been an accident and we should all go back to bed but I stayed."

"Why?"

The woman shrugged. "Force of habit, if you'll excuse the pun. I'm used to being around crises."

Lorimer let this go. It was probably true. "So, what happened then?"

"Mrs Baillie tried to calm her down and Peter let me come into the staff room to make some tea. They didn't seem to mind me being there," she added, as if this had only just occurred to her. "Mrs Duncan was shaking and sobbing by this time and I heard Mrs Baillie tell Peter she was going to telephone the police. That was when she told me to go back to my room."

"And did you?"

"Yes," she hesitated as if there was something more she wanted to say but couldn't form the words.

"Did you see anything strange that night, Sister?" Lorimer looked intently at the nun,

"Not strange, not really. Just," she gave her head a shake as if to clear her brain. "Just unusual."

"What was that?"

"When I got back to my room one of the other patients was kneeling by my bed. Praying."

Lorimer stopped and caught her arm. "I would say that was very unusual."

Sister Angelica gave a sigh. "More's the pity, I say. But, you're wrong as it happens. They all knew I was a nun and some of them would come into my room to talk about spiritual matters. I encouraged them. I even held a time of prayer each week. Well, they needed guidance if they were in a clinic for neural disorders, didn't they?" she said briskly.

"Who was in your room, Sister?"

The woman sighed again, her large white face turned up to Lorimer's. "It was Leigh," she said. "And he was crying."

147

20

"Well, what do you think? Does Leigh Quinn fit your profile?" Lorimer asked, taking his eyes off the road for a moment and turning to Solly with a scarcely contained excitement.

Solly said nothing. This was the moment he'd been dreading. He'd been waiting for just such a question from the DCI and had absolutely no answer. No answer and certainly no criminal profile. His mouth shifted into a little bitter twist. Not so long ago Lorimer had thrown scorn upon the veracity of such techniques as profiling and here he was now, all eager to have a response as if Solly were some conjurer pulling a rabbit out of his hat. The truth was that he didn't have a clue. This case had puzzled him from the time he had visited the Grange. Nothing seemed to add up about the two killings. The different locations were odd for a start. The murder of a prostitute and a respectable nurse were at variance, too. Nor was there any matching DNA material. Yet the things that should have been significant remained: that flower and those praying hands. It had to be one and the same killer.

Not a soul outside the murder investigation knew about these details; even the Press had depicted a corpse with praying hands like an effigy, palms towards heaven, not like their victims at all. So he'd ruled out any possibility of a copycat killing. Now Lorimer wanted answers and he had none to give.

"You don't think it's Quinn? Is that it?"Lorimer's voice held just a hint of querulousness as Solly remained silent.

Solly heaved a sigh. "To tell you the truth, I'm not sure at all. It would be better to re-interview the man, of course, but from his notes he seems a pretty withdrawn sort. Not the type to have easily consorted with a prostitute."

"I would have thought those kind of loners were exactly the sort who'd need a woman like that!"

"But he's practically non-verbal. He'd have needed some conversational skills to persuade the woman to go into the station with him," Solly protested.

It was Lorimer's turn to fall silent. His sudden euphoria at the nun's revelation had evaporated. Solly's words made sense. And yet? Perhaps Leigh Quinn had been a different person back in January? Maybe his illness manifested itself in different ways? They'd have to re-examine the case notes thoroughly, that was for sure.

The sign for Callanish appeared and Lorimer turned off the road without consulting his companion. Right now he needed some fresh air and a chance to think without a nun and a dog at his heels.

As Lorimer switched off the engine and opened the door he glanced over to Solly, who was staring out of the windscreen as if he were miles away. Something was troubling the younger man. He got out, leaving Solly sitting where he was. If he wanted to follow him, fine. If not, he was happy with his own company. Aware that a rift had developed between them, Lorimer turned his back on the Visitors' Centre and walked purposefully towards the ancient ring of standing stones that stood out like giant fingers pointing skywards. There were no sounds of other vehicles on the road nor of aircraft overhead, only the thin cry of a bird that might have been a curlew. Lorimer squinted against the brightness of the sky and the water, shading his eyes to look for the bird.

Yes, there it was, almost hidden against the muddy

browns of the lochan's shoreline: unmistakeable with that long, curving beak. Another note made him look up suddenly to follow the flight of a lark, soaring into the pale skies. Still gazing heavenward, he heard the tread behind him.

"Quite a place, isn't it?"

"Indeed," Lorimer replied, not looking down but still following the flight of the skylark as it became a dot against the clouds. When it had disappeared he turned to Solly and was gratified to see his face raised in similar rapture.

"The Lark Ascending," Solly nodded. "He captured it so perfectly. Vaughan Williams. Yet the real thing never fails to work its magic, does it?"

Lorimer raised his eyebrows. "Didn't know you were a bird lover too."

"Ever since I was a little lad being taken around Saint James's Park. It's all part of my scientific curiosity, I suppose. How about you?" Solomon looked quizzically at Lorimer through his horn-rimmed spectacles. There was a kindness to his tone as if he were speaking to one of the patients in the Grange. Trying to sound me out, Lorimer thought. Was there a tentative suggestion here for him to open up his private thoughts?

Or had Solomon already drawn some profiling conclusions of his own? Lorimer was tempted for a moment to reveal his desires to this young man in a way that he had once shared with Maggie. He wanted to tell how he sometimes longed for wild open spaces like these and fresh air to fill his lungs instead of living within the confines of the city's grid; how he wanted to turn his back on the paper trails that Mitchison left him to follow; how he felt that surge of freedom when gazing into the soul of a painting or following the song of a simple bird. These were desires of a kind that he kept strictly to himself.

But there was always that other desire, too, the desire to hunt out the truth. Sometimes it was like an itch that he automatically started to scratch without thinking, the kind of itch that made him demand answers to hard questions. Such as, who had killed a young nurse in Glasgow? Whoever it was had robbed her, forever, of the right to stand here as he stood now, simply glad to be alive.

Lorimer expressed none of these whirling thoughts to the man at his side, however much he might understand, but simply stood looking out over the landscape, his face as inscrutable as the mealiths themselves. The slanting grey stones thrust themselves out of the grass high above their heads. For a moment they stared at them silently. Lorimer felt the weight of years pressing down on the landscape. Did Solomon feel that too, he wondered?

"Yes. Tomorrow or the day after. That's right. The whole day, I'm afraid. The boats out of here aren't frequent. Sorry? Oh, just a small hotel near the harbour. Nothing fancy." Lorimer put a hand onto his stomach. That meal downstairs had been plain home cooking but the portions were obviously meant for appetites larger than his own.

"Yes, Solly's fine. Okay. See you sometime tomorrow night or else I'll phone you. 'Bye." Lorimer replaced the telephone on its cradle before realising he hadn't asked Maggie how she was or what had been happening at home. Cursing himself, he lifted the handset again to redial but just at that moment a knock on the bedroom door made him drop the phone back with a clatter.

"Thought you might fancy a drink. The bar downstairs looks friendly enough. What d'you think?" Solly grinned from the doorway, his eyebrows raised in anticipation of his reply.

"I'll just grab my jacket." He slipped his wallet into the inside pocket, picked up the room key and closed the door behind them, all thoughts of another phone call forgotten.

Maggie put down the phone thoughtfully. It was the same as usual. No information about what was going on with the case nor any inquiry as to how *her* day had been. Okay, so she was used to being told the minimum information or else none at all. That was standard procedure. So why did she suddenly feel so sidelined by her husband?

Maggie shivered despite the heat wafting from the radiator. She was sitting on the carpet by the phone, her back against the hall table. The wooden spar dug into her spine but she hardly noticed it. For a few minutes she closed her eyes, trying to imagine what he was doing up there in the Island of Lewis. It was a place they'd talked about visiting but never had. Like so many of the things they'd intended to do. Opening her eyes, Maggie's gaze fell upon the envelope. It looked like any other plain buff A4 envelope, nothing that should give rise to any excitement, but Maggie experienced a sudden lifting of her spirits just by seeing it there. It could be her passport to a different way of life. A life she'd be able to control for the first time in years. Why hadn't she done something like this ages ago? When they'd finally given up trying to have a family, for instance? She'd let things drift just as much as he had. That was the plain truth of the matter. And it had taken that American woman to make her see things in a different light. Divine Lipinski had made an impact on her, that was for sure. Maggie cast her mind back to the night of the nurse's murder when they'd been left so abruptly. She and Divine had talked for hours. About being a policeman's wife. About all the dreams she'd shelved because of his job. And about how she yearned to travel. Divine had provided such colour and warmth that night. She'd made Maggie laugh about her life in Florida. She even made her involvement with crime in that part of the US sound amusing. Then she'd spoken about the Everglades, the sunsets over the Keys, the lazy flight of the brown pelicans; listening to her, Maggie was spellbound.

"Come over, why don't you?" Divine had said. She'd brushed away all the excuses about Lorimer's job. Maggie remembered the gentleness of her voice and the way she'd looked into her eyes. "I'm talking about *you*, Maggie, just you. Don't you want to spread your wings just a little?"

Maggie stretched out her hand for the envelope and drew it towards her. The pages of the white form were stapled together at one corner. She flicked through the contents speculatively. There was a closing date for this application. It was ages away but still she felt an urgency to do something now. She should discuss it with him first, surely? Almost as soon as the thought had come into her mind she dismissed it. No. This was for her to decide alone. It was her future. Her career.

There was no knowing whether they'd take her anyway, another little voice reasoned. Besides, hadn't there been an element of fate in seeing that leaflet on the staff room noticeboard?

It hadn't taken her long to collect the necessary references, either. Things had fallen swiftly into place as if it was meant to be. But she still hadn't told a soul outside the school. Well, except for Divine.

Maggie pulled herself to her feet and strode through to the kitchen in search of a pen. She cleared a space and spread the form Pout on the table. A few minutes later it was completed. All she had to do to finish this application for a teacher exchange was to sign her name at the bottom. Then the wheels would be put into motion and she might just find herself flying out to the US for an academic year while another teacher came to take her place. Would he miss her? Would she feel differently about things when she came back? Questions reeled through her mind as the pen hovered over the last page of the document. Where was he now? a voice demanded. Away. As usual. Maggie bit her lip. Then suddenly she knew what she had to do.

The pen flew over the dotted line with a flourish and Maggie sat back in satisfaction, smiling at the two words: Margaret Lorimer. It was like looking at the name of a new and exciting stranger.

21

Solly and Lorimer strode towards the narrow staircase that led to the hotel foyer and thence to the bar. The hum of talk was as thick as the cigarette smoke that hung like a hill mist in the airless room. In one corner a large individual in jeans and grubby t-shirt battled against aliens in the shape of a games machine. From his curses it sounded as if the aliens were winning.

"What'll you have?"

"Oh, why not a local malt, eh?"

Lorimer grinned. There was something about being with Solly tonight that made him feel as though he were on holiday. It wasn't a feeling he was very used to, he thought as he pushed his way between the rounded shoulders of two burly seamen. Lorimer caught the barman's eye and gave his order then, turning to see where Solly had gone, he watched as the man weaved his way to a vacant table by the window. His beard nodded up and down as he responded to some friendly remark from a total stranger. There was a touch of the exotic about Solomon Brightman that drew eyes to him, thought Lorimer. On his own patch, Lorimer knew he was pretty easy to identify as Plain Clothes. But that didn't seem to apply up here. He studied the faces around him, noting the weather-beaten complexions of the fishermen and trawler men who slouched against the bar.

There was a knot of older fellows dressed in shabby jackets and tweed bunnets. Lorimer pigeon-holed them as local worthies. Maybe they'd be good for information after a dram or two, he mused, the policeman's train of thought taking over. Behind them Lorimer's eyes made out the paler faces of a group of skinny boys lounging in a dingy corner. They were likely drinking up the week's giros, if he read them aright. He'd no illusions about the unemployment difficulties in these parts but as he watched them his thoughts turned to those other youths who had left the islands to find work.

Inevitably his mind turned to Kirsty.

As Lorimer carried back the drinks to where Solly was sitting he glanced this way and that, watching for a stare or a wondering eye to catch but nobody seemed the least interested in him. He was just another tourist passing through. So it was with some surprise that he felt a tug at his sleeve.

"Mind if I join you?" Lorimer turned to see Rowena Evans, an insouciant grin on her face. Lorimer hesitated. Was the girl underage or not? Her manner suggested that she was quite used to coming into the hotel for a drink but that meant nothing. He followed the girl's eyes towards their table where Solly sat reading the Gazette. So that was her little game, was it? Well, Solly was more than a match for a warm-blooded teenager.

"Why not. We're just over here." Lorimer stepped aside to let Rowena slither through the gap between the tables.

"Oh, hallo," as soon as he caught sight of the girl, Solly rose to his feet, the newspaper slipping on to the floor.

"Here. A local malt, you said?" Lorimer put down the drinks as Rowena slipped into the chair opposite Solly. "What about you, Rowena?"

"Oh, just a diet coke, thanks. I'm driving," she replied, a twinkle in her eye as if she had already guessed Lorimer's thoughts. As he left the pair at the table Lorimer wondered if Rowena Evans had deliberately chosen to come to the hotel knowing that Solly and he were staying over. Or was it just a coincidence?

"You're a criminal profiler, Dad says," she began. "Does that mean you have to interview lots of really nasty folk?"

Solomon laughed. "I don't really interview people much at all during an investigation. That's up to the investigating officer and his team. In this case, Detective Chief Inspector Lorimer."

Rowena turned to glance at Lorimer who was patiently waiting his turn at the bar once more. She shrugged. "So what do you do, then? Weren't you up here to question Sam and Angelica?"

Solly's smile died on his lips. The girl's eagerness to find out about his professional techniques seemed feigned suddenly. Had John Evans put his daughter up to this, perhaps?

"Rowena, this is a murder investigation. A young woman from Harris died in pretty horrible circumstances and we are all trying to find out everything we can about the world she came from and the people who knew her. Anybody from the clinic who had met her might be of help," he told her, his voice deliberately grave.

"So you don't think it was Sam or Sister Angelica?"

Solly stared at the girl, not answering, until she dropped her gaze and flushed.

"Sorry. I'm being a nuisance, aren't I?"

"You haven't known these two patients very long, Rowena. Why all this solicitude for them?"

"What?"

"Solicitude." Solly stopped. The girl wasn't one of his students; perhaps this was a term she might not understand. "Do you care about them a lot?"

"Are you kidding?" Rowena gasped with laughter. "I just want to know if I'm sleeping across the landing from a murderer!"

"And do you have any reason to think you might be?" Lorimer broke in, placing a bottle of Coke on the table.

"Gosh, you gave me a fright. I didn't hear you coming!"

"Nervous type, are you?" Lorimer joked, trying to make light of the girl's reaction.

"No, not usually."

"But you're worried about the present house guests?"

"Well, sort of. Not Angelica, really. She's all right. Sam's a bit creepy, though. Dad says he's been through hell and back. I suppose I should feel sorry for them all. They've been so ill and all they want up here is a bit of peace and quiet. Well, they get that okay, I can tell you. This place is *dead*. Okay, so I'm going with my pal to a disco tonight but that doesn't happen very often."

"Sam Fulton. Is there any reason to feel a threat from him other than your own imaginings?" Solly asked.

"What do you mean?"

"Has he actually done or said anything that gave you cause for concern?"

Rowena took a sip of her drink, considering Solly's words. "No. It's just that Dad seems to be with him all the time as if he's worried to let Sam out of his sight. Like he'll take him into town or they'll both go up the hill with Sula. They even watch T.V. together. I mean, Dad never watches T.V. He'd rather sit with his nose in a book."

"Me, too," Solly said and smiled as Rowena made a face at him.

Lorimer regarded the girl. She was restless on this island, a city girl who had been brought up here because of her parents' work. "How long have you been living at Failte?"

"Three years next August. I started at the Nicholson just after we came up."

"And have you any plans of your own for the future?"

"Depends on my exam results, doesn't it? Dad wants me to go to university but I'd rather get a job."

"In Glasgow?"

"No way. I'm off to London first chance I get," she scoffed. "As far away from Lewis as I can manage."

"You're not happy here, then?" Solly inquired.

"Oh, I'm happy enough. Mum and Dad are fine, you know. But I miss my friends from down South. Wish I could cadge a lift with you two or get a flight with Angelica tomorrow."

Lorimer raised his eyebrows. "She's leaving? Sister Angelica's leaving the island tomorrow?"

"Uh-huh. She told Dad she was going back to Glasgow just after you had left. Why?" the girl looked from one man to the other sensing the impact of her revelation.

"No reason," fibbed Lorimer though his mind was racing with all sorts of possibilities.

"Oh, here's my pal Heather," Rowena stood up suddenly, waving to a dark haired girl who was standing looking around the bar. "Thanks for the drink. Be seeing you." She gave the two men a quick smile as she left, her mind already on her friend and the evening ahead.

"So," Lorimer said, cradling the malt whisky in his hands. "Sister Angelica has had enough of the quiet life already."

"I wonder," returned Solly. "Is she regretting telling us about Leigh Quinn?"

"Or is there some other reason that's taking her back to Glasgow?" Lorimer frowned. The sooner they were on that boat back to the mainland, the better. This trip to Lewis and Harris had left him with more questions than answers.

22

It was the tune on the radio that brought everything back. Just a simple thing like that, Tom marvelled, and he was once more sitting by Nan's bed, her face turned to his, tired as always, slightly puzzled as if she still hadn't worked out why this disease had chosen her body for its host. Even when its final strains died away and the presenter began announcing something entirely different, the memories lingered like the scent of a woman's perfume, subtle yet all-pervasive.

Tom had battled with all his psychologist's expertise against the demons that had threatened to submerge him until he'd finally taken his own advice and sought professional help. But sometimes there would be a trigger, like that song, and he'd be swept into a series of pictures in his mind that refused to be dislodged.

Yet today it was not scenes of utter desolation and sickness that came to mind but the better days when he'd taken Nan for drives down the coast. She'd been light enough to carry out to the car, her wasted limbs slack beneath the rug, her arms not twined about his neck but hanging useless as he placed her gently in the passenger seat. He'd always played the car radio on those journeys rather than trying to make one-sided conversations. Nan's voice had reached that piping stage when it was impossible to make her out over the car engine.

Once they'd sung along to the radio, he remembered, when they'd been first married. Journeys into work had been happy, he suddenly realised, despite the daily grid-lock. Wasn't it always thus? To find a memory of pleasure that had seemed so mundane at the time? That's what everyone had told him at the funeral. Hang on to the good memories. And he'd tried. God knows how he'd tried.

Another picture: Nan on her exercise bike, her feet strapped into the pedals in an attempt to strengthen her ankles. She'd not been able to walk but Kirsty had insisted that it was of benefit anyway. The routine had been well established by then. Mornings when he'd washed and dressed his wife, leaving for work only when the Community nurse and her assistant arrived. The full time carer came after that and was gone by the time he'd returned, his morning note embellished with words of her own. Often his classes were over in time for Tom to be there when Kirsty arrived for her third visit of the day. He'd watched her tend to his wife, her lilting voice utterly normal, never condescending like some of them. Nan had hated the ones who had treated her like some imbecile child. Thankfully they'd usually had Kirsty up until the end.

"You'll be wanting *Countdown* then?" she'd ask Nan. "I'll leave you to it. Never could do anagrams myself," she'd say with a self-deprecating laugh. She'd known somehow that Nan's mind was still quick even if her fingers couldn't hold a pencil any more. That was what he'd admired about the young nurse, her ability to see beneath the illness to the whole person inside. Not many people had realised what an asset the girl had been to them. And how many people would miss her now?

The radio presenter's voice brought Tom back to the present as he handed over the programme to the news-caster. Another bomb had exploded in the Middle East.

He listened as the facts presented themselves to his brain, Nan's face still floating before him, still smiling up at Kirsty as she made to turn on the television. Now last night's FA Cup results were being analysed. Her face became hazy, indistinct. A different voice told Tom that a band of rain would be sweeping across the country. He tried to hold onto the image dissolving in front of him, to keep the smile at least, but all he could see was that empty pillow.

Lorimer switched off the car radio. The weather forecast told him only some of what he needed to know. If only there could be a crime forecast, he thought wryly. *A band of robberies will sweep across England and Wales today, followed by a combined forces occluded front. A high of serial killings will be present over Scotland leaving floods of victims in its wake. Outlook: grim.* His mind toyed with more comparisons, their flippancy a relief from the thought that had been haunting him all morning. Mhairi MacLeod was all alone now, the last of her family now that Kirsty was gone. Just what thoughts she had hidden away under that wise exterior, he couldn't say. Did she ever wonder about the possible link between a Glasgow prostitute and her own darling girl? Nobody in the investigation had even begun to tar the nurse with the same brush as poor Deirdre McCann. Even the Press had shown some sympathy. Their take on things was that the killer was some nutter and Kirsty his random victim. But was she?

Victims were not restricted to the dead women in the mortuary, either. The old lady herself was a victim just like the McCann family. And the ripples spread outwards to all whose lives had been touched. The Grange had its own victims, too. How many poor souls were still shaken by their loss?

Lorimer glanced across at Solly who seemed absorbed in the landscape, miles away from thoughts of death and its consequences. Behind him on the back seat his mobile began its insistent ringing, making him look ahead for the nearest place to stop. Despite these fairytale mountains sweeping above, Glasgow could still reach out with its persistent demands.

Phyllis didn't really care if the new nursing assistant was an improvement or not.

"What d'you think of her, then, dearie?" Brenda had asked for her opinion and was watching Phyllis's face closely for a sign. The woman in the bed gave none, simply stared back into space as if she hadn't heard a thing. Muttering to herself, Brenda swept her hand over the creaseless counterpane and waddled from the room. Behind her a pair of bright eyes followed her progress and a small sigh escaped into the air. Phyllis fixed her eyes on the door that was always kept ajar. Beyond it there was another world. But here, for a time, was her territory. She let her gaze focus on a fly that was crawling steadily up the grey paintwork. Its erratic progress might let it reach the top of the door. Would it take flight then? The question for Phyllis was far more absorbing than anything big Brenda could offer.

Brenda Duncan knew fine that Phyllis had heard her. "Just can't be bothered, I expect." She told herself, adding a whispered, "Poor soul."

Time and again she'd tried to make a connection with the sick woman. Even a flicker of the eyelids would have been something. But, no.

Kirsty had had the knack, of course, Brenda thought. That one had been able to charm the birds off the trees and no mistake. They'd all been daft about young Kirsty. And she had even seen Phyllis nodding in response to the nurse's questions. Nothing great, mind. Just that slight movement. But it was a dash sight more than she ever got. These thoughts were going through Brenda's mind as she pulled her shopping bag out of her locker and dragged on her raincoat. Those other thoughts were suppressed now. She'd had counselling from that woman her GP had recommended. Hadn't wanted it, but she'd had no choice in the end. It was that or trail about forever like a zombie, doped up to the eyeballs.

"That you off, then, Brenda?" Sister Pearson was looking pointedly at the clock at the end of the corridor. It was still four minutes to the hour but Brenda had to clip the minutes off if she were to catch her bus. Pearson knew that fine well, she thought crossly to herself. Mrs Baillie didn't mind, so why should she?

"Aye," she responded shortly and heaved open the front door, activating the bleeper as she did so. The glass door swung shut, stopping the alarm abruptly. Brenda quickened her stride. She didn't want to be hanging about in this drizzle. There was no shelter at her stop and this was the kind of rain that soaked through everything. She visualised her umbrella, hanging from the coat hook in the hall. Fat lot of good it was doing there. So much for this morning's forecast, she told herself, clenching her teeth against an easterly wind.

It was supposed to be nearly summer, for God's sake. What bloody awful weather! Her glasses were streaming now and she had to keep her head down to avoid the worst onslaughts of the gusts. Her rubber-soled shoes made wet imprints on the pavements under the watery light from the street lamps. The dark sky had activated their photo-sensitive cells on an evening that was more like autumn than spring. Brenda's stout legs quivered with the effort of increasing her pace. She had turned the bottom of the hill and now it was that climb up to Langside Monument. Determined not to miss her bus, the woman plunged on, bag over one arm, clutching at her collar to stop the raindrops seeping in. She felt a sharp pain in her chest as the incline steepened. Too much weight, her GP had scolded her when she'd complained about her aches and pains. Brenda was conscious of her glasses slipping down her nose now, but she tried to ignore them, fearful of loosening her grip on the coat collar.

Just as she made her way to the brow of the hill she saw the bus pulling away from her stop.

"Damn!" she uttered aloud. "Damn and blast!" Her shoulders sagged and the shopping bag slipped from her grasp as she watched the bus sail past her, tyres swishing on the wet road. It was at least fifteen minutes until the next one, unless this was an earlier one running late. Brenda knew all about the erratic timetables. Bitter experience had taught her that it was no use taking a chance to go off to the café for a hot cuppa. You had to wait, just in case there was another bus coming.

She took her place at the head of the queue, tucking wet hands into the sleeves of her coat. She was oblivious to the other passengers forming a line behind her. The rain that was now coursing in runnels down the back of her neck had sapped all her energy and she stared moodily towards the direction from which her bus would come. She didn't notice a figure half-obscured beneath a golf umbrella in the queue behind her. Nor was she aware, when the bus did eventually arrive with a harsh squeal of brakes, of the same figure leaving the queue and heading instead towards the taxi rank by the Victoria Infirmary.

Brenda slumped into the nearest seat and stared out past the streaming windows at absolutely nothing at all. Her mind was jumping ahead to the meal she'd cook for herself at home; her body was simply grateful to be seated at last. Behind her two women chattered. If Brenda had cared to listen in to their patter she might have heard all about that-one-in-the-next-close and her fancy men. But the women's voices were simply part of the overall noise of bus engine and the presence of humans around her, a comforting sound that made her eyelids droop. She paid only the briefest of attention to the outside world; a flicker of a glance outwards to make sure she didn't pass her stop.

Here it was. She rose slowly from the seat with a creak of leather and shuffled forwards towards the platform. Her hands grasped the cold metal rail as the bus veered around a corner then shuddered to a halt.

Now she was walking, walking, forcing her legs to carry her up the familiar street. The red sandstone tenements looked warm and welcoming through the misty drizzle.

Not far now.

The close mouth yawned open, the security door latched back on its metal hook. The stone corridor with its glazed wall tiles that led from the front steps to the back-court was exposed for all to see. Yet it was only residents who were supposed to have keys for either entrance. She peered in, uncertain for an instant as to why this door was lying open. Then the smell reminded her. Of course. This was the day the painters were to be in. Brenda tiptoed past the Wet Paint sign chalked on the stone floor of the close.

Mustn't get any of that on my raincoat, she thought, pulling its folds tighter around her rotund frame. It was a fair step to the second landing.

Puffing, she stopped from time to time, admiring the newly painted walls. The lower half was a bright sky blue, defined by a neat black stripe from the cream upper walls and ceiling.

Brenda gave a sigh of relief as she reached the top step then rummaged in her raincoat pocket for the keys. The sigh became a yawn and she took off her glasses to rub tiredly at her eyes, fitting the Yale in the lock with her free hand.

Just as the solid wooden door swung away from her, she felt a tap on her shoulder. Brenda turned around with a start, surprised and instantly puzzled that she'd heard nobody coming up behind her. Her face, which had been tensed in alarm, relaxed immediately.

"Oh," she said, "it's you." Then, cocking her head to one side, she added, "What on earth are you doing here?"

Brenda's eyes widened in disbelief as the figure lunged towards her, hands suddenly grasping her throat. Her mouth opened in protest, then there was a gargling sound as she struggled against her attacker.

As Brenda jerked backwards onto the hall carpet, her glasses flew upwards into the air. They curved in a perfect arc then broke with a tinkle against the rows of brass hooks screwed into the wall. For a moment the landing held its breath. Then several small sounds interrupted the silence. Wood clunked on wood as the golf umbrella was propped carefully against the doorframe. Feet in wet shoes brushed back and forth, back and forth on the doormat; the sound of coming home; familiar, nothing to alert the neighbours.

The front door banged shut against the newly painted close, echoes spiralling down the stairwell. These were the sounds that everybody listened to at the time, but afterwards nobody remembered that they'd heard them.

Within the house, behind the solid door, Brenda Duncan lay sprawled where she had fallen, ungainly even in death.

23

The Cross café wasn't the nicest place to have tea and a chat, but it was a safe haven from the deluge outside. The rain had not stopped all day and runnels of water were swirling down the slopes of the pavement outside. Angelica sipped the hot brew, sighing with a mixture of pleasure and relief. It would be okay, now, she told herself. It was all over. Trying to make Leigh see things that way might be tricky but she had hopes.

As if on cue, the Irishman staggered into the café, his hair plastered black against his head. He gazed around him, lost for a moment in the sea of tables and chairs until he spotted her at the window. She'd sat there deliberately so he could see her but the window had steamed up, foiling her strategy.

"Angelica." Leigh's eyes softened as he sat down opposite her. "I thought… for a minute … you'd not come."

"I said I'd be here, didn't I?"

"Aye, that's so."

"I haven't let you down yet, my boy, and I'm not about to start now. Got that?"

Leigh nodded.

"What d'you want? Tea? Coffee?" Angelica asked as the waitress approached.

He shrugged as if it wasn't important so Angelica gave the waitress an order for another pot of tea.

"Now, down to business. The police were up at the respite centre in Lewis. That Chief Inspector wanted to know what you'd been doing the night of Kirsty's death."

Catching sight of Leigh's sudden frown, she hastily added, "I told them that you were with me, of course. We'd been praying together. But somehow he seemed to think that was suspicious."

"Why?"

"It's the praying hands, Leigh. That's what they can't see past. You know and I know the significance for us both but they don't look at things quite in the way that we do. D'you understand?"

The man nodded then flinched as the waitress set down a pot of tea on the table. Angelica poured it for him, knowing he was still too shaken for even a simple task like this. The man's nerves were shot to pieces, she told herself. How he was going to stand up to that Lorimer when he came back from Lewis, only God knew.

"You still keeping an eye on Phyllis?"

"Aye."

Angelica nodded her approval. That was something at least. She leaned forward and patted his hand. "Now you're not to worry, but the police will be coming back. They want to talk to you again."

Leigh looked puzzled but said nothing.

"Here's what to do. Now listen. When they ask where you were the night Kirsty died, tell them you were with me. I'll back you up."

Leigh Quinn shifted in his seat, squirming around as he looked around the cafe. Suddenly every person there seemed to pose a threat. Angelica watched him intently, sensing his moods as she always did. She could almost smell the fear rising from him.

"Look, Leigh, it's going to be all right. Trust me?" Angelica fixed her eyes earnestly on the man's white face until he looked at her. Then he gave a grudging nod.

"Good. Now drink up your tea. We have plans to make, you and I."

24

Lorimer's eyes were gritty from peering into the swishing windscreen wipers hour after hour. He'd been reasonably circumspect on the journey through the Highlands, given the rain sweeping across the winding roads, but after that call on his mobile the car had hurtled down from Loch Lomond, breaking every speed regulation in the book. Now they were entering the city boundaries at last. Solly had slept a lot of the way from Ullapool, folded into his black raincoat like one of those cormorants he'd seen around the Harris coastline. Lorimer was glad of the silence between them. It had given him time to think, time to digest that phone call from HQ telling him to get himself over to the south side double quick, there'd been another death.

He'd called Rosie at the University to see if she'd be at the scene of crime. Yes, she'd said shortly, and not with Mitchison if Lorimer could get his arse into gear. Her tone expressed distaste for Lorimer's boss that had made him chuckle. But his mirth was short-lived. There was nothing remotely funny about this.

"Brenda Duncan," Lorimer spoke softly to himself. "Who on earth would want to do you in?" It didn't make sense. First a prostitute in Queen Street station, then a nurse working the night shift. Now another member of the clinic's staff murdered in her own home. Had she seen something the night of Kirsty's death? Had she been keeping something back from Strathclyde CID? Or had something happened that she'd failed to register as significant? Either way it took him back to the same place: the Grange. One thing was certain, though; neither Sam Fulton nor Sister Angelica could have committed this latest murder.

Lorimer braked sharply as the lights turned to red.

"Here already?" Solly turned to look out at the familiar urban landscape. "How long till we reach Govanhill?"

"Another fifteen minutes, if we're lucky." He stared ahead at the build up of rush hour traffic. It would take them at least that to cross town, he reckoned. Maybe he should have crossed the Erskine Bridge. Hunger was gnawing at his guts. He should have made more time for a lunch stop. Maggie would be home by now. Maybe even cooking something decent for him, he thought wistfully. God, he'd missed her these last few days.

The journey across town via the Clyde Tunnel was a nightmare. Lorimer fretted and fumed aloud, cursing each and every driver that slowed him down. To cap it all, the tunnel was down to one lane. Solly, sitting beside him, kept a tactful silence. The psychologist looked out onto the darkening skies. He'd already worked one thing out for himself. Whoever had killed Brenda Duncan had known exactly where she lived and when she'd be off duty. Someone she knew, possibly. A colleague? A patient? Again, Solly felt a frisson as he thought of the killer and the risks he'd taken. There was both recklessness and a sense of calculation about the man that seemed at odds with one another. More than ever Solly was disquieted by the three murders; it was as if they had been carried out by a different hand each time. Still, there was a new crime scene ahead and that might throw light upon the puzzle. Solly shivered. The sight of a corpse was not something he relished.

It was well after six o'clock when Lorimer turned the car into the street in Govanhill. Rosie Fergusson's BMW was parked outside the close mouth, a squad car just beyond.

"Coming up?" Lorimer asked, unbuckling his seat belt.

Solly just looked at him and nodded. He had to see it for himself. There was no other option.

Brenda Duncan's flat was on the second landing. Lorimer acknowledged the scene of crime officer with a nod as he reached the open doorway. He could see a uniformed officer at the far end of the passage where the glare of the arc lights washed over the scene. Rosie was examining the body as they entered the hallway. It was a surprisingly large area, reminding Lorimer of the old-fashioned room and kitchen belonging to an aged relative, long since deceased. The Glasgow tenements had fairly teemed with family life a century ago. But he was here to deal with death, he reminded himself, his eyes returning to the body beyond Rosie's white-coated figure.

The pathologist looked up at the sound of their footsteps. "Hi. Oh, Solly. You're here too. Good!" She waggled a glove-clad hand in their direction before continuing her examination.

Brenda Duncan's body lay close to the wall. Above her a huge gilt mirror reflected the grim tableau of Rosie and Lorimer now crouching over the body. Solly held onto the wall for support, his stomach suddenly queasy. Yet he could not look away from the mirror. It was there, all right. Clasped between her podgy fingers was a single red carnation.

His signature, thought Solly, his calling card. Sliding along the wall, he took in the whole length of the woman's corpse, the raincoat riding up above the fleshy thighs, legs falling apart. The hands were pressed together and pointing downwards. It was just like the others.

"You okay?" Rosie looked up suddenly, concern on her face.

"Not really," he replied. "Think I'll go outside for a minute."

Lorimer and Rosie exchanged glances as Solly made his

way out of the flat.

"Who found her?" Lorimer asked.

"The neighbour across the landing. She has a spare key. Got worried when nobody answered the door all day."

"Didn't she think the woman was out at work?"

Rosie shook her head. "She knew it was Brenda's day off. Said she'd arranged to call in and have coffee with her." The pathologist crooked her finger at him and Lorimer drew closer. "See this?" Rosie turned the head gently to one side and pointed to the bruising. "He used both hands and you can see where his fingers pressed into the larynx."

"Any sign of a struggle?"

"Nope. She was dead by the time she'd hit the floor, I reckon."

"Then he had his little ceremony."

"The flower? Yes. We saw that right away."

"Was she in this position when that neighbour called?"

"Yes, the body hasn't been shifted much at all."

"So whoever killed her just locked the door and walked away?"

"I see what you're getting at," Rosie replied. "But there was no need to use a key to lock up. The door locks simply by pulling it to."

"Time of death?"

"She's been dead since last night. I should think around mid-evening. I can't be more accurate than that, yet."

"What about sexual activity?" Lorimer pointed at the exposed thighs.

"None. I'm not sure why he pulled her skirt up like that. There's a question for Solly, perhaps."

"Any chance of fingerprints on the throat?"

"I shouldn't think so. He wore gloves. Again. But there may be some traces under Brenda's fingernails. That's something we'll have to investigate."

"Evidence. We need some evidence," Lorimer muttered. He stood up and turned towards the door. "Solly and I had better head over to the clinic. I'll be in touch."

Lorimer looked down as a flashlight from the SOCO's camera illuminated the corpse. He blinked then nodded briefly towards the body. The dead woman was in safe hands with Rosie Fergusson.

"Chief Inspector," Mrs Baillie's hand was outstretched as soon as they entered the reception area. "This is unexpected," she said, ushering Lorimer and Solly into the Grange.

"I'm afraid we have some rather distressing news. Is there somewhere private we could talk?" Lorimer said.

"In my quarters. We won't be disturbed there," she added, tucking a bulky file under her arm.

Mrs Baillie's rooms were situated on the top floor of the building. She unlocked a door in the corridor that gave way to a tiny square hall. A set of golf clubs lay propped against a shelf that contained a few dusty looking books.

"In here, please," she motioned them through to the sitting room. The windows overlooking the front of the grounds gave a view of the road all the way down to Queen's Park. Lorimer looked around him. Whatever he had expected from the woman's living quarters, it certainly wasn't this. The room was practically bare. An open door gave him a glimpse of a tiny kitchenette; another door, firmly closed, probably led to her bedroom. It, too, would give that view over the front. The walls were painted in the same pale wash that he'd seen throughout the rest of the Grange and were totally unadorned; no prints, no photographs, nothing but a blank expanse. Or was it?

Moving closer to the wall opposite the windows, Lorimer noticed faint rectangular shapes where pictures of some sort had once been hanged. Was she preparing to have the decorators in, maybe? Would that explain the empty mantelpiece and bare walls? Sweeping a practiced eye over the rest of the sitting room, he saw only a plain teak coffee table placed between a basic two-seater sofa and one upright chair. A grey metal filing cabinet stood to one side of the chair as if Mrs Baillie was accustomed to doing her paperwork in the privacy of her own rooms. It reminded him suddenly of Kirsty's bedsit with its second-hand furnishings, except that Kirsty had tried to project some of her personality into her room. This place had been stripped of any personal touches.

It looked as if someone had packed up all the usual bits and pieces that transform a living space into a real home; the little clues his detective's eye instinctively sought. Curious, he thought. Was the woman preparing to move out? Did that explain why it all looked so spartan? Catching Solly's eye, he raised an inquiring eyebrow. Solly's glimmer of a smile told him that the same thoughts had occurred to the psychologist.

Behind the door there was a cheap telephone mounted on the wall. His eye fell on the box fixed to the skirting board. At least she seemed to have her own private line.

"Please take a seat," Mrs Baillie said, immediately opting for the upright chair so that Lorimer and Solly had to share the sofa. "I was just about to begin checking the time sheets," she said, patting the folder on her lap.

Lorimer was aware of Solly's eyes still roving over the room as he began. "I'm sorry to have to disrupt your evening, Ma'am, but there's been another murder."

Mrs Baillie's face remained impassive, her eyes waiting for the information Lorimer was about to give.

"Brenda Duncan's body was found this evening by a neighbour." Lorimer watched the woman's face turn pale. Her hands clutched briefly at the folder but then she stayed stock still as though frozen by the news.

"It appears that she was killed last night, shortly after she had returned from her shift here," Lorimer went on. "You have my commiserations," he told her, wondering just what emotions were circulating under that bloodless face.

"I can't quite take this in, Chief Inspector," Mrs Baillie began slowly. "*Brenda*? She was such a harmless big woman. Who on earth would want to kill her?" she said, echoing Lorimer's earlier thoughts. "Where did it happen?"

"In her own home."

Mrs Baillie frowned. "So, do you think it was the same person...?" she tailed off, her eyes flitting from one man to the other.

Lorimer took a deep breath. "We aren't at liberty to divulge details right now," he began, then took a swift look at Solly.

"If it was the same person, then there is an obvious link between the clinic and the killer," Solly said.

"We could station a uniformed officer here if you wished," Lorimer told her.

"No. No. That won't be necessary. There's been enough disruption already. This business has set back a good number of our patients. Imagine how they will feel if they think they're being watched. Some of them suffer from paranoia, you know."

"There will have to be a police presence here at some time, though. We still have to question your staff about Mrs Duncan."

"But why? If she was killed in her own home? Why bother us here?" The woman clenched her fists, her expression defiant.

"Brenda Duncan," Lorimer began, smoothly. "I understand she left here yesterday evening. What time would that have been?"

Mrs Baillie opened the folder that lay across her knees. She turned the pages of the file with great deliberation, unaware of the eyes firmly fixed on her, intent on every emotion flickering across her face, watching for every sign revealed by her body language.

"According to Sister Pearson's sheet, she left at four minutes to eight yesterday evening, Chief Inspector. Today was her day off."

The papers had stopped being rustled and Lorimer had the impression that Mrs Baillie could have given that information without the need to sift through the time sheets.

The woman's white hands were folded in front of her on the documents. She looked from Lorimer to Solly with an apparent coolness that was betrayed by two pink spots highlighting her cheekbones.

"The shift doesn't finish until eight on the dot but we are fairly flexible with our staff." There was a pause as she eyed them both. "She had a bus to catch over the hill. Anyway," she tapped her fingers in irritation, "Brenda was a good time keeper. Never had a problem with her."

The woman's words jarred. She'd said much the same about Kirsty.

"Even after Kirsty MacLeod's murder?" Lorimer swiftly interjected. Mrs Baillie's shoulders tensed. Lorimer could feel the anger being controlled. It was a cruel question but he wasn't in this job to ask easy ones.

"She went for counselling at my request. Through her own GP, of course."

"So she was off work?"

"Not for very long. Five days in all. She seemed fine once she was back into the routine." Mrs Baillie leaned forward slightly to press home her point. "That's what the Doctor recommended, a return to the normal working day. And it worked," she added defiantly. Lorimer didn't doubt it.

"But I thought she worked nights?" Solly asked innocently.

"It wasn't thought suitable for her to return to night-shift work. A later shift beginning at noon and finishing at eight was deemed more appropriate," Mrs Baillie fixed Solly with a stare that brooked no nonsense then turned to Lorimer.

"Actually," the matron gave him a lopsided smile, "Brenda had spoken to me privately about handing in her notice."

The smile stayed glued to her mouth but failed to reach the eyes that continued to betray their hostility towards the two men. Her hands were clasped firmly in front of her.

Lorimer was instantly reminded of his guidance teacher way back in secondary school when he and his mates had been caught drinking Carlsberg Specials in the boys' toilets. He stared her out too, if he remembered rightly.

"And did she?" he asked.

"I persuaded her otherwise," she said. "She didn't enjoy being grilled by the police. None of us did. You seemed to ask the same questions over and over as if you didn't believe what we were telling you. Brenda was most upset."

And now she's dead, Lorimer wanted to say. The woman didn't appear to have taken that news in properly, yet. There was a hostility here that he couldn't comprehend, something that threatened to create a chasm between the Director and himself. Fear could cause that, he knew. Had she something to hide, he wondered?

"This is quite normal procedure, Mrs Baillie," he began, keeping his tone neutral, almost bored. "You may expect to answer the same questions several times. Memory's a funny thing. Suddenly there are aspects people remember days later. Even when they were certain they'd recalled everything there was to recall."

Mrs Baillie inclined her head in a token of deference.

She doesn't buy that one, thought Lorimer. Let's try a different tack.

"We visited Failte in Lewis and spoke to Sam Fulton and Sister Angelica."

"Well, I'm sure they enjoyed that little change to their routine," she remarked, the sarcasm scarcely concealed.

"Sister Angelica told us that Leigh Quinn had been very upset the night of Kirsty MacLeod's murder. He'd actually been in her room shortly after the body was discovered. Praying."

"Really?"

"Where was Leigh Quinn last night, Mrs Baillie?"

For the first time the woman looked flustered. She unclasped her hands and wiped them down either side of her skirt.

"Here, I suppose. They're not prisoners, you know, Chief Inspector. Only those patients who might be a danger to themselves are kept under close scrutiny."

"And Leigh Quinn doesn't come into that category?" Solly asked mildly.

"No. Leigh has severe problems but he may come and go as he pleases."

"And does he?" Lorimer asked.

The woman hesitated before answering. "Sometimes he'll go out for a walk. He doesn't sleep well, you see. Other times," she broke off, biting her lips as if she had already said too much.

"Yes?" Lorimer prompted.

"Other times he sits with Phyllis in her room." She looked from one man to the other. "Phyllis doesn't mind," she insisted. "We'd know if she didn't want him to visit her room."

Lorimer nodded. Could anything be gleaned from that crippled patient downstairs to confirm Quinn's where-abouts last night?

"Brenda Duncan," Lorimer switched tack again. "Have you any record to show when she and Kirsty worked together and with whom? Nursing staff as well as patients."

Mrs Baillie clasped then unclasped her fingers and Lorimer saw the knuckles white and bloodless under her tight grasp. He suddenly had the impression of a physically strong woman beneath the navy suit.

"That's not a problem, Chief Inspector. We have duty rosters made up and signed after every shift. I can let you have a photocopy of the more recent ones." She paused and gave a small frown as if they were two tiresome small boys taking up her valuable time. Lorimer thought back to Kirsty's diary. It had yielded very little after all. No personal information had been recorded other than birthdays; her work rotas had simply been marked *early* or *late* depending on the shifts.

"And I believe you were not here yesterday evening, Mrs Baillie," Lorimer added.

"That's right. I..." The woman stopped mid-sentence, staring at him as the full import of his words hit home.

"You're not suggesting that I had anything to do with Brenda's death? Dear God!" she exclaimed, her hand clutching the pearls at her throat.

"I'm not suggesting anything, ma'am. But it would be helpful to know where you were last night." Lorimer sat up abruptly, his shadow now cast over the coffee table between them. Mrs Baillie stared at him blankly then twisted round to search for something in the handbag that was looped over the arm of the chair, head lowered to cover her confusion.

When she looked up her face was flushed.

"I can't find it," she began. "My cinema ticket. I thought I'd kept it but I must have thrown it away." Then she straightened up and smoothed her hands along the front of her skirt. "But I don't suppose you're really looking for an alibi for me, are you?" She smiled again, her confidence returning.

"No, no. Not at all," Solly reassured her before Lorimer could speak. "What a pity you hadn't been here, though. Isn't it?" Solly smiled and shrugged.

"Anyway," she stood up and turned towards the filing cabinet, "I can give you the duty rosters for the last month." Lorimer watched as she walked her fingers through the files. At last she stopped and pulled out a green folder. Her back was to them as she leafed through its contents but even so, Lorimer and Solly could see the raised shoulders stiff with tension.

"Here," she pushed the file across the table to Lorimer. "All the rosters for April and May. You should find what you're looking for in there."

"Really?" It was Lorimer's turn for sarcasm now. "We're looking for a murderer."

Their eyes met in a frozen stare then, to Lorimer's

satisfaction, Mrs Baillie dropped her glance.

"Thank you," he said as if nothing untoward had happened between them. "I'll see this is returned to you as soon as possible," he added, tapping the green file and easing himself out of the sofa. Solly followed his lead, springing to his feet. Mrs Baillie simply stood there for a moment, her tall figure ramrod stiff.

"I'd better show you both out," her voice was dry.

Nothing was said as the three made their way downstairs to the main entrance. The woman's hand flicked over the security buttons then pulled the door wide open.

She made no attempt to return Lorimer's "goodnight" as he strode towards the drive, Solomon in his wake.

Once in the driveway Solly tugged his sleeve.

"What was all that about? You were practically rude to her. Don't you want her co-operation, Lorimer?" Solly raised his arms then let them fall in a moment of bewilderment.

"Oh, she'll co-operate all right," he smiled. "She'll be only too pleased to co-operate once we've gone through the other files."

"What other files?"

Lorimer looked down at his quizzical expression and smiled. "Before we left Stornoway I got a rather interesting fax."

"Go on."

"I didn't mention it at the time but it seems that this clinic has been experiencing financial difficulties after all. Despite the accountant's previous assurances."

"So?"

"So. A number of things. On their own they could be nothing to worry about but put together they make me uneasy. For a start the last accounts show a big loss. That could be okay on its own but the most recent accounts haven't been lodged and they've recently changed their bankers. That's always a bad sign." Lorimer paused. "But there's something else that's got me worried."

"What?"

"The building contractors who were doing renovations have slapped an inhibition order on the whole business."

"You don't think any of the contractors could have kept a key to the basement door, do you?"

Lorimer shrugged. "Who knows? They've been questioned just like everybody else who has something to do with this place. No. What's concerning me is money. The builders haven't been paid and they've obviously run out of patience so what they can do to get their money is to take steps to stop any of the properties being sold until the directors cough up."

"But I thought Phyllis Logan owned them. Surely the directors can't market the properties without her permission."

"I don't know. There's something odd going on and it's not just to do with her saving money on airline tickets to Lewis. Did you see that place of hers? Didn't you think it looked like she was in the throes of moving out? There was hardly a decent stick of furniture in the entire flat."

"I still don't see what it's got to do with the murder of three women," Solly replied.

"Nor do I," Lorimer frowned suddenly. "But my policeman's nose tells me something's rotten in that place. Maybe something Kirsty and Brenda knew about, too. I want to sniff around a bit and find out what it is." He unlocked the car and leaned on the door. "And another thing. I've rarely seen anybody display so little grief. Shock, maybe, but not a word of sorrow. Explain that to me, eh?"

Solly pulled open the passenger door and slid into the leather seat. "Can't fault her there. Some people hide their emotions very well. She may well be crying her eyes out right now for all we know."

"Hm," Lorimer sounded sceptical.

"Anyway, aren't you forgetting Deirdre McCann? She's got nothing to do with the Grange," Solomon bit his lip suddenly. This was what he had wanted to discuss with

Lorimer but each time he came close to it something stopped him. He'd been trying to see and feel his way into a killer's mind and all he could think was how disparate it all was, especially since Brenda Duncan's murder. He gnawed at the edges of his moustache. How could he tell Lorimer how he felt? It was as if there were two shadows following them, just out of sight, each intent on strangling some poor woman.

As the car roared into the night, Solly looked out into the streets and all he could see was a red flower crushed between dead fingers.

"It's me," the familiar, husky voice breathed through the intercom.

"Come on up."

Solly grinned. Rosie was just what he needed right now, he realised, his tiredness vanishing. It was late. She would stay the night, surely? Or was she merely bringing him up to speed with this latest murder? Solly caught sight of his boyish expression in the hall mirror and laughed softly. She'd have phoned if it was just about work.

Leaning over the banister, he looked down at the fair head bobbing below him as she climbed the stairs. His hands gripped the metal rail. Brenda Duncan might have stopped at such a place watching out for her assailant. But had she? Or was the freshly painted close with its yawning mouth an open invitation for a stranger to walk right in? Solly shook his head. No way. Brenda might not have expected a visitor but she would have known who he was.

Thoughts of the woman's corpse disappeared as Rosie smiled up at him.

"Hallo, you."

She raised herself up on tip-toe to kiss him full on the mouth. Solly's arms were around her in a welcoming embrace, drawing her to him.

"Mm. That's better," she murmured. "Can I come in, now?"

Solly gave a laugh, pulled the door wider and then

closed it firmly behind her.

"Oh, what a day!" Rosie flopped into the nearest comfy armchair, dropping her handbag and jacket onto the floor.

"Drink?"

"Any of that gin I brought you?"

"I even bought in some tonics, specially for you."

"Ah! That's my man!"

Moving into the kitchen to fetch her drink, Solly warmed to her words. *Her man*. Not her waiter, her butler, but her *man*. *Her* man.

He sat at her feet, his head resting companionably against the chair as they drank in silence. It was comfortable, secure, so he could tell her what he'd been thinking, couldn't he?

"I've had some thoughts about the profile."

"Because of tonight, you mean?"

"Not really, but this death does rather consolidate my ideas."

"Go on."

Solly remained silent for a few minutes. Rosie let it linger. She was familiar enough with those silences of his by now so she waited, sipping the gin slowly.

"It's the flower that bothers me most."

"His signature?"

"Hm. Signatures can be forged, don't you know."

"Solly. What're you trying to say?" Rosie leaned forward, her eyes on his dark profile.

"Not all of it makes sense. A murderer who kills a prostitute in a station then two nurses, one at her work and the other in her own home. What kind of man is that?"

"Reckless? A risk-taker?"

Solly shook his head. "Not just that. There aren't any proper links. Just that flower and the praying hands."

Rosie laid her glass down suddenly. "Hey! Are you saying we've got more than one guy doing these killings? Or is there some sort of religious fundamentalist gang targeting women victims?"

Solly heaved a sigh. "Not a gang. Nor do I think the two killings show a pattern."

"Three. Three killings," Rosie corrected him.

Solly turned and faced her, his expression suddenly grave. "Yes, but there are only two killers and I doubt very much if they have ever met."

"But the flowers?"

"Yes, that's what I keep coming back to. In profiling you must look at the location first to see what opportunity the killer might have had and if he lives anywhere near the choice of locus. With the station that was difficult at first."

"He could've come by train?"

"Not in the middle of the night. He has to have something to do with Queen Street station. He knows the layout well, gets away without anybody noticing him or being caught on a security camera. Now, if the second murder had been in the vicinity of the city, even a mile or so away, I wouldn't have bothered so much. But the Grange is away over on the south side."

"So?"

"So, there's no pattern. You see, serial killers tend to work in ever increasing circles away from a base, which is usually where they live. With each killing they become bolder and travel a bit further afield. Okay. It's not a rigid model. There are cases like the long distance lorry driver who murdered those children. But even then there was a pattern defined by his delivery schedules. Here I can't find any evidence to show me a killer who progresses from a prostitute in a station to a nurse at work."

"Unless he's a nutter inside the Grange already."

Solly didn't answer her. For a moment he stared into space, unblinking.

"With Brenda Duncan's death I feel justified in proposing that we have two killers. Whoever killed Deirdre McCann is a person in serious need of help. He's a danger to himself as well as to society."

"And Brenda? Kirsty?"

185

"Ah. I'm not entirely happy with the disturbed personality theory everyone is so eager to believe. There's a reason for those deaths. Someone badly wanted these two women out of the way. The flowers are a blind."

"You mean someone is trying to make you think there's a serial killer on the loose?"

"Exactly. There are two profiles here and my job right now is to untangle them."

"What does Lorimer think about this?" Rosie took one look at Solly's face and laughed. "You mean you haven't told him yet?"

"No. But I will. I'll have to, won't I?"

Solly pulled himself up and perched on the arm of the chair. "What about you? What's next on your agenda?"

"Oh, back to the lab. *Early*," she added with a grimace.

"Well," he hesitated and then smiled as if a happy thought had just occurred to him.

"Hadn't we better go to bed now, then?"

25

It was still daylight when Lorimer reached his street. The longest day was barely a month away and there was a pearly glow from the sky that comes after a rain shower in late Spring. It could have been any hour of the day.

Lorimer pulled into the driveway, carefully avoiding the stone gateposts, and parked outside his door. The front drive was ancient tarmac with the weeds poking through. It did fine for a parking space, if Lorimer had ever thought about it (which he didn't). It was Maggie who mowed what little lawn their property possessed and fitfully tended their ragged flowerbeds. Lorimer turned the key in the car door, reminding himself yet again to buy new batteries for the key fob. He looked up automatically at the lounge window. There was a light flickering against the glass. The television was on. Surely it wasn't *Newsnight* already?

The slam of the door behind him sounded hollow, as if all the carpets had been lifted. The house had an abandoned feel to it but Lorimer knew Maggie was in there somewhere.

"Hi. Anybody home?" he called up the unlit hallway. There was no response but he could hear the sound of voices from the television beyond the lounge door.

Lorimer rapped twice on the door before pushing it open. "It's only me," he joked, then stopped as Maggie leaped up to switch off the television, a look of alarm on her face. The alarm changed to something else. Relief? Lorimer couldn't decide. Then she was in his arms, clinging round his waist as if she'd never let him go. Lorimer felt her tension. Maybe she'd been watching a scary movie. He stroked her hair and kissed the top of her head. Suddenly his tummy rumbled below Maggie's clinging grasp and they broke apart, laughing together.

"No dinner again?" she shook her dark curls reprovingly.

"Sorry, Miss," Lorimer pulled a contrite face. "Didn't have time."

"How about poor Solly?"

"Oh, he never seems to remember such mundane things as meals. Time we found him a good woman."

"Like Rosie."

"Indeed." Lorimer slumped into a sagging armchair. "Oh, it's good to be home. Just the two of us."

Maggie nodded. It seemed ages since they'd been at home together.

"Anything to eat, kind lady?" Lorimer put on his most disarming face.

"Typical," she rejoined. "Doesn't see me for days and what does he miss? My home cooking!" And with a great pretence at being offended she set off for the kitchen.

Lorimer stretched his long legs out and, giving a huge yawn, muttered, "Too right." Then he closed his eyes.

When Maggie returned five minutes later with a tray full of soup and sandwiches she found her husband fast asleep.

Quietly she set the tray down on the coffee table then lifted the remote control. The videotape ejected noiselessly. Holding her breath she retrieved the tape, fitted it back into its sleeve then slid it deep down into her open briefcase. For an instant the echoes of those American voices reverberated in her brain telling her all about the opportunities teacher exchange could bring. Opportunities Maggie wasn't ready to share with her husband. Not yet. She looked down at the man sleeping below her gaze. His mouth was open slightly and she could see two days' stubble round the slack jaw. The lines round those bad blue eyes seemed deeper than usual. We're getting older, thought Maggie wistfully, both of us. But she wasn't past it yet. Oh, no. Not by a long way.

"Hey," she whispered at last, "soup's getting cold."

Lorimer came to, blinking as if he'd slept for hours rather than minutes.

"'S'nice of you to bother," he mumbled, sitting up and taking the tray onto his lap. Maggie watched as her husband spooned up the soup and munched on the ham sandwiches, never pausing for breath.

A lock of dark hair tumbled over his brow and she had to stop herself from putting out her hand to smooth it aside. Finally he put down the spoon and laboriously cleared the sandwich crumbs from his plate. Maggie observed the sagging shoulders and outstretched limbs. She'd seen the signs often enough to know that he'd sleep where he lay if she let him.

"Come on," she said softly, "let's get you to bed."

Lorimer reached out and slammed the top of the alarm clock, killing its insistent, drilling ring. He could feel Maggie's warmth curling around his legs, her hair soft against his naked back. He wanted to stay in this bed forever, slumbering against his wife's closeness. The sigh he exhaled told him a million things. How he'd be better off in a nine-to-five job, how he really missed the comforts of a proper home life. Lorimer straightened out under the duvet as sleepiness evaporated and he began taking stock, recalling Mrs Baillie's responses to his questions. What was going on over there? Was the clinic in such dire straits that it faced closure? The woman's flat looked as if she was planning to move out. But what would happen to the patients? And who would care for that poor woman lying paralysed down in the back room?

Maggie, sensing the shift in her husband's preoccupation, was up and out of bed before he'd had time to notice.

He watched her for a few minutes as she went through the morning routine of opening the bedroom curtains then pulling a hairbrush through her unruly dark hair. His eyes followed her as she unhooked her negligee from the back of the bedroom door then she was gone. Lorimer listened to the sounds of the bathroom door closing then the shower shushing its spray onto the tiled walls. He heard Maggie slamming shut the cabinet door. Closing his eyes, he imagined her body reaching up to the jets of water, her skin turning to wet silk under the spray.

There was a dull thud as the newspaper hit the hall carpet and he flung off the covers, grabbed his dressing gown and padded barefoot downstairs.

The headlines were predictable. Yesterday's news had been full of Brenda Duncan's murder. Now today's paper had inevitably linked it with Deirdre and Kirsty. There were some quotes from the residential patients to make it look as if there was a general panic amongst them. Mrs Baillie wouldn't like that. There was a quote, too, from Mitchison.

Investigations by senior officers have been taking place both in Glasgow and the Island of Lewis. It is too early yet to make a definite link in respect of the deaths of three women in Glasgow but forensic evidence may prove to be crucial in that respect. I would urge the families of patients at the Grange to remain calm and support the excellent staff who are doing their utmost to keep the clinic running as normally as possible.

Lorimer grimaced. Here was one senior officer who wouldn't mind a quick report from forensics. He'd give Rosie a ring just before he left, just on the off-chance that she'd come up with something. Then there were the computer checks on all the patients and staff at the Grange. And at Failte, he reminded himself.

Lorimer waved briefly as Maggie clattered out the front door, her jacket slipping off her shoulder as she struggled to close the bulging briefcase. It wouldn't fasten so she hoisted it up under her arm, feeling with her free hand for the car keys somewhere deep within her shoulder bag. He watched her from the open door, biting his lip as he waited for Rosie to come to the phone. The car started up then his wife was gone.

"C'mon, Rosie, where are you woman?" he whispered under his breath, listening into the airwaves that were blessedly free from any taped music-while-you-wait. At last Rosie's "Hi, Lorimer," came down the line. She sounded weary.

"Okay, Doc, whatcha got for me?" Lorimer put on his jokey Columbo voice, but his face became serious as he listened. Rosie Fergusson took her time as she filled him in on what she'd found since last night.

"We've run tests on the fibres from all three and there are definite matches between Kirsty's and Brenda's, so far. There were traces that may have come from surgical gloves. There's static showing up in several sets of fibres, particularly around their throats."

"That makes sense," Lorimer said, visualising only too clearly how the women had been strangled.

"No matches with Deirdre McCann, then?" he frowned.

"Nope, but there are still loads of things to work on. There is something else, though."

"Go on."

"There were traces on the hall carpet that show a dirty footprint. Remember it had been raining really heavily that day."

"Any indication of foot size?"

"A size eight shoe as far as we can determine."

"So. You're saying it's a man's print?"

"Come, on. You know me better than that. When did I ever jump to those kinds of conclusions? No. I'm simply saying someone had on a pair of wet shoes in a particular size. Not necessarily a man." Lorimer grinned at the indignation in her voice. "Anyway, the imprint suggests a size eight shoe. The heel mark was quite distinctive. And the traces from the carpet fibres showed all sorts of stuff. Mostly to be found in the Glasgow streets," she added wearily.

"So. A very big lady or a small man?"

"Even a man of average height might have a smaller shoe size. You know that, Lorimer," Rosie protested. "My cousin Ruth's only five foot three and she takes a size seven."

"What about the post mortem?"

"This morning sometime. Coming down?"

"Will I make it by ten? The Super wants to see me first thing."

"Okay. Have fun," Rosie's voice was loaded with sarcasm. Mitchison obviously wasn't her flavour of the month either.

Lorimer gazed into space, thinking about what Rosie had just told him. Surgical gloves. A man's footprint. Were they dealing with a member of staff from the Grange, then? That's what had been running through his mind since last night. The sooner they had these computer checks available the better. Then he could focus on the picture more clearly. For now it was blurred round the edges, just like that grainy Press photo lying on the floor.

Mitchison was on the warpath. The latest broadside from the Press had obviously got under his skin. And now there was another victim to add to the tally of unsolved murders.

"How do you account for the time spent? One interview with a relative and a brief visit to Failte! You've been away three days, Lorimer!"

Lorimer ground his teeth. Whose case was this anyway? He was the investigating officer, for God's sake! But he kept the thought to himself, refusing to give Mitchison the satisfaction of his outrage.

"Another thing. I don't see anything in writing from the second victim's relative," Mitchison went on, flicking through a file that was indeed painfully thin. Lorimer knew he'd not be happy until there was a Bible-sized report on his desk.

He ached to take the man by the collar and give him a good shaking. Victim. Relative. They were statistics to this man, not the flesh and blood figures that peopled Lorimer's every waking thought.

"There hasn't been time yet to write up a report. With the discovery of Brenda Duncan's body I decided to go straight over to the Grange last night. Besides," he continued, "Dr Fergusson's report should be included."

"Anything new there, yet?"

"Dr Fergusson's team have found traces of latex on Kirsty and Brenda's bodies. It may suggest the involvement of a member of the medical staff." Lorimer stopped short of divulging any other information. He wasn't prepared to go into the whys and wherefores of the Grange's finances just yet. He'd follow that up as and when he could. But he certainly didn't need this kind of earache.

Mitchison pressed his fingertips together and frowned. "I don't want the Press involved with members of staff until we know more. Tell Mrs Baillie."

Bit late for that now, thought Lorimer, remembering the morning's headlines. Let the Police Press Office sort that out. He had enough on his plate right now.

The Superintendent sat up as if he were about to dismiss Lorimer then changed his mind, leaned forward and added, "A Press conference with members of the Duncan family might be helpful after the PM. Get the TV boys in to video it. See how the family members react."

Lorimer shrugged. Was Mitchison hedging his bets or did he simply want to control the Press boys as well? He'd be lucky, thought Lorimer; there was no way he was going to go down that path. The less the public knew right now, the better.

"You missed the course with Miss Lipinski," Mitchison told him. "Pity, that. You might have learned something."

The Superintendent's change of tack didn't fool Lorimer for a minute. It was his way of reminding his DCI who was

Boss. Reminding him who sat in the Super's chair. Reminding him yet again that he hadn't got George's old job.

The City Mortuary was situated in one of the oldest parts of Glasgow, rubbing shoulders with the modern High Court building next door. Lorimer had often conjectured that the killers up before a judge and jury could be mere yards away from their victims held in cold storage in the mortuary.

Brenda Duncan's body was already in Rosie's "In-tray" as one of the mortuary assistants had jokingly coined it. Rosie was in her bright yellow wellies and green plastic apron, her assistant, Don, by her side as she performed the post mortem examination. Lorimer stood at the window that looked into the PM room. He had no problem with this aspect of detective work. Some policemen and women simply couldn't take it even after years of seeing dead bodies revealing their innermost secrets on the pathologist's slab. There was an intercom between him and the PM room. Not only could he hear Rosie's instructions to Don while they worked, but it enabled her to keep a running commentary of her examination for Lorimer's benefit.

Lorimer looked at the body of Brenda Duncan. She'd been a large, heavily built woman in life, he remembered. But now death had shrunk her body as she lay, the vital organs openly displayed to curious eyes. Her killer had taken everything from her, even her last dignity.

"Yes. There we are. Larynx compressed against the cervical spine. Injury to the hyoid bone. The cricoid cartilage has been damaged also. Someone pretty strong who knew exactly what they were doing, Lorimer. The element of surprise, too, of course. But she was a big woman and you might have expected her to fight back. He had used both hands so she'd have had her hands free."

"So, why didn't she?"

"Fright. Coupled with the fact that she was breathless from climbing the stairs. She had a weak chest. Being overweight was really to her disadvantage. And she was of an age that made fractures to the laryngeal cartilages more likely. A younger, fitter person would have fought back."

"Any resemblance to the injuries Kirsty MacLeod sustained?"

"He came at Kirsty from in front, too. But Kirsty's death was inflicted by one hand while he held an arm across her chest."

"And Deirdre McCann was strangled with her own scarf," Lorimer mused.

"No carbon copies of murder for you, I'm afraid. Just the killer's signature for Solly to deal with," she sighed.

"But I can tell you we are probably looking for a strong, fit person of at least average height, someone who works out, maybe. It takes a lot of strength to strangle a person who's standing upright."

Lorimer tried to picture the man in his mind. A shadowy figure that leapt at the women's throats, someone of significant strength to force them to the ground. He bit the end of his fingernail. There was something not right. He thought about the latex gloves and the security door.

Everything seemed to indicate that this was a murder where the victim had known her assailant. And had Kirsty known her attacker also? Was he in fact one of the patients at the clinic? And had he been responsible for Deirdre McCann's murder several months ago?

He felt a pulse in his temple throb against his hands as the image of Mrs Baillie came to mind. She was tall and probably strong. But was she strong enough to strangle two of her employees? Wonder what shoe size she takes, Lorimer mused, gnawing at his lip as he dismissed the idea. It had to be a man. Deirdre McCann's killer proved that. And the red carnation, as Rosie had reminded him, linked all three women. That part of the signature was known to the general public, all right, but the actual position of the praying hands was information that only the investigating team knew. Solly, Cameron, Alistair Wilson,

Rosie... the list went on to include those who had discovered the bodies, he realised. And Brenda had discovered Kirsty's body.

Perhaps he should talk again to that chap from British Rail. Push a little harder. But, try as he might, he couldn't rid himself of the feeling that an answer to these murders was to be found in the Grange.

26

These spring mornings gave Phyllis new heart. It happened every year. Even with this disease wasting away her body, she experienced a surge of optimism each bright morning. In her waking hours Phyllis could close her eyes against the tedium of the room and see once again the avenue of trees unfurling their green leaves. By now the beech hedges would be a mass of bright green and the chestnuts would have uncurled their sticky buds. The azaleas would be a swathe of colour, the scent of the yellow blooms sweet and damp. In her mind Phyllis walked once more through the estate. She'd had dogs then, silly spaniels that raced through the woods after rabbits, real or imaginary. She smiled to hear them barking as she lay inert below the spotless sheets. Outside her window she could hear the sound of a pair of collared doves as they croocrooed. In her mind they rose above the treetops heading towards the house. She could feel the tread of her feet on the earthen track. She could smell the wild garlic that wafted up from the banks of the stream.

Phyllis had been born at this time of year. Deep down she suspected that was why it was special to her. Other folk felt it too, she realised, opening her eyes as she heard someone singing in the corridor. It was little wonder. May was such a relief of light and colour after the long yawning stretch of grey winter months. Phyllis treasured these spring days. Would they be her last? There was no thudding of the heart as she anticipated death. Her illness was so far advanced now, realistically there couldn't be much time left. There was little more to be done. Her affairs were tidy. She was a financial burden to no one. Very few would mark her passing. Her solicitor, maybe. One or two of the staff here, perhaps. She really didn't care. Tying the house up as a clinic had been quite selfish, really, giving her a safe haven without the need to part with her own home.

In the long hours before daylight, Phyllis thought about death and what it would bring. An end to everything? Or a release into a new dimension? It was frightening to contemplate a new life free from the prison of this useless body. Not that she didn't want to believe in a life after death, an existence where her spirit swept untrammelled by flesh and bones. No. It was frightening because she wanted to believe in it so much. She had been let down by too much wanting already.

It was better to concentrate on outside. On the birds frantically feeding their young or the light that pierced the blinds and fell in shafts of dust towards the floor.

She hadn't been disturbed again by that voice or by those searching eyes. Maybe it was all over now. Maybe she'd never have to think about them again. Yet even as she tried to recapture the vision of her old garden in all its spring glory there came to mind the cries in the night and the threat that had followed.

Ellie Pearson's hands shook as she replaced the handset. That was another one calling in sick. She doubted if they'd come back at all. Not that she blamed them, really. Who'd want to work in a clinic for neural disorders where one of the patients might be a mad strangler? Stevie had been hinting only last night that she should find another post. The NHS was crying out for staff, he'd told her. Ellie had just shaken her head and tried to concentrate on *University Challenge*. She didn't want to leave. A stubborn loyalty for the Grange subdued any fears she might have. Anyway,

Stevie picked her up at night now, like so many of the husbands. And the night staff all came in by taxi, Mrs Baillie had seen to that. She smiled wryly. After Ellie's own breakdown the Director of the Grange had been surprisingly sympathetic. Losing the baby had been the worst thing ever to happen to Stevie and her. The doctors had been terrific, though, really helping her to focus on positive things and to take time to mourn the baby properly. It was as if they'd all been through exactly the same kind of grief.

Ellie's eyes fell on the dust cover shrouding the computer on the reception desk. Cathy had been the first to leave and so far there was nobody to take her place. Glancing at her watch, she realised that the next shift was due in soon. She'd commandeer one of the girls to take the receptionist's place until they could find an agency temp.

A shadow on the frosted glass door made her look up a split second before the bell rang out. It would be the police. Again. They were practically on first name terms with some of them now, but not the man in charge, Chief Inspector Lorimer. There was an authority about him that made people keep their distance, Ellie thought.

"Good morning, come in," Ellie held open the door and looked up. She kept forgetting how tall the Chief Inspector was. Professional interest made her scrutinise his face.

The tired eyes were heavy with creases as if he hadn't slept much and the downturned mouth merely straightened into a polite line as he took her hand. That dark brown hair flopping over his forehead was badly needing a cut, she thought absently. Still, it was a good head of hair, not like Stevie's premature baldness. DCI Lorimer was good-looking, too, in a rugged sort of way. Ellie wondered absently if he was married. There was no sign of a wedding ring.

"Mrs Baillie's away today," Ellie told him. "So you'll have to make do with me."

Lorimer raised his eyebrows in surprise as Sister Pearson took them through the hall to the reception foyer.

Now the sun filtered in through the vertical blinds casting slanted shadows across the room.

"We'd like to speak to Leigh Quinn," he began. Alistair Wilson hovered deferentially at his elbow as Lorimer waited for the Sister to reply.

"He's due to be with his psychiatrist in half an hour, will that be enough time for you?" Ellie Pearson looked at Lorimer doubtfully. The police had spent so much time interviewing staff and patients alike in the days following Kirsty's murder that she'd thought they must know about everyone by now.

"I think under the circumstances we might just take priority, Sister," Lorimer told her quietly.

Ellie felt her face begin to burn. She felt suddenly like a small child in a grown-up world that was beyond her. "Yes, yes, of course. If you'd like to wait here I'll find out where he is."

"Think you'll get anything out of him this time?" Wilson asked.

"Who knows? He was practically non-verbal last time we interviewed him. *Lost in a world of his own.* Wasn't that what his case notes said? *Post traumatic stress disorder resulting in non-communication.*" Lorimer remembered.

"What sort of treatment has he had?"

"They seem to have tried all sorts. One-to-one counselling. What did they call it? Brief therapy, or something like that. And group sessions."

"I bet they were a pure waste of time. I can't see Quinn participating in anything."

Lorimer shrugged. Solly had filled him in on some of the methods the clinic employed. His colleague, Tom Coutts, had been really helpful in that direction. Coutts was due to go to Failte, too, he thought. Perhaps he could see what the Psychology lecturer made of that experience. The patients' case notes had been made available to the team. Some of them made heavy reading; several depressed souls had tried to end it all. Those for whom life had become intolerable seemed to have reached a black hole, yet the patience and dedication of the staff here had helped not a few of them out of these pits of despair. Coutts had been lavish in his praise of the Grange. But then, it had worked for him, hadn't it? Whether Leigh Quinn, the Irishman, would succeed in throwing off his demons remained to be seen.

Lorimer had spent plenty of time reading the man's file. Born in Dublin, the son of a Union leader, there had been a background of involvement in grassroots politics, especially in the years he'd spent at university. After graduation he'd been in local government for a few years but had lost that job through his heavy drinking.

That hadn't been all he'd lost, though, the case notes told Lorimer. Quinn had been married with a baby son. Both wife and child had perished in a house fire. Quinn had escaped, physically unhurt but with unseen scars that refused to heal. The file had recorded how he'd left Dublin to look for work in Glasgow. For six months he'd held down a job as a hotel porter before slipping into spells of depression that led him onto the streets. Rescued by the Simon Community, it had appeared that Quinn had tried to pull himself together but the depression had worsened until he'd been admitted to the Grange.

Lorimer had tried to make enquiries about his admission, but had drawn a blank so far. How could a down-and-out like Quinn afford the private fees demanded by a place like this? He recalled Sam Fulton. Something was going on here that didn't make any sense. How could men like that pay for such specialist attention?

His thoughts were interrupted by Sister Pearson's return.

"I've asked him to talk to you in his own room, Chief Inspector, if that's all right?"

"Fine. Thank you," Lorimer replied. The woman turned to lead them back along the corridor but Lorimer stopped her.

"Nobody on reception today?" he asked.

"Oh." The woman bit her lip. "Actually, our receptionist left us suddenly. We haven't had time to find a replacement yet."

"Did she give a reason for leaving?" Wilson asked.

Sister Pearson's shoulders slumped suddenly. "You can't blame her really. Two nurses dead like that. We've had other resignations as well." She looked up at Lorimer, meeting his gaze defiantly. " It's hard for the patients, too. Until you catch this man they feel they're under suspicion," she said.

"Well, Sister, that's just what we're trying to do," Lorimer said quietly.

Ellie dropped her eyes. The man sounded so tired. God knows what sort of job he had to do. Of course the police would be doing their best. She looked up again. "Leigh's in here," she motioned towards an open door off the main corridor.

She rapped on the door. "Leigh. Visitors for you." Ellie pushed open the door and stood back to let Lorimer and Wilson into the room then, catching the Chief Inspector's eye, she retreated.

Behind her, Lorimer pushed the door shut. The Irishman was sitting by the bay window with his back to them. Instinctively Lorimer looked out at the trees framing the sky. Leigh Quinn's accommodation certainly didn't lack for a good view. Again the question of how he came to be there in the first place niggled at the edges of his mind. A quick look around the room showed a bed and a couple of easy chairs clad in matching turquoise fabric. The walls were painted in pale green emulsion broken up by prints of Monet's garden. A pair of slippers lay neatly by the bed and several books were piled up on the bedside table. Apart from that there were no signs of personal possessions. The man could have been a hotel guest on an overnight stay rather than a long-term patient.

"Mr Quinn," Lorimer said, expecting the man to turn at the sound of his voice but the Irishman stayed motionless as if glued to whatever he was seeing. Lorimer shifted his position so that his reflection was directly in the man's line of vision, noting a slight movement of the dark head. Even seated, he could see that Quinn was a tall man, though his frame was so gaunt that Lorimer supposed that his depression had affected his appetite.

With a nod, he motioned to Alistair Wilson and his sergeant placed himself on one side of the patient while Lorimer took a chair from the side of the bed and sat down on the other.

"Mr Quinn," he began again. "We would like to ask you some questions." The man continued to stare out of the window but Lorimer had the distinct impression that he was taking in every word.

"I went to visit Sister Angelica. She told me you had been very upset on the night Kirsty MacLeod was murdered. Can you confirm that, please?" Lorimer's voice was quiet but firm, devoid of any supplication.

Leigh Quinn turned his head and stared at Lorimer. The man was breathing in short spurts as if he'd been running hard. Was he about to suffer a panic attack? He fervently hoped not.

Then a long sigh escaped the Irishman and he shook his head wearily. "She should not have been killed," he said at last, looking away from Lorimer and gazing into his cupped hands. "She was a wee flower."

Over his head, Lorimer caught Wilson's eye.

"You were fond of Kirsty?"

The dark, shaggy head nodded again and Quinn put his hands over his eyes as if to blot out a memory.

"Sister Angelica told us she found you praying in her room. Is that right?"

The hands were still covering his eyes as the man nodded again.

Outside a blackbird called in liquid notes from the tree-tops, heightening the silence within the room. Lorimer waited for a moment before speaking.

"Brenda Duncan has also been killed, Leigh. Did you know that?" Lorimer's voice dropped to a conspiratorial whisper. He saw the man's head nod into his hands.

"Who told you?"

Quinn took his hands away from his eyes, clasping them together on his knees. "A nurse."

"Have you been out of the clinic in the last two days, Leigh? For a long walk maybe?" Alistair Wilson asked, diverting the man's attention from Lorimer.

Quinn's head turned towards the sergeant, a puzzled frown on his pallid face.

"Do you know where Brenda lives, maybe?"

Quinn's face froze in sudden understanding.

"No. I've been for... walks, sure," he began slowly, stumbling over his words. "Not out of the grounds." He shook his head and turned to Lorimer as if this was something he should know.

"Can anybody confirm this?" Wilson persisted. Quinn shook his head, his eyes still fixed on Lorimer's. The man's gaze was shrewd, Lorimer thought. He knows fine what we're asking him.

"Do you remember the night before last, Leigh? It was pouring with rain," Lorimer asked.

Leigh Quinn pushed back the chair and stood up, putting his hands out against the glass of the window. Lorimer watched as the man's breath clouded up in little circles against the cold pane. Wilson started as if he was going to pull him back down but Lorimer raised a hand and shook his head, seeing Quinn push his face right up against the glass.

What was the gesture meant to signify, he wondered, suddenly wishing that he had Solly Brightman there in the room. Was the Irishman trying to escape from them or was he simply trying to make the two policemen disappear?

"You're not thinking of leaving the Grange, are you, Leigh?" Lorimer asked suddenly.

He heard a sniff from the man and a muffled "No" then

watched as the man rested his head on his forearms and began to sob.

Lorimer stayed still. Were those tears of remorse? Or was Leigh Quinn still grieving for a young Island girl who'd befriended so many of the patients here? He waited until the sobs quietened. Quinn pulled out a pocket-handkerchief and blew his nose then slumped back down on the chair.

"I didn't kill anyone," he sighed. "That's what you're thinking, though." He looked across at Lorimer, defeat in his eyes.

"We need to check the whereabouts of everybody who was here two nights ago," Lorimer told him. "If you can find somebody who would vouch for your presence here from eight-thirty onwards, that would be a help."

Quinn nodded then stared back into space.

"Can you?"

There was no reply as the Irishman failed to react. He'd said all he was going to say, for now, Lorimer realised, watching the dark eyes glaze over. Still, having him talk at all was a major breakthrough. He signalled to Wilson and they got up to leave. Turning before he left the room, Lorimer saw the face of Leigh Quinn reflected in the glass like a faded print, the luminous eyes unblinking.

"Chief Inspector." Lorimer turned to see Ellie Pearson hovering in the corridor.

She beckoned them with a finger as if afraid to disturb the silence in the room. "Dr Richards would like a word with you." Lorimer and Wilson followed her down the corridor to a room simply marked "Staff."

Sister Pearson knocked and opened the door. "Dr Richards. Chief Inspector Lorimer and Sergeant Wilson."

Lorimer smiled. Solly had told him about this psychiatrist. A miracle worker, Tom Coutts had called him. Perhaps Leigh Quinn's ability to verbalise had more to do with the doctor's expertise than a sudden need to defend himself.

A man of medium build, with thinning hair and a pair of half-moon glasses perched on his nose rose from behind his desk to greet them. "Maxwell Richards," he said, hand grasping Lorimer's firmly. "Chief Inspector, thank you for giving me a little of your time. Gentlemen, please sit down. Ellie, is there any chance of some tea or coffee?" He beamed at the Sister before turning his attention to the two men before him. Lorimer took in the dark pin-striped suit and pink polka-dot bow-tie. On Maxwell Richards the ensemble was sartorial rather than effete, he realised. He looked like a psychiatrist and somehow that immediately dispelled any mystique. Lorimer found himself warming towards the man who continued to smile at him.

"You came in to see Leigh, I believe?"

"That's correct, sir,"

"Perhaps I can fill you in on my patient, gentlemen. He won't have spoken much to you?"

Richards' eyebrows rose questioningly above the glasses. "No, I thought not," he continued as Lorimer hesitated. "Let me see. Where should I begin?" he mused, steepling his fingers and twirling his thumbs around as he considered.

"Perhaps you might tell us how Quinn came to be here in the first place," Lorimer broke in.

"Ah, I wondered if somebody might ask me that. Hm. Confidential, really, but in the circumstances..." Dr Richards took off his spectacles and rubbed the side of his nose before replacing them. "The Logan Trust," he began. "It was set up by the owner of the Grange some time ago. When she was still in charge of all her faculties, you understand."

"Phyllis Logan? The Multiple Sclerosis patient?"

"Indeed. Phyllis established her Trust to enable the clinic to treat people with neural disorders. There are funds set aside for several patients who could not otherwise afford our fees. Leigh Quinn is one such," Dr Richards explained.

Lorimer nodded. Sam Fulton, no doubt, would be another.

"Why should she do something like that?" Wilson wanted to know. "I'd have thought she'd have given preference to MS patients like herself."

Dr Richards smiled. "Yes. One would think so but there are aspects of her life that make such provisions understandable," he hesitated to look closely from Wilson to Lorimer. "This is in the strictest confidence, of course, gentlemen," he added. "Phyllis Logan's husband committed suicide after suffering depression for many years. Giving help to other people has been a sort of catharsis for her."

Lorimer nodded. That explained a lot.

"Doesn't she have any family?" Wilson asked.

Dr Richards shook his head. "No, nor many friends. Since her illness she has become something of a recluse. The clinic was set up to give her a permanent home with the best of care. She is very well looked after here."

Lorimer picked something almost defensive in the man's tone. Had there been any comments made to the contrary?

"What happens when, well," Wilson hesitated, "when she goes?"

"Ownership of the Trust reverts to the Grange and its Directors."

"I see."

"Leigh Quinn," Lorimer put in. "What can you tell us about him?"

Dr Richards sat back in his chair. "Well, now. What can I say that you haven't read in his case notes? He's basically a very kind man. He cares about other people far more than he cares about himself. You'll have noticed that already, though. His personal grooming is quite neglected. Not a materialistic sort of man at all, though he does value his books," Dr Richards smiled. "He actually has a soft spot for Phyllis," he went on. "Goes into her room to sit with her.

As far as we know he doesn't say anything, just sits or rearranges her flowers."

Lorimer stiffened. The image of Brenda Duncan's cold hands clasping that solitary red carnation came unbidden into his mind.

Richards continued as if he hadn't noticed the policeman's discomfiture. "He is usually very withdrawn. Didn't communicate at all when I first met him. But he does keep a diary."

"Oh, yes?" Lorimer was suddenly interested.

"Yes. But he scores everything out and begins again each day. Not a healthy sign, I'm afraid. The denial of his day-by-day experiences, I mean. Perhaps one day he'll allow himself to acknowledge that he has a life. Meantime he seems to find solace in the world of nature. He takes long walks by himself. My colleague in the Simon Community tells me that he used to spend hours simply staring into the river."

Dr Richards clasped his hands on the desk in front of him and fixed Lorimer with a penetrating stare. "What you really want me to tell you, of course, is if I consider Leigh Quinn capable of murder."

"And is he?"

"In my opinion, no. There's a gentleness about the man that I think precludes any ability to hurt another person. Besides, he's been diagnosed as suffering from manic depression. He's not psychotic."

"And would you be prepared to stand up in court and say this?"

"Of course. But I don't really believe you're going to charge Leigh with murder, Chief Inspector."

Lorimer clenched his teeth. There certainly wasn't enough evidence for that but there were coincidences that bore further scrutiny, like the flowers in Phyllis Logan's room and the image of the man on his knees after Kirsty's death.

Psychiatrists had been wrong before, in his experience.

No matter how highly this one was rated, he might not be correct in his assessment of the Irishman.

27

The embankment was covered in brambles and elder saplings pushing up through the litter that seemed to grow like some perennial weed. No matter how often he picked it up and bagged it, the cans, papers and other foul stuff simply returned. His legs were beginning to ache from walking along the steep slope for so long. Trying to keep balanced while holding the sack in one hand and the grabbers in the other made unreasonable demands on his calves and thigh muscles. Still, there was a sense of duty in it all. He was performing a cleansing task. The green would re-emerge once he'd cleared the rubbish away and someone travelling along might see God's gift of beauty in the wee flowers that were struggling to appear. All along the track itself were pink weeds that threw out their suckers year after year. How they survived the trains sweeping over them, he couldn't imagine. But they were brave, these little flowers, and persistent, like himself.

He felt a glow of pleasure as he thought of his work. To clean up the embankments was not his only occupation, oh, no. Sighing with pride, he recalled the voice that had appointed him to rid the stations of other foul weeds.

Then, as if to spoil his morning, a sudden memory of the woman and her temptations shamed him.

She'd lured him towards his sin. But this time he wouldn't weaken. All through the cold months of winter he'd waited for a sign and then had acted upon it. Now he felt the restlessness that had preceded that first sign. Was it time to commit another act of cleansing?

28

It was time to come clean. All day Maggie had felt a restlessness that had more to do with guilt than with the anticipation of Lorimer's reaction. More than once she'd found a pair of eyes staring at her from the rows of desks, waiting for a reply to a question she'd never even heard. It was totally unlike her not to be on the ball. Not within the sheltered haven of her own classroom, anyhow. She'd fought for months to have her own room, a place where she could keep papers and books, where she could work undisturbed. There was a poster opposite her desk, just above eye level. It was a souvenir from last year's trip to Stratford. They'd taken the Fifth and Sixth Years in the slot after exam leave and before they all scooted off for the summer. It had been an idyllic interlude for the kids, and for Maggie. She'd felt a hundred years younger walking through the cobbled streets with those kids. The weather last June had been hot and breezy. If she thought about it hard enough she could still conjure up the feeling of her long linen skirt wrapping itself around her legs and her hair blowing free as they'd walked along the banks of the Avon. But the memory that stuck longest was the sense of disappointment at having to come home to an empty house.

As ever, her husband had been out on some police matter or other.

Maggie had wept that night in sheer frustration at having no one, no one at all to communicate her days of pleasure and nights of magic, transported by the spell of The Bard. It wasn't the same to phone her old mum, even if she'd been awake at that hour. She'd wanted someone to talk to; a soulmate who would hold her in his arms and look at her in understanding of all she had to tell. She'd wanted Lorimer.

The clock on the wall told her it was high time she took herself out of there. The rush hour traffic would be its usual slow, gas-guzzling mass with motorists caught between rolling back the sunroofs or cooling themselves with recycled air. Maggie made a sour face. It was all right for Lorimer with his Lexus. Ancient it might be, but the comfort and air-conditioning were there okay. Still she sat on, torn between a desire to have it all over and done with and a fear at what he would say. What would he say? She'd gone over and over this question for days, steeling herself to come to this moment of truth.

Maggie stretched herself and pushed back the metal chair. Okay. She'd do it. Now. Tonight. She was sure he'd be home tonight. After how tired he'd been he would try to come home at a reasonable hour. Surely. Maggie straightened her back and gave her dark curls a shake. She was going to America for a year and her husband would just have to accept it.

Jo Grant's brow creased in a frown as she scrolled up the list of figures. Lorimer had been right. There was something out of order in the clinic's accounts. At first she'd assumed that the Logan Trust had been responsible for the gaps, but they were way too frequent and didn't tally properly. She could see that now. Jo gave a smile.

I.T. had a way of showing up things that could save hours of old-fashioned detective work. She pressed the print button. Lorimer would like this. There were several large sums of money missing from the Grange's accounts. The patients' fees simply weren't covering the expenditure.

Someone had been on the fiddle, she guessed. Her years in the fraud squad had given Jo a nose for that sort of thing.

"We need to see the clinic's own paperwork," Lorimer told her. "Mrs Baillie keeps the records. See what you can worm out of her."

He watched as Jo left the room. She was good, that one; sharp as a needle. He'd felt there was something wrong about the finances and now she'd proved him right. But was there any link to the murders? Lorimer leaned back in his chair, swivelling it back and forth as he pondered. Mrs Baillie had been so tight with information. She'd also shown little real remorse after the deaths of her two nurses. He'd like to be a fly on the wall when DI Grant started to ask more questions. The Procurator Fiscal had issued a new warrant to search locked premises so Mrs Baillie couldn't refuse access to any of the clinic's files. Lorimer smiled to himself. Something was beginning to unfold.

Maggie had prepared a pot of chicken broth. It was totally unseasonable but she had felt the need for comfort food and the soothing feeling that came from cutting up the vegetables as she'd listened to Classic FM. Now the soup was congealing in the pressure cooker as she waited for the sound of his car.

She'd rehearsed over and over in her mind what she would say to him, but she still jumped nervously as the Lexus braked in the drive below. She could hear him take the stairs two at a time as if eager to be back home.

"Hey, something smells good. That wouldn't be one of your brilliant soups by any chance?"

Suddenly he was there and Maggie shrank back into a corner of the kitchen as if seeking refuge by the cooker.

She turned to face him, tried to smile and failed miserably.

"Mags?" Lorimer reached out for her, immediately sensing her distress.

One moment she was in his arms and the next she was

struggling to be free of him, angrily pushing him away. Lorimer took a step backwards, trying to see his wife's expression but Maggie had turned away. He stood, hands helplessly by his side.

"What the hell's going on?"

"I'm sorry." Maggie looked at him, seeing the puzzled, hurt look in his eyes then, she took a deep breath. "I think we'd better talk." She motioned through to the sitting room.

Lorimer sat on the edge of the sofa but Maggie chose the armchair opposite as if touching him would somehow weaken her resolve. He watched her chest heave in a sigh that made him want to fold her up into his arms.

Her eyes were cast down towards the carpet as she spoke. "I've applied for a new post. A temporary post. It's just for a year. An exchange, actually." Maggie's voice rose in a squeak that betrayed her nervousness. She looked up to see her husband frowning at her, trying to figure out what she meant.

There was a tentative smile hovering around Maggie's mouth as she told him.

"I'm going to America."

"What?" Lorimer stared at his wife in disbelief. He wanted to replay that last moment, let her words sink in. America? She hadn't just said that, had she?

There was a silence between them that seemed to go on and on. In the silence Lorimer's worst fears about his marriage were brought to the surface like scum on a pot of bubbling stock. What was she saying? He listened numbly as Maggie suddenly rattled on about teaching opportunities and career advancement. He wasn't hearing this properly at all. All he could think of was that he felt like she'd swung a wet dishrag across his face.

"Hang on. Let me get this right. You want to spend a year abroad. On your own?" He heard his voice rise in protest. When he spoke again the words came out in a mere whisper. "Why? Why do you have to do this, Mags?"

"For me. I've wanted to do something like this all my life. Can't you understand? I'm tired. So tired. All the time I wait for you to come home. I feel as if I've spent, no let's be truthful about this, I've *wasted* so much of my own life. You're never here. I want to talk to you. I want to spend my evenings with you. Oh, I know all about the pressure of police work. Believe me I've tried so hard to put up and shut up."

Lorimer flinched at the bitterness in her voice.

"I need to do something for myself. Before I end up simply an appendage of DCI Lorimer."

"Maggie, this is beginning to sound all very mid-life crisis to me," Lorimer began.

"Don't you dare start to tell me I'm becoming menopausal or whatever. Just don't dare!" Maggie's eyes were so fierce with passion that Lorimer sank back against the sofa cushions wondering what on earth to say next.

"What have I got that's my own? Eh? Tell *me* that? A job. A house. Okay we couldn't have kids. No one's fault. I'm not trying to lay any blame. All I want is a year to myself doing something I might enjoy." Her eyes were pleading with him now. "Don't you understand? I want to be me. Do something on my own."

What about us? Lorimer wanted to say, but something he couldn't define stopped him from uttering the words. Instead, in a voice stiff with emotion, he asked, "And at the end of the year?"

Maggie shrugged her shoulders. Her eyes were focused on the pattern of the carpet again. "We'll see."

Lorimer took a deep breath. He spent a lot of his working life trying hard to put himself into the shoes of other people; victims of crime, hoods, murderers, witnesses too scared to speak. But it seemed he'd failed to empathise where it mattered most, in his own home. He gazed sideways out of the window at the still clear blue sky. America. Suddenly a thought struck him.

"Why America? This wouldn't have anything to do with

that woman, Lipinski, would it?"

Seeing Maggie's expression gave him his answer. "I might have known! She's been encouraging you to make a break for freedom. Is that it?"

"Don't you think I've got a mind of my own? Okay so Divine told me a bit about Florida and, yes, that's where I'm going on an exchange. But you're entirely wrong in imagining that she put me up to it," Maggie snapped back at him. Then her face softened as she added, "I wouldn't be doing this if I didn't want to."

Lorimer nodded. He wouldn't let this escalate into a row. Looking at his wife's face he realised how important this moment was. If he made too much fuss then he could alienate her all together. All his expertise as a police officer had taught him that he must play this quietly. The best thing now was to reassure her, not to let her see how she'd hurt him.

"Right. Come over here and tell me about it all over again," he patted the sofa cushion beside him.

Maggie hesitated for a fraction of a second then got up to join him. Lorimer resisted the urge to hold her tight and simply took her hand, giving it a friendly squeeze.

He tried to make out that he was listening carefully as she told him all over again; about the job in Sarasota, about the high school system, about the accommodation being made available to her, and about the holidays.

"I could see you at Christmas," she whispered, a little sadly.

"I should hope so," Lorimer replied, his tone light, belying the heaviness he really felt inside.

29

It was a perfect night. The moon had slid behind the blue-black clouds leaving just the glow from city streetlamps shining on the parked cars. He leaned against the wall and waited. There was no hurry and certainly no fear of being seen. Apart from the fact that the CCTV cameras didn't work in the staff car park, he was simply part of the natural background of the station, a railway worker going about his lawful business.

He shivered, anticipating the real business of the night. It was more lawful than anyone could guess, commanded by the highest authority. The woman had been hanging around for three nights in succession, eyeing up the stragglers from the last Edinburgh train, flashing her bare legs around the taxi rank. She'd disappeared with a man every night and somehow he knew she would keep coming back. A quick glance at his watch told him it was nearly time.

He heard her high heels click-clacking over the pavement before he saw her walking briskly towards the automatic doors, her short red skirt riding up against those white thighs.

"Hey!" he called out softly and grinned as he saw her pause mid-stride and peer into the darkness.

Moving out of the shadow he waved his hand, gave a flick of the head indicating that she should come over.

As she smoothed down her skirt and sashayed over he

could see that she was younger than he'd thought. A momentary qualm was quickly replaced by disgust at how much she'd sullied her youthfulness. The grin on his face was a rictus. It would never do to reveal how he really felt towards her. The woman stopped in front of him, flicking back her white-blonde hair, a black shoulder bag clutched tightly with one hand. He could see beyond the caved-in cheekbones and the dull eyes to the girl she might have been before she'd chosen this way of life. With one crooked finger he beckoned her further into the shadows.

"Ye wantae do the bis'ness?" She was chewing gum, her jaw moving in wide circular movements. The sound of saliva slapping against her tongue was like a dog wolfing its meat. Something turned in his stomach.

He swallowed hard, nodded and took the woman's arm. "Over here," he said, leading her into the shadows of a small building tacked on to the back of the station. It was where all the green rubbish bins were corralled together behind a mesh fence. A padlock swung loose on its hasp.

"Ah'm no gonnae go in therr," she protested, tugging against his grip.

"Aw, c'mon," he coaxed. "Give's a kiss." With one hand he swung open the gate and pushed her inside the compound, his body already hard against hers. There was no struggle as his mouth enclosed her thin lips, more an acquiescence. He could feel her body relent as he pulled her hands around his waist, walking her slowly over to the nearest bin.

It was when she fumbled for his zip that he uncoiled the scarf from his neck and slipped it around her throat.

The "Noooooooo!" was cut off abruptly as the ligature tightened. He felt her body struggle against his in a passion that had nothing to do with sex any more. Her leg came up in a vain attempt to lash out at his crotch but he sidestepped, hanging on to the scarf, yanking against it with all his strength. Suddenly a gurgling noise issued from her throat and she buckled under his grasp. He let go and she fell to the ground with a soft thump.

He took a step back, looking at her for a moment then knelt beside her. The grin that hadn't left his face was like a mask now, something he couldn't remove. Not yet. There was still the ceremony to perform.

He clasped her fingers straight within his own, glad of the leather that separated their flesh. How small they were, the warmth seeping through the gloves. He was aware of these things even as he uttered the prayer. The words that he spoke were of forgiveness for sins. She would not commit any more acts of depravity. Sitting back on his heels, he turned to look for the package that he'd left here earlier that evening. It was still there, hidden under the concrete edge of the shed. He slid it out and unwrapped the carnation from its cellophane wrapper. There were tears in his eyes as he forced the stem between her dead palms. It was such a lovely flower, so fresh and sweet. But it was a mark that she was saved now. They would find her and know she'd been redeemed.

He rubbed his gloved hands against his trousers as he stood up. Finished. He was done. The gate made virtually no sound as he fastened the padlock onto its hasp.

It was only a short walk back to the car and there was nobody about to see him slip into the driver's seat. He peeled off the heavy gloves, letting them fall to the floor. There would be new ones issued tomorrow, unsullied by her kind of filth.

Two black cabs turning into the area made him stop for a moment. Then he released the brake and drove slowly out of the station, up the hill towards Cathedral Street and away, his night's work complete.

30

They'd arranged to meet late afternoon. Solly would be free by four o'clock, he'd said, but Lorimer knew from past experience that he was rarely on time. He'd taken the clockwork orange (which was the locals' name for the Glasgow Underground) as far as Hillhead station, deciding to stroll along Byres road to clear his head.

The woman's body had been identified as Geraldine Lynch. She was a known prostitute in that area, the railway staff had said. Already there were punters coming forward with information about her. Lorimer's mouth hardened. She'd been dead for hours before they'd found her, dumped beside the huge industrial rubbish bins at the back of Queen Street station. One of the Transport officers had made the discovery. That, at least, had had the advantage of keeping the area sealed properly for forensics.

There had been an angry scene outside the Gazette's offices, girls and women who had known Geraldine Lynch and Deirdre McCann making their presence felt. Jimmy Greer's piece about Glasgow prostitutes had enraged them. None of them ever denied what they did, but to have the city's newspaper deriding them the way Greer had done was particularly insensitive. It was the usual ploy, Lorimer guessed, to generate letters to the editor.

The Police liaison team had invited the women into Pitt Street to discuss their security. It was doubtful that many would turn up, though. These Glasgow girls liked to think themselves tough, and some of them were, but others were just wee lassies finding themselves at the bottom of the drugs spiral.

Lorimer tried to rid his mind of the murdered girl's face as he walked along the road, taking note of the shops and buildings. Much of the area had changed dramatically since his own student days, but there were still landmark pubs like the Rubaiyat further down where he was to meet Solly, and of course the Curlers next to the Underground. They'd been revamped over the years but they continued to provide that ethos of camaraderie and heavy drinking a student clientele had come to expect.

Outside the station Lorimer side-stepped the flower vendor with his basket of brightly coloured blooms. He paused for a second. He'd never been in the habit of buying flowers for Maggie except on the rare occasions when they'd been supermarket shopping together. The vendor, a slim boy with lank, dark hair, caught his eye even as Lorimer hesitated.

"Nice roses. Two bunches for a fiver?" the boy held up several bunches of the long-stemmed blooms for Lorimer to see.

"No thanks," he shook his head briefly, eyeing the single carnations stuck into a green bucket. Inquiries had been made all over the city. This boy had probably been questioned more than once. Should he stop and buy some flowers for Maggie? He had walked away from the stall even as the thought crossed his mind. No, they'd only wither by the time he reached home, he argued with himself. Anyway, she'd maybe think he was trying to apologise for something.

As Lorimer waited for the lights to change on the corner of University Avenue his attention wandered to the shops on the other side of the road. On day-glo orange stickers, Going Places travel agency was proclaiming cut-price fares to Florida. He could always see what flights were available in October, say?

The lights changed to the wee green man and Lorimer strode across, his mind drifting away from fares and flights to Geraldine Lynch. The only place she would be going was into Rosie Fergusson's post-mortem room.

As he crossed over, his eye was caught by three older men deep in conversation. Two had greying beards compensating for what they lacked on top and the third was a tall, angular fellow whose mane of white hair made him an imposing figure.

Three academics, Lorimer smiled to himself as they swept past. They still seemed to favour baggy linen jackets and distressed leather briefcases, just like his old Prof. He'd felt at home here once, Lorimer realised. What would life have been like if he'd pursued his original studies to their conclusion? Would he have ferreted into all the intricacies of Art History instead of investigating contemporary crimes? Would Maggie have been happier married to an academic?

Walking in the direction of Partick, he caught sight of another familiar landmark. The newsagent was still there. Lorimer saw with a pang that several youngsters were busy taking down details of flats to let from the cards in the window. This unofficial letting agency had been there for as long as he could remember. He had a sudden memory of standing in the pouring rain in his ancient duffel coat scanning the cards for a room to let where he and Maggie could set up home. They'd talked such a lot about moving in together but it had never happened.

Instead Lorimer had left university for his police training while Maggie had finished her degree. They'd done the conventional thing after all, working and saving to buy the house before they'd finally married. His young man's dream of a love nest had been set aside when he'd left the university world behind for the new experiences of the police force.

The pub on the corner seemed caught in a time warp,

Lorimer thought as he pushed open the door. The Rubaiyat might have a name that conjured up a literary world but it wasn't so far from the traditional spit and sawdust. The same scuffed brass foot rail had been there in his day and although the banquettes were newer, their vivid patterns continued the attempt at evoking the idea of ancient Persia. Lorimer ordered a pint and settled into the curved seat opposite the door.

"Lorimer. Hallo," Solly's face displayed his usual boyish grin as he caught sight of him. Seemingly oblivious to the warmer weather, he was wearing a long gabardine raincoat over his leather jacket; he unravelled himself from these layers of clothing, discarding them in a heap over his bulging briefcase.

Lorimer smiled. Solly would never change.

"What are you having?"

"Ah. Something nice and cold. I don't mind," he answered vaguely.

"White wine? Beer? Orange juice?"

"Yes, lovely," he replied.

Lorimer raised his eyes to heaven and ordered another pint for himself and a glass of squash for Solly.

"So," Solly suddenly put the drink down, giving Lorimer a considered look. "We have another young woman who's been strangled."

Lorimer sighed. "I can't believe four women have been killed and we've no trace of their killer."

"No," Solly replied. "It's a difficult one." There was a pause as he seemed to examine his glass carefully, then he placed it on the table and shifted close towards Lorimer. "More difficult than I think you realise."

"Oh? How's that?" Lorimer looked at Solly. There was something familiar in the sad smile, something that told him Solly was about to be the bearer of bad news, as if he hadn't enough to contend with.

"We don't have one killer. We have two."

Lorimer nodded slowly. It was something that he'd

fleetingly considered himself. "That would be a lovely idea, pal, but how do you account for the modus operandi? Besides, the guy places flowers into her praying hands each time. Same signature."

"But a different locus. And a different type of victim," Solly tapped the edge of the table to underline his point.

"Granted. But how can you explain the hands? Even the Press didn't get hold of a picture of any of the bodies. Their mock-up shows a different position altogether. It has to be one and the same person who's carrying out these killings."

"I don't agree," Solly told him quietly. He heaved a sigh. "The whole picture didn't make sense from the time of Kirsty MacLeod's death. I simply couldn't build a profile. Now I think I know why. There are two people to profile, not one."

Solly watched as the policeman's mouth set in a grim line. The murder case sat heavily on his shoulders. Until they could solve it there would be a feeling of inadequacy heightened by something he couldn't yet put his finger on, an extra weight that he was bearing. His energies were directed at finishing off this job if he could. That was good for the case and good for Strathclyde CID, but was it good for William Lorimer?

Just then a crowd of students piled into the pub, their voices loud with post-exam relief. Soon it would be standing room only in the Rubaiyat.

Lorimer bent forwards, suddenly aware of any ears that might be tuning into their conversation. "Look, why not finish off here and we'll go for a walk? Fancy the Botanics? It's a nice night."

Solly nodded and raised his glass. The two men sat back opposite one another, drinking in a silence that was full of questions.

"We'd have to check all the members of the team, too," Lorimer told him. "If your theory's correct, and I'm not saying you're wrong, then someone inside the investigation has let slip details of the signature." Lorimer didn't dare voice any other thoughts than that. Carelessness, that was the only crime any of his team could be guilty of, wasn't it?

"It could have been the railwayman who discovered the first victim," Solly reminded him.

Lorimer gnawed a raggle on his fingernail. Nobody had noticed the flower until he'd arrived at the scene. Still, it was worth checking out. "If the nurses have been killed by a copycat killer then we're still left with a helluva lot of questions. Like, why?"

Solly didn't reply. He was walking slowly along the path, face towards the ground as if he was looking for a lost penny. Lorimer glanced sideways at him.

What was going on in that brain? He'd given the psychologist the benefit of the doubt and, in an uneasy way, he felt he was on to something.

"What about the prostitutes, then?"

Solly looked up and stopped, smiling sadly. "Oh, that's easy, I'm afraid. The killer is suffering from some kind of delusions. Religious delusions. Fairly common, I have to say. He's probably hearing voices telling him to take away the bad women of the night."

"A religious nut, then? What we thought all along?"

"Yes. And I think this latest crime shows he's definitely got a link with Queen Street station."

"The staff car park's close circuit camera is out of order," Lorimer told him gloomily.

"There. Have a closer look at who has access to that area at night. Or even during the day."

"Anything else?"

"If forensics haven't found any DNA matches between railway personnel then maybe you could dig a little deeper into each member of staff's background."

"What are you looking for?"

"White, single male. Thirty to forty. There's possibly a history of being in an institution. I suppose he must have a

226

car, too," Solly mused, stroking his beard absently as if he were seeing a shadowy figure in the recesses of his mind.

"And the other murders?"

"Ah. Now that's more difficult. We're dealing with somebody very clever indeed."

"Someone inside the Grange?"

Solly frowned before answering. "I'm not sure. It's possible, but then again…" he trailed off.

"Look, why don't we go for a curry? See if we can get into the Ashoka?" Perhaps with some food inside him Solly would become more expansive, he thought. Besides, Lorimer wasn't in the mood to go home just yet.

It was dark by the time the taxi drew up outside the house. Maggie stumbled a little in her high heels as she tried to tip-toe to the door. She failed to see the swish of curtains from upstairs as her key turned in the lock.

Her husband appeared to be asleep when she crept into the bedroom.

Maggie slipped easily out of her skirt and top, letting them fall onto the carpet. She was unfastening her suspenders when Lorimer spoke suddenly, making her jump.

"Been out on the town?"

"Good God! You gave me a fright. I thought you were asleep."

Lorimer half sat up, regarding his wife in the darkness. She saw him shake his head.

There was a silence as she finished drawing off the stockings and underwear, a silence that was charged with embarrassment as if he had no right to be watching her. She fished out a nightdress from under the pillow and slipped it hastily over her head. His eyes were still on her as she climbed into bed beside him. There was a continued silence that was full of unspoken questions about where she'd been, who she'd been with.

Heaving a sigh, Maggie gave in.

"I was out at the Rogano having a drink with Sheilagh. Okay?"

There was no reply. She turned her head towards him and in the darkness she could make out the smell of onions on his breath.

"Been out for a curry?"

Lorimer gave a laugh. "Want to join my team, Sherlock? Or is it that obvious?"

Maggie giggled, the tension suddenly evaporating. "You stink! You always eat far too many spiced onions," she complained.

"I was seeing Solly," Lorimer said, as if that was an explanation for the state of his breath.

"And?"

"He's got this idea that we're dealing with two separate killers."

Maggie twisted towards him, interested in spite of herself. "And is he right?"

Lorimer lay back on the pillows, one hand behind his head. "I don't know. If he is, though, I may have to start looking a lot closer to home."

"You mean someone in the force?"

Maggie could hear her husband sigh in the darkness. It was sigh that went all the way through him. She snuggled up closer, her cold skin touching Lorimer's warm body. He didn't answer her question but wrapped an arm round her shoulders, pulling the duvet in tighter to keep her cosy.

There was nothing sexual in his action, it was a gesture of pure affection, the kind of thing she'd been missing for so long. After only a few minutes Lorimer's breathing became heavier and Maggie knew he was asleep. Still he held her close, folded into his arm. So why did she feel that overwhelming sense of loneliness?

As Maggie laid her head against his chest she felt the tears hot against her lashes.

31

It was already daylight and he'd only slept for about three hours but Lorimer felt wide awake as he lay on his back staring at the bright gap in the curtains. He'd been dreaming about the St Mungo's case. In his dream he was being chased by a figure in the park that had somehow turned into to Maggie. He'd woken with a start, relieved to see her sleeping soundly by his side. But it had got him thinking.

He remembered the moment in that other case when he'd suddenly realised he'd been looking at things all the wrong way round. Maybe he was doing it again. Lateral thinking, he told himself. Open up your mind.

The image of the rusted railing leading to the basement of the Grange came back to him. If the killer had come in that way then how had he crept up on Kirsty? Lorimer traced the whole route in his mind from the stairs leading into the corridor and through the double doors leading to the main building. No. Wait a minute. There was something missing. The room where Phyllis Logan lay, her body full of tubes. Lorimer recalled those bright eyes. She couldn't talk, he'd been told. But nobody had said she couldn't hear, had they?

For a moment he lay quite still. They'd interviewed the other residents, but not her. Was it worth a try? If the woman had heard something maybe there could be a way of finding out what it was?

Phyllis felt the sun warming her hands. She observed them on the white cuff of the sheet, drained of colour in the brightness, thin membranes stretched over knobs of bone. Her nails grew hard and gnarled, pale ochre, the colour of an animal's hoof. It was an irony (one of many she'd noted with a bitter smile) that she'd suffered split and brittle nails in her younger days when such small vanities had mattered, and now her fingernails grew strong and hard when nothing like that was of any importance. It was simply a result of the drugs she had to take. That's what young Kirsty had told her.

Phyllis remembered her lilting voice and the way she'd made conversation as if Phyllis could actually answer her back. She'd felt easy and comfortable with that young girl. She'd longed to be able to talk to her, to share some of her own past, the way Kirsty had shared hers. She knew all about the drowned father, the loss of her mum, the growing up years she'd spent on the croft with her old auntie. They'd been kindred spirits in some ways, though she'd never been able to tell Kirsty that of course. Phyllis, too, had been a solitary child. No brothers or sisters. She wondered what life would have been like having siblings. Would they have cared for her at home? Or would she have ended up staying here, no matter what? The ideas she pushed around her head were totally objective. Phyllis was long past the stage of self-pity. Yet it was pity she felt for Kirsty. Pity and grief that her young life had been so cruelly cut short.

A spasm passed through her hand, making it flicker with a sudden illusion of life. It was a nervous shudder, no more. The sun must have passed behind a cloud for the warmth had gone out of the room and now her hands were like two dead fish, pale and untwitching.

Phyllis turned her eyes at the noise of swing doors opening and shutting a small distance away. She could hear voices. There were people coming along her corridor, a man and Maureen Baillie. She couldn't mistake her voice.

She was in and out of Phyllis's room quite often these days, making sure everything was in order.

Mrs Baillie didn't knock.

She watched the woman stride into the room, hands bunched into fists at her side. There was a determined set to her jaw as she spoke.

"This is Chief Inspector Lorimer, Phyllis. He's investigating the events that happened here. He'd like to talk to you. Is that all right?"

Phyllis's eyes travelled over the man as he came into view. She saw a tall figure whose dark hair straggled over his collar. She focused on the face. There was a certain weariness etched into the lines around his mouth but the eyes that regarded her were a bright, unforgettable blue. It was him. The one who'd come before. That night. So he was a policeman, was he? That pleased her. She liked to know who was on her side.

Lorimer had noticed that the Director had failed to knock but simply swept into the room and now stood with her back to the window. He looked from her face, which was in shadow, to the immobile figure in the bed. The eyes looked back at him, unflickering. Lorimer saw a keen intelligence there.

Mrs Baillie folded her arms, looking as if she were waiting for Lorimer to begin. Just then there was a light tap on the door. PC Annie Irvine stepped into the room, a large square bag slung over her shoulder. The policewoman smiled then gave a nod to the Director. Lorimer stood aside to let her move into a position where Phyllis could see her.

"You can go now, Mrs Baillie. My officer will let you know if there's anything we need. Thank you." Lorimer held the door open as if to emphasise the point. She wasn't wanted. Police interviews were conducted in private, no matter what the circumstances.

Mrs Baillie looked as if she might argue the toss but a glance at Lorimer's face showed she'd decided against it. They heard the sound of her feet quietly padding down the corridor as Lorimer closed the door.

"Here's a couple of chairs, sir," Annie had spotted the grey stacking chairs and was lifting them over the side of Phyllis's bed. "Is it okay, ma'am?" she added, looking directly at Phyllis.

The woman in the bed gave a tiny nod and Lorimer saw a faint smile play about her lips. Maybe this wouldn't be so impossible after all. He positioned his chair close to the bed so that the woman and he were facing one another.

"Hallo again," he began. "You do remember me, don't you?" His tone was gentle but firm. He didn't intend to insult her by being condescending. There was nothing worse for disabled folk than being talked down to like children. She gave that slight nod again and her smile deepened.

"The last time I was here it was to investigate the death of a nurse, Kirsty MacLeod," he continued, still gazing at her face, her penetrating eyes.

She closed them and opened them again. Was she trying to blot out the memory of that night? He hoped she wouldn't, for his sake and for Kirsty's.

"May I ask you about that night?"

Phyllis frowned at him as if he'd said something out of place so he added quickly, "Look, I know you can't talk to me, but I'd like to think we can communicate all the same. Give a nod if you mean "yes". Close your eyes if it's a "no". Can you do that?"

There was a tiny movement of the woman's head that Lorimer took to be a nod. Lorimer turned to Annie, who was busy unpacking the video camera she'd brought.

"We'd like to make a recording of this interview. It's a little unorthodox, perhaps, but then your situation is, let's say, a bit different."

The woman had her gaze trained on his, he noticed. She could hear him, no bother, then. But just what was going on behind that steady expression?

"PC Annie Irvine recording in the Grange clinic for neural disorders. DCI Lorimer interviewing Mrs Phyllis

232

Logan. Date and time pre-set," Annie's voice broke into his thoughts. Okay, this was it.

He took a deep breath before asking, "We need to know exactly what took place in the clinic on the night that Kirsty died. And I'd like to know if you heard anything."

The nod she gave was quite definite now and her eyes were staring at him, huge and fearful. She'd heard something all right. Lorimer edged his chair closer to the bed. He spoke slowly and deliberately, watching Phyllis's every reaction. Her eyes flickered once in Annie's direction then passed back to him as if she was indifferent to the presence of the camera.

"Right, now. Did you hear anything unusual outside your door on the night of…"

Lorimer broke off. The woman in the bed was making high-pitched mewing sounds, as if she was trying to tell him something. Tears threatened to spill over from those huge eyes.

Lorimer leaned closer. "You heard something?"

Phyllis gave a nod. Her eyes were round and staring.

"Was it a sound like something being dragged past your door?"

Again that tiny jerk of the head meant yes.

"Did you hear any noises coming from the far end of the corridor?"

The woman's brow furrowed for a moment.

"A noise like something heavy falling down a flight of stairs?"

She gave another frown then shut her eyes quite deliberately before nodding again.

Was she telling him "Yes and no"? How the hell could he draw out all the details? For a second Lorimer clenched his teeth in frustration. Then he looked at the woman in bed. Dear Christ! If this was how he felt what on earth must it be like for her? He breathed in and out, deliberately relaxing himself before continuing.

"Did you hear a door banging shut? A heavy door?"

233

The nod confirmed her answer this time.

Lorimer paused, still holding her eyes in his, trying to see what she had seen.

"Phyllis, did you hear footsteps coming *back* along in this direction?"

Lorimer watched as her mouth worked noiselessly, trying to form words that nobody could hear. A plaintive sound came from within her, repeated over and over again as her head tilted up and down in agitation. Then suddenly her eyes flitted past him and stared wildly at the door, making Lorimer turn to see who had come into the room.

There was no one there. What was she trying to tell him?

He could feel a growing excitement inside as he asked her, "Phyllis. I want you to think very carefully before you nod again. Did you see anybody in here just after you'd heard the noise of the door banging?"

Her eyes switched back to his. He could see the sigh unfold in her chest as if she'd been waiting for this question that he'd finally asked. She gave a nod.

"That's "yes", Phyllis. You're telling me that you saw someone in here that night?"

The nod came again but Lorimer could see the strain on her face. The effort of making even these small movements was exhausting the sick woman.

"Was it anyone you knew?"

Her eyelids fluttered. Was that a "no" or was she simply unable to keep her eyes open?

"Did Leigh Quinn come into your room that night?"

The movement of the woman's head was imperceptible. Not a nod at all, more of a gesture of inquiry as if she was puzzled by the question.

"Phyllis. Did a man come into your room?"

She nodded but the movement was clearly an effort as her head hung forward, its weight drawing Phyllis's face towards the sheets.

"Was this man a stranger to you, then?"

Had she nodded? He couldn't be sure.

Lorimer gazed at her wasted body. Could he really put his faith in this invalid? A niggle of doubt began to bother him. Was she a reliable witness? Should he even be questioning her like this?

Lorimer's eyes travelled back to her face. The body might be wasted but here was no doubting the intelligence locked inside that impaired nervous system. As Phyllis's eyes met his, he realised that he had no need to doubt her. That steady expression told him that she was willing him to see whatever she had seen.

"Did he speak to you?"

Lorimer saw the muscles in her face twitch as a spasm passed through them. Her eyes widened in fear but her head nodded forwards.

"And threaten you?"

Her eyes bored into his as she gave a nod.

Lorimer glanced up at Annie Irvine. They were on the brink of something momentous.

"Phyllis. Do you believe that you saw the person who killed Kirsty MacLeod?"

There came a small weeping from the woman in the bed, tiny stifled cries as the tears flowed down into the pillow. Slithers of mucus dropped from her open mouth. For an instant Lorimer stared at her, absorbing her grief. Then he felt in his pocket for a clean handkerchief. Folding it around his index finger, he wiped away the tears. Carefully he gathered up the wet trails hanging from Phyllis's mouth and dried her chin.

Her breath shuddered suddenly. Lorimer's simple actions seemed to have calmed the woman. Her head was drooping low and she looked awkward, propped up on a bank of pillows that no longer gave her any support. Lorimer didn't hesitate. He knew he was probably breaking all sorts of rules, nevertheless he thrust an arm around the exhausted woman's shoulders then pulled her further down into the sheets until her head was resting against the pillows once more. Well, he'd broken rules before and, hell,

235

all those leading questions might be thrown out in a court of law anyway.

This video could turn out to be a total waste of time. Lorimer sat back looking at the patient. Her body was rigid with pain. It was not only pointless but cruel forcing any more out of her now. Besides, she'd given him plenty to work on already.

"DCI Lorimer terminating the interview," he said. He heard the buzz from the video camera as Annie retracted the zoom and ended the recording. He was pretty sure that there were several leads he could follow from what Phyllis had given him. Part of him wanted to be up and off to study the footage they'd just recorded but there was something he had to do first. Right now he had a duty to protect this vulnerable witness.

"Ask Mrs Baillie to come back in here, would you, Annie?"

As the policewoman left the room there was a low moan from the woman in the bed. Lorimer returned to his place beside her and took her hand. It felt cold and bloodless.

Phyllis turned her head away from him and then moved it back to look into his eyes, making sure he was watching her. Then she turned once more, staring at the large vase of flowers set on top of her locker.

"Is it the flowers, Phyllis?" Lorimer felt the cold hand in his, motionless. She continued to stare at him, then, imperceptibly, she nodded.

Suddenly Lorimer realised what it was she had been trying to tell him. The flowers!

"Did the man take a carnation from your vase, Phyllis? A red carnation?"

The woman gave Lorimer a long hard stare then, quite deliberately, nodded her head, once, in definite affirmation.

Her shoulders relaxed in the sigh that followed. Now she really had expended all her energy. Her eyes closed and Lorimer heard her breathing steadily until he was sure that she had fallen asleep.

"You may also think you have a witness statement from the Logan woman but it might be quite inadmissible in a court of law, you know," Mitchison continued, the finger wagging just a fraction too close to Lorimer's face.

"If you would just take a look at the recording, sir?"

Mitchison gave a theatrical sigh, "Oh, very well, then. Let's have a look."

The Superintendent watched as Lorimer slotted the tape into the video machine. The two men listened as Annie Irvine's voice began the interview. Lorimer stared at the face on the screen. He had every detail of the tape off by heart now. There was no interruption from Mitchison as they listened to the recording. At last it was over and Lorimer looked questioningly at his superior.

Mitchison was frowning at the empty screen, an expression on his face that Lorimer couldn't quite fathom. It was almost human, he thought cynically.

Finally the Superintendent broke the silence between them. "She's a very sick woman," he began slowly.

"Yes, she is," Lorimer replied. There was no point in denying it after what they'd both witnessed on the tape.

"I wonder if the courts would consider her a reliable witness?" Mitchison seemed to be asking the question of himself. Then he shook his head. "Oh, I don't know. We'd need all sorts of expert medical witness statements to back up the validity of this statement. If you can even call it that."

Lorimer clenched his fists out of sight, under the desk. Would Mitchison try to stop the tape being used as evidence after all her efforts? He mentally rewound the video, seeing the woman's anguished face. It took all his powers of restraint to keep the passion from his voice.

"Sir, although she has no power of speech, she's no dummy. Mrs Baillie can vouch for her mental health."

Mitchison's face twitched as if a spasm of annoyance had passed over it. For a moment he didn't speak but simply continued to stare at the blank screen. Lorimer wondered what was going on in the man's mind. At last Mitchison swung around in his chair, his usual expression of superiority back in place. "Oh, very well, let's get on with it. But I have to warn you, Chief Inspector, I'm really expecting some results now. There have been too many man hours frittered away on this case already."

Lorimer took a deep breath. "I'll be showing this to Dr Brightman, sir."

Mitchison looked askance at his DCI. "Our criminal profiler? Why not. He hasn't come up with anything yet, has he?" he asked, as if Solomon was yet another tiresome burden he had to bear.

"No, sir," Lorimer lied, his fingers crossed under the table. Let Solly's theory about two killers simmer for a bit, he decided.

Having Mitchison's blessing about Phyllis Logan meant more right now, especially with the idea that had taken root in his brain. If Solly was correct and a killer was closer to home than they thought, then Phyllis Logan might be in more danger than they imagined.

Solly recrossed his legs thoughtfully. They had watched the video footage twice together now and he'd not offered any comment. He could feel Lorimer's eyes burning into him, waiting for some word of encouragement.

"Well, what do you make of her?" Lorimer asked, obviously bursting for a response from the psychologist.

Solly shook his head slowly, tugging absently on the curls of his beard. Then he sighed. "What a terrible imprisonment for her. To be so confined. Just like poor Nan Coutts. Yet she must have developed an inner self." He spoke softly, almost to himself as he stared at the screen. "She's been terrorised all right, though, don't you think?" he added, turning to make eye-contact with Lorimer.

"Oh, I don't think there's any doubt about that. Only by whom? That's where our problem lies. Leigh Quinn was my first thought, but now I'm not so sure. It's certainly a man, so we can eliminate the female staff and patients from

238

the scenario along with the cleaners and other women. Including Mrs Baillie," he added.

Solly tried to hide a grin. The director of the Grange had ruffled DCI Lorimer's feathers considerably during the investigation. And there was still that question mark hanging over the finances of the clinic.

"Phyllis Logan's been there long enough to know the staff and long term patients by name, surely," his voice trailed off and Lorimer was left watching him as Solly's face took on the dreamy attitude with which he was becoming so familiar. There was something brewing in that brain of his.

"I took a long walk around the whole area," Solly began. "It struck me that somebody walked straight into the Grange and straight out again the night that Kirsty was murdered. I think we're pretty much agreed that this killer knows his way about. He knew Brenda's movements too. There's a coolness about his character. He has something to do with the clinic, that's clear enough to me. He can disappear into the background like so much wallpaper. Nobody sees him as out of place."

"Nobody seems to have seen him at all except Phyllis Logan!" Lorimer protested.

"I wonder," Solly mused. "Brenda Duncan and Kirsty MacLeod were doing their usual rounds, checking up on the patients. They had to go into everybody's room, isn't that so?"

Lorimer nodded, puzzled. They'd been over this again and again. What was Solly getting at now?

"Well, it's a pity we can't ask either of them, but I wonder…"

Lorimer bit his lip impatiently.

"The patients on suicide watch have a designated nurse with them during the night, don't they?"

"Yes," Lorimer frowned. What was he trying to say?

"Well, suppose one of them left their post for a bit? Both they and their patient would be vulnerable, wouldn't they?"

"Vulnerable to what?"

"Suspicion, of course!" Solly exclaimed, surprised that Lorimer hadn't followed his line of thought. "And I don't see any of the nurses owning up to being away from a patient's bedside when that would provide a perfect alibi, do you?"

"But, hold on, let's look at this another way. Say you're right and there's one killer of prostitutes who likes to hang around Queen Street station then another who bumps off two nurses, what about motive? Are we looking for two nutters, d'you think?"

Solly shook his head. "Whoever murdered Kirsty and Brenda knew exactly what they were doing and why. The real problem is how they came to find out about the signature." Solly looked hard at the policeman. "Rape can escalate into murder. The women in Queen Street may well have been raped. Sexual activity was present in both cases."

"But they were prostitutes! Of course there were signs of sexual activity!"

"But neither Kirsty nor Brenda were assaulted like that. He simply walked up and strangled them. The element of shock was that they knew their attacker and trusted him."

"Would they have trusted a patient?"

"That depends. If they knew him well enough, yes. Still considering Leigh Quinn?"

Lorimer's face twisted in a grimace. It fitted almost too neatly: a depressive who had some sort of flower fetish. But why would he have killed Kirsty? He'd liked her. And Brenda Duncan? What possible reason could he have had for stalking her home like that?" Lorimer shook his head. "Not really," he sighed. "He had no grudge against either woman as far as we know."

"Interesting you should use the word *grudge*. Something may have happened to poison a mind already holding a grudge. Something that triggered off this chain of events."

Lorimer reached forward to eject the tape. The MS patient had given them both plenty to think about.

Solly would try to develop his profiles while his own team would continue the painstaking work of cross-checking the background of every man connected to the Grange. And now that included every member of the team itself.

32

Father Ambrose let his spectacles fall on top of the evening paper. Four women had been strangled now and still he sat here worrying about them. Praying too, he admitted, but he would have done that anyway. The picture in the evening paper showed a young woman smiling into a camera. The headline had shouted out her crime, and his. Poor child, he thought, to have stooped so low. The journalist had painted a life of drugs and deprivation. Father Ambrose could imagine what that might have been like. One of his parishes had been in the inner city, long ago, before they'd torn down the sagging tenements and given people decent homes. He'd been party to some terrible confessions in those days, he remembered.

It was the flowers that had first bothered the priest. Red carnations slipped between the praying hands of a killer's victims. There had been a shiver of unease to begin with until memories came flooding back, memories of other hands that had selected the choicest blooms. A vivid picture of a body in a coffin came back to him, the flower like a gash of blood against the whiteness of the shroud. The hands that had placed those flowers had been clasped in prayer each day, right by his side. Until the scandal that had shocked them all.

Father Ambrose picked up the paper with shaking hands. He knew what he must do. All along he had known it, but he'd suppressed that event over the years until it had almost ceased to exist. Now he had to face the truth.

33

Lorimer could have gone home but tonight he just didn't feel like sitting staring at the television while Maggie was up to her eyes marking these interminable papers. So here he was, waiting to be served in the canteen. The fluorescent bulbs glared overhead, at odds with the spring light that poured into these upstairs windows. Mitchison could make a start by saving dosh here, thought Lorimer moodily. Like the waste of money Maggie was always going on about in her school where the heating was kept turned up all year round, even in the holidays. Maggie again. He must stop thinking about her.

Lorimer looked around the canteen. There weren't many folk in tonight but he recognised DC Cameron sitting alone, hunched over a plate of spaghetti. Lorimer noted with interest that he wasn't eating it. He was stirring the strands of pasta round and round his plate with a fork but was making no attempt to put any of it into his mouth. Lorimer's curiosity made him watch the young officer.

"Chief Inspector, what's it to be?" Sadie, a wee woman with a voice that could have scoured a burnt pot was standing, ladle in one hand, looking at him expectantly. Lorimer turned to give her his full attention. No one messed with Sadie.

"Just some soup, thanks. Oh, and one of your brilliant Danish pastries, Sadie," Lorimer gave her his best smile as usual but this was one woman who was oblivious to the Chief Inspector's famous blue eyes.

"Wan soup, Betty!" she shouted towards the kitchen. "Yer Danish is up therr, son," she added, jerking her head to the plastic-covered shelves that Lorimer had already passed. Lorimer nodded and turned to fetch his pastry, marvelling as he always did at Sadie Dunlop's ability to make them all feel like school kids. She was wasted here. She should've been Governor of Barlinnie at least.

"Mind if I join you?" Lorimer grasped the back of the metal chair next to Cameron's. The DC sat up with a start as Lorimer spoke.

"Not fancy Sadie's pasta special tonight, then?"

Cameron shook his head and attempted a smile.

"How about a drink? I was going to drop into the Iron Horse. Okay?"

Cameron's pale face flushed slightly as he answered, "I don't usually drink, sir. I'm TT, you know."

"Ah, the strict Hebridean upbringing," Lorimer teased. Then his face grew more sombre as the germ of an idea began to form in his head. An idea that might take root, depending on what Cameron could tell him.

"Come on down anyway. The ginger beer's on me," Lorimer's voice held a note of authority that he knew Cameron recognised. The DC looked up at his boss then pushed the congealing mess of spaghetti away from him.

They were practically out of the canteen when a familiar voice stopped them in their tracks.

"Haw, ye's've left yer dinners. Ah thought ye wanted that Danish? Right waste of good food that is, 'n'all!"

Lorimer glanced at Cameron who was dithering in the doorway. "Come on, before we get arrested for dinner neglect!" Lorimer grinned conspiratorially and gave the DC a friendly wink.

It was quiet in the pub. Seven o'clock was a watershed between the quick after office pint and quiz night. Seeing the bar staff polishing glasses and catching up with the day's paperwork, Lorimer knew they wouldn't be disturbed.

He had chosen a booth at the rear of the bar. On the table sat a pint mug of orange squash and Lorimer's two preferred drinks, a pint of draught McEwan's and a half of Bunnahabhain. Lorimer stretched his long legs under the table, feeling the heels of his shoes dig against the ancient wooden floor. The Iron Horse had made few concessions to modernity, which, for Lorimer, was part of its charm. He sank against the burgundy-coloured padded seat, feeling something close to relaxed. Pity he'd have to spoil the moment.

"How are you settling in to the job, now? Glad to be out of uniform?"

Cameron shot Lorimer a wary look before giving a shrug.

"You could tell me to get lost, but I think it might do you good to have a wee talk if there's anything on your mind."

"There's nothing, really," Cameron began in a tone that told Lorimer just the opposite.

"Is it the case that's bothering you? Still feeling bad about Kirsty MacLeod?"

Lorimer looked intently at Cameron. The lad's mouth was tightly shut and he could see his jaw stiffen. If it had been anyone but Lorimer asking such questions he'd probably have been told to mind his own damned business. Except that Cameron didn't even swear. The young detective constable had been looking past him as if intent on the framed engraving of James Stewart on the wall above their booth, but then he turned suddenly, meeting his superior's gaze.

"Yes, I feel bad. I thought I could handle it, but maybe I was mistaken."

"You handled yourself well enough at the mortuary. Dr Fergusson even commented on that."

"Well, that was different. It wasn't so personal."

Lorimer took a mouthful of beer and licked his lips. Just

what did the lad mean by personal, he wondered.

"Did you ever meet Kirsty down here in Glasgow?"

"No." The answer came just a shade too quickly.

"Sure about that?"

"Of course. Why would I lie?" the flush had crept back over Cameron's neck.

"You tell me."

"Look, Chief Inspector, Kirsty was a girl from home. She was a friend of my wee sister's. I hadn't seen her for years, okay?"

"Okay, calm down. How about that place Failte, then? Did you know anybody there?"

Cameron shook his head. "Before my time. It was a holiday place for as long as I can remember. There are plenty of houses empty most of the year just waiting for incomers. It's only been a respite centre, or whatever, for the last two years or so."

Lorimer nodded. That had been his information too. Phyllis Logan's family had kept the house as a summer residence then it had lain empty for years before becoming a part of the Grange.

"D'you remember that first murder back in January?"

"Of course. I'm not likely to forget it."

"The woman who was killed had a flower between her hands. Did you actually see it that night?"

Cameron stared at him, surprised by this sudden change of tack. He frowned as if trying to recall the images of that freezing January night.

"I remember seeing her lying there and DS Wilson calling her Ophelia. That was after we saw the flower, wasn't it?"

"Can you remember how her hands were held?"

"Well, I know how they were held, it's in all the reports, isn't it?"

"But do you *remember* it?"

"I think so. Why?"

"You didn't by any chance describe it anybody outside

247

the case, did you? Anyone from home, for instance?"

Cameron looked at him curiously then shook his head. "I don't talk about my work to the folks," he said. "They don't even know I'm involved with Kirsty's murder."

Lorimer was looking at him keenly as if to weigh each of the DC's words carefully. Niall Cameron returned his gaze with apparent coolness. There was no longer any tell-tale flush warming that Celtic pallor.

He wanted to believe the younger man. Experience told him he was hearing the truth, but there was someone who had inside knowledge of the first case, someone who had used it to copy the killer's signature. And Niall Cameron had known the girl from Lewis. It had been his call, too, that had alerted Lorimer that night, he remembered. He picked up the whisky and drained the glass in one grateful swallow, suddenly needing the burning liquor to take away a taste he didn't like.

The vibration from his mobile made him put down the glass with a bang. "Lorimer?"

Cameron's eyes were on him as he listened to the voice on the other end. He was vaguely aware of the younger man picking up his jacket and giving him a wave. He nodded in return, watching the Lewisman walk out of the pub and into the Glasgow night.

"Who is this Father Ambrose?" Lorimer asked, listening as the duty sergeant told him of the priest's telephone call.

"And he's coming up to see us?" Lorimer bit his lip. This was news indeed. A priest from the Borders who had information about Deirdre McCann's murder, or so he claimed. As he pressed the cancel button, his thoughts drifted back to Lewis and to the house called Failte where he'd met the nun. Where was she, now? And had she anything to do with this sudden need for an elderly priest to speak to Strathclyde CID?

34

Father Ambrose was a small rotund gentleman dressed in clerical black. His thinning hair showed a well-scrubbed scalp that shone pinkly through wisps of white curls. A cherubic face smiled up at Lorimer's.

"Chief Inspector. I'm so glad to meet you," Father Ambrose said in a voice as gentle as a girl's. But the hand that grasped Lorimer's was firm and strong.

"Father Ambrose. You rang last night, I believe?"

The priest ducked his head as they walked towards the stairs. "Yes. Though I should have contacted you sooner."

Lorimer raised his eyebrows. Ideas of confessionals sprang to his mind. But weren't those secrets told during the confessional sacrosanct? As he pulled open his door and ushered the little man inside, his head was buzzing with speculation.

"Some tea, Father?"

"No thank you. I will be seeing an old friend later this morning. She will be filling me with pots of the stuff, I assure you," he smiled, a dimple appearing on his cheek.

"Well, what can we do for you, sir?"

"Ah. Now, it's what I can do for you, Chief Inspector. What I should have done for you months ago, when that poor young woman was killed."

"Deirdre McCann?"

The priest nodded sadly. "I read about it in the papers.

It troubled me greatly at the time but it was not until this latest death that I made myself face some unpleasant facts."

"Oh?" Lorimer leaned back slightly, appraising the man. Father Ambrose had folded his hands in front of him as if to begin a discourse. Lorimer waited to hear what he had to say.

"There was something that happened several years ago, something that I had wished to forget. It's no excuse, of course, for procrastinating. Indeed, had I acted sooner perhaps these other women might not have been murdered." Father Ambrose's voice dropped to a whisper. He gave a short, resigned sigh and continued. "I became a priest and was trained by the Jesuits. I have probably had one of the finest educations in the land, you know," he remarked. "Anyway, my work took me into teaching for a time and I was responsible for the young men in a novitiate in the Borders."

"A novitiate? Is that like a seminary?"

"No, Chief Inspector. A seminary exists to educate those who wish to become diocesan priests. Rather like students for the Ministry in other denominations."

"So what does a novitiate do, exactly?"

"Well, we have a year of discernment where men, usually young men, learn about the Order. The novices study but also do many tasks around the Parish House." Father Ambrose smiled wryly. "We like to give them quite menial jobs as a way of testing their resolve."

Lorimer nodded, encouraging the priest to continue.

"This is not something we take lightly, Chief Inspector. It is the highest of callings and any novitiate must be suitable as well as serious in their intentions. About fifteen years ago we had a young man who had come from a farming family in Lanarkshire. He was a huge chap, great shoulders on him, hands like hams. He had the physique of a farmer. But Malcolm wanted to join our Order and I was appointed to be his novice master. He was so eager and willing to help and I admit he was of great use around the Parish House when anything of a practical nature was required. That was how he came to help us with the funerals." He paused and stared at Lorimer.

"We were part of a large Parish at that time and our own church was shared with the local parishioners during massive renovation work. Malcolm began by doing the heavy work, lifting coffins, packing away hurdles, that sort of thing. But then he began to take an interest in the laying out of the deceased." Father Ambrose tightened his lips in a moue of disapproval. "Normally there would be vigil prayers the evening before a funeral and the coffin would be kept overnight in church. One evening, just before leaving, we caught sight of Malcolm placing a flower in the hands of a young woman who had passed away. It was a red carnation."

Lorimer sat up smartly.

"It was a nice idea, we thought, and the relatives rather liked it, so it became a habit of Malcolm's to select a flower for the coffin thereafter. Of course that stopped when he went away."

"He left the Order?"

Father Ambrose sighed once more. "Not exactly. He was asked to leave. There was an incident," he hesitated, his pearly skin flushing. "Malcolm was found interfering with a corpse, Chief Inspector."

"What exactly do you mean? Interfering in what way?"

"Normally the coffins were screwed down after vigil prayers and somehow that job always fell to Malcolm." The old man wiped a hand across his eyes as if trying to erase a memory. "One of the other novices had left something in church and went back for it. That's when he saw Malcolm."

"What was he doing?"

"He was trying to make love to the corpse." The priest's voice had sunk to a whisper again as if the memory of that shame was too much to bear. "We realised then what we had suspected for some time, that he was not quite right. Academically Malcolm was fairly poor and his progress towards the priesthood would always have been in question, but there was more to it than that. I think there may have been some problem. There was talk of behavioural difficulties when he was little. Perhaps I'm trying to find an excuse for what happened, I don't really know. Anyway, it was a terrible time. We managed to keep it out of the papers but it rocked the whole novitiate. Malcolm was sent home and I left shortly afterwards."

"But it wasn't your fault, surely?"

"I was responsible for the boys and their welfare, Chief Inspector. My integrity was in question. There was no way I could continue as a novice master," the priest replied firmly.

"So," Lorimer began, "you think this Malcolm may have had something to do with the murder of Deirdre McCann and the other women?"

"I do. Although," the man hesitated again, "I worried about the nurses. I couldn't see him murdering good people like that. Still, the mind does odd things, isn't that so? No, it was the killing of the two prostitutes that concerned me."

"Why was that?"

"Malcolm was adopted, Chief Inspector. His parents were farming folk who had no children of their own and they took him in and gave him a good home and a loving upbringing. Perhaps that love was just too giving, in the end. You see, they told Malcolm about his real mother. She had been a prostitute in Glasgow and had given up her baby for adoption. That was the reason Malcolm gave for wanting to enter the priesthood. He had a vocation, he said, to rid the world of that kind of sinfulness. Of course, we took that to mean that he wanted to save their souls."

"And now you think he may have been on an entirely different crusade?"

"Yes."

"Tell me a bit more about this man. Malcolm...?"

"Malcolm Docherty. There's not a lot I can tell you. He must be in his late thirties by now. I can give you the address he had in Dumfries," he said, handing Lorimer a piece of paper. "But I don't know what became of him after he left us."

"And there's nothing else?"

"No. Just my feeling, I suppose. Well, more a certainty, really." Father Ambrose looked Lorimer straight in the eye. "I just know that Malcolm is the man you're looking for."

It didn't take long after the priest had left for Lorimer to run a computer check on their existing data. The names and details of all who had been interviewed were listed in a file. Running his eye down the names, Lorimer wondered if Malcolm Docherty, disgraced novice priest, had even kept his own name.

He had. There, amongst the list of railway employees, was one Malcolm Docherty, aged thirty-nine. Lorimer sat back, stunned. They had him! After all his team's intensive investigating it had been the conscience of one elderly priest that had cracked it for them. Taking a deep breath, Lorimer lifted the phone.

"Alistair, get the team together. Now. There's been a development."

Malcolm was picking up an empty lager can when he saw them approach. His stick froze in his hand as he watched the figures draw closer. There were about five of them, all in uniform, and they were coming down the side of the railway line. His first instinct was to warn them off, they were too close to the rails. But these were no wee school kids shouting names at him as he chased them away from his line. These men walked towards him with a purpose. Malcolm dropped his plastic sack and turned to run. But just as he began the ascent of the embankment he saw two more uniformed figures sliding down the grassy slope towards him.

He raised his stick and charged, yelling at the top of his

voice. Suddenly his legs were swept away from him and he felt a sickening thud as his mouth connected with the hard turf. As he stared at the ground and listened to the harsh voice telling him that he was under arrest, all Malcolm could see were the pale blue speedwells shivering on the grass. He put out his hands and grabbed the tiny flowers, squeezing them tightly in his huge fists, then felt them being wrenched away and cuffed tightly behind his back.

All eyes were on the man as he was led away through the station to the waiting police van. The platforms that had been cleared for this operation were now full of commuters alighting from their trains. Even a Press bulb flashed, prompting an officer to throw up an arm as if to protect his prisoner. But there would be plenty of stories told by the passengers held back by the police cordon. Once the news broke, they'd be able to tell how they'd actually witnessed the arrest of the man who'd become known as the Station Strangler.

35

Solly shook his head as he read the evening headlines, *Killer of Four Women Caught*. They were wrong of course, just as Superintendent Mark Mitchison was wrong. Malcolm Docherty had not murdered Kirsty MacLeod or Brenda Duncan. Solly's mouth twisted at the irony of it all. The signature that had identified the man was being used as evidence that he had murdered all four women. And so far Lorimer had not intervened. Mitchison had insisted that he be charged with all four killings. Was Lorimer really doing nothing to prevent this? Somehow he couldn't imagine the DCI condoning a miscarriage of justice, not to mention the fact that Solly was convinced that a killer was still at large. And Lorimer knew that.

He hadn't been invited to sit in on the interview. In fact, there had been no communication at all from Strathclyde Police. Perhaps he ought to make it his business to be there all the same, Solly thought, watching as a black cab rolled down Byres Road, its orange light glowing. Making a sudden decision, Solly raised a hand and watched as the vehicle drew in to the kerb.

There was an atmosphere of jubilation at headquarters when Malcolm Docherty arrived. Lorimer felt guilty that he was about to spoil it. The last months had been a slog for all of them and Docherty's arrest seemed to be the culmination of all that painstaking effort. He'd called the whole team together once Docherty had been safely conducted to the cells for a medical examination.

Lorimer looked from one smiling face to another. Jo Grant was looking positively smug, as well she might. Even the serious Lewisman had a grin on his pale face, though it wouldn't be there for long.

"I'm sorry to spoil the party," he began, "but there is a development that I want you to be aware of."

All eyes turned to him and he could see their smiles fading as they heard the gravity in his tone.

"As you know, Dr Brightman has been attempting to profile our killer. I'm pleased to tell you that Malcolm Docherty fits a profile that has been drawn up."

There were murmurs of approval but among them Lorimer detected Alistair Wilson, hand on his chin, giving his boss a speculative look. The detective sergeant knew Lorimer well enough to tell when something was wrong.

"However, this profile was developed with some difficulty. Dr Brightman did not find it possible to draw his profile until he came to a conclusion about the murders." Lorimer paused to see if he had their attention. There was a kind of hush as all eyes were turned his way.

"He believes we have not one, but two killers," Lorimer told them.

"But that's impossible!" someone exclaimed.

"What about the flowers?" another voice demanded.

"I know, I know. I've been asking myself exactly the same question. There's a chance, however, that the murders of Kirsty MacLeod and Brenda Duncan have been carried out by a copy-cat killer. Until we interview Docherty, we can't be certain of this, of course. It may well be that he confesses to all four murders. If so, we can open a few bottles and go home. And no one would be happier than me, I can assure you," he added. "However," he raised his hand to quell the murmurs that had broken out, "If we have no real evidence to link Docherty with those other two deaths, we may have to consider something else." Lorimer took a deep breath before continuing. "If Dr Brightman is correct then we have a real problem on our hands. It would mean that information has been leaked from somebody on the team. Now, I don't have to tell you about security during an investigation. You all know how things operate. But the fact remains that the killer of those two nurses knew exactly how Deirdre McCann's hands were folded around that flower. The Press got that aspect wrong and we weren't about to correct them, I can tell you. So. Whoever killed Kirsty and Brenda had to have seen an incident report."

"Or been the same killer!" Jo Grant declared, a mutinous look on her face. Lorimer's heart sank. Jo had been one of Mitchison's sidekicks in the past. Would she make trouble for him now?

"That's right," he told her. "But we have to prove that, ladies and gentlemen. I wanted you to be aware of this before I have Docherty up for questioning. If any of you have been guilty of a breach of security then now's the time to tell me. Otherwise we may have to turn this place upside down."

"Superintendent Mitchison does not share Dr Brightman's theories, I might add," he said, looking deliberately at Jo. But the DI showed no triumph at his remark. In fact, she was frowning now and Lorimer wondered just what she was thinking.

"I'll have a copy of Docherty's statement circulated to all of you as soon as it's available. Let's just hope he tells us what we want to hear."

Lorimer took his detective sergeant aside as the other officers departed. "I want you downstairs with me when Docherty's brought up," he told him. "We'll not have his DNA results for a bit and they may prove crucial. Meantime he's in for a grilling."

"You really believe Brightman's theory, don't you?" Wilson asked, a rueful smile on his lips.

Lorimer nodded. "Aye, more's the pity. It just makes so much sense, you know. The logic of it all hangs together apart from anything else."

"And has he come up with a profile for killer number two yet?"

"I think he's still working on that. But I'll let you know. *If* Mitchison lets him carry on, of course."

"Any chance that the Super will halt the investigation?"

"Don't even ask me that yet. Wait till we've heard what Docherty has to say."

It was a different figure from the man they'd seen escorted between two burly police officers. Malcolm Docherty's shoulders were slumped and his head hung down as if a weight drew it earthwards. The police doctor handed Lorimer a file, nodding towards the prisoner seated at the table.

"No problems, Chief Inspector. We'll let you know the results ASAP. Okay?"

"Thanks," Lorimer replied and walked around the table to face Malcolm Docherty. The man did not look up as Lorimer stood at the table, nor did he flinch when the DCI scraped a metal chair across the floor, its grating squeal setting everyone's teeth on edge. At first Lorimer simply stood there appraising the prisoner. His mind flicked back to the January night when this case had begun. The swirling fog had cleared away now and he felt a weird sense of peace in the interview room. Euphoria had given way to calmness now that the man was finally here in front of him.

One glance at his feet made the line on Lorimer's mouth tighten. This man's shoes were size twelve, at the very least.

Alistair Wilson waited patiently out of Docherty's line of vision. His boss would begin whenever he was good and ready. At last Docherty looked up as if some magnetism stronger than his own will was forcing him to acknowledge Lorimer's presence. Lorimer sat down, Wilson beside him.

"Interview with Malcolm James Docherty beginning at 15.00 hours. June sixth. Detective Chief Inspector Lorimer and Detective Sergeant Wilson in attendance," Lorimer began in a voice that sounded utterly bored by what he had to do. It was a useful ploy. It made a suspect feel both inferior and at ease, often resulting in a sense of outrage. *How dare this cop treat me as if I were some unimportant part of his daily grind?*

Docherty's eyes gave a glitter that told the two policemen that the ruse had worked.

"You are Malcolm James Docherty of 19 Peninsula Crescent, Springburn?"

Docherty glared at Lorimer then shifted his eyes to take in Wilson who nodded encouragingly. "Aye," he said at last.

"Where were you on the night of January 12th this year?"

Docherty licked his lips nervously, eyes shifting from Lorimer to Wilson and back again. His silence was not unusual. Many suspects were at a loss how to begin answering questions in an interview room, especially those who had no previous experience of the situation. Lorimer waited as if he had all day. If Docherty stalled too long, he'd simply pick up the Gazette and begin to read bits out to Alistair Wilson about last night's football results. That was another ploy that got under their skin, he knew.

But he hadn't long to wait. Docherty sat up a bit straighter and looked at Lorimer.

"It's my work," he began.

Lorimer nodded encouragingly, but not too eagerly. He'd make Docherty do the talking if he could.

"You see, I clean up the railways." He paused, uncertain of how to continue. "There's a lot of rubbish everywhere. Everywhere," he added, a dreamy look appearing in his eye.

Lorimer tried hard to sit still although his impulse was to lean forward to catch any nuance of speech.

"I was *asked* to do these other jobs," he told Lorimer, a note of querulousness creeping into his tone.

"What other jobs?" Lorimer asked.

Docherty looked surprised. "Clearing up the station. Those women can't come in and do things there," he protested, sitting up in his chair with an air of righteous indignation.

"What women?"

Docherty bent across the desk and glared at Lorimer as if he were stupid. "Prostitutes," he hissed, his teeth showing in a grimace of hatred.

"What method did you use to clear these women from your station, Malcolm?"

"I put them down."

"Could you describe exactly what you did, Malcolm?"

Docherty hesitated as if he were trying to find the correct answer then he moved his hands up and clasped them together as if they were round an invisible throat.

"Like this," he said.

"You strangled them?"

Docherty nodded.

Lorimer swallowed hard. His next question was crucial. Trying to sound as if this was a normal conversation he asked, "How many women have you strangled, Malcolm?"

The sound of Docherty's feet shuffling under the table could be heard as Lorimer waited for the answer.

"Just two," he said. "I'm sorry."

Lorimer took a deep breath, suddenly understanding what the man was apologising for. It was not contrition about taking lives. It was that he'd only taken two of them.

"Are you sure it was only two?"

Docherty nodded sadly. "Aye. Two prostitutes, they were."

"Tell me what you did after you'd strangled them, Malcolm."

The man seemed to brighten up a little at the question. "Oh, I sent them on their way. I gave them a flower and let their hands do a prayer. I said a prayer too. They're quite safe now, you see. They'll not harm anything ever again."

Beside him Lorimer could feel Wilson shift uneasily in his seat. They had a right one here and no mistake.

"Did you give a flower to any other young women recently, Malcolm?"

"No. Just those two. It's not my fault," he told them, round-eyed. "I didn't get any other orders."

"You said earlier that you were told to do these clearing up jobs, as you put it. Who exactly was it who told you to kill these women, Malcolm?"

Docherty gave a smile. "God."

Lorimer nodded as if this was something he heard every day in the course of his investigations.

"And how did God make his instructions clear, Malcolm?"

"He talked to me. He showed me the flowers. *His* flowers. They're perfect, you know. All His creation is perfect. But *they* weren't perfect. They had to be cleared away. Like the rubbish."

A nutter, Lorimer thought. A twelve-carat nutter. Voices in the head from God. Sometimes they actually heard them from the television. That kind of mental illness wasn't really so uncommon. But had he had anything to do with the killing of the two nurses? Lorimer had to ask.

"Where were you on the nights of May 7th and May 14th?"

Docherty shook his head. "I don't know. What days were they? I work during the day. But I don't go out much at night."

Lorimer told him.

"No, I'd be at home. I watch TV at night then go to my bed. Sometimes I go out for a fish supper. Can't remember, really." He shrugged as if the dates were of no importance to him.

"Two nurses were killed on those dates. They were strangled and somebody left a flower in their praying hands, Malcolm. Just like you did."

"What?" Docherty suddenly sat up, a horrified look on his face. "But that's terrible! Who'd do a thing like that?" The man's expression was almost comical, thought Lorimer, one serial strangler condemning another. But then his expression changed as the awfulness of the news sank in.

"You don't think...? No. Oh, just a minute, hold on now," Docherty rose from his seat, fists clenched, his face a mask of fear.

"Mr Docherty has got up from his seat," Wilson intoned into the listening tape.

His words seemed to calm the man for he sank back down, a look of horror still on his face.

"Do you deny strangling Kirsty MacLeod and Brenda Duncan?"

"Of course," he whispered. "I never killed them!"

Lorimer believed him. But would Mitchison expect him to grind the man down in order to elicit a confession from him? If so, he'd be sadly disappointed. That wasn't Lorimer's way. The DNA results might confirm what they were hearing and what Solly had suggested. For a moment Lorimer wished that he could have the psychologist here with them. He might know how to tune in to Malcolm Docherty in a way that would prove his innocence as well as his guilt.

A tap on the door made all three men and the uniformed officer turn round. DC Cameron's face appeared, signalling for Lorimer to join him outside.

"DCI Lorimer leaving the interview room."

Lorimer stopped in his tracks. Beside Cameron was the familiar figure of the psychologist. It was as if his wish had suddenly spirited Solly there. Was the man psychic as well as everything else?

"What are you doing here?"

"I wasn't asked to come in, if that's what you mean. I just wanted to be here," he explained with his usual little smile.

"Well. I'm not sorry you did," Lorimer told him. "We're in the middle of interviewing the suspect. He's already confessed to the two station murders but says he knows nothing about the other two."

"And you believe him," Solly said. It wasn't a question. He could see his answer in Lorimer's face.

"Will you come and sit in?"

"Thanks."

"Chief Inspector Lorimer re-entering the interview room accompanied by Dr Brightman," Alistair Wilson told the tape recorder.

"Malcolm, this is Dr Brightman from Glasgow University."

Docherty stood up and took Solly's outstretched hand in his large fist. "But I've seen the doctor already," he muttered, giving Solly a dubious look. "Why do I have to see another one?"

"Dr Brightman is here to keep us company, Malcolm," Lorimer reassured him. It was like talking to a wee boy, he thought, except that most wee boys of his acquaintance were a dash sight more streetwise than Malcolm Docherty appeared to be.

There was something otherworldly about this man that had nothing to do with his experience as a failed novitiate. Lorimer had seen so many criminals whose lives were lived in a world so different from his own, yet all worlds impinged on each other, he thought. There was never really a place to hide from the evils that existed. Not even in the Jesuit Order.

Solly had listened as Lorimer and Wilson took turns to ask the man questions. His behaviour intrigued the psychologist. It was as if he were a perfectly normal citizen in his own eyes, assisting the police with their enquiries. Any minute now, he thought, and he'll get up and ask if he can go home. There was no remorse, no worry at all about the crimes he had committed, nor any awareness of the boundaries that he had trespassed. That was the real difference between the criminally sane and those criminals who were mentally ill. Culpability was indeed a state of mind.

As he heard the questions and answers about Docherty's methods of strangling the two prostitutes, Solly's stomach turned. To dispatch these poor women as if they were so much dross! Lorimer and Wilson kept their feelings well under check, he noticed, though he knew well what they thought. *Any murder is an affront to humanity*, he remembered Lorimer insisting. And he agreed. But this man, this huge man who looked like a farmer with his weather-beaten skin and massive shoulders, he had no sense of humanity at all. Only a warped brain that took twisted messages from a false god.

Malcolm Docherty was well capable of murder. The man's physique was such that it was no longer difficult to imagine a swift strangulation at these hands. Rosie had worried about that, he knew. How could someone kill these women with no sound of a struggle?

The same applied to Kirsty MacLeod's death, though, a little voice reminded him. She'd been dealt with swiftly, too. But there was no way on earth that Solly could believe the man in front of Lorimer was responsible for that death. Nor for Brenda Duncan's. Solly was still a way from completing his profile but he knew the mind that he sought was altogether sharper and clearer than Docherty's. That was a calculating, reasoning person who was not quite in focus, yet. And it was not Malcolm Docherty.

36

Rowena sighed as the pick-up gathered speed. She could see the new man's hair curling sweetly around the curve of his ear and over the brown cord collar of his waxed jacket. Dad was wittering on about the flight and telling the man how much he was going to enjoy Failte. Give Dad his due, it sounded so sincere and welcoming, but Rowena had heard the same spiel each time a new one arrived at the airport.

She was glad that last one had gone. Sam Fulton had given her the creeps. Dad had kept a real good eye on him, though. Mum had insisted on that. After Sister Angelica's abrupt departure, the Glasgow man had sought out Rowena's company just a bit too often. She'd been pretty uncomfortable with him, not liking the way he joked about women as if they were all an inferior species. It was all a bit of fun, he'd told her. No harm meant. But Rowena had kept her distance from him all the same. Dad never told any of them what a patient's background was. She understood how it was important to maintain their privacy. She wouldn't like any of them to know all of her secrets either, Dad had once pointed out. Still, she had the feeling that Mum knew more about Sam Fulton than she was letting on. And this fact alone had increased her uneasiness. Still, he was gone now, back to Glasgow, supposedly over the worst of his depression.

Rowena smiled to herself. The new patient had shaken her hand as if she was a proper grown-up, not some silly wee schoolgirl. She recalled his grave eyes and that tired, kindly smile. She'd maybe ask him to come for a wee walk up the road with the dog after dinner, though Dad liked his guests, as he called them, to have complete rest after they arrived. Still, this one was only here for a long weekend.

Funny about the other man, though. They'd waited for him yesterday with a placard that said Failte in bold lettering, but nobody from the Glasgow flight had acknowledged them. Dad had phoned Mrs Baillie who had shrugged it off but there was always a worry that somehow a patient would simply slip past them and roam about the island, unsupervised. It hadn't happened yet, but there was always a first time, Mum had warned them. Still, they had another new one now.

Rowena settled back to enjoy her thoughts. She'd rehearse what to say before they went out. Then maybe she'd be able to slip in questions about that Dr Brightman. Had they met at the Grange? Was he married? Her fantasy continued down towards the house, the passing landscape a familiar blur of greens and blues.

37

"You want *what*?" Superintendent Mitchison's voice rose in a squeak that might have been funny in other circumstances.

"Complete freedom to carry out a surveillance operation. I've spoken to the patient and she has agreed to my suggestions."

Mitchison sat silent for a while, his face showing the struggle within. Lorimer could almost hear the cogs turning. Would the cost of the operation, never mind its risks, be outweighed by the capture of the second killer? Mitchison had railed long and hard against Lorimer's decision not to charge Docherty with all four murders. But the DNA results were pretty conclusive. Whoever had killed Brenda and Kirsty, it was not now likely to be the prisoner currently undergoing psychiatric testing. Which left them with a huge problem. Lorimer had sat down with Solly to confess his innermost fears; someone on the team was involved. Mitchison had been reluctant at first to have them all DNA-tested but it made sense for the purposes of elimination as well as to restore some kind of peace in the ranks. This weekend all his men and women would be in for their tests, whether they liked it or not. Lorimer and Solly would be there too.

Undergoing the test would give the team a sense of solidarity as well as letting him observe their various reactions. Staff and patients at the Grange had already been tested by the police doctor, giving Rosie's lot plenty to keep them busy.

At last the Superintendent looked up. "I don't like your ways, Lorimer, but that's neither here nor there. A surveillance operation like the one you are suggesting carries a high risk. Not just for the patient, but a risk of failure. And I don't need to tell you how much the Chief Constable abhors a waste of time and money."

"We really need to try, sir. It's almost certain that we have another killer on the loose and that he has something to do with the clinic." Lorimer paused. Should he reveal his disquiet about the Grange's financial affairs or would that muddy the waters at this stage? No. He'd beaver away at that problem on his own, for now.

"Give me a complete breakdown of all the personnel you would need and the timescale, then," Mitchison decided. "And," he paused and drew a hand across his brow, "take care of that poor woman, won't you?"

Lorimer was taken aback. Concern for Phyllis was not what he'd have expected from the Super. Maybe the man had a heart after all.

"Mind if I come into your room, missus?" The man in white overalls carrying a cantilevered toolbox stood uncertainly at Phyllis's door. Phyllis eyed him with curiosity. That new nurse said that someone would be arriving today. To fix the television set. A wave of the old frustration swept over her. She couldn't explain she didn't watch the thing. It was pointless to do anything to a set that hadn't been used in years. Why not dismantle the whole thing and take it away?

As she watched him there were other questions that digested themselves in her brain until Phyllis had produced a satisfactory answer; questions that were explained by the repairman's unusual activities. She didn't know the first thing about televisions but she didn't think the set would function in its normal way with all its innards removed and replaced by what seemed to be a smallish camera.

They were watching her. Perhaps she should be relieved that those secret eyes were looking after her but all she could feel was a sense of intrusion into a world that was already far too confined.

Lorimer swung round in his chair to face the window, the solicitor's words still singing in his brain. There had been a lengthy delay in responding to his query about the woman's will. He glanced down at the figure on his notepad as if to check that it was correct. Phyllis Logan's estate was estimated to be in the region of three and a half million pounds. What would his team make of this? One thing was certain, they'd have to be especially careful of the sick woman now.

Lorimer looked back at the solicitor's report. The main beneficiary of the woman's estate was the clinic itself, wrapped up in a trust fund. There were several provisions made to help patients who could not otherwise afford the fees, that money coming from interest in share capital. Lorimer frowned. With the collapse of so much on the stock market in recent years, just what were these shares worth? But it was the other beneficiary that caught his attention. To the director of the Grange, Mrs Maureen Baillie, Phyllis Logan had left £250,000. A sweet quarter of a million!

Recalling the woman's spartan living quarters and the suspicion that all was not well with the clinic's finances, Lorimer felt a niggle of worry. People had been murdered before for a lot less than that. But why would Kirsty and Brenda have been killed over a financial scam? It didn't make sense, unless they knew something that made their continued existence a danger to somebody. You've got a dirty mind, Lorimer, he told himself. Still, he'd keep digging this particular seam until he hit gold.

Why would Kirsty have been killed that night? Phyllis had been so vulnerable to the killer's hands. It would have been so easy just to have dispatched her there and then. If that was the underlying motive. He gnawed his fingernail until he felt it split under his teeth. There was something there, but what?

A bird flying past his window made him glance up and catch sight of the clock on his wall. Time to go. They'd all be waiting for him.

They were all in the muster room. Lorimer walked in to face the semi circle of officers who sat on steel chairs. He noticed that Jo Grant had chosen to perch on the wide windowsill that overlooked the car park.

"Right. We've got the go-ahead. I want to introduce you to two of our undercover officers from D. Division, Patricia Crossan and Marion Warbrick." He turned towards two young women who were sitting at the edge of the circle. One, a blonde girl hugging a stone-coloured raincoat around herself, was slouched into her chair. She gave a perfunctory nod. The other girl raked back her seat and stood up. Her black leather jacket and short cropped hair showed drops of water from the recent rain shower.

"Hi there," she smiled at the other officers. "I'm Pat and this is Marion." There were murmurs of acknowledgement from the rest of the room. As she sat down again, all eyes turned towards Lorimer.

"Next time you see Pat she'll be on duty at the Grange. Marion has come in specially to meet you before she hits the sack." The blonde girl managed a watery grin as Lorimer continued. "Erica, the third of our undercover officers, is keeping an eye on Phyllis Logan right now and Pat will be doing the next shift later on. I don't need to tell you how important it is that you treat all of these officers as if they were perfect strangers. As far as you are concerned they are agency nurses who are helping out at the clinic, okay? The one thing we don't want to do is to arouse anyone's suspicions. And I'm talking about staff, patients, visitors, anybody who comes through their doors on a regular basis."

Lorimer let his gaze travel over every officer's face as he went on. "If their cover's blown the whole operation could be scuppered. As far as the people in the clinic are concerned they're simply three new pairs of hands. Luckily, each of them has bona fide nursing experience. Guess the glamour of police work lured you away from your last jobs, eh, girls?"

There were snorts of derisive laughter from several directions, including, he noticed, Jo Grant tucked into her windowsill.

"There's been no suspicion at all at the clinic, has there?" Lorimer addressed Pat.

"They've accepted us without question, sir. Frankly, they're all relieved to have some agency nurses," she replied.

"Yes. There's been a bit of an exodus amongst the staff since Kirsty and Brenda's deaths," Lorimer agreed.

"So, ladies and gentlemen, we now have a round-the-clock presence at the Grange." He measured each word carefully as he continued, letting his blue gaze fall on each officer in the room as he spoke. "Now, here's the risky bit. We've let it be known to the nursing staff that Phyllis Logan has information about the night of Kirsty's murder." He paused to let his words sink in.

"We've not said in so many words that she actually saw the killer but the implication is there all the same. Pat, Marion and Erica have been asking both staff and patients all about the murders like the rookies they're supposed to be," he told them. "One way or another we've made sure that word has spread. Not too difficult in a small community like that. The patients will no doubt pass on the gossip to their nearest and dearest. I just hope to God the Press don't get wind of it."

He tapped his thigh as if considering what to say. Sometimes stating the obvious helped to concentrate the mind.

"The murders of those two nurses took place exactly one

week apart. Okay, the loci were entirely different but each of them took place on a Monday night. Now that may have absolutely no significance but it's never something that can be ruled out of an equation, as you all well know. So this coming Monday is our choice. We've got the weekend to let the rumour factory do its worst, then we move in."

Lorimer heard their sounds of approval with a sense of satisfaction. There had been some voices of dissent when Solly had dropped his bombshell but now it seemed that they had come round to respect his opinion.

"We set up surveillance over the weekend and then wait to see if Phyllis Logan has any unexpected visitors."

"What if nothing happens, sir?" Niall Cameron was red in the face but he seemed determined to risk the question nonetheless.

"I expect Superintendent Mitchison will send us to the salt mines for wasting public money, Cameron," Lorimer growled at him.

"We've laid our bait in the trap. With her full co-operation, remember. Now we have to watch and wait. You're all experienced enough to know that's the hardest bit in any operation. You'll be on duty from just after nine o'clock right through till I say when."

He turned to the board behind him. A large-scale plan of the Grange had been fixed to the board with pieces of masking tape at each corner. Lorimer pointed to each area as he spoke.

"We'll have officers in unmarked cars all along the road to the front. There's waste ground at the rear. Alistair, you and Davie will take up positions between the basement door and the shrubbery. The gardeners have been given a holiday that week," he grinned. "You'll cover that exit. The patients will all be receiving visits from Health Board "officials" in the shape of Eddie and Vince," he indicated two of his detective constables, "since neither of you have been out at the clinic. The story is that you're there for a routine check. We've done the homework on it and it's a normal procedure. There should be nothing to create suspicion. The camera's in place and it'll be monitored from our British Telecom van out in the street. That's where I'll be with Dr Brightman and DC Cameron. We'll be out of sight but in constant contact with all units. Erica and Pat will alert us to anyone coming into or going out of Phyllis's room. She's a target but remember she's also our main witness. Right?"

He turned to the board again and drew aside a fresh sheet of paper. "And," he added, "there's this." Taking a marker pen, Lorimer wrote down the figures he'd obtained from Phyllis Logan's solicitor and a brief note of her will.

He heard an incredulous whistle as he faced them again. "So now we have even more reason to look after our witness. *And* keep an eye on certain members of staff. Okay?"

There were murmurs of assent as the team prepared to leave the muster room. Lorimer found that he was surprisingly calm. Cameron's question had been quite valid, even if unwelcome. What if nothing did happen? He was gambling with the hope that the killer would take action, believing Phyllis to be a real threat. But what if the information so carefully dropped simply made him take to the hills? Was there any reason to suppose that the killer was still around anyway? Solly firmly believed that he was, and right now that was enough for Lorimer.

38

Niall Cameron was sweating. Lorimer had chosen to take him personally under his wing. What could that mean? Did the DCI have doubts about his ability? Did he feel that as the relative newcomer to the job he needed to be supervised? Or was there another reason?

As he walked along Bothwell Street, the young man kept looking out for the clocks that signified the Standard Life building. That was where he was to meet the guy. Lorimer had indicated that the Grange's accountant had been trawling through the clinic's books with a fine toothcomb and that he wanted to discuss certain things with Strathclyde Police. Cameron had been dispatched for this particular duty, and right now he was feeling more like an office boy sent on a simple errand than an officer involved in a murder case.

There they were, great gilt clocks high up at either end of the building. Automatically he checked their time against his watch to see if the time was correct. It was. Cameron stepped into a vast lobby flanked by elevators on each side and a list of names indicating the firms that occupied the building. A quick glance told him the third floor was his destination.

Minutes later he was shaking the hand of a man not too much his senior who introduced himself as Tommy Stirling.

"Fancy a coffee? The drinks machine's not bad," Stirling told him.

Cameron shook his head. "No thanks." The idea of coffee in a polystyrene cup didn't appeal. He'd be bound to spill it and make a fool of himself in this plush office with its matching blue carpet and padded chairs.

"Right, then, the Grange's account has only recently come into our hands. It's the sort of bread and butter thing we do all the time, really. There was nothing to show that this was an unusual client until those murders happened."

"The clinic's accounts were all in order, then?"

"Well, the last audit had been done by our predecessors fairly recently so we weren't due to check the books as soon as this. But of course you folk made us look a bit closer."

"And?"

"And there are discrepancies in the accounting. It took a while for me to spot them but I can show you," Stirling handed over a sheaf of papers folded back at a particular page. A turquoise highlighter pen marked several figures in a column.

"What do they indicate?" Cameron wanted to know.

"Unauthorised withdrawals from the main account."

Cameron frowned. "How could that happen?"

"Any withdrawals above a certain amount require two signatures. These only show one."

"Ah," Cameron nodded, understanding what the accountant meant. Against each of the turquoise figures was the name of the person who had taken several large sums of money from the clinic's account. Cameron flicked over the sheets of paper, seeing the same name again and again. It was Mrs Maureen Baillie.

"What exactly does this mean, then?" he asked. "Mrs Baillie is the Director of the clinic."

"She's *one* of the Directors," Stirling replied firmly. "And unless the other Directors are aware of her taking out these sums of money then there's only one conclusion we can come to, I'm afraid."

"What's that?"

"Embezzlement."

"How did you find out?"

"It showed up in the accounts."

Mrs Baillie gave a resigned sigh. "So you know, then?"

"We know that you misappropriated funds for your own use, yes. But we don't exactly know why. Care to enlighten me?"

For the first time since he had met her, Lorimer saw a tremble in the woman's face as if she might actually begin to cry. He could see her swallowing and heard her breaths coming in short gasps as she tried to regain some control.

"I needed the money," she began. "I had debts to repay."

"Uh-huh. And just who were your creditors?"

"Oh," the woman's eyes flew to meet his suddenly. "Just one. A man called Joseph Harrigan." She smiled a bitter little smile. "Perhaps you've heard of him?"

Lorimer had. Harrigan was a notorious bookmaker in Glasgow who had come to the attention of the fraud squad on more than one occasion.

"What on earth were you doing mixed up with someone like that?"

Mrs Baillie straightened herself up and looked Lorimer straight in the eye. "I gamble," she said.

Lorimer saw the steady way she regarded him as if waiting for some condemnation. She wouldn't get any from him. Other people's weaknesses were not something he despised but pitied.

"Ironic, isn't it?" she continued. "I run a clinic for patients who have various disorders and I can't even help myself."

Lorimer nodded. Those bare rooms at the Grange made sense now. She'd whittled down her possessions as she'd gambled their worth away.

"There is the matter of a legacy in Phyllis Logan's will that I was hoping you would explain to me," he told her.

Suddenly the woman's face changed. Her smile was

wistful as she shook her head.

"Ah, yes, poor Phyllis. I did wonder if you would ask me about that."

And then she told him.

Maureen Baillie looked down at the sheet of paper on her desk. She was surprised that her hand was so still, given the turmoil of emotion within. Her resignation as Director of the clinic would take effect from the end of the month in compliance with her terms of employment.

What would become of her after that? Lorimer had told her that there would be a court case pending. But fraud cases could drag on and on. Perhaps she'd have time to cut her losses and simply disappear. But it was her lack of assets that was holding her back, she thought with some bitterness.

The car she drove couldn't be turned into cash as it was on lease hire, her own house had long since gone, which was her main reason for taking up residence in the Grange. If they ever thought about it, which she doubted, the staff probably believed she was simply being over-conscientious in her duty to the patients.

Harrigan had fleeced her. There was nothing left at all, now that the police had discovered her secret. Her salary would be paid into the bank but that few hundred pounds wasn't going to take her very far. Besides, where was she to go?

Mrs Baillie sat very still, fingering the pearls at her throat. They were all that she had left of her mother. Her face twitched in an ironic smile. Sentiment had proved stronger than her compulsion to gamble.

She could hear the chatter of two of the women as they passed by her room on their way to the television lounge. Her thoughts turned to Angelica who had been here so recently, providing an oasis for them all. And, of course, there was Phyllis to consider. She wondered about Phyllis and that new nurse who was so determined to learn what she could about Multiple Sclerosis. Patients like Phyllis were so vulnerable, she thought. Always prey to infection. How long she could survive was anyone's guess, but she'd seen other cases like hers before and knew that a sudden onset of pneumonia was the thing most likely to dispatch her patient.

Maureen Baillie's fist clenched the paper into a ball.

No. She wouldn't leave right away. She had a duty to patients like Phyllis, even if that duty meant a little bit of suffering.

39

They were all set.

Mitchison had been surprisingly co-operative all of a sudden. Maybe it was the lack of DNA evidence, though they'd never really suspected anyone from the team. Lorimer had feigned astonishment when he'd been told of Sir Robert Caldwell, the Chief Constable, proclaiming his desire to follow the criminal profiler's advice. There were wheels within wheels. He knew fine that Solly had mentioned his case to the Professor of Psychology on the very evening when the Prof. was due to have dinner with Strathclyde's finest. He must have taken the hint and bent the Chief Constable's ear. It gave Lorimer some satisfaction to know that the Superintendent was not the only one capable of manipulating people. He wondered just what had been said between Sir Robert and the Professor. Still, it was enough that the Superintendent was giving them the authority to mount this operation without any hindrance.

Maggie had packed him a flask and a box of food. There was enough to feed an army, not just the three men, he'd complained, juggling with plastic carrier bags. But then she'd reminded him that Solly probably wouldn't even think about meals and he'd given in. It might be a long night.

The driver of the British Telecom van was DC Beattie, a

lad who'd come into the force around the same time as Niall Cameron. He was dressed in the regulation navy uniform of British Telecom engineers, a mock-up badge clipped to his woollen jersey.

Lorimer and Cameron sat in the back amongst the paraphernalia of sound engineering and close circuitry, backs against the metal sides of the van with Solomon facing them. Beattie sat up front. Despite the cramped interior of the telecommunications van, Lorimer had a decent view of all the monitors. His eyes wandered over them all but kept returning to those fixed in Phyllis Logan's room. If she were to have an unwelcome visitor they'd be the first to know.

The van was parked facing the crest of the hill that ran down towards Queen's Park, only yards away from the entrance to the Grange's driveway. Lorimer had walked around the area before giving his officers their various positions. There was some advantage in this road being a dead end, he'd realised; whatever vehicle came up this way would have to turn into the driveway or make a slow U-turn behind them before it could accelerate away again.

More than ever Lorimer felt that their killer was somewhere not too far away; perhaps, as Solomon had suggested, he was even inside the clinic already. Beattie was logging every vehicle that came up or turned to leave. So far his list included residents of the surrounding tenement flats as well as known members of staff and previous visitors to the clinic.

Lorimer's eye was caught by a movement from one of the monitors. Pat Crossan, her slim figure hidden beneath the regulation overall, was bending over Phyllis. From what Lorimer could see, the policewoman appeared to be checking the sick woman's pulse. One of Pat's credentials for the job had been her years as a Royal Alexandra nurse. She'd even seen action in the Gulf before coming home and joining the police force.

He saw her straighten up then give a small wink at the

camera just to let them know she was aware of their presence. Below her, Phyllis lay inert, her eyes shut. It was impossible to know if she was asleep or not.

"Do you have a list of who's on duty?" Solomon asked, suddenly breaking the silence in the back of the van. He nodded, handing him a copy of the paper that had already been circulated amongst his team. They'd tried to cover every member of staff from the director down. The late shift would continue until ten o' clock, by which time the night staff would have taken over. Before the change of shift the visitors and day case patients would have come and gone. Mrs Baillie was there all day. Not only was she on duty but her off-duty time seemed to be spent more and more in her flat on the top floor of the Grange or wandering in and out of the residents' rooms, according to the undercover girls.

"Erica takes over in four hours," Solly noted aloud.

"Right, but Pat will still be in the building. She's going to be writing up her essay on the clinic's computer. Or so she's told Mrs Baillie."

"I wonder what she'll really be typing onto the screen?"

Lorimer shrugged. He trusted Pat Crossan to cover her tracks effectively. She'd think of something plausible.

The next hour passed in a haze of boredom as Lorimer switched his attention from monitor to monitor, only calling up the members of his team to check out their positions.

It was a quiet Monday evening in a peaceful Glasgow suburb when all good residents were out walking their dogs or strolling in the park. There was nothing to suggest that the surroundings contained small pockets of watchful police officers waiting for something sinister to happen. And that was the way it should be, Lorimer thought, looking out from the restricted view they had in the back of the van. He could see the pavement that curved up towards the clinic then turned into its drive. Beyond the dense shrubbery there was nothing else in sight. Above them the sky was full of house martins dipping and diving for insects. Lorimer watched their swooping movements as a relief from studying the monitors. Already it was June. Only a few more weeks remained of the school term, then Maggie would be away on her travels.

Lorimer stretched his long legs out in front of him. Earlier they'd been able to slip out for brief comfort breaks to the pub across the road but now he'd told them to stay put. He was aware of Cameron squirming beside him; cramped muscles no doubt. The monitors flickered as a car passed by, sunlight bouncing off its wing-mirrors.

Phyllis had been watching the woman all day with a growing curiosity. Pat had revealed her identity on her first visit to the room. It was their secret. Nobody else knew that the agency nurses were plainclothes policewomen. It gave Phyllis a small feeling of triumph to be part of this clandestine operation when so much of her existence depended on other people. She had understood the need for the policewoman's presence. Their witness must be protected, Pat Crossan had stressed, especially now that Phyllis had agreed to this.

The paralysed woman told herself that she ought to feel frightened or even excited; after all, she was the bait being dangled to attract the person she thought was the killer. But today she was too exhausted to summon up such emotional energy.

Instead she had merely observed the policewoman's movements, watching her intently until sleep had overtaken her.

Since Lorimer's interview the sick woman had slipped into sleep more and more. Observing her, Pat had wondered at the tenacity of the human thread that held onto life. From time to time she bent over the bed, just to listen to the whisper of her breathing. It could scarcely be heard above the rise and fall of the machinery below the bed that hissed and sighed. She'd been sleeping now for almost an hour. The room was warm although Pat had closed the blinds against the direct sunlight. She wanted Phyllis to have a decent sleep. The poor woman seemed so weary.

A buzzer sounded suddenly so Pat reached up to the red button on the patient's water line to switch off the noise. But Phyllis did not even blink. Below the sheets she was somewhere else, dreaming and drifting as the shadows shifted around the room, oblivious to the fluids being pumped into her body. The policewoman looked at the watch pinned to her uniform. Two more hours and Erica would be here to relieve her. Quietly she left the room, closing the door behind her. She had other things to check; the whereabouts of other members of staff or visitors. And she needed to go to the loo. She wouldn't be away all that long.

Meantime the camera fixed inside the television set would watch over Phyllis.

As Pat walked briskly along the corridor a figure emerged from the shadows, looking after her.

Then, as silent as a cat, Leigh Quinn slipped into Phyllis's room and sat beside the sleeping woman. His hands strayed towards the vase of flowers on her bedside locker, touching their petals, re-arranging their stems. Then he drew one of them out of the vase and regarded it for a long moment.

Alistair Wilson circled his head slowly, hearing the crunch of fibres around his cervical vertebrae. At least he was out in the open air. Lorimer and the others would be roasting inside that BT van. So far all was quiet. The only communication they'd had was to check out all the visitors to the Grange. There had been no strangers among them, nobody who was out of place. The detective sergeant was sitting with PC Davie Inglis opposite the back entrance to the Grange, the gardening tools at their feet, screened from view by the thick branches of the rhododendrons.

"Reminds me of playing hide and seek at my auntie's garden in Saint Andrews when I was wee," Davie had whispered after they'd scrambled out of sight.

The door to the basement had been left locked, as it

normally would be. It was vital not to arouse any suspicions on the part of anyone who might have access to the basement area, Lorimer had insisted. Whoever had murdered Kirsty MacLeod had been able to make their escape this way. But had they? Alistair wasn't so sure about that and he knew Lorimer himself had doubts about the access. Had the door been left open to make it look as if an intruder had broken in? And had the real killer remained in the clinic during the hours that had followed? Whatever theories they might have, there was no way they could fail to keep this exit under close surveillance.

"I need to stretch my legs," Cameron said suddenly.

"Don't we all," grumbled Lorimer.

"No, sir. I mean I really need to stretch my legs," Cameron told him. Lorimer noted the flush around his collar and sighed.

"Okay. But don't be long," he warned. Trips back and forth to the pub were okay for so long. Someone behind the bar might begin to comment if they weren't discreet enough. If the lad really needed to go to the toilet, he couldn't very well stop him, could he? Perhaps Maggie had been a bit over-generous with her refreshments after all.

Cameron clambered over their legs and slid open the van door. The sun had made the metal hot and he winced as he touched it. It was a relief to be out in the air again. He bent down slowly, massaging his calves, then stood up to walk carefully around the van.

Inside, Lorimer craned his neck to watch Cameron walking towards the pub but he was either out of sight or had sprinted across, more desperate than he'd admitted. He tried to catch Solly's eye but the psychologist was engrossed in the papers in front of him. Even in the sweltering heat of the van, the psychologist was trying to keep up with his exam marking.

Sister Angelica was happy. It had been a beautiful day, just like the summers when she was a girl. She'd been telling the other patients in the lounge all about the summer holidays of her youth when the family had spent weeks on the farm in Melrose. She'd walked the Eildon Hills until she'd known every crag of them, she said. Then she'd told them about Lewis and how peaceful it could be in Failte.

The weekly prayer meeting was due to begin soon. There was only one person left to arrive then they could start. She'd lit a fat scented candle and placed it on the table by the window. The breeze stirred its flame beside the muslin curtains, sending the fragrance of sandalwood into the room.

Angelica beamed at them all. It was so heartening to do something for these people who had become her friends. Mondays were quite special for her, now. Her vocation was not over, after all. That was something else she had found out during her stay here.

It happened so suddenly that nobody quite knew how to react. First there was a whooshing sound followed by the table being upset as Angelica lumbered to her feet and one of the girls began to scream. The fire caught hold swiftly, spreading to the wallpaper and sending sparks of tinder onto the soft chairs.

"Out! Everybody! Get out!" Angelica ordered, shooing them all like sheep from the room just as the smoke alarm began its insistent beeping.

They were coughing in the corridor and gasping for air by the time the nun joined them. One man had picked up the fire extinguisher and was heading back into the room, followed by Peter, one of the male nurses. The front door gave its alarmed ring as they all spilled out into the fresh air. Angelica did a swift head-count. They were all there, she told herself. All, that is, except the one person they'd been waiting for. Where was Leigh?

"Something's up. The fire alarm's gone off," a voice came over the radio as Lorimer and Solly crouched in the back of the van. They exchanged glances but Lorimer shook his head.

"Not yet. This could be a false alarm." He switched his mike to talk. "Okay. Let us know the details as soon as you can. We won't make a move unless we have to." His gaze returned to the monitor.

The room where Phyllis Logan lay was bathed in a gentle half-light filtering through the blinds. There was no movement at all; the figure beneath the sheets seemed quite peaceful. There was no sign of the Irishman sitting by her bed.

"D'you think they'll need to call out the fire service?" Solly asked anxiously.

"We'll know soon enough, I suppose," he replied. "Maybe you should back the van up a bit, Beattie," he told the driver."And what's keeping Cameron?"

As the van shuddered into life the monitors were shaken into blurred lines of grey and white, making observation impossible. The sound of the smoke alarm could be heard faintly from the building.

Lorimer had to know what was happening inside. He tapped out the numbers on Pat's mobile. The ringing went on and on until he gave up in disgust. She was supposed to keep in contact. Where the hell was she? He glanced back at the monitor showing Phyllis's room. Only the patient in her bed could be seen. There was no sign of the undercover officer.

Pat flushed the toilet and unbolted the door. As she turned towards the basins to give her hands a thorough wash with the liquid soap she was aware of another person coming into the ladies' washroom.

The policewoman only had time to glance at the reflection in the mirror before she felt the sudden pain in her skull then everything went hazy as the sound of a high-pitched bell rang out in her brain. There was nobody to see her limp body being dragged into the cubicle, nobody to witness her nurse's overall being buttoned over another person's clothes.

Lorimer breathed a sigh of relief. The fire seemed to be under control by all accounts and he could see Pat's white-coated figure standing by the window. Any minute now she'd turn towards the camera and give him a reassuring signal.

Only she didn't. As the figure turned to face the screen, Lorimer found himself confronted by a different person altogether.

For an instant he was speechless then he felt the adrenaline rush as he grabbed the radio control.

"Alert all units. Find Pat Crossan. There's a stranger in Phyllis's room. We're going in."

He thrust the doors aside, not waiting for Solly who sat staring at the monitor in a daze of disbelief.

Phyllis woke up, suddenly aware of the shadow above her. But perhaps she was still asleep.

This wasn't the policewoman.

This wasn't meant to be happening.

She tried to scream, but the thin noise that came was quickly stifled by a feather pillow thrust over her mouth.

Now she was underwater, gasping and blowing for air that would not come. A ringing sound began far away then nearer and nearer, filling her ears. Her chest hurt with an unfamiliar pain as if she had been running hard.

Then she heard a cry and suddenly the room was full of whirling shapes as the pillow was pulled away.

Leigh was struggling with another man who had his hands against his throat. She watched, terrified, as they edged towards the wall, the man's fingers pressing into Leigh's neck. There was a thump and both men fell to the ground out of her sight. She stared, open mouthed, as another commotion erupted into the room. Then Lorimer was wrestling with her attacker, pulling his arms away from the bed. She watched as his tall figure grabbed the man from behind. He struggled against the policeman's grip, legs kicking wildly, knocking over the drip stand beside the bed. The crash as it hit the floor reverberated

287

through every nerve in Phyllis's body.

The sound of running feet brought several more people bursting into the doorway, Solly and Mrs Baillie among them.

"Tom!"

Solly came to a sudden standstill. Lorimer had his colleague in a tight grip, the handcuffs already pinioning the man's wrists. The Chief Inspector looked from Solly standing white-faced in the doorway to Tom Coutts. Solly was gazing at the man's face, then his eyes dropped to the killer's shoes.

"I look towards his feet, but that's a legend," he quoted softly. Lorimer saw the slight shake of Solly's head and the brightness behind those horn-rimmed glasses. Trust and betrayal; weren't they always the cruellest wounds?

Tom Coutts twisted once under Lorimer's grasp then, meeting Solly's eyes at last, Lorimer felt him slump in defeat.

"I'm sorry," he whispered. "I'm so sorry."

Nobody spoke for a moment, the sound of whirring machinery the only noise as the two men stared at one another.

Then Leigh Quinn stumbled to his feet. Ignoring the other people in the room he went over to Phyllis and crouched beside her.

"Are you okay, wee lady? Are you okay?" Tears were streaming down the Irishman's face as he stroked Phyllis's hands. "He didn't get you, my dear. You're safe, now," he told her tenderly.

Phyllis watched as they led that man, the man they called Tom, out of the room. She saw Dr Brightman following them, escorting Maureen Baillie gently by the arm. Leigh stood up and the policeman clapped his shoulder. For a moment Leigh flinched but then his expression changed and a grin spread over his face. He gave Phyllis a wave as he turned to go but she knew he'd be back later, sorting her flowers, talking to her about things he was unable to tell another soul in the whole world.

Then there were only the two of them left.

Lorimer came towards the bed.

"I'm so sorry you had to go through all that. Are you all right?"

Phyllis tried to nod but felt her eyes close instead. His voice was gentle.

"It's all over now," he said.

And Phyllis knew that it was.

40

There was a breeze blowing in from the sea, rippling through the new grass as Lorimer stood outside Saint Clement's Rodel. The psalms had been sung with no music, the voices raised in Gaelic song to their Maker, giving Lorimer the feeling that he was hearing words that had been uttered since time began on these islands. He had come alone on the morning plane to Stornoway but now he stood beside Niall Cameron, their heads bowed as the minister intoned the final words of the service. He could see Mhairi MacLeod leaning on her stick, Chrissie by her side as always. The cemetery was so packed with people that he was sure every member of the community must be there to pay their final respects to Kirsty.

At last the minister raised his hand in benediction and a resounding *Amen* came from every mouth.

Lorimer had watched as the simple coffin was lowered into the earth; Kirsty was there at last, laid to rest with her father and mother. There were no flowers. The funeral notice had indicated that anyone who wished might send a donation to the MS Society of Scotland. Everyone knew the nurse's vocation had been to care for such patients and even Lorimer's team had donated a cheque for the charity.

Overhead a buzzard mewed, a sad cry like a lost child's. Lorimer felt Cameron's hand on his arm then saw the mourners turning to leave.

"One minute. I'd like to see Miss MacLeod, if I may," Lorimer told him quietly.

"I'll wait in the car, then."

Lorimer stood aside as one by one they passed him by. Dougie from the hotel gave him a nod but no smile. When there was only the minister by the graveside with the two old ladies, Lorimer strode across the clipped turf.

"Miss MacLeod," he offered her his hand.

"Ah," Mhairi MacLeod turned at the sound of his voice, then, seeing who it was, she gave him a sweet smile. "You came!" she said. "I'm so glad."

"Yes."

"She's at peace now, Mister Lorimer. Far from any harm the world can do to her. Safely home with her Saviour," she said. Her words carried such simple conviction that Lorimer felt immediately humbled. Here was an enduring faith that carried on from generation to generation.

"And how are you?" he asked.

"Oh, I'm just biding here till it's my time. Chrissie sees that I have everything I need, don't you dear," she added, turning to the lady in black who was holding her arm.

"Aye. But we should be going now. There will be tea in the hotel if you wish to join us, Chief Inspector," Chrissie told him.

"Thank you, but no. I must get back to Stornoway for the return flight to Glasgow."

"You go ahead, Chrissie. Mister Lorimer and I will take a wee daunder along the path. It's fine," she added seeing the other woman's doubtful expression. "He'll take my arm. Won't you," she added, looking up into Lorimer's eyes.

They did not speak until they reached a green painted bench that faced the sea and Lorimer had helped the old lady onto the seat.

"Well, now. Are you going to tell me all about it or do I have to wait until the rumours and the papers mangle it up?"

Lorimer grinned at her and she returned with a smile of her own and patted his hand. "I may be old but I'm not afraid of the truth. Now, tell me everything that really happened."

"Tom Coutts was a patient at the Grange. He'd been receiving treatment for depression in the wake of his wife's death. Kirsty had been one of Mrs Coutts' nurses during her final illness."

"Yes, I remember Kirsty told me all about her. A right poor soul she was. Couldn't do a thing for herself. Hard on the man, I'm sure."

"Yes," Lorimer replied. He couldn't begin to imagine what kind of life Tom Coutts may have had, trying to care for a wife who had no sight and was completely paralysed. "So hard that he couldn't endure her suffering." Lorimer told her gently. The man's sobs rang in his ears as he recalled his confession; how he had smothered his wife with a pillow. Then a combination of guilt and paranoia had driven him to despair.

"He took her life, then?" Mhairi guessed.

"Yes."

"And did Kirsty know?"

"I thought you might tell me that," Lorimer replied. "The missing pages of her diary corresponded with the dates of Nan Coutts' death and Kirsty's resignation from her job."

"Aye," Mhairi MacLeod sighed. "I knew something was wrong, then, but she never told a soul, Chief Inspector. I promise you that."

"Dr Brightman thinks that those torn pages from Kirsty's diary simply showed how much she wanted to obliterate the events from her mind. She was never a threat to Coutts. Still, he took fright when he met her again at the Grange. He couldn't rid himself of the belief that Kirsty knew what he had done. So he had to kill her. He was really ill, you know."

"And the other woman? The nurse he killed in her own

home?"

"She was on duty the night Kirsty was killed. I think Tom Coutts was afraid she had seen him."

Mhairi MacLeod shook her head sadly. "Such a waste," she sighed. "Such a terrible waste."

Lorimer took her hand in his and felt its warmth. As they sat together in the midday sun the policeman felt strangely comforted by the old lady; her weight of years and greater wisdom a kind of solace to him.

"He copied the methods of another killer," Lorimer began.

"The flower and the praying hands. I remember."

"What puzzled us was how he knew exactly what that other man had done. Right down to the last detail. We hadn't even worked it out at the end," he admitted.

"And how had he found these things out?"

Lorimer shrugged. "Like most things, it was just too easy. Tom Coutts was in and out of the University even during his illness. He expressed an interest in the case. Even helped us with information about the clinic! What we didn't know was that he had been in Dr Brightman's office months before and had found that first forensic report. It was all there. Even down to the position of those praying hands."

"The poor man," she remarked. "To have suffered such guilt!"

Lorimer looked at her in surprise. Here was a large heart indeed that could feel for such a devious killer. Nothing excused the act of murder in his book, and never would.

"And the woman in the clinic? How is she?"

"Safe," Lorimer told her. It was perhaps the best thing he could say about Phyllis Logan. She was safe and well cared for as long as she remained in the clinic.

He recalled Maggie standing at the top of the stairs after he'd returned home, hugging her arms around her body as if she were shivering with the cold. She had asked the same question then promptly burst into tears when he'd told her it was all over.

"Here comes Chrissie. We'd better go," the old lady told him. Lorimer helped her to her feet, handing her the walking stick as Chrissie marched along the path towards them.

"Thank you, Chief Inspector. Thank you for everything," she whispered, leaning across to touch his cheek with her lips.

As the plane circled away from the island, Lorimer wondered if he would ever return. There was something about the place that he found beguiling. In some ways he envied Niall Cameron. It might have been his choice to work in Glasgow, but Lewis was still home. He'd been glad of his DC's company today. It had made him feel less of an outsider. Niall had taken some leave. There were things he had to do, people he needed to see, he'd said. Lorimer suspected one of them might be a girl. His shyness whenever Kirsty's name had been mentioned was merely a reminder of another lassie from home, he thought.

Then he considered Mhairi MacLeod, and her calm acceptance of all that had happened. If only they could all emulate that old lady's wisdom.

This had affected so many lives. Maureen Baillie might never work again as a nurse, though he had a notion that she would be there until Phyllis Logan passed her final breath. Leigh Quinn was still there, too, watching over Phyllis as he and Sister Angelica had done during that troubled time since Kirsty's death. Their partnership had been more than a bond of faith, they had kept watch over the MS patient, fearing for her life. Would this set Quinn back? Or would the incident give him a renewed confidence? Only time would tell.

His thoughts returned to Mrs Baillie. Who would have thought that the Director had spent so many years as the sick woman's private nurse? She'd been fiercely protective of her relationship with Phyllis. And Solly had been right. Her cold manner had hidden a flawed, but caring, personality. Maybe time would heal her wounds, too.

Time, Lorimer thought. Time. Everything passed eventually. Even this year of Maggie's would wind to a close. He smiled ruefully to himself. She wasn't away yet and here he was trying to wish her back. Solly had said little when he'd told him about his wife's decision, but he'd laid a friendly hand on his shoulder that Lorimer had found oddly comforting. Solly and Rosie were closer than ever these days.

He wished them luck. Rosie was just the balm to soothe any hurt the psychologist was feeling over his colleague's revelations.

Two men were now in custody awaiting their fate. Would their cases ever come to trial, he wondered? Or would their acts be seen as some kind of sickness? Malcolm Docherty's twisted sense of religion was a far cry from the faith he'd just witnessed down there, on that little patch of green that was fast disappearing into cloud.

And Tom Coutts? Solly could console himself that his final profile had not been so far out after all: a highly intelligent man with some sort of personal motive for murder. At least he had succeeded in unwinding the twists of those two threads that had bound their victims together for so long. And the last piece of the puzzle had come from Coutts himself. They'd known the details about the signature had to have come from someone on the team. Forensics had drawn a blank, though. Coutts had simply walked into Solly's room and read the file on Deirdre McCann. And his supposed weekend in Failte had been cleverly timed so that he was the only patient not to have given a DNA sample.

Lorimer looked out at the clouds banking up against the window. Such intricate planning! And yet there was still a chance Coutts would wriggle out of it all as unfit to plead. Well, his destiny was in other hands now, Lorimer knew. But it was a thought that gave him little satisfaction.

41

The preliminary hearing had been postponed again. Maureen Baillie knew she should have been pleased but the tension of those last months was finally getting to her. Her post at the Grange would be terminated whenever a suitable candidate was chosen but her fellow directors were being surprisingly slow about finding a replacement. Mrs Baillie had her suspicions that a certain DCI was pulling strings on her behalf. There was no way she'd be reinstated once the case had come to court, but until then her duties continued as normal. Phyllis was still here too, languishing under that cruel disease. She'd been horrified when Lorimer had revealed the extent of the legacy left to her. As Phyllis's nurse for so many long years she had been told to expect a "little something". Shame had made her seek out Maxwell Richards. He'd been quite matter-of-fact about her problem. Now she was determined never to gamble again. No matter what happened.

It was some relief that she had been kept on after the arrest of that man, Coutts, especially when Phyllis was so poorly. The woman needed her, though she might not know it. The Director of the clinic had made it her personal business to have the Multiple Sclerosis patient nursed with extra special care those past few weeks. She knew from experience what that disease could do, remembering her own mother dying far too young, and had vowed that

Phyllis should be given as much personal dignity as was possible.

The Chief Inspector had become a regular visitor. Mrs Baillie, who left Phyllis and DCI Lorimer discreetly alone at visiting times, often wondered what he said to her.

It was early morning. Phyllis could hear the blackbirds on the lawn outside her window. Their dawn chorus roused her from a shallow sleep every morning. Even with the blinds shut she knew the sunlight would be making the sky a pearly pink. It had rained last night; she'd heard it against the glass. Now she could imagine the sweet scent of newly cut, wet grass as the sun steamed it dry. Her shoulders felt cold. The bedclothes had slipped off her thin cotton nightdress some time during the night.

There was another new nurse on duty. Phyllis had rather wished that policewoman could have stayed on but of course that was impossible. She was all right, now. Just a knock on the head, Lorimer had told her. The events of that night had left their mark on her, too. Maureen had fussed in and out for days afterwards.

Phyllis tried to breathe deeply and heard the rattle in her chest. She'd been so hot during the night but now her arms were covered in gooseflesh. All she could think of was how tired she felt and how noisy the birds were outside. Maybe she'd slip into a decent sleep again before the nurse came to begin the morning routine. She'd been so weary after Lorimer's visit yesterday. He'd not stayed too long, but he'd told her things about that man, things she didn't really want to hear. It was over now and all she longed for was the blessed oblivion of a deep, deep sleep.

Phyllis closed her eyes as the blackbird on the lawn opened his throat in celebration of another new day.

"Sure you've got everything you want?" Lorimer asked anxiously.

"I'm sure," Maggie replied, biting the flesh inside her mouth to stop the sudden tremor in her voice. It wouldn't do to let tears spill at this stage.

"Phone me when you get in. Okay?"

"I will. I promise," she said.

Lorimer gave her a hug then Maggie turned away before he could see her face.

The slope up towards Passport Control seemed to go on forever.

"Don't look back," she told herself. "Don't look back."

At the desk, Maggie Lorimer handed over her passport to a woman in uniform. In front of her a queue was forming at the baggage x-ray. Most of them would be holiday-makers off to Florida for a fortnight of sunshine and Disney. She should feel so lucky, shouldn't she? After all, she was going to spend the next ten months in the Sunshine State.

Maggie took back her passport and hesitated, just for a moment, then turned her head to scan the crowds below her. The Costa Coffee seemed full of yuppies with mobile phones. Outside the avenue of shops, people were milling around, their holiday clothes bright splashes of colour against the cool airport interior.

Maggie looked and looked, trying to see her husband among the crowd below.

But he was gone.

DATE DUE

PRINTED IN U.S.A.

Debates in Economic History

Edited by Peter Mathias

Science, Technology, and Economic Growth in the Eighteenth Century

Science, Technology, and Economic Growth in the Eighteenth Century

edited with an introduction by
A. E. MUSSON, 1920-   comp.

METHUEN & CO LTD
11 NEW FETTER LANE LONDON EC4

First published in 1972 by Methuen & Co Ltd
Introduction © 1972 by A. E. Musson
Printed in Great Britain by
Richard Clay (The Chaucer Press), Ltd,
Bungay, Suffolk

SBN 416 08000 6 hardbound
416 08010 3 paperback

Distributed in the U.S.A.
by Barnes & Noble Inc.

3/73   C+H   # 4086

Contents

PREFACE   *page* vii

ACKNOWLEDGEMENTS   ix

EDITOR'S INTRODUCTION   I

1 PETER MATHIAS
   Who Unbound Prometheus? Science and Technical
   Change, 1600–1800   69

2 A. E. MUSSON
   The Diffusion of Technology in Great Britain during
   the Industrial Revolution   97

3 T. S. ASHTON
   Some Statistics of the Industrial Revolution in
   Britain   115

4 CHARLES C. GILLISPIE
   The Natural History of Industry   121

5 ROBERT E. SCHOFIELD
   The Industrial Orientation of Science in the Lunar
   Society of Birmingham   136

6 ARCHIBALD CLOW AND NAN L. CLOW
   Vitriol in the Industrial Revolution   148

7 D. W. F. HARDIE
   The Macintoshes and the Origins of the Chemical
   Industry   168

8 F. W. GIBBS
   Bryan Higgins and his Circle   195

SELECT BIBLIOGRAPHY   208

Preface

This volume in the *Debates in Economic History* series is concerned with one of the important, though less publicized, of recent debates in economic history: the role of science in technical change during the Industrial Revolution. One may predict that much more attention will be given to it over the next few years as research into the springs of technical change and the diffusion of technology continues. It has all the attributes of the best historical controversies. Both the Scientific Revolution and the Industrial Revolution are clearly of the very first historical importance and intrinsically fascinating. Both occurred in Western Europe, uniquely so in the history of mankind, in close juxtaposition in time. Each is also of such a degree of generality, sufficiently unspecified conceptually, with such a complex of variables – most of them unquantifiable – interacting in such a bewildering variety of ways, that the debate about how they are causally related is, in the final analysis, unresolvable. Because 'scientific' proof of causation is thus impossible, all participants in the debate can rest happy in the awareness that their contributions, whether of more data, new hypotheses or judicious trimming between old ones, cannot be absolutely discounted as provably false or demonstrably irrelevant.

A controversy in such a happy state flourishes as the generations pass, bringing new evidence as well as new ideas to the traditional stock-pot. In the present case new research, not least that of Mr Musson and Dr Robinson, is much enlarging the awareness of economic historians about the extent of scientific interests among eighteenth-century entrepreneurs and innovators. In no field of common interest are there larger gains to be made by the collaborative efforts of economic historians and historians of science. For a general editor who finds himself caught in the debate as a contributor, that provides a discreet note upon which to end a preface.

All Souls College, Oxford   PETER MATHIAS
31 August 1971

Acknowledgements

The editor and publishers wish to thank the following for permission to reproduce the articles listed below:

Cambridge University Press for 'Who Unbound Prometheus? Science and Technical Change, 1600 – 1800', by Peter Mathias (*Science and Society, 1600 – 1900*, 1972); *Chemistry in Britain* and Mrs F. W. Gibbs for 'Bryan Higgins and His Circle', by F. W. Gibbs (*Chemistry in Britain*, vol. I, 1965); *The Economic History Review* for 'Vitriol in the Industrial Revolution', by A. and N. Clow (vol. XV, 1945); D. W. F. Hardie for 'The Macintoshes and the Origins of the Chemical Industry' (*Chemistry and Industry*, 1952); *The Manchester School* for 'Some Statistics of the Industrial Revolution in Britain', by T. S. Ashton (vol. XVI, 1948); Manchester University Press for 'The Diffusion of Technology in Great Britain during the Industrial Revolution', by A. E. Musson (from A. E. Musson and E. Robinson (eds.), *Science and Technology in the Industrial Revolution*, 1969); *Isis* (Quarterly Journal of the History of Science Society) for 'The Natural History of Industry', by Charles C. Gillispie (vol. 48, 1957) and 'The Industrial Orientation of Science in the Lunar Society of Birmingham', by Robert E. Schofield (vol. 48, 1957).

Editor's Introduction

I

The study of the relationship between science, technology, and economic growth during the Industrial Revolution necessarily involves consideration and attempted integration of a vast amount of work, both empirical and theoretical, in different academic disciplines. The greatest quantity of factual evidence has been collected by economic historians, though a good deal of research has also been carried out by scientists, engineers, and others interested in scientific, technological, and industrial history. At the same time, current interest in economic development and growth has made such studies of closer relevance to the theoretical work of economists and sociologists. It is therefore the main purpose of this introductory chapter to trace the evolution of economic and sociological theories in regard to the problems presented by scientific and technological progress, and against this theoretical background to view recent historical studies on these aspects of the Industrial Revolution.

The scientific and technological achievements of the past two centuries are so overwhelmingly obvious in their transformation of economic and social life that it seems almost incredible that, until very recently, most modern economists, building theoretical growth 'models', left them entirely out of account. These immense forces of change – revolutionizing industrial organization and production, prodigiously expanding trade and transport, requiring vast amounts of capital, and altering the whole structure of the labour force and society in general – have been regarded as 'exogenous' or external to the economic system! Economic historians, on the other hand, have always given great prominence to industrial–technological developments: inventors and entrepreneurs crowd the stage in economic history, together with the workers and population generally whose lives have been so profoundly affected by their innovations. Economic history has retained a much greater realism, a much broader approach, and, on account of the multiplicity and complexity of the factors involved, has tended to be strongly empirical, utilizing only a loose framework of theoretical ideas. But now the resurgence of interest in business studies and technological growth among economists raises the possibility of closer collaboration with economic historians, who, on their side, are now recognizing more clearly the uses of theoretical and statistical tools in historical analysis.

The neglect of scientific and technological developments by economists became pronounced only in the late nineteenth century, when economics tended to become increasingly academic and theoretical, narrower and more remote from industrial and commercial reality than earlier economic writings, in which there was a much broader approach.[1] Mercantilists, for instance, in the seventeenth and eighteenth centuries,

> stressed the importance of invention and technological improvements and the need to introduce them speedily and effectively into industry ... by encouraging the development of empirical science and its application, not only to the solution of military problems, but also to the solution of mining, transport, and other problems of economic import. ... The practical application of science received continuing stimulus from mercantilist Francis Bacon's endorsement of innovation and gradual change and from his philosophy of utility. ... Because the importance of invention was recognized by many English mercantilists (e.g. Grew and Petty), some under the influence of Bacon, by French mercantilists (especially Colbert), and by various others, they looked with

[1] There is a vast literature on theories of economic development from Adam Smith onwards. See, for example, G. M. Meier and R. E. Baldwin, *Economic Development: Theory, History, Policy* (New York, 1957); B. Higgins, *Economic Development: Principles, Problems, and Policies* (New York, 1959; new ed. 1968); B. F. Hoselitz *et al.*, *Theories of Economic Growth* (Glencoe, Illinois, 1960); I. Adelman, *Theories of Economic Growth and Development* (Stanford, California, 1961); Y. S. Brenner, *Theories of Economic Development and Growth* (1966). See also general histories of economic thought, such as J. A. Schumpeter, *History of Economic Analysis* (New York, 1954); R. Lekachman, *A History of Economic Ideas* (New York, 1959); O. H. Taylor, *A History of Economic Thought* (New York, 1960); M. Blaug, *Economic Theory in Retrospect* (1962; 2nd ed. 1968); W. J. Barber, *A History of Economic Thought* (New York, 1968).

favour upon the establishment of academies and schools to promote and diffuse science and its application.[1]

The later classical economists, while generally attacking mercantilist restrictions and advocating *laissez-faire* and free trade, showed a similarly broad concern with industrial–technological and social as well as more narrowly 'economic' factors.[2] Adam Smith's *Wealth of Nations* (1776) shows a strong awareness of the dynamic forces behind economic growth. In particular, he emphasized the importance of division and specialization of labour, resulting from expanding markets and leading to improvement in skills, technology, and productivity; he also stressed social factors such as growth of population, changing consumer wants, and ambitions of merchants and manufacturers to acquire wealth, prestige, and power. Moreover, Smith pointed out that improvements were introduced not only by practical craftsmen but also by 'philosophers, or men of speculation', and he remarked how with the growth of trade and specialization 'the quantity of Science is considerably increased'.[3] This observation, according to Professors Carter and Williams, shows how much he was 'ahead of his time';[4] but these authors, while notable among present-day economists for their emphasis on the importance of applied science to modern industrial growth,[5] have repeated uncritically the traditional view of the Industrial Revolution as almost entirely the product of uneducated empiricism, though they make an exception of James Watt and the steam engine. In fact, however, Smith was simply observing the developments of his own day,[6] although, of course, it is true to say that at the time when

[1] J. J. Spengler, 'Mercantilist and Physiocratic Growth Theory', in Hoselitz, op. cit., pp. 46–8. To Bacon, Grew, and Petty we can add Hartlib, Evelyn, and others who similarly emphasized the importance of applied science in industrial development.

[2] J. M. Letiche, 'Adam Smith and David Ricardo on Economic Growth', ibid., pp. 65–88, and E. McKinley, 'The Theory of Economic Growth in the English Classical School', ibid., pp. 89–112; B. E. Supple (ed.), *The Experience of Economic Growth* (New York, 1963), pp. 12–14.

[3] *Wealth of Nations*, book 1, chap. 1.

[4] C. F. Carter and B. R. Williams, *Investment in Innovation* (1959), pp. 149–50.

[5] In addition to the above-mentioned work, see their *Industry and Technical Progress* (1957) and *Science and Industry* (1959).

[6] A. E. Musson and E. Robinson, *Science and Technology in the Industrial Revolution* (Manchester, 1969), p. 59 *et passim*.

he was writing, the Industrial Revolution had not gone far, and that he therefore 'wrote more about pin factories than about iron fabrication',[1] or other technological changes then in their infancy.

Smith's successors in the English classical school, living in the midst of the Industrial Revolution, were also very much concerned with the growth process, though they tended to be pessimistic about long-term prospects, envisaging ultimately a stationary state, as a consequence of scarcity of natural resources, population pressure, falling profits, etc.; they underestimated the future flow of technological improvements and investment possibilities. It must be remembered, however, that they were writing amid the uncertainties of revolution, war, and their aftermath, causing profound economic and social upheavals. But Ricardo did observe that British manufacturing superiority was brought about 'by the improvements in machinery, by the better division and distribution of labour, and by the increasing skill, both in science and art, of the producers'.[2] With much greater emphasis, John Stuart Mill included among the principal forces responsible for increased production the progress of science and technology, education, and entrepreneurial enterprise, as well as capital formation, population growth, division of labour and improved skills; education, indeed, he regarded as the most dynamic factor, both for its general socio-economic stimulus and for its contribution to the development and diffusion of scientific-technical knowledge. He has been described, in fact, as 'the first British economist to stress the importance of applied knowledge'.[3]

The neo-classical economists of the late nineteenth and early twentieth centuries, however, including Jevons, Edgeworth, Marshall, Wicksteed, Menger, Walras, Pareto, Clark, Fisher, Wicksell, and Pigou, turned their attention away from long-term growth to short-run functioning of the market mechan-

---

[1] Barber, op. cit., p. 24.

[2] *The Works and Correspondence of David Ricardo*, ed. P. Sraffa (Cambridge, 1951–5), vol. I, p. 94.

[3] J. J. Spengler, 'John Stuart Mill on Economic Development', in Hoselitz, op. cit., pp. 113–54.

ism – from 'dynamic' to 'static' analysis.[1] This also involved a shift away from the study of large aggregates to the examination of the detailed working of the economic system – the decisions of producers and consumers, interacting to determine market prices – so 'macro-economics' was mostly abandoned for 'micro-economics'. Thus was developed the theory of the margin and general equilibrium. More narrowly academic than their predecessors, and impressed by the methods of the physical sciences, the neo-classical economists discarded the empirical socio-historical approach and adopted more rigorously theoretical and mathematical techniques. 'Neo-classical authors . . . replaced real-world firms and households for analytical purposes by relationships couched in mathematical language, e.g. by production functions and utility functions.'[2] Simulating scientific laboratory techniques, they constructed abstract models, from which they sought to eliminate uncertain, random, or disequilibrating variables. They not only made the unrealistic assumption of 'perfect competition', but also focused their attention on a narrow range of factors in a static situation, eliminating time and long-term variables from their analysis (*ceteris paribus*), especially those of an 'exogenous' or 'non-economic' character – among which, of course, were science and technology, population, natural resources, etc.[3] This concentration on static analysis of limited problems was not, as might perhaps be thought, through any recognition of their inability to deal with the complexities of long-term development; their writings indicate, in fact, an assumption that, under the beneficent influence of free competition, economic growth would take care of itself – that it was not really a problem at all – a complete change in attitude and interests from those of the classical economists. This was probably a reflection of the contemporary optimism and faith in progress,

[1] J. Buttrick, 'Toward a Theory of Economic Growth: the Neo-classical Contribution', ibid., pp. 155–92. See also above, p. 2 n. 1.

[2] H. J. Bruton, 'Contemporary Theorizing on Economic Growth', ibid., pp. 239–98. Some, such as Walras, were more 'purely' theoretical, mathematical, and 'scientific' in their approach than others, such as Marshall, who were closer to the realities of life.

[3] It is true that Marshall, for example, did include both 'short-run' and 'long-run' in his analysis, but these vague time-periods were not historical in scale. His treatment of 'the secular period' was comparatively brief and inadequate.

resulting from a century of continued and unprecedented economic expansion.

It is true that all economic theory during this period was not characterized by static, micro-economic methods. The German Historical School of economists, including List, Hildebrand, Bücher, Schmoller, and Sombart, emphasized long-term factors and developed various theories of 'stages' of economic growth.[1] These were variously concerned with changes from primitive to modern societies, from barter to money and credit, from agricultural to manufacturing and commercial activities, from village to urban to national economic organization. They attached considerable importance to social and technological, as well as economic factors,[2] but were generally weak in their explanations of the dynamics of change. Marx, of course, similarly formulated a stages theory – developing from primitive society, through feudalism, to capitalism, and finally to socialism – in which basic changes in technology and productive organization determine class relations and other social, political, and cultural parts of the superstructure.

These historical theories, however, were never accepted into the general body of economic analysis during the neo-classical period. With the exception of Marx, and one or two individual theorists, it has been stated, 'for almost a century after 1850 there was no fresh systematic discussion of the nature of economic development'.[3] This is perhaps going too far: even in the neo-classical period, economists such as Marshall wrote broadly on the development of industry and trade, and his theory did contain some 'dynamic' or evolutionary elements

[1] B. F. Hoselitz, 'Theories of Stages of Economic Growth', in Hoselitz, op. cit., pp. 193–238, and Brenner, op. cit., pp. 150–74.

[2] We find Sombart, for example, writing of the growth of 'the capitalist spirit' in the early modern period: 'The same spirit out of which was born the new state and the new religion, the new science and the new technology, also created the new economy.' W. Sombart, *Der Moderne Kapitalismus* (1921), vol. I, p. 327. But he considered that seventeenth-century technology was essentially empirical, almost completely divorced from contemporary science (ibid., pp. 466–7).

[3] Supple, op. cit., p. 14. See also W. A. Lewis, *The Theory of Economic Growth* (1955), Preface, where it is stated that 'no comprehensive treatise on the subject has been published for about a century. The last great book covering this wide range was John Stuart Mill's *Principles of Political Economy*, published in 1848.' See also S. Kuznets, *Economic Growth and Structure* (New York, 1965), pp. 4–5.

(he recognized, for example, the effects of technological progress); Juglar, Tugan-Baranowski, Spiethoff, Robertson, Pigou, Kondratieff, Kitchin, and others studied industrial fluctuations; while historically-minded economists such as Chapman and Daniels wrote about industrial development. There were also some outspoken contemporary critics of the narrow unreality of neo-classical theory, notably Thorsten Veblen, with his sweeping attacks on the exploiting role of 'Big Business', capitalist 'absentee owners', financiers, and advertising salesmen, and his lauding of scientists and technologists as the true creators of the vast (but still artificially restricted) increase in modern industrial production and wealth.[1] Doubtless his writings contain a good deal of historical and theoretical nonsense (together with many discerning insights), and he was almost pathologically distorted in his attitude towards 'business men' and their activities, but he was undoubtedly right in his emphasis on the realities of applied science and technology, so utterly neglected by most economists of his day. Particularly interesting from our present point of view was his discernment not only of the effects of applied science upon industry, but also of the reverse effects of industrial–technological developments on science,[2] interactions which he traced back to the Industrial Revolution, though developing mainly in the modern period.

Veblen's views were beyond the pale of economic orthodoxy, but even among traditional economists there was some awareness of the importance of technology in economic development. Particularly interesting are the views on inventions and patents expressed by some economists in the later part of the

[1] See, for example, T. B. Veblen, *The Theory of Business Enterprise* (New York, 1904); *The Instinct of Workmanship and the State of the Industrial Arts* (New York, 1914); *The Place of Science in Modern Civilization* (New York, 1919); *The Engineers and the Price System* (New York, 1921); *Absentee Ownership and Business Enterprise in Recent Times* (New York, 1923).

[2] 'Science has flourished . . . somewhat in the same degree as the industrial interest has dominated the community's life. And science . . . has made headway in the several departments of human life and knowledge in proportion as these several departments have come into closer contact with the industrial process and the economic interest . . . modern science may be said to be a by-product of the industrial process.' *The Theory of the Leisure Class* (New York, 1899), chap. XIV.

period.[1] These views, however, were often contradictory. Some emphasized the importance of 'autonomous' or 'spontaneous' invention. Taussig, for instance, considered that great inventors are moved mainly by 'the instinct of contrivance' – 'an inborn and irresistible impulse' – although he recognized the powerful influence of pecuniary gain or profit.[2] Pigou also considered inventions to be, 'for the most part, spontaneous'.[3] Sir Josiah Stamp expressed similar views in a Watt anniversary lecture: 'He [the inventor] is still *sui generis*, and emerges from the ranks of engineers, physicists and chemists, not indeed as a "sport", but as a special product, which is touched by no "economic spring". The sense of curiosity and the idea of fame play a greater part than the economic reward.'[4] J. B. Clark, on the other hand, emphasized the importance of inducements such as the patent system and profit prospects.[5] Sir Arnold Plant, similarly, while conceding that some 'amateur' inventors are 'prompted by curiosity rather than hopes of gain', and that some inventions are products of chance or accident, considered that most inventions are 'induced', that they are products of 'the circumstances of time and place'.[6] One very potent influence was the rate of growth of scientific knowledge; another was the patent system, though opinions differed profoundly on its effects;[7] but Plant and other economists emphasized the predominance of economic influences, such as relative factor prices, the state of trade, and profit prospects.[8]

II

Neo-classical micro-static theory held sway until after the First World War. The shock of war, however, and the severity of

---

[1] The best discussion is that in A. Plant, 'The Economic Theory Concerning Patents for Invention', *Economica*, N.S. vol. I (1934), pp. 30–51.

[2] F. W. Taussig, *Inventors and Money-Makers* (New York, 1915), chap. I.

[3] A. C. Pigou, *Economics of Welfare*, 2nd ed. (1924), p. 163.

[4] Sir J. Stamp, *Some Economic Factors in Modern Life* (1929), p. 113.

[5] J. B. Clark, *Essentials of Economic Theory* (New York, 1907), chap. XXI.

[6] Plant, op. cit.

[7] See below, p. 49.

[8] Cf. the similar conclusions of present-day economists such as Schmookler, below, pp. 25–6.

post-war economic crises, accompanied by widespread and massive unemployment, caused economists to look afresh at the problems of economic growth and fluctuations, and since the Second World War the situation of the 'underdeveloped' countries, and the rivalry between capitalism and communism, particularly in the scientific–technological sphere, have also revived interest in the factors responsible for long-term economic development and growth. There has been renewed concern with those factors previously regarded as 'exogenous', including science and technology, entrepreneurial activity, investment, population, and social structure.

Schumpeter was one of the first to emphasize these long-term aspects, particularly the factors producing economic fluctuations, in which entrepreneurial 'innovations' played a dominant role, whether in new technologies, or new forms of economic organization, new products, new markets, or new resources.[1] He emphasized particularly the importance of major technological innovations, which accounted to a large extent for discontinuous economic growth, in great 'leaps and bounds', e.g. with the introduction successively of the steam engine and its application in cotton, coal, and iron, then the development of railways and steel, followed by electrification, motor transport, and chemicals. Schumpeter tended, however, to neglect the scientific–technological aspects, stressing the entrepreneurial side of innovations rather than technical inventions. The entrepreneur need not be the inventor of the process or product that he introduces, nor need he himself provide the capital: he is essentially an innovator, a business leader, often utilizing the inventions or capital or others, grasping and exploiting potentially profitable opportunities.

In many ways, however, Schumpeter's writings were outside the field of dominant economic theory[2] and more akin to

---

[1] J. A. Schumpeter, *The Theory of Economic Development*, first published in German in 1911, translated into English in 1934, reprinted in 1961. See also his *Business Cycles* (New York, 1939), 2 vols.

[2] He considered that 'economic theory in the traditional sense contributes next to nothing' to the analysis of problems of long-term or historical development (*Theory of Economic Development*, p. 59). Neo-classical theory assumed unrealistically that economic growth was 'a continuous and almost automatic process that does not harbour any phenomena or problems of its own' (*History of Economic Analysis*, pp. 892–3).

economic history, which, in fact, he personally considered to be more fundamentally important and interesting.[1] New ideas did develop, however, within established economics schools during the inter-war period, with increasingly radical revisions of neo-classical theory.[2] 'Perfect competition' was abandoned; uncertainty and risk, and the problems of business expectations were brought under analysis; Keynesian macro-economic analysis explored the interconnexions between the aggregates of income and consumption, savings and investment, in a revolutionary new *General Theory*. But this new theory was still static, or very short-run, dominated by the idea of maintaining or restoring 'equilibrium': it excluded long-term 'dynamic' factors affecting economic growth such as capital accumulation, science and technology, population, etc. Post-Keynesian theory, however, developed notably by Harrod and Domar,[3] created 'dynamic' models, taking account of changes over time in investment and output, income and savings, with the aim of achieving 'dynamic equilibrium' or a steady rate of growth, the rate of investment being a particularly key factor. But scientific–technological and other largely unknown or non-quantifiable variables were still treated in such theories as 'given', as 'non-economic' or 'exogenous'.

In short-run analysis such assumptions may be justifiable and useful, but in the long-term they are untenable.[4] Changes in science and technology, for example, certainly cannot be disregarded, since they are crucial to investment decisions and continued growth.[5] What, in fact, are the links between techno-

[1] *History of Economic Analysis*, pp. 12–13.

[2] For an intriguing investigation into the beginnings of this 'revolution' in economic thought, see G. L. S. Shackle, *The Years of High Theory. Invention and Tradition in Economic Thought 1926–1939* (Cambridge, 1967).

[3] See especially R. F. Harrod, *Towards a Dynamic Economics* (1948) and E. D. Domar, *Essays in the Theory of Economic Growth* (New York, 1957). For an elaboration of the Harrod–Domar analysis, see W. J. Baumol, *Economic Dynamics* (New York, 1951), W. Fellner, *Trends and Cycles in Economic Activity* (New York, 1956), and D. Hamberg, *Economic Growth and Instability* (New York, 1956).

[4] It is true, as Kuznets, for example, has always emphasized, that 'economic growth is essentially a quantitative concept' (Kuznets, *Economic Growth and Structure*, p. 6), but to *explain* the statistics it is necessary to consider many non-quantifiable factors, often regarded as 'non-economic'.

[5] As Hirschman has pointed out, investment decisions are very closely related to technical progress and inventions, which do not necessarily occur in a

logical advances and investment, how do they change capital–
labour and capital–output ratios, how do they affect employment and income, what determines their rate and direction, how
can they be measured or controlled? Mere figures of capital
accumulation may be quite misleading, since all capital is not
homogeneous – quality is important as well as quantity – and
such statistics may not, therefore, truly indicate a country's
economic–technological progress. Technological improvements may be capital-saving rather than, or as well as, labour-
saving; productivity may be increased by more efficient use of
existing capital and labour resources (by economies of scale,
better training, improved organization), with relatively little
new capital formation; capital investment may be 'deepening'
or 'widening', it may be in improved machinery or merely
(though not usually) in more of the same; it may be in new,
fast-growing industries or in old, slow-growing ones; it may
be in more or less capital-intensive sectors; it may be in heavy
industry or in housing, in scientific research or in education,
roads, etc., with varying effects on productive capacity, some
largely unquantifiable.

An associated weakness of these macro-economic models is
their aggregative and abstract character: couched in terms of
national income, consumption, savings, investment, and output, they take no account of the varied realities at the level of
particular industries and firms. A tendency has developed, in
fact, to refer to these aggregates as if they moved on their own
volition, without human agency, under some sort of im-
personal, mathematical compulsion: a tendency to talk in
'compound interest' terms, which one finds in some studies of
economic growth, e.g. Patel refers to 'the immense power of
compound growth at higher rates',[1] and Rostow typifies a
country's 'take-off' as a critical phase when 'compound interest
gets built into the society's structure' (his term 'self-sustained
growth' is similarly misleading).[2] With all the statistical mani-

steady stream, so that economic growth is unstable. A. O. Hirschman, *The
Strategy of Economic Development* (New Haven, Conn., 1958), pp. 34–5.
[1] S. J. Patel, 'Rates of Industrial Growth in the Last Century, 1860–1958',
Economic Development and Cultural Change, vol. IX, no. 3 (April 1961).
[2] W. W. Rostow, *The Stages of Economic Growth* (Cambridge, 1960), p. 36.
Rostow does, however, stress the need for 'disaggregation' (see below, pp. 42–3).

pulation of national aggregates, there is little apparent contact
with scientific–technical–industrial reality, little awareness of
the complex problems facing the business-man or engineer on
both the supply and demand sides.

At the same time, micro-economic theory has also tradition-
ally been dominated by narrow, short-run considerations, as
in the theory of the firm, rather than with dynamic factors
such as technological change.[1] This raises many complex
questions. How, for instance, in the midst of uncertainties,
do individual firms make their output and investment decisions? To what extent are technological changes responses to
demand, or to what extent do they create new markets? How
are they affected by, and how far do they bring about, changes
in industrial structure? What are the links between scientific
research, technological inventions, and investment?

Faced with these problems, economists have reacted in
various ways. Some, still trying to retain theoretical rigour and
mathematical techniques, have constructed more complex
dynamic models on modified Keynesian–Harrod–Domar or
neo-classical lines, including 'disaggregated' or multi-sectoral
models of the Leontief type.[2] These have included technological
progress along with land, capital, and labour among the factors
of production determining economic growth, but in a highly
abstract manner, with many unrealistic assumptions. Other
economists, therefore, have abandoned these artificial rigidities

[1] Nordhaus has recently pointed out that 'the conventional theory of the
firm . . . has neglected the role of new technology', assuming changes in scientific
and technical knowledge to be 'exogenous'. W. D. Nordhaus, *Invention, Growth
and Welfare: A Theoretical Treatment of Technological Change* (Massachusetts,
1969). He has therefore constructed a theoretical model including inventive
activity.

[2] Early examples of these new 'growth models' were those of R. Solow, 'A
Contribution to the Theory of Economic Growth', *Quarterly Journal of Economics*
(February 1956), and 'Technical Change and the Aggregate Production Function', *Review of Economics and Statistics* (August 1957), and N. Kaldor, 'A Model
of Economic Growth', *Economic Journal* (December 1957), reprinted in his
Essays on Economic Stability and Growth (1960). A flood of articles and books soon
followed: see, for example, F. Hahn and R. C. O. Matthews, 'The Theory of
Economic Growth: A Survey', *Economic Journal* (December 1964). More recent
and extensive bibliographies are to be found in the works by Lave, Nelson *et al.*,
and Mansfield cited below, p. 17 n. 4, and p. 22 n. 2. There is a very thorough
discussion of the literature, theories, and statistical techniques in Lave's book,
particularly with regard to technological change.

in favour of a looser framework, combining general concepts with a broader more empirical approach, in the classical tradition. These 'development' economists have also shown considerable sympathy towards inter-disciplinary studies, since many psychological, sociological, political, historical, scientific, and technological, as well as economic, factors are involved in the growth process.[1]

From our present point of view, the most significant feature of this ferment in economic growth studies has been the gradually dawning realization among economists that science and technology cannot any longer realistically be treated as 'exogenous' – that applied science is, indeed, the major force behind modern economic growth and must somehow be brought into economic theory. This has been associated with a growing demand for 'disaggregation', for studies of applied science and technology in particular industries and firms, so as to produce more detailed empirical information on which to base developing theory: somehow, it is felt, micro- and macro-economics should be married in a comprehensive dynamic analysis.

Both before and after the 'Keynesian revolution', Schumpeter had, as we have seen, laid strong emphasis upon the importance of technological and other innovations. Another great American scholar, Simon Kuznets, has stressed even more strongly the vital role of science and technology in economic growth. His earliest publications emphasized the 'sectoral'

---

[1] An outstanding example of this wide approach is provided by W. A. Lewis, *The Theory of Economic Growth* (1955). Another is E. E. Hagen, *On the Theory of Social Change. How Economic Growth Begins* (Homewood, Ill., 1962). Hagen, having become convinced of 'the inadequacy of economic theory' to solve the problems of economic growth, supplemented it with psychology, anthropology, sociology, and history. For other wide-ranging studies, in addition to the previously cited works by Schumpeter, Meier and Baldwin, Higgins, Hoselitz, Kuznets, Rostow, and Supple, see also C. E. Ayres, *The Theory of Economic Progress* (Chapel Hill, North Carolina, 1944); B. S. Keirstead, *The Theory of Economic Change* (Toronto, 1948); M. Abramovitz, 'Economics of Growth', in B. Haley (ed.), *A Survey of Contemporary Economics* (Homewood, Ill., 1952); H. F. Williamson and J. A. Buttrick (eds.), *Economic Development* (New York, 1954); N. S. Buchanan and H. S. Ellis, *Approaches to Economic Development* (New York, 1955); L. H. Dupriez (ed.), *Economic Progress* (Louvain, 1955); C. Clark, *The Conditions of Economic Progress*, 3rd ed. (1957); C. P. Kindleberger, *Economic Development*, 3rd ed. (New York, 1965); H. J. Bruton, *Principles of Economic Development* (Englewood Cliffs, N.J., 1965).

theory of growth[1] – that at any given period of time one or a few industries are leading sectors, experiencing rapid techno-logical innovation and pulling the rest of the economy along, but that eventually they experience 'retardation', after the 'innovation effects' have worn off and the possibilities of rapid technological progress have been fully exploited, so that if the economy is to continue to grow, new industries must take up the running. This pattern of sectoral growth has been further demonstrated in Great Britain's industrial development by Hoffmann and has been taken up and publicized by Rostow, firstly with emphasis on the role of the cotton industry in Britain's 'take-off' during the Industrial Revolution and then, more generally, along lines similar to the earlier Germanic 'stages of growth' theories.[2] Kuznets meanwhile has continued to provide quantitative evidence of growth patterns in different countries, which, he points out, have everywhere been charac-terized by rising productivity, which is

> possible only through major innovations, i.e. applications of new bodies of technical knowledge to the processes of eco-nomic production. . . . In these days it is hardly necessary to emphasize that science is the base of modern technology, and that modern technology is in turn the base of modern economic growth. Without the emergence and development of modern science and science-based technology, neither economic production nor population could have grown at the high rates indicated for the last century to century and a half in the developed countries. True, growth of tested know-ledge, both scientific generalization and empirical informa-tion, and of modern technology based on it, were necessary, not sufficient conditions: knowledge itself does not suffice.

[1] S. Kuznets, 'Retardation of Industrial Growth', *Journal of Economic and Business History*, vol. 1 (1929), and *Secular Movements on Production and Prices* (Boston, 1930). He pointed out that 'questions of industrial development in their general aspects have become suspect to all conscientious economists and statis-ticians. We find hardly any discussion of the problem in the standard treatises which have appeared since the great days of the English Classical School . . . economic theory proper has restricted itself largely to static problems', almost totally neglecting 'the really dynamic elements of economic life'. *Secular Move-ments*, pp. 2, 323.

[2] W. Hoffmann, *British Industry 1700–1950* (English translation, 1955), and Rostow's works previously cited. See below, pp. 42–3.

... Yet the growth of science and technological knowledge has distinct patterns of its own; difficult as it is to discern them (particularly for a mere economist), some attempt should be made to do so, for they are relevant to the pattern ... that modern economic growth exhibits.[1]

In attempting to trace these patterns, Kuznets distinguishes between (*a*) a scientific discovery, an addition to knowledge, (*b*) an invention, the application of existing knowledge to a useful end, (*c*) an innovation, the first industrial use of an invention, (*d*) an improvement, a minor application, and finally (*e*) the spread of an innovation, usually accompanied by improvements. Between these successive phases there is a feed-back effect, as industrial development and usage may lead to further improvements, inventions, or scientific discoveries. But there are also bottle-necks between them, for all scientific discoveries do not necessarily lead to inventions, all inventions are not exploited, and all innovations are not successful. About these interconnexions, Kuznets points out, there is 'still little known',[2] but at the point where innovations transform new technical knowledge and inventions into productive use, three factors are important: (*a*) capital investment, (*b*) entrepreneurial talents, and (*c*) the market. Economic growth is thus a product of economic and social as well as scientific and technological factors.

More recently, Kuznets has emphasized even more strongly the importance of science and technology, pointing out the inadequacies of capital investment as a measure of economic growth. The most important capital of an industrially advanced nation, he considers, is not its physical capital, but its human capital, its scientific and technical knowledge, resulting from improved education and training. It might even be possible

[1] S. Kuznets, 'The Meaning and Measurement of Economic Growth', *Six Lectures on Economic Growth* (Glencoe, Ill., 1959), pp. 13–41. Kuznets has written voluminously on this subject. See his recent volumes on *Economic Growth and Structure* (1965) and *Modern Economic Growth* (1966), which include references to his numerous earlier publications.

[2] This is also the view of those who have been involved in modern 'research and development', e.g. D. A. Schon, *Technology and Change* (New York, 1967), emphasizes the difficulty of differentiating between 'invention' and 'innovation', 'research' and 'development', and points out that the whole process is often viewed as being more clear-cut and rational than in fact it is.

for technological progress to increase output rapidly 'without any additions to the stock of capital goods'. Capital investment, therefore, cannot be regarded as the one strategic factor. The growth of applied scientific knowledge 'must account, in large part, for unusually rapid rates of economic growth in recent centuries', though it has obviously been closely related to broader economic and social forces: it is this, in fact, which has been 'the strategic factor'.[1]

These views have been supported in recent years by an increasing number of other economists. Fellner, for instance, has emphasized the importance of a continued flow of 'technological and organizational improvements', particularly inventions, as the main factor behind long-run growth – the force which has staved off the Ricardian prospect of diminishing returns and a stationary economy – although he discusses their development in narrowly economic terms.[2] Higgins has put technological progress foremost among the causes of economic growth, linked with entrepreneurial enterprise, acquisition of new managerial and technical skills, and capital accumulation.[3] Cairncross has similarly stressed the predominance of technological progress and innovation, while pointing out how little we know about the forces governing them.[4] Blaug has criticized the unrealistic assumptions in growth theory regarding process-innovations, and suggests that the 'neglect of technical change' can no longer be 'justified by its intractability to the traditional tools of economics'.[5] Bruton, reviewing contemporary ideas on

[1] *Economic Growth and Structure*, pp. 34–8, 60–2, 70–1, 83–92, 127–30, 194–212. In *Modern Economic Growth*, pp. 8–15, Kuznets expresses a similar view: 'The epochal innovation that distinguishes the modern economic epoch is the extended application of science to problems of economic production.' The most outstanding early example of this was Watt's development of the steam engine. Other early inventions may have been mainly empirical, but Kuznets stresses that 'the intellectual and cultural milieu within which the basic steam inventions were made also produced the burgeoning of modern science and brought about its more extended applications.' His views reflect very strongly the recent emphasis by other economists on the importance of scientific–technological progress, rather than on capital investment. See below, pp. 16–29.

[2] Fellner, op. cit., pp. 118, 126–9, 137–8, etc.

[3] Higgins, op. cit., pp. 202–4.

[4] A. K. Cairncross, *Factors in Economic Development* (1962), part II.

[5] M. Blaug, 'A Survey of the Theory of Process-Innovations', *Economica*, N.S. vol. XXX (1963).

the subject in 1960, demonstrated the inadequacy, indeed the non-existence, of any integrated general theory of economic growth.[1] Modern dynamic models, he pointed out, have proved largely unrealistic, because of their artificial assumptions, particularly their exclusion of so-called 'exogenous' factors, which are, in fact, inextricably part of the economic system, such as entrepreneurial behaviour, scientific and technological changes, inventions and innovations, changes in population structure and consumer tastes, labour mobility, trade-union policies, and general social and cultural patterns. He emphasized that 'the growth process must be viewed in a larger context than simply the arithmetic of capital–output ratios, savings–income ratios, and population growth rates'. He stressed particularly the lack of any theory of technological change, and considered that such theory could be developed only from 'case studies of the history of inventions and innovations in different industries'.[2] In such empirical studies, there could be no valid distinction between 'economic' and 'non-economic' factors: the tools and methods of the economist must be altered and combined with those of the sociologist, psychologist, scientist, engineer, and historian to achieve an all-round understanding. This necessity for inter-disciplinary effort has also been emphasized by Meier, in his investigations into the role of science and technology in future economic and social development.[3]

III

These criticisms of the inadequacies of growth theory have given rise, during the last decade or so, to a swelling flood of research and publications on the links between science, technology, and modern industrial development.[4] A few of the more

[1] Bruton, in Hoselitz., op. cit. Kuznets has said much the same thing: *Economic Growth and Structure*, pp. 4–5.

[2] Reference is made particularly to A. A. Bright, Jr., *The Electric Lamp Industry: Technological Change and Development from 1800 to 1947* (New York, 1949), and W. R. Maclaurin, *Invention and Innovation in the Radio Industry* (New York, 1949). See also A. E. Musson, *Enterprise in Soap and Chemicals* (Manchester, 1965).

[3] R. L. Meier, *Science and Economic Development* (New York, 1956).

[4] There is a very full bibliography in R. R. Nelson, M. J. Peck, and E. D. Kalachek, *Technology, Economic Growth, and Public Policy* (1967). Note particularly

outstanding examples will illustrate the strength of this changing academic current. Professor Jewkes and his collaborators have made a wide-ranging but detailed survey into the sources of invention, dealing with a large number of cases in many different industries, in an effort to explain the forces behind modern scientific technology, 'one, if not the main, spring of economic progress'.[1] Unlike most economists, who tend to assume that applied science is only of twentieth-century importance, they have demonstrated that, in fact, from the Industrial Revolution onwards there has been an increasingly close relationship between science and technology in the making of inventions. They have thus shown – though only in broad outline, since their major emphasis is on the twentieth century – that knowledge of the historical background may serve to dispel many false illusions about technological development. It will tend, for instance, to modify the still widely-held belief in the distinction between 'pure' and 'applied' science, or between theoretical science on the one hand and industrial empiricism on the other. As they suggest, and as has since been demonstrated in great detail,[2] there were close links between industrialists and scientists even in the eighteenth century; long before the development of modern State education, there were many agencies for the development and diffusion of scientific and technical knowledge. Jewkes and his collaborators have emphasized particularly the importance of individuals in the making of inventions; although in modern times the growth of 'big business' and establishment of corporate research and development organizations have tended to alter the situation, the individual's role is still important. They have emphasized, too, that the underlying motives are by no means entirely

the important collection of articles in R. R. Nelson (ed.), *The Rate and Direction of Inventive Activity* (National Bureau of Economic Research, Princeton, 1962). For more recent publications, see E. Mansfield, *The Economics of Technical Change* (New York, 1968) and *Industrial Research and Technological Innovation* (New York, 1968); W. P. Strassman, *Technological Change and Economic Development* (New York, 1968); and Nordhaus, op. cit.

[1] J. Jewkes, D. Sawers, and R. Stillerman, *The Sources of Invention*, 2nd ed. (1969).

[2] By Musson and Robinson, op. cit., whose ideas were first published in 'Science and Industry in the Late Eighteenth Century', *Economic History Review*, 2nd ser., vol. XIII, no. 2 (December 1960).

economic, but also psychological and social: 'the intuition, will and obstinacy of individuals spurred on by the desire for knowledge, renown or personal gain [remain] the great driving forces in technical progress'.

Salter likewise has emphasized that merely to measure productivity, as econometricians have done, 'is not to understand', and that 'behind productivity lie all the dynamic forces of economic life: technical progress, accumulation, enterprise, and the institutional pattern of society. These are the areas where our understanding remains rudimentary.'[1] His opinion is that, among the causes of increased production and productivity, 'primary emphasis must be placed on technical progress and economies of scale'. Technical progress has been based on 'improving technical knowledge', both scientific and empirical. It is true that generally accepted 'economic' factors, such as relative prices of capital and labour, and investment, have also been important, but it is 'extremely difficult to distinguish' between economic and technical factors. Changes in relative factor prices may stimulate invention and innovation, but, equally, scientific and technical developments may alter relative factor prices and influence investment decisions. Scientific–technical knowledge and economic factors are continuously changing and interacting in this way, but existing economic theory has failed almost completely to take account of technological factors, so that discussion of the problems of productivity has to take place 'in a theoretical vacuum'.

More recently, Nelson, Peck, and Kalachek in the United States have similarly emphasized 'the leading role' of scientific–technological progress in economic growth, and the vital contribution of education and training in producing entrepreneurs, managers, and workers with scientific and technical competence and flexibility.[2] But, like Kuznets, while they stress the importance of science and technology as a necessary condition of economic growth, they emphasize that it alone is not sufficient and that inventions are stimulated mainly by economic factors, especially changes in demand, resulting from population

---

[1] W. E. G. Salter, *Productivity and Technical Change*, 2nd ed. (Cambridge, 1966).

[2] *Technology, Economic Growth, and Public Policy.*

growth, expansion of exports, changes in income, tastes, etc.[1]
Here, of course, they are also following Adam Smith, and, like
Salter, they see these market forces operating on technology
through changes in relative factor prices, leading to labour-
saving or capital-saving inventions (as the case may be) and
factor-substitution. They see examples of these causes and
effects in the English textile inventions during the Industrial Revolution, beginning with the invention of the fly-
shuttle:[2]

> The result was a fall in the price of cloth, more cloth out-
> put, and more demand for yarn to make cloth, thus raising
> economic returns to technical advances in the spinning
> processes. The profit prospects for successful invention were
> further enhanced by labour shortages and rising wages
> since the supply of spinners increased slowly. . . . The work
> which led to the water frame, the spinning jenny and, later
> on, the spinning mule . . . was directly stimulated by this
> increase in demand for yarn and in wages of spinners. This
> spurt of induced invention in spinning eventually overshot,
> and shortages of weavers began to materialize. These new
> shortages were met in part by a shift of labour into weaving,
> and in part by the shift of attention of inventors from
> spinning to weaving resulting in the development of the
> power loom.

[1] They admit that 'many of the technological advances . . . have stemmed, at
least in part, from the work of a single man or a small group of men with zeal for
an idea and only limited concern for profit, social value, or cost', but point out
that these have generally required outside financing and thus came 'within the
orbit of economic calculation'.

[2] Op. cit., p. 29. They do not explain how the fly-shuttle came to be invented;
it does not fit in with their demand theory, because the existing shortage was in
the spinning not the weaving section. They also draw on H. J. Habakkuk's
American and British Technology in the Nineteenth Century (1962), to illustrate the
different effects on invention of differing factor prices in the two countries,
e.g. in Britain, where fuel was relatively scarcer and more expensive, fuel-saving
inventions were more important, as demonstrated by the inventions of Watt
and Bessemer, whereas in the United States, where labour was relatively costly,
labour-saving inventions predominated. Habakkuk's theories, however, have given
rise to some argument: see, for example, the review article by D. S. Landes in
Business History, vol. VII, no. 1 (January 1965). For further examination of these
factors, see S. B. Saul, *Technological Change: The United States and Britain in the
Nineteenth Century* (London, Methuen, 1970).

Yet while they emphasize this 'demand–pull' effect, they also counterbalance it with the statement that 'a strong demand . . . is not sufficient' to produce technological advance. 'Capability [i.e. supply] is important as well as demand.' This depends on scientific–technical knowledge and its diffusion, material resources, etc. But, unlike Jewkes and his collaborators, they follow most economists in distinguishing the 'science-based' inventions of the twentieth century from the allegedly empirical developments of the eighteenth and nineteenth centuries.[1]

Scientific and technological developments are not easily manipulated by economists' statistical tools, but in recent years attempts have been made to quantify them. Some of these efforts have been very strained. Maclaurin, for example, has endeavoured 'to break down the process of technological advance into elements that may eventually be more measurable', with particular consideration of the key 'propensities': to develop pure science, to invent, to innovate, to finance innovation, and to accept innovation.[2] But some of the proposed indicators while certainly reflecting significant developments, cannot bear much weight of interpretation, e.g. numbers of Nobel prize-winners, scientific publications, etc. Others, such as research expenditure and patents, though requiring careful handling, are undoubtedly useful,[3] but there still seems little possibility of directly measuring scientific–technological developments with anything like mathematical accuracy.[4]

[1] See also, for example, Mansfield, *Economics of Technical Change*, pp. 11–12 and 43–5.

[2] W. R. Maclaurin, 'The Sequence from Invention to Innovation and its Relation to Economic Growth', *Quarterly Journal of Economics*, vol. LXVII (1953). See also his article, 'The Economics of Invention; A Survey of the Literature', *Journal of Business*, vol. XXXII (April 1959).

[3] See, for example, in addition to the previously cited works by Jewkes, Salter, Nelson, Mansfield, etc., L. Silk, *The Research Revolution* (New York, 1961); N. E. Terleckyj and H. Halper, *Research and Development* (New York, 1963); J. Bright, *Research, Development, and Technological Innovation* (Homewood, Ill., 1964); R. Tybout (ed.), *The Economics of Research and Development* (Columbus, Ohio, 1965). For patents, see below, pp. 24–8, 49–53, and 115–20.

[4] Abramovitz, op. cit., for example, though confident that scientific and technical advances account for 'a very large share, if not the bulk, of the increase in output', has admitted that 'measurement of the relation between changes in the stock of knowledge and the pace of economic growth has so far proved impossible'. Adelman, op. cit., has more reluctantly recognized that technological

Many economists, therefore, have continued to place their main emphasis on economic factors. Blaug, for example, in discussing innovations, points out that firms have to consider not only technical possibilities, but also probable costs, output, sales, prices, and profits. Innovations are 'market-induced'.[1] But he recognizes the prevailing ignorance and the need for 'detailed case-studies of innovating activity' in particular firms and industries (as Maclaurin, Brunton, and others have also urged). 'Until then we shall not be able to choose decisively between the concept of a technically determined "life-cycle of capital–output ratios" and the theory of market-induced innovations.' At the aggregate level there is as yet no possibility of any quantitative assessment: 'No one has yet managed to measure the state of technical knowledge, much less the rate of change of technical knowledge.'

The most recent studies in this field have tended to confirm this observation. Despite intensive econometric efforts, it still remains true that 'there is no way to measure the rate of technological change directly',[2] even in the present-day economy, and resort has therefore to be had to indirect measurements, such as estimates of 'labour productivity' (output per man-hour) or of 'total productivity' (relating changes in output to those in both capital and labour inputs); but these are not really adequate for the purpose (quite apart from the serious theoretical and practical problems of aggregate measurement). Such analyses of the 'production-function' – an abstract economic-theoretical concept rather than a scientific-technical

---

progress and socio-cultural factors, though of vital importance, cannot be quantified.

[1] Op. cit. See also his article 'Technical Change and Marxian Economics', *Kyklos*, vol. XIII (1960), in which he similarly emphasizes that technical changes may be capital- as well as labour-saving, that they are, in fact, responses to changes in relative factor prices, and are consequent upon 'market pressures'. But he admits that this theory cannot apply to 'product-replacing or demand-creating innovations for which there is no basis of comparison with previous cost-outlays', and that 'little can as yet be said' about these, or about 'variations in the level of inventive efforts'.

[2] Mansfield, *Economics of Technical Change*, pp. 15, 33–4. In addition to Mansfield's works, see also M. Brown, *On the Theory and Measurement of Technological Change* (Cambridge, 1966), and L. B. Lave, *Technological Change: Its Conception and Measurement* (Englewood Cliffs, New Jersey, 1966).

reality – are concerned with the effects rather than the causes of technological change.

Econometricians have, however, succeeded to some extent in getting round these problems of measuring technological change directly, by subtracting measurable elements and leaving 'residuals'. Abramovitz was one of the first to discern that much the greater part of the increase in net product *per capita* was associated with something other than inputs of physical capital and labour.[1] Solow estimated that of the increased productivity in the United States from 1909 to 1949, only 10–13 per cent was attributable to increase in capital and that most of it resulted from technological progress.[2] Fabricant, Domar, and others reached similar conclusions,[3] and Denison's broad study of recent American and European growth rates[4] has shown that, in the USA and UK, for example, education and improvements in technological knowledge have together accounted for between 40 and 50 per cent of total growth – far more than capital investment – and they were also, no doubt, partially responsible for other growth factors, such as increased labour and managerial efficiency, economies of scale, and improved allocation of resources.[5] Other economists, in both the USA and Great Britain, have reached a similar conclusion,

[1] M. Abramovitz, 'Resource and Output Trends in the United States since 1870', *American Economic Review* (May 1956).

[2] R. M. Solow, 'Technical Change and the Aggregate Production Function', *Review of Economics and Statistics*, vol. 39 (August 1957). See also his articles on 'Investment and Technical Progress', in *Mathematical Methods in the Social Sciences* (Stanford, 1960), ed. by K. Arrow, J. Karlin, and P. Suppes, and 'Technical Progress, Capital Formation, and Economic Growth', *American Economic Review*, vol. 52 (May 1962).

[3] S. Fabricant, 'Economic Progress and Economic Change', *34th Annual Report of the National Bureau of Economic Research* (New York, 1954) and *Basic Facts on Productivity Change* (NBER, New York, 1959); E. D. Domar, 'On the Measurement of Technological Change' *Economic Journal* (December 1961).

[4] E. F. Denison, *The Sources of Economic Growth in the United States* (New York, 1962), and *Why Growth Rates Differ* (Washington, D.C., 1967). For a similar comparative study, see A. Maddison, *Economic Growth in the West* (1964), which also stresses the importance of science, technology, and education, but places more emphasis on the general level of demand and its effects on entrepreneurial expectations, thus determining investment and technological advance.

[5] In fact, 'technical progress' defined more broadly could account for 70 per cent or more of the US growth rate. E. F. Denison, 'United States Economic Growth', in P. M. Gutmann (ed.), *Economic Growth* (Englewood Cliffs, N.J., 1964).

C

that technological progress has been far more important than capital accumulation in causing economic growth.[1] Their views have been supported by researches into the 'economics of education',[2] which have led to growing emphasis on the importance of 'human capital' and 'investment in human beings', on the 'stock of knowledge' as against the 'capital stock' of buildings, machinery, etc. The statistical estimates are subject to very wide margins of error, and some economists, such as Solow, have had second thoughts on capital investment, on account of its vital relationship to technological progress (much of which is 'capital-embodied'). An immense and controversial literature has accumulated on this subject. Nevertheless, there is now no doubt whatever of the considerable importance of technical progress, including intangible factors such as educational improvement and growth of scientific and technical knowledge, in the process of economic development.

Another, more direct, approach towards quantitative measurement of technical progress and assessment of its causes has recently been made by Schmookler, using patent statistics as an index of inventions.[3] His overall aim is extraordinarily ambitious: to discover 'what laws govern the growth of man's mastery over nature'. He points out that existing economic theory has done little or nothing to solve this problem: 'Technological change is the *terra incognita* of modern economics.'[4] Recent research has demonstrated that the growth of

---

[1] Kuznets, for example (see above, pp. 15–16: see also his *Modern Economic Growth*, pp. 63–85). Cairncross, op. cit., has also expressed the view that capital accumulation has probably accounted for no more than about a quarter to a third of economic growth, and that technical progress and innovation have been the real dynamic forces.

[2] By Mincer, Schultz, Becker, and others in the USA, and by Vaizey, Robinson, and Blaug in Great Britain. See also, on a closely related topic, F. Machlup, *The Production and Distribution of Knowledge in the United States* (Princeton, N.J., 1962).

[3] J. Schmookler, *Invention and Economic Growth* (Cambridge, Mass., 1966). Among his various articles, see especially 'Economic Sources of Inventive Activity', *Journal of Economic History*, vol. XXII (1962). For a much earlier use of US patent statistics, in the study of cyclical and secular changes in various industries, see R. K. Merton, 'Fluctuations in the Rate of Industrial Invention', *Quarterly Journal of Economics*, vol. XLIX (1934–5).

[4] A similar view has more recently been expressed by Mansfield (op. cit., pp. ix, 17), who points out that a decade or so ago 'the economics of technological change . . . was almost totally unexplored', and that 'existing theory is still in a relatively primitive state'.

'intellectual capital', the development and diffusion of new technical knowledge, has been much more important than accumulation of physical capital, and has thus tended to play down the importance of 'economic' factors, since conventional economic theory treats technological progress as 'exogenous', i.e. 'determined by non-economic forces'. But, Schmookler points out, inventions are products of supply and demand: on the supply side they result from accumulated technical knowledge, while on the demand side they are produced for utilitarian purposes, to satisfy consumer wants. He therefore seeks to answer the question whether they are 'mainly knowledge-induced or demand-induced'. And after examination of the patent statistics in several American industries over the past century, he comes down heavily on the demand side, mainly because of the close correlation, both short- and long-term, which he observes between numbers of patented inventions and output (or sales) and investment in the industries concerned, with patents usually lagging slightly behind. Thus he concludes that economic growth determines the rate of invention and technical progress, rather than vice versa, and that economic growth is determined by socio-economic forces, such as the state of the economy, population growth and structure, changes in *per capita* income, etc. It would appear that we have come full circle and are back with Adam Smith again. Inventors, Schmookler considers, do not usually make discoveries by chance: they are influenced by market forces, by prices and profit prospects; they invent 'for gain'. Scientific discoveries and technological knowledge are 'necessary, but seldom sufficient, conditions for invention'.

Schmookler's evidence and arguments are certainly very impressive and compelling. There is no doubt that they will have a generally favourable reception among economic historians, who in recent years have tended to become increasingly Smithian in their emphasis upon demand factors among the causes, for example, of the Industrial Revolution.[1] It must be

---

[1] See below, pp. 40–42. Among growth economists, moreover, Kuznets is now inclined to accept the view that technological inventions are mainly 'responses to demand', though he still emphasizes the complex interplay between scientific-technological and socio-economic factors. *Modern Economic Growth*, pp. 8–15.

pointed out, however, that there are some weaknesses in both his evidence and arguments, and that his conclusions cannot be regarded as decisive. Patents do not cover all inventions, nor are all patented inventions of equal importance.[1] Schmookler admits that the patent statistics refer predominantly to minor improvements, not major inventions, and he can only surmise that his conclusions may 'probably' apply to 'basic inventions which establish new industries', though in their case he has uncertainly to postulate 'latent demand' as the determining influence. He does not explain how this latent demand becomes operative, and how inventors are made aware of it: clearly, in the case of a new basic invention, or new product, an inventor cannot be influenced by present output or sales of that product, though he may discern future market possibilities. Generally, in fact, except for establishing the aggregate statistical relationship between patents and sales or output, Schmookler is very brief and vague in his examination of the socio-economic forces affecting demand, and how individual inventors are affected by them. He also admits to a theoretical weakness in his argument, in that, in actual business operations, research expenditure leading to patents and new or improved products must necessarily occur *before* such products are marketed, i.e. before they can affect output and sales figures. Moreover, whereas his statistical evidence shows patents coinciding with or lagging somewhat behind sales, other scholars have pointed to the time-lags, often very considerable, between scientific discoveries and technical inventions and their eventual embodiment in industrial innovations.[2]

On the supply side, moreover, Schmookler is very vague and inadequate in the evidence which he produces on the motives of particular inventors, especially those of major importance in the industries concerned: his conclusions are mostly deduced from the quantitative aggregates. He makes the significant confession that 'for most of the roughly one thousand inventions in our four categories the literature available unfortu-

[1] For some discussion of the serious limitations of patent statistics, see the contributions by Kuznets and Sanders, with Schmookler's comments, in Nelson (ed.), *The Rate and Direction of Inventive Activity*.

[2] See below, pp. 27–9, 52–3, and 82–3.

nately fails to identify the initiating stimuli', though in a minority of cases the evidence showed the stimulus to be largely economic.[1] Schmookler also admits that he made little investigation into the role of chance or accident.[2] He deliberately excludes the motives of scientists.[3] He admits that scientific and technical knowledge must, of necessity, be anterior to inventions and to their 'intended, socio-economic, functional *future*'. What, then, originally motivated new scientific and technical knowledge? Is this still to be treated as 'exogenous'? 'In our context [says Schmookler] science and engineering appear as given, to be used to explain but not themselves to be explained. In the larger context, however, these too would require explanation.' He suggests that the explanation might be largely in terms of market demand, to which scientific and engineering progress is probably responsive, but this is obviously debatable.[4] Is it not, in fact, a vain quest to seek which is more important, demand or supply, markets or technology, when *both* are essential to economic growth and both are continuously changing and interacting?

These criticisms of Schmookler's mainly statistical approach receive support from the views recently expressed by various people with wide and direct scientific and industrial experience. Not only is there historical evidence of long time-lags between

[1] Op. cit., p. 66.

[2] Ibid., p. 197. We may contrast Schmookler's vagueness in these matters with the earlier findings of Rossman, who in an extensive investigation among professional inventors found that the motive most frequently mentioned was the 'love of inventing', closely followed by 'the desire to improve'; accidental discoveries also played an important role. J. Rossman, *The Psychology of the Inventor* (Washington, D.C., 1931). H. Hart, *The Technique of Social Progress* (New York, 1931), reached similar conclusions: that 'the pleasure of the inventive process, the zest for pitting one's powers against a puzzling obstacle, the fun of using one's mental and mechanical abilities, the satisfaction of rendering a service to one's fellowmen', were pre-eminent motives. See also H. S. Hatfield, *The Inventor and his World*, 2nd ed. (1948), and the views of Jewkes and earlier economists, above, pp. 7–8, and 18–19. On the other hand, there is no doubt that in modern times the individual inventor has tended to be displaced by corporate research in large firms, motivated by economic considerations. But as Jewkes, Nelson, Schon, Nordhaus, and others have pointed out, inventions continue to come from the supply as well as the demand side.

[3] Op. cit., p. 177.

[4] For the debate on the early modern 'Scientific Revolution', see below, pp. 37, and 56. For modern works on the psycho-sociological motivations of scientists, see below, p. 38 n. 1.

inventions and their commercial exploitation, but even in the modern period the lags appear to have been longer than is often supposed.[1] It has been pointed out that an 'invention tends to come before society needs it or is willing to buy it. Therefore you usually have to wait for the invention to become saleable to the public. More frequently than not you have to wait a very long time. Few inventions are made that a society is willing to pay for immediately.' Entrepreneurial drive, capital, and risks are required to get new products on to the market: there is often strong consumer resistance, and opposition from those whose position is threatened by innovations. The market has to be 'invaded': market research, advertising, etc. are required. In fact, a market has often to be *created* for new products.[2]

Very similar views, backed by much empirical evidence, have recently been put forward by Schon,[3] who emphasizes that even under modern 'research and development' programmes, invention, innovation, and marketing are full of uncertainties and risks. The process of invention takes unpredictable 'twists and turns'; in trying to solve one problem, unexpected discoveries are often made in another scientific–technical field, or discoveries in another field impinge unexpectedly on the problem in hand; costs and results are highly uncertain, and accident plays a significant part. The notion that invention is a direct response to clearly discerned 'needs' is 'a myth', except where small improvements are concerned. In the case of a major new invention or product, the 'need' for it does not pre-exist, and a market has to be developed; 'market research' tends to follow rather than precede technical invention and innovation.

---

[1] From studies of a number of important modern examples, the average time-lag appears to have been around fourteen years in the period since the Second World War, though having declined considerably during this century. Mansfield, op. cit., pp. 100–3.

[2] A. W. Warner *et al.* (ed.), *The Impact of Science and Technology* (New York, 1965), pp. 137–9, 211. Schumpeter similarly emphasized the risk-taking role of the entrepreneur in introducing new processes and products, and Kuznets pointed out many years ago that 'demand for tea, cotton cloth, radios, electric light and automobiles appeared only after the progress of technique had made all these commodities available'. *Secular Movements*, pp. 8–9.

[3] Schon, op. cit., *passim*. Cf. also the evidence collected by Jewkes and others.

Marketing pressures do not, in any case, automatically bring forth technological solutions, and 'most new products and processes fail'.

Clearly, then, both in theoretical analysis and in statistical investigation, economists are a long way from the precise understanding of the process of economic growth, particularly with regard to technological development. But the broadening of scope and inclusion of long-term variables has brought growth theory into closer relationship with economic history.[1] The eclectic approach of Adam Smith and the classical economists, with their inclusion of long-term factors such as population growth, technological change, etc., and their more general theorizing, has always appealed to economic historians, who have necessarily been concerned with dynamic problems of growth rather than with static equilibrium, and who have also tended to attach more importance to empirical facts, however diverse and complicated, than to simplistic and often unrealistic theorems.[2] The development of neo-classical micro-static theory tended to create a gulf between economists and economic historians, although, as we have seen, the links were never entirely broken. But the post-Keynesian resurgence of interest in economic growth has brought them much closer together, e.g. the recent common interest in the growth of national income and capital accumulation. On the particular aspects of growth which concern us here – the links between technological progress and economic growth – there is now an obvious possibility of mutual stimulus and collaboration, since economic historians have always laid great emphasis on these interconnexions.

[1] As we have previously noted, however, most economists still repeat the traditional view of the almost entirely empirical character of industrial changes before the twentieth century (see above, pp. 3, 18, and 21). Even the most wide-ranging and erudite of them say the same thing, e.g. Lewis (op. cit., p. 169): 'the great inventions of the eighteenth and nineteenth centuries . . . were all invented by practical people who knew no science, or very little'. Jewkes and his collaborators are remarkable exceptions.

[2] See, for example, Clapham's famous article, 'Of Empty Economic Boxes', *Economic Journal*, vol. XXXII (1922).

IV

The possibility of an interdisciplinary approach is also opened up by the increasing interest of sociologists in the problems of economic growth and scientific–technological development. It is now many years since Talcott Parsons first drew attention to the shortcomings of economic theory in its neglect of sociological and psychological factors.[1] More recently he has reiterated these views, seeking to integrate economics into a 'general theory of social systems'.[2] He has stressed the importance of 'non-economic' factors such as social structure, institutions, cultural patterns, values, wants, and motivations. Economic development is thus closely related to social changes, e.g. the growth of modern industry is associated with the break-up of relatively static societies based on hereditary status and custom, and emergence of new social groups rising through economic achievement, with an accompanying revolution in social values and motives, social mobility, and changed attitudes to work, all conducive to exploitation of profit possibilities including technological innovations.[3] On the last, however, Parsons merely follows Schumpeter in emphasizing the key role of entrepreneurial enterprise, influenced mainly by consumers' wants and profit prospects.[4] He refers to 'new ideas' or 'new combinations of the factors of production', to 'technological know-how', and to 'scientific resources potentially available for technological application', but his discussion of these factors

[1] See his articles in the *Quarterly Journal of Economics*, vols. XLVI (1931–2), XLVIII (1933–4), and XLIX (1934–5).

[2] T. Parsons and N. J. Smelser, *Economy and Society. A Study in the Integration of Economic and Social Theory* (London, 1956). (See also N. J. Smelser, *The Sociology of Economic Life*, Englewood Cliffs, N.J., 1963.) For Parsons's general sociological theories, see *The Structure of Social Action*, 2nd ed. (New York, 1949); *Essays in Sociological Theory Pure and Applied* (Glencoe, Ill., 1949); *The Social System* (Glencoe, Ill., 1951); T. Parsons and E. A. Shils (eds.), *Towards a General Theory of Action* (Cambridge, Mass., 1951); *Sociological Theory and Modern Society* (New York, 1967). Parsons's efforts to combine economic and sociological analysis are in line with the earlier works of Marx, Weber, Durkheim, Pareto, and Veblen.

[3] There are obviously close similarities here to Marx's views on the evolution of bourgeois capitalist society and to Weber's thesis of the 'Protestant ethic' and rise of capitalism.

[4] *Economy and Society*, pp. 43–4, 96–7, 203, 207–9, 264–7.

is terribly vague and repetitive, e.g. technological know-how is 'differentiated into modes of application and adopted to realistic production situations';[1] technological innovation results from 'some dissatisfaction with the current economic mode of activity';[2] it somehow 'evolves' from scientific knowledge, etc., 'but several stages are necessary before concrete technology results . . . various forms of social organization and concrete factors of production are added to make the facilities fully operative in the production process'.[3] There is little evidence here of any contact with industrial–technological reality.

Parsons, in fact, follows Weber in regarding technological progress mainly as an outcome of social changes, changing wants and thus changing market demands.[4] At one point, however, he does observe vaguely that 'changing processes of production' are not determined solely by 'demand conditions', but also partly by 'changes originating in the conditions of production themselves'.[5] Here again one notices a similarity to the view of Weber, who recognized that 'this economic orientation [profit-making] has by no means stood alone in shaping the development of technology': a part has been played by imaginative 'dreamers', by purely 'artistic' interests, and other 'non-economic factors'.[6] Nevertheless, both Weber and Parsons place predominant emphasis on economic and social factors, and refer very sketchily to actual scientific–technological developments. Indeed Parsons has recently expressed a view, now becoming outdated among economists, that technology 'is the outcome of non-economic processes and for economic purposes should be treated as given'.[7]

The importance of socio-cultural factors in economic growth has been increasingly emphasized in recent years by other

[1] Ibid., pp. 131–2.
[2] Ibid., p. 276.
[3] Ibid., pp. 132–3.
[4] Cf. Weber, *The Theory of Social and Economic Organization* (trans. by Henderson and Parsons, 1947), where there is similar emphasis on the market economy; technological development is considered to be 'largely oriented . . . to profit making' (p. 163).
[5] *Economy and Society*, pp. 42–3.
[6] Weber, *loc. cit.*
[7] Parsons, *Structure and Process in Modern Societies* (New York, 1964), pp. 134–5.

sociologists, who have made comparative studies of early industrializing Western economies and modern 'under-developed' countries. Hoselitz, for example, has stressed the need for a general theory of growth, which should include social, cultural, and political, as well as 'purely economic' factors.[1] He considers that, in the development of western European capitalism, 'cultural and socio-structural variables . . . created the conditions for economic change'.[2] Of particular interest, from our present point of view, are his observations that many of the early manufacturers, not only in Britain (e.g. early ironmasters), but also in France and Germany, were 'chiefly contrivers of new technical procedures, rather than men of commercial or financial genius', that many came from humble social origins, were often themselves originally manual craftsmen, and owed much of their success to their technical-innovating and managerial abilities.[3]

Similarly, Hagen, searching outside the boundaries of economic theory for explanations of economic growth, has stressed the importance of the complex sociological and psychological motives of innovating entrepreneurs, the agents of technological progress. An economist himself, he recognizes that economic thought since the late nineteenth century has completely ignored 'technological creativity', the main cause of economic growth.[4] And Hetzler, casting aside the prevalent theories of both economics and sociology, has recently become almost phrenetic in his worship of technology and the machine, discerning the sources of technological growth 'in the nature of technology itself', with engineers instead of entrepreneurs as the heroes of the whole process.[5]

Most sociologists, however, tend to maintain a social-determinist point of view. Notable among those who have studied technological development more deeply is Gilfillan, who,

---

[1] B. F. Hoselitz, *Sociological Aspects of Economic Growth* (Glencoe, Ill., 1960).

[2] But 'economists may query whether this process of social change is autonomous or whether . . . it is related to changes in the more purely economic variables . . . no causal primacy can be assigned to anyone or any one set of variables' (ibid., pp. 42–3).

[3] Ibid., pp. 151–3. See also below, pp. 54–6.

[4] Hagen, op. cit., pp. 49–51. See below, p. 62.

[5] S. A. Hetzler, *Technological Growth and Social Change* (1969).

however, opposes Marxist materialist determinism – 'the idea that invention, technological change, determines economic life and hence all history' – by putting forward the view that social forces are of most fundamental importance.[1] Technical inventions are an 'inevitable' response to changing social needs or demands. His conclusions are thus similar to those of some economists, such as Schmookler, who, however, disagrees with him on some points.[2] They also lend support to the currently popular opinion among economic and social historians as to the importance of demand factors (changes in population, social structure, and tastes) in the causes of the Industrial Revolution. They therefore merit our serious consideration, as an important example of the sociological approach to this subject.

Gilfillan emphasizes the evolutionary character of inventions and attacks the 'heroic' or 'great man', theory. Inventions depend not only on past knowledge and practice, but also on numerous interrelated developments in many technological fields: 'the great inventions are enormous and never-ceasing aggregations of countless inventions of detail'. He therefore criticizes the excessive emphasis on original discovery and the

---

[1] S. C. Gilfillan, 'Invention as a Factor in Economic History', *Journal of Economic History*, Supplement V (1945). See also his earlier book on *The Sociology of Invention* (Chicago, 1935), and his later article on 'The Prediction of Technical Change', *Review of Economics and Statistics* (November 1952). Gilfillan, however, was by no means the first scholar to put forward such views. Veblen, for example, while admitting the role of individuals, had stressed that technological improvements are products of previous socio-cultural and technological development in the general community, e.g. in *The Instinct of Workmanship* (1914; new ed. reprint, 1922), pp. 103–4. See also W. F. Ogburn and D. Thomas, 'Are Inventions Inevitable? A Note on Social Evolution', *Political Science Quarterly*, vol. XXXVII (March 1922), and W. F. Ogburn, *Social Change*, new ed. (New York, 1950); R. C. Epstein, 'Industrial Inventions: Heroic or Systematic', *Quarterly Journal of Economics*, vol. XL (February 1926); W. B. Kaempffert, *Invention and Society* (Chicago, 1930); and H. Hart, *The Technique of Social Progress* (New York, 1931). The ideas, in fact, go back much further, to the eighteenth- and nineteenth-century opponents of the patent system, e.g. the view expressed in *The Economist*, 26 July 1851, that 'nearly all useful inventions depend less on any individual than on the progress of society. A want is felt . . . ingenuity is directed to supply it; and the consequence is, that a great number of suggestions or inventions of a similar kind come to light.' See F. Machlup and E. F. Penrose, 'The Patent Controversy in the Nineteenth Century', *Journal of Economic History*, vol. X (May 1950). See also below, pp. 37, 45–9, 52–6, and 61–2.

[2] Schmookler, op. cit., chap. X.

neglect of subsequent improvements. 'Big starting ideas come cheap and are often duplicated; it is the vast labour of development that is most worth while.'

There is undoubtedly much substance in these views. In marine engineering and shipbuilding, for example, as Gilfillan demonstrates, there are many claimants to the original invention of the steamship, including Fitch, Rumsey, and Fulton in America, and Symington and others in England and elsewhere, and these inventions depended on prior or parallel inventions in the manufacture of iron, engineering, and steam-engine construction. Similarly in the evolution of the steam engine, many scientists and engineers were involved, including various seventeenth-century figures as well as Newcomen and Watt in the eighteenth, and they also depended upon related improvements in construction of boilers, cylinders, etc. Nor is there any doubt that the later, very substantial improvements of Newcomen's engine by Beighton, Smeaton, and others, and of Watt's engine by Hornblower, Trevithick, Wolf, etc., including development of the high-pressure engine, have been comparatively neglected. Similarly, how little we know about the later improvements in spinning and weaving machines, after the initial inventions of Kay, Paul and Wyatt, Hargreaves, Arkwright, Crompton, and Cartwright. It is also right to ask how original were some of the 'heroic' inventors, and how much they were helped by comparatively obscure men. Gilfillan points out that undue importance is attached to those who managed to secure patents or who made inventions commercially successful. That there is much truth in these observations is certainly evident to anyone who has waded through the voluminous reports of patent cases, such as those of Arkwright, Watt, and Tennant, with all the legal and technical wrangling about what constitutes a 'new manufacture' or original invention and all the conflicting evidence by rival claimants.[1]

Gilfillan's general theory, however, is open to question, and some of his supporting arguments are themselves contradic-

[1] For a recent study of the legal cases concerning Watt's patent, see E. Robinson and A. E. Musson, *James Watt and the Steam Revolution* (1969). For the weakness of Tennant's claims, see the chapter on chlorine bleaching in Musson and Robinson, op. cit. For Arkwright, see below, p. 47.

tory. For instance, how is it possible, by his own social-evolutionary theory, for there ever to be any 'big starting ideas'? And, if such ideas are admitted, do they, in fact, 'come cheap' and easy, as he says? Gilfillan considers that the falsity of the 'great-author theory of invention' is demonstrated particularly by 'the frequency of duplicate inventing, when two or more seekers make the same invention about the same time independently'.[1] There are, of course, many such examples, but is it right to conclude that no inventor is indispensable, that 'if the great So-and-so had died in infancy we should have got his inventions just the same', through someone else? Are inventions 'inevitable', do social forces determine that somehow or other, somebody or other, at some time or other, will produce solutions to technical problems (if not the same inventions then others 'functionally equivalent')? Is it possible, as Gilfillan claims, to state with any certainty what would have happened in the past if, say, the steam engine, or the power-loom, had not been invented? And is it likewise possible, as he also claims, to predict the technological future with any accuracy?[2] Gilfillan's own technological forecasts have not been very impressive, nor can one place much confidence in his musings as to what might have happened in the past. (It is interesting, however, to compare Gilfillan's notions with the idea of 'counter-factual propositions' more recently put forward by Fogel and others, in regard, for example, to what might have happened if the railways had not been built in America.)

Gilfillan has to admit that the time factor is important, that history might have been different if an invention had not been made when it was. He also casts doubt on his own what-might-

---

[1] This parallelism in scientific discovery and technical invention had been earlier demonstrated by Ogburn and Thomas, op. cit., and had been noticed by many people since the late eighteenth century. See also R. K. Merton, 'Singletons and Multiples in Scientific Discovery', *Proceedings of the American Philosophical Society*, vol. 105 (1961).

[2] It has been pointed out that this theory of social 'need' and inevitability 'gives better hindsight than foresight', and that it ignores the fundamental role of the individual, influenced by a complex of social and psychological motivations. H. J. Barnett, *Innovation: The Basis of Cultural Change* (New York, 1953), chap. IV. It also neglects the question of time-lags (see above, pp. 26–9, and below, pp. 52–3).

have-been surmises: 'imagined unrealities mean trouble aplenty when we attempt to mix them with the complex vastness of real economic history'. Moreover, such surmises clash with his social-inevitability theory: the invention of steam power, for example, '*was* made; and it *had* to be made', at that time, because of 'the advances of population, wealth, technical knowledge, and related sciences'. Gilfillan admits, however, 'the value and contribution of the inventor': that 'inventors as a class are completely indispensable'. Inventive men are in short supply: 'Particularly scarce are men with the high quality of the great inventors, imagination, insight, learning, tenacity, persistence under great obstacles, sometimes no recompense for years. Such men deserve high rewards. . . . They merit credit as well as cash; but not credit for doing what they never did.' This statement is strangely contradictory to his main argument. If inventions are the inevitable products of economic and social forces, if there are usually several claimants to any invention, if an invention (or its 'functional equivalent') would have been made by somebody or other, and if 'big starting ideas' come easily, how is it possible to admit the existence of 'great inventors'? On the other hand, if their existence and value are admitted, how can one argue against giving them 'credit for what they never did', if in fact they *did* do something original and important? In regard to the patent system, Gilfillan is equally contradictory. In places he condemns it, because of its support of 'the great-author theory', because of the duplication of inventions, dubious claims, etc., but elsewhere he refers to it as 'the chief institution for paying for the invaluable work of invention', and largely responsible for the increasing number of inventions in England in the eighteenth century. If invention is the inevitable product of social forces, and individual inventors are of no account, why should it be necessary to encourage them in this way?

Gilfillan eventually concedes that 'the only concept of history that will hold water is one of a network of causation, with social, technic, biologic, geographic, and accidental factors intermingled and each causing the other, so that we cannot properly speak of the primacy of anything'. He admits, for example, that in the early modern industrial development, the

Renaissance and the growth of science were significant, and that 'Watt and most others of the early great had considerable scientific training'; but he does not regard the role of science as really important until the twentieth century, when individual inventors became submerged in corporate research and development.

Other sociologists, while adopting similar social-determinist views of historical development, have placed much greater emphasis on the role of science. Merton, for example, has similarly attacked the 'great man' or 'heroic' theory, stressing the determining importance of social forces in scientific discovery and applied science, as evidenced, for example, in the 'Scientific Revolution' of the sixteenth and seventeenth centuries, springing from the Renaissance and Reformation and motivated by social and religious changes, with strong emphasis on utilitarian objectives.[1] His ideas have been strongly challenged by some historians of science,[2] who maintain the distinction between 'pure' and 'applied' science, and who consider that the development of scientific ideas has been little influenced by either social or industrial changes. The controversy between Merton, Hall, and others in regard to the 'Scientific Revolution' has developed from the earlier debate on the 'Protestant ethic' and the rise of capitalist individualism, as expressed in the works of Weber, Tawney, and Robertson. Marxist historians, of course, such as Bernal, stress the close interconnexions between scientific, industrial, and social developments, in both the early modern and modern periods,[3] while others have tried to combine both points of view.[4]

[1] R. K. Merton, 'Science, Technology and Society in Seventeenth-Century England', *Osiris*, vol. IV (1938). See also his *Social Theory and Social Structure*, rev. ed. (Glencoe, Ill., 1957), part IV, 'Studies in the Sociology of Science'; his article on 'The Role of Genius in Scientific Advance', *New Scientist*, 2 November 1961; and the one referred to above, p. 35 n. 1.

[2] Most notably by A. R. Hall. See, for example, 'Merton Revisited, or Science and Society in the Seventeenth Century', *History of Science*, vol. II (1963).

[3] J. D. Bernal, *The Social Function of Science* (1939; reprinted 1967), and *Science in History*, 3rd ed. (1965). Veblen had expressed similar ideas much earlier (see above, p. 7).

[4] R. Taton, for example, while stressing the role of individual 'genius' and 'originality' (*Reason and Chance in Scientific Discovery*, trans. by A. J. Pomerans, 1957, *passim*), at the same time admits that 'a considerable number of discoveries were made almost simultaneously by different scientists, working independently',

V

Our review of economic and sociological theories concerning the role of science and technology has demonstrated the increasing awareness of the importance of these factors in economic growth. At the same time, it has revealed that, while certain general theoretical propositions have been produced, together with many shrewd insights based on empirical research, there certainly does not exist anything like an agreed general theory, integrating science and technology into the older theories of economic growth. The view of many economists and sociologists appears to be, in fact, that in the present state of ignorance progress can only be achieved through more detailed case-studies of particular industries, firms, and inventions, i.e. by 'disaggregation'. It also seems evident that, despite efforts to achieve statistical precision, through analysis of patent statistics, research and development expenditure, capital investment, etc., the sources of scientific discovery, technological invention, and industrial innovations are unlikely, in the near future (if ever), to be reduced to quantifiable terms, especially at the aggregate level; indeed, it would appear not unlikely that sociological and psychological analysis may be able to provide as much insight as economic theory and statistics, since the underlying motives are by no means entirely economic.[1]

---

and that such discoveries 'often arise when the general level attained by the science of the times renders them almost inevitable' (ibid., p. 108); moreover, scientific discovery may be regarded as 'the reflection of the civilization of an epoch', with political and economic factors playing an important role (ibid., p. 155). See also E. G. Boring, *History, Psychology, and Science* (ed. R. I. Watson and D. T. Campbell, New York, 1963), part 1, where the importance of 'the psychosocial matrix' is emphasized, but the existence of individual genius is affirmed. For Usher's views, see below, p. 49.

[1] In addition to previously cited works on sociological and psychological motivations of scientists, inventors, and entrepreneurs, see also the following: P. A. Sorokin, *Social and Cultural Dynamics* (New York, 1937); A. Kardiner, *The Psychological Frontiers of Society* (New York, 1945); B. Malinowski, *The Dynamics of Culture Change* (New Haven, Conn., 1945); J. B. Conant, *On Understanding Science* (New Haven, Conn., 1947); D. H. Killeffer, *The Genius of Industrial Research* (New York, 1948); B. Barber, *Science and the Social Order* (New York, 1952); B. F. Skinner, *Science and Human Behavior* (New York, 1953); H. H. Anderson (ed.), *Creativity and Its Cultivation* (New York, 1959); K. R. Popper, *The Logic of Scientific Discovery* (Toronto, 1959); D. C. McClelland, *The Achieving*

Nevertheless, examination of developing theories does provide us with a framework of ideas and many intriguing questions for application to economic history. What contributions did science and technology make to the Industrial Revolution? To what extent were technological changes scientific or empirical? What agencies were there for general, technical, and scientific education and for the diffusion of technology? To what extent was the Industrial Revolution knowledge-induced, or the result of 'an instinct of contrivance', or the product of market forces? What were the links between changing technology and changes in population, social structure, incomes, and tastes, or changes in export markets? What parts were played by capital, labour, and natural resources, and what changes occurred in the price-relationships between these factors of production? Were technological changes labour-saving or capital-saving or both? What statistics are there of capital investment, patents, etc.? What was the role of the patent system? What distinction can be discerned between inventions and innovations? What were the motives of inventors and entrepreneurs? Was there a general advance, all along the line, or can we distinguish 'leading sectors', spearheads of technological advance? Did the changes occur with dramatic suddenness, were they revolutionary, or were 'preconditions' gradually established and was the process evolutionary? What evidence is there for the sociological theory of 'inevitability', or for economic or scientific–technological determinism?

To answer all these wide-ranging questions adequately – if they *can* be answered – would require volumes, rather than these few pages. Indeed, one could fill a sizeable library with relevant books that have already been written. We shall not endeavour to deal here with the commercial aspects, such as expanding trade and marketing, or with social aspects such as the growth of population and changing social structure, which have been the subjects of other volumes in this series.[1] Our

---

Society (Princeton, N.J., 1961) and *Motivating Economic Achievement* (New York, 1969); B. T. Eiduson, *Scientists: Their Psychological World* (New York, 1962); C. W. Taylor and F. Barron, *Scientific Creativity: Its Recognition and Development* (New York, 1963).

[1] D. M. Hartwell, *The Causes of the Industrial Revolution in England* (1967);

D

particular concern will be with the interactions between science, technology, and economic growth during the Industrial Revolution, though stressing all the time that these cannot realistically be considered in isolation.

The prevalent tendency among economic and social historians is to place more emphasis than hitherto upon the demand side, upon market forces at home and abroad. It is a good many years now since Ashton pointed out that the popular view of the Industrial Revolution as 'a wave of gadgets' is no longer tenable,[1] and more recent work has tended to reinforce his opinion. Habakkuk, in particular, has strongly affirmed that although 'the main stimulus to growth came from changes in industry', Adam Smith's explanation of these changes is 'still the most reasonable': that they resulted from the increase of trade, extension of the market, increases and shifts in demand, which led to more division of labour, greater efficiency, invention and improvement of machines. 'Most of the economically important inventions of the Industrial Revolution period can more plausibly be ascribed to the pressure of increasing demand rather than to the random operation of the human instinct of contrivance, change in factor prices, or the Schumpeterian innovator (who became an important agent of advance only at a relatively late stage).' True the effects of trade expansion were 'enhanced by changes in religious belief' which stimulated business achievement, and also 'by accessions of scientific knowledge', but 'extension of the market' was the real driving force: 'there is still a good deal to be said for the old view that the acceleration of economic changes in the late eighteenth century was primarily the result of the great expansion of overseas trade in the two preceding centuries'.[2]

Supple similarly has placed the main emphasis on economic and social factors – population, social structure, markets, entrepreneurial ability, etc. – and considers that 'the older

W. E. Minchinton, *The Growth of English Overseas Trade in the Seventeenth and Eighteenth Centuries* (1969); M. Drake, *Population in Industrialization* (1969).

[1] T. S. Ashton, *The Industrial Revolution 1760–1830* (1948), p. 58 *et passim*.

[2] H. J. Habakkuk, 'The Historical Experience on the Basic Conditions of Economic Progress', in L. H. Dupriez (ed.), *Economic Progress* (1955).

interpretation of the British Industrial Revolution, which sees it as the outcome of an almost spontaneous wave of heroic inventions, is no longer fully tenable'. But he clearly recognizes the importance of technology: 'The Industrial Revolution may not have been "caused" by, but it was certainly carried forward by, the application of machinery and power to textile production, by advances in the technology of iron manufacture, by the invention of the steam engine and the birth of engineering and the machine-tool industry, and by the overhauling of methods in a host of other industries.'[1]

The most recent general survey has produced much the same conclusions:[2] 'in every instance it was the general movement of the economy, and not the technical innovations as such, that dictated the pace of change. The inventions came – or at any rate were seriously developed – when economic conditions were ripe', i.e. when market demand was growing both at home and abroad, and when the resultant industrial expansion was putting pressure on traditional methods and resources (e.g. of wood fuel and water power). But, of course, demand might have gone unsatisfied, had it not been for the dynamic force of capitalist enterprise, stimulated in Britain by changing class structure, social mobility, the profit motive, and free competition. However, in Lilley's view, once the Industrial Revolution got under way, it gradually acquired an almost independent technological impetus, in which applied science played an increasingly important role.

Lilley's conclusions are based on a number of general studies of the Industrial Revolution which have appeared in recent years.[3] Most of these, with varying emphasis, stress the funda-

[1] Supple, op. cit., p. 35.

[2] S. Lilley, 'Technological Progress and the Industrial Revolution 1700–1914', in the Fontana *Economic History of Europe*, vol. III (1970), chap. 3.

[3] For example, D. S. Landes, 'Technological Change and Development in Western Europe, 1750–1914', in the *Cambridge Economic History of Europe*, vol. VI (1965), since revised and extended in *Prometheus Unbound* (1969); M. W. Flinn, *The Origins of the Industrial Revolution* (1966); R. M. Hartwell (ed.), *The Causes of the Industrial Revolution in England* (1967); Phyllis Deane, *The First Industrial Revolution* (1967); and various technological histories, such as A. P. Usher, *A History of Mechanical Inventions* (1929; rev. ed. 1954); C. Singer *et al.* (ed.), *A History of Technology* (6 vols., 1954–8), condensed by T. K. Derry and T. I. Williams, *A Short History of Technology* (Oxford, 1960); W. H. Chaloner and A. E. Musson, *Industry and Technology* (1963); M. Kranzberg and C. W. Pursell,

mental importance of expanding markets, and there would now seem to be little doubt that growing demand was the main driving force behind technological change. But, as in most intellectual swings of opinion, there is danger of reaction going too far. There is evidence that, even two centuries ago, as in modern times, leading innovators, such as Boulton or Wedgwood or Manchester cotton manufacturers, to a very considerable extent *created* the markets for their new products by vigorous sales promotion.[1] No doubt in making technological advances they had strong commercial motives, but invention and innovation often preceded exploitation of market possibilities. And without the technological advances, which made possible greatly increased production at lower costs, markets could not possibly have expanded as they did. There are two blades to the scissors of supply and demand.

Among recent historians of economic growth, Rostow has acquired most notoriety, with his terminology of 'take-off', 'leading sectors', 'self-sustained growth', and other 'stages' of development. Many earlier economists and historians, however, had developed similar 'stages' theories, and many had previously emphasized the role of cotton in the Industrial Revolution. Rostow adds little or nothing in detailed factual information. He refers, for example, to the key roles of science and technology in the 'take-off', but says remarkably little about them; his main emphasis is upon economic and social factors, especially the postulated growth in the rate of investment as a proportion of national income (or net national product) from around 5 to over 10 per cent.[2] He points out, however, that the

Jr. (ed.), *Technology and Western Civilization*, vol. 1 (1967). See also Lilley's earlier *Men, Machines and History*, 2nd ed. (1965).

[1] N. McKendrick, 'Josiah Wedgwood: An Eighteenth-Century Entrepreneur in Salesmanship and Marketing Techniques', *Economic History Review*, 2nd ser., vol. XII, no. 3 (April 1960); E. Robinson, 'Eighteenth-Century Commerce and Fashion: Matthew Boulton's Marketing Techniques', ibid., vol. XVI, no. 1 (August 1963); M. M. Edwards, *The Growth of the British Cotton Trade*, 1780–1815 (1967).

[2] The references below are from *The Stages of Economic Growth* (1960). But a similar impression is gained from *The Process of Economic Growth* (1953; rev. ed. 1960), e.g. his discussion in chaps. II and III of the 'propensities' to develop and apply science is extremely vague, while in chap. XII, dealing with the 'take-off', he deliberately sets aside 'the question of how new production techniques are generated from pure science and invention', a really colossal omission.

use of such aggregate economic statistics 'tells us relatively little of what actually happens and of the causal processes at work . . . nor is the investment-rate criterion conclusive'. He therefore stresses the need for 'disaggregation', or sectoral analysis: to see 'how rapidly growing manufacturing sectors emerged and imparted their primary and secondary growth impulses to the economy'. On these developments, however, Rostow is very brief and vague. He emphasizes particularly 'the supply of loanable funds' and 'the sources of entrepreneurship', social mobility, and the profit motive, though he leaves aside 'the question of ultimate human motivation' and hints at the need for 'further empirical research' on the motives of entrepreneurs. He talks about different 'growth sectors', about 'the introduction and diffusion of changes in the cost–supply environment', and about 'new production functions', but he provides no details whatever about the scientific and technological developments upon which industrial expansion was based, or about particular individuals or firms which played leading roles. One gets the overwhelming impression of vague, repetitive jargon and generalization, though Rostow's work is certainly of value for its demonstration of the necessity for an interdisciplinary approach to the problems of economic growth – involving consideration of psychological, social, political, and historical, as well as economic factors – and of the necessity for more empirical research.

Rostow's stages theory includes the notion of 'pre-conditions' for 'take-off', but, here again, much work had already been done, and more has since been done, on developments before the Industrial Revolution. Markets had been expanding, with slowly rising population and exports, in the sixteenth and seventeenth centuries. Nor was technological change new or revolutionary. Indeed, there appears to be little justification, either in terms of capital formation or technological development, for Rostow's sharp differentiation between the 'preconditions' and 'take-off' periods.[1] Studies in the history of technology show that even in the Middle Ages there had been

[1] See Kuznets's criticisms in 'Notes on the Take-off' in Rostow (ed.), *The Economics of Take-off into Sustained Growth* (1963), reprinted in Kuznets, *Economic Growth and Structure*. See also below, p. 53.

important developments in the application of water and wind power (e.g. in grinding corn, working forge-hammers, etc., and fulling cloth: Professor Carus-Wilson has even discerned 'an industrial revolution of the thirteenth century'[1]); there had been improvements in textiles (e.g. the introduction of the spinning wheel and development of the handloom); while in the iron industry the blast-furnace and cast-iron had been introduced in the later Middle Ages. Technological change continued in the sixteenth and seventeenth centuries: Professor Nef's 'industrial revolution' in that period may not have been as revolutionary as he at first suggested,[2] but he was obviously right to emphasize the importance of the growing British coal industry and of new coal- or coke-burning processes in the manufacture of glass, bricks, salt, sugar, etc.[3] Meanwhile, the 'new draperies' were being introduced, together with further improvements in spinning and weaving; these, along with the invention of the stocking frame, ribbon loom, and gig-mill (for raising the nap), foreshadowed the textiles revolution of the eighteenth century. In the metallurgical industries, moreover, the use of coal or coke fuel in the smelting of copper and lead similarly preceded the better-known discoveries of Darby, Cort, and others in iron smelting and forging. Likewise, one can trace earlier important if not revolutionary changes in printing and paper-making, in clock- and instrument-making (with development of precision metal-working tools, such as drills, lathes, and 'wheel-cutting' or gear-cutting 'engines', preparing the way for the later development of heavy mechanical engineering), and also in embryo chemical and allied manufactures producing alum, dyestuffs, saltpetre, acids, potash and soda, soap, etc. From a technological point of view it is very difficult to discern anything really revolutionary in the eighteenth century: even the steam engine was a seventeenth-

---

[1] E. M. Carus-Wilson, 'An Industrial Revolution of the Thirteenth Century', *Economic History Review*, vol. XI (1941).

[2] J. U. Nef, *The Rise of the British Coal Industry* (2 vols., 1932), and 'The Progress of Technology and the Growth of Large-scale Industry in Great Britain, 1540–1640', *Economic History Review*, vol. V (1934).

[3] His views have recently received support from W. Rees, *Industry before the Industrial Revolution* (2 vols., 1968), mainly concerned with Welsh coal and metallurgical developments.

century product of scientific theory and experiment. 'The early stages of the Industrial Revolution – roughly up to 1800 – were based very largely on using medieval techniques and on extending them to their limits.'[1] Water power, for example, long continued to be much more important than steam power.[2]

It would appear, then, that technological change was a long-continued response to gradual expansion of markets. But Coleman's researches into the 'new draperies' suggest that the origins and development of these early technical changes are very difficult to trace, and that one should not jump too quickly at the apparently more obvious commercial explanations.[3] The same is true of the Industrial Revolution. It is very difficult, because of lack of evidence, to discover what precisely were the motives of individual inventors: in most cases we simply do not know exactly what impelled them to invent new machines or processes, whether it was expanding trade and profit prospects, or a desire to rise in society, or 'an instinct of contrivance', or an interest in mechanical or chemical experiment, or an innate desire to 'improve', or some other psychological impulse. Very few inventors of that period have left letters, diaries, or other evidence explaining their motives.

The sociological theory of the 'inevitability' of inventions, like the modern emphasis on demand among economic historians, leaves many questions unanswered when applied to the Industrial Revolution. It tends to assume an almost automatic response to market or social forces, and greatly to simplify, or even ignore, precisely how and with what difficulties 'supply' was revolutionized. There is an assumption that if economic and social factors are 'ripe', then hey presto! technological solutions will somehow be produced by some-

---

[1] Lilley, *Technical Progress*, p. 8.

[2] Ibid., pp. 8–9, and Musson and Robinson, op. cit., pp. 67–71.

[3] Coleman has shown how difficult it is to disentangle the complexities of supply and demand, of the new techniques and their inventors, of changing markets, prices and profits, and of technical diffusion, migration, etc., in this field: 'economic causes alone may well be inadequate to explain' these changes, and 'anyone going model-building in the history of new products needs to walk with more than usual care.' D. C. Coleman, 'An Innovation and its Diffusion: the "New Draperies"', *Economic History Review*, 2nd ser., vol. XXII, no. 3, (December 1969).

body or other. Such a view is naïve and unhelpful. It is akin to easy modern assumptions that somehow, someday, Man will reach the planets or the stars, or cure cancer, or perform other scientific–technological miracles. But such assumptions are of little help to the scientists or engineers who are faced with the detailed problems of finding out precisely how to achieve such goals. In the same way, there is danger of easy historical hindsight: we *know* that certain inventions were made during the Industrial Revolution, and it is easy to produce arguments as to their 'inevitability', though they certainly did not seem 'inevitable' to the contemporaries concerned. James Watt (or somebody else), it is said, was bound to invent the separate condenser, etc., because the economic situation 'demanded' it. But exactly how was this demand transmitted to Watt? What evidence is there that he personally was impelled by market forces? What about the qualities of his own individual mind and personality? Was he a 'genius' or not? What were his scientific and technical interests? How did he come to tackle the problem of steam power, and how did he overcome the technical difficulties involved? About Watt, in fact, we do know a good deal,[1] and it is clear that, while he was certainly indebted to existing technology and scientific knowledge, he also carried out a series of original experiments, mainly out of scientific–technical curiosity, with no apparent economic motive in the first place, and that he combined careful experiment with extraordinary insight and imagination. There is equally no doubt that he very soon became aware of the economic possibilities of exploiting his invention. The same is also true of his later development of chlorine bleaching, regarding which we also have his surviving letters;[2] but his prolonged experiments and disappointments demonstrate the naïve over-simplicity of an after-the-fact theory of 'inevitability' in this case.

The evidence regarding Watt and other inventors also shows the difficulty of distinguishing between invention and innova-

---

[1] See Musson and Robinson, *Science and Technology* . . . , and *James Watt and the Steam Revolution*; also E. Robinson and D. McKie, *Partners in Science* (1969). See also below, pp. 62 and, 108–9, for Watt's scientific interests.

[2] Musson and Robinson, *Science and Technology*, chap. VIII.

tion (or commercial exploitation).[1] Watt not only invented the separate condenser, but was also involved in the prolonged technical, financial, and managerial problems of developing it, and development required further inventions or improvements. Watt, in fact, regarded the development problems as the more difficult, not only in his own case, but also in that of Arkwright, in supporting whose claims he declared that, 'whoever invented the spinning machine, Arkwright certainly had the merit of performing the most difficult part, which was the making it useful'.[2] The water-frame appears to have been invented originally by Thomas Highs (if it was not an improvement on the earlier roller-spinning machine of Paul and Wyatt), but it was not successfully developed, either technically or commercially, until Arkwright himself took it over (almost certainly from Highs); but Arkwright appears to have shown considerable technical ingenuity if not originality (helped though he undoubtedly was by Kay and others), as well as commercial acumen, and further technical inventions and improvements were necessary to the water-frame's eventual success.[3] Arkwright, however, unlike Watt, seems to have been driven from the beginning almost entirely by commercial motives, being well aware of the profit potential of a successful spinning machine.

Research into other inventions similarly reveals the complexities of the processes and motivations involved. But too often historians, economists, and sociologists have produced simple explanations, based mostly on inference or deduction from some general theory of economic or social causation, with inadequate empirical evidence. Other scholars, however, have stressed the rare intellectual qualities of outstanding inventors and innovators, such as Watt or Arkwright. Lewis, for example, considers that such men are probably products of

[1] As A. P. Usher has pointed out, 'Technical Change and Capital Formation', in M. Abramovitz (ed.), *Capital Formation and Economic Growth* (Princeton, 1956). See also Schon's views regarding modern 'research and development', above, pp. 28–9.

[2] A. P. Wadsworth and J. de L. Mann, *The Cotton Trade and Industrial Lancashire 1600–1780* (Manchester, 1931), p. 492.

[3] Unpublished paper by A. E. Musson, read to the Midlands section of the Institution of Mechanical Engineers, Birmingham, 1969, on the occasion of the bicentenary of the Watt and Arkwright patents.

'biological accident', or 'statistical accident', though he recognizes the influence of circumstances, and Hagen also emphasizes the importance of superior innate intelligence, imagination, and energy, though these are affected by socio-cultural factors.[1] Recent research into a great many of the engineers, chemists, etc. who played leading roles in the Industrial Revolution reveals the complexity of factors involved:[2]

> Although economic and social factors were undoubtedly of immense importance in motivating scientific and technological changes – growth of population, expansion of trade, development of transport, availability of capital and credit, social mobility, and the profit motive all impelled or encouraged men to develop new industrial techniques – we have been impressed by the fact that many of the leading scientists and scientifically-minded industrialists were motivated also to a considerable extent by innate curiosity, by a desire to discover more about how industrial processes worked, by an urge to make improvements, and to be esteemed by their fellows, not merely for the money they made, but [also] for their contributions to scientific and technological advance. This impression tends to suggest, indeed, that psychology and sociology may have as much as economics to teach us in such matters.

These conclusions are very similar to those of Professor Jewkes and his collaborators, resulting from equally detailed investigation into the sources of modern invention.[3] There is, in fact, plentiful evidence to support Schumpeter's view that entrepreneurs were motivated not simply by a hedonistic desire for profits, but also by a will to achieve, to acquire power and renown, to found a 'dynasty', and other psycho-sociological drives.[4]

Few, if any, scholars nowadays would subscribe to a naïve

---

[1] Lewis, op. cit., p. 55; Hagen, op. cit., *passim*.

[2] Musson and Robinson, op. cit., p. 8.

[3] See above, pp. 18–19.

[4] Cf. also the views of Hagan and McClelland, who (in their works previously cited) similarly emphasize the 'need to achieve' and 'urge to improve', though they also recognize that economic and social circumstances and opportunities are important.

'heroic theory' of inventions. Most would agree with Usher[1] that technological progress is not autonomous but is a social process, influenced by the economic and cultural environment, and that an invention is not an isolated achievement, but the culmination of a long process of improvement, often achieved only after repeated trial-and-error, and often also requiring many modifications before coming into practical use. This is certainly true of the famous textile and metallurgical inventions of the Industrial Revolution, the development of the steam engine, sulphuric acid and soda manufacture, etc. But if one studies at first-hand the detailed contemporary evidence – revealing the prolonged thought, experiments, disappoint-ments, and innumerable practical problems involved in pro-ducing an invention, from the first original idea to eventual industrial application, not forgetting also the countless failures and bankruptcies – then a theory of 'inevitability' appears ludicrous: it completely ignores the realities of individual achievement, the imaginative insight, sustained effort, and mixture of motives involved.

VI

A possible factor encouraging invention was an 'institutional' one – the patent system – illustrating the role of governmental or parliamentary policy.[2] This is another field in which econo-mists have been interested, but have reached contradictory conclusions.[3] Some have regarded the patent system as vitally important in encouraging invention and enterprise, but others have strongly criticized its monopolistic aspects, its arbitrary unfairness, and the huge amount of litigation to which it has

---

[1] Usher, *History of Mechanical Inventions*, chap. IV, in which he puts forward a theory, based on 'Gestalt' psychology, half-way between the individualist ('heroic') and social ('inevitability') theories, seeing the process of invention 'as a cumulative synthesis', but involving 'acts of insight' or 'imaginative construction', with chance playing a random role.

[2] It may be argued, of course, that the development of the patent system was a product of economic and social forces, such as the growth of capitalist enterprise, influencing political policy. A similar factor was the growth of tariff protection, etc., restricting foreign competition and encouraging native manufactures. Parliament also made numerous grants to inventors.

[3] See above, pp. 7–8.

given rise. This division of opinion is of long standing: during the Industrial Revolution, there were similar arguments and legal wrangles, but no one has yet made a detailed study of how the system operated in that period.[1] Some general attention has been paid, however, to patent statistics as indicators of technological progress. Witt Bowden was one of the first to emphasize their importance.[2] He compiled the following figures from the Patent Office publications by Bennett Woodcroft:

Number of Patents Issued

1660–9	31	1730–9	56
1670–9	51	1740–9	82
1680–9	53	1750–9	92
1690–9	102	1760–9	205
1700–9	22	1770–9	294
1710–19	38	1780–9	477
1720–9	89		

Bowden also pointed out that whereas many of the early patents had been granted for vague and often worthless ideas, or merely for bringing a new process into use, by the late eighteenth-century specifications had to be much more precise and patents were only granted for genuine inventions. It is not clear how far inventors were encouraged by the somewhat dubious protection afforded by patents, which were costly to obtain and often challenged in the law courts; many inventions were apparently never patented and secrecy was often preferred. Moreover, patent statistics measure only quantity, not quality, of inventions; the majority were for minor improvements, and many proved abortive.

Ashton put the patent statistics under more revealing analysis.[3] He was, of course, well aware of their shortcomings: he stressed that technical change is 'a continuous process', much of it occurring 'behind the scenes' in innumerable small and

[1] For some recent references, however, see above, p. 34 n. 1.

[2] W. Bowden, *Industrial Society in England towards the End of the Eighteenth Century*, 2nd ed, (New York, 1965), pp. 12–14, 25–30.

[3] T. S. Ashton, 'Some Statistics of the Industrial Revolution in Britain', *Manchester School*, vol. XVI (1948), pp. 214–34, extracts from which are reprinted below, chap. 3.

mostly unpatented improvements (a view which has been confirmed by the researches into modern industry of economists such as Salter). Nevertheless, he considered that the patent statistics provide a useful 'rough index of innovation'. He pointed out that they showed not only the expected 'strong upward trend' observed by Bowden and others, but 'also the cyclical variations typical of most economic data'. Peaks in the figures coincided with 'years when the rate of interest was low, and when . . . industry and trade were active', whereas comparatively few were taken out in years of depression, suggesting that invention was motivated by 'the hope of gain, rather than avoiding loss'.[1] Moreover, Ashton discerned a connexion between invention, on the one hand, and the rate of interest and capital investment, on the other, cheap money being a major incentive.[2] Like many modern economists, he related technological change to the relative prices of the factors of production, capital and labour – the downward trend in interest rates being responsible for the labour-saving bias in most inventions. 'It is at least clear that, whatever the nature of the connecting thread, the inventions were not a force operating more or less casually from outside the system, but were an integral part of the economic process.' Only in recent years, as we have seen, have economists generally come to recognize this fact of economic life.

Ashton had, however, been influenced in his ideas by Sir Arnold Plant's earlier article on the patent system.[3] Kuznets had also previously pointed out the significance of patent statistics,[4] and Merton had carried out similar researches upon them in tracing fluctuations in American industry.[5] Schmookler's more recent and much more exhaustive investigations have, as we have seen, tended to confirm Ashton's conclusions. Hoffmann, in his investigations into the growth of British industrial production, followed Ashton in tracing 'a close correlation between changes in the number of patents taken

[1] A similar conclusion has been reached by R. S. Sayers, 'The Springs of Technical Progress 1919–39', *Economic Journal*, vol. LX (1950).

[2] See also Ashton, *The Industrial Revolution*, pp. 9–11.

[3] See above, p. 8.

[4] Kuznets, *Secular Movements*, pp. 54 et seq.

[5] See above, p. 24 n. 3.

out and changes in the volume of output of the producer-goods industries' during the Industrial Revolution and later:[1] plotted graphically, the curves of patents and output correspond exactly in their 'long waves' (of approximately twenty years). Patents increase with output in booms and decline in slumps, while there is an inverse relationship with bankruptcies: 'as bankruptcies rise, so patents fall'.

Hoffmann has to admit however – and his admission also undermines Ashton's theory – that the date at which a patent is taken out may be of little economic significance, 'since many years may elapse between the patenting of an invention and its practical application; and in any case, the full economic effects of an invention may not be felt for some time after its first application'.[2] This time-lag between invention (whether patented or not) and development and diffusion has also been admitted by the sociologist Gilfillan, although he fails to appreciate adequately how damaging it is to his theory of social 'inevitability'.[3] It is equally damaging to Schmookler's theory of inventions, especially in the case of major ones, and particularly during the Industrial Revolution, when the time-lag was often much longer than in the later period. (One may mention, for example, Darby's coke-smelting process, Huntsman's crucible steel, Kay's fly-shuttle, Paul and Wyatt's roller-spinning, Cartwright's power-loom and combing machine, Watt and Murdock's steam locomotive, and Trevithick's high-pressure engine.) If these inventions were simply products of pressing economic and social forces, why was there such a long time-lag before their widespread application? Surely, if they were sociologically or economically 'determined', 'inevitable', and 'necessary', they should have been brought into

---

[1] W. Hoffman, *British Industry, 1700–1950* (English trans., 1955), pp. 171–4, 300, and table 54.

[2] Ashton, in fact, admits this elsewhere: that 'there was often a lag of years between an invention and its application, and it was this last, rather than the discovery itself, that was influenced by such things as a growing shortage of materials or a change in the supply of labour or capital' (*The Industrial Revolution*, p. 92).

[3] Gilfillan, *The Sociology of Invention*, chap. V. The time-lag may be 'ten to fifty years'. Ogburn, *Social Change*, similarly recognized these 'cultural lags'. Gilfillan did actually admit (op. cit., p. 152) that in many cases invention may arise from 'an individual, not a social, need, and is an inner aspect'.

widespread use immediately. It has been argued that such inventions were 'before their time', and were not adopted till the market was 'ripe'. But what, then, prompted their original invention? Ashton's more limited and cautious observation – that patents rose and fell with the state of trade, and that this was a factor influencing inventors – is obviously borne out by the statistics, but it fails to distinguish adequately between invention and the later (and economically perhaps more significant) stages of innovation, development, and diffusion, the necessity for distinguishing between which Kuznets has emphasized.

There seems little doubt, however, that – whatever the motives of inventors – innovators or entrepreneurs were certainly very much influenced by economic factors, such as relative factor prices, market possibilities, and profit prospects. Of this there is plentiful evidence in specialized historical studies of particular firms, too well known and numerous to list here.[1] On the other hand, Ashton's emphasis on the role of increasing capital investment, reiterated by Rostow, has tended to be somewhat deflated by recent statistical investigations, which have shown that the proportion of national income invested during the Industrial Revolution did not rise so remarkably as surmised,[2] and suggest that capital-saving was perhaps more important than hitherto thought (as emphasized by Blaug), that technical advance was not simply a product of capital accumulation, and that the growth of scientific, technical, and managerial knowledge was of considerable significance. In the cotton industry, in particular – Rostow's 'leading sector' – it has been shown that fixed capital formation was a good deal less than has hitherto been thought.[3] It was probably only

[1] Good examples are G. Unwin, *Samuel Oldknow and the Arkwrights* (Manchester, 1924); T. S. Ashton, *An Eighteenth-Century Industrialist* (Manchester, 1939); A. Raistrick, *Dynasty of Iron Founders* (1953); R. S. Fitton and A. P. Wadsworth, *The Strutts and the Arkwrights* (Manchester, 1958).

[2] P. Deane and W. A. Cole, *British Economic Growth 1688–1959* (1964), pp. 263–4. Their estimates indicate a rise in net national capital formation from about 5 per cent at the end of the seventeenth century to only about 6½ per cent in Rostow's 'take-off' period, with a gradual rise thereafter to about 9 per cent in the second quarter of the nineteenth century.

[3] Edwards, op. cit., chap. IX; S. D. Chapman, 'Fixed Capital Formation in the British Cotton Industry, 1770–1815', *Economic History Review*, 2nd ser., vol. XXIII, no. 2 (August 1970).

in the second quarter of the nineteenth century, with the large-scale development of machine-tools and mass-production engineering, that technological developments became very capital-intensive and labour-displacing.[1] But how far inventors and innovators were influenced by relative factor prices – whether by the prevailing abundance of relatively cheap capital, as Ashton has argued, or by relatively dear (and troublesome) labour, as others have suggested – and how far by 'non-economic' factors, is still far from clear.

In regard to inventors, there is some evidence to support the view that they are just as likely to have been motivated by intellectual or practical curiosity, by a love of 'tinkering' or an 'instinct of contrivance', or by a non-economic interest in 'improvement', as by economic factors.[2] We have already referred to the differences among economists on this subject.[3] Study of some leading figures in the Industrial Revolution indicates that the economic incentive was certainly not the only one, nor necessarily the most powerful. Watt is a particularly good example of this mixture of motives, not only in his improvement of the steam engine, but also in his other scientific-technological interests.[4] Berthollet, discoverer of chlorine bleaching for textiles, expressly disclaimed, as a scientist, any personal economic interest in its development.[5] Edmund Cartwright, inventor of the power-loom, was driven mainly by a creative urge and desire to improve: he never stopped inventing, almost to the day of his death, and produced a multifarious list of schemes for industrial and agricultural improvements.[6] Richard Roberts, inventor of the self-actor mule, was even more prolific, impelled chiefly by a profound interest in mechanical engineering, and apparently lacking in sound business sense.[7] John Kennedy, the famous cotton-spinner and machine-maker, 'never pursued business for the

---

[1] Musson and Robinson, op. cit., chap. XV.

[2] As suggested by Rossman, Hart, Hatfield, Jewkes, etc.

[3] See above, pp. 8, 18–20, and 24–9.

[4] See above, p. 46, and below, pp. 62, and 108–9.

[5] Musson and Robinson, op. cit., p. 266.

[6] Taussig, op. cit., pp. 25–6; Hart, op. cit., p. 656, based on J. Burnley, *The History of Wool and Wool-Combing* (1889), pp. 132–3.

[7] H. W. Dickinson, 'Richard Roberts, His Life and Inventions', *Newcomen Society Transactions*, vol. XXV (1945–7).

sake of money, but for love of improvements in his favourite mechanical pursuits'.[1] William Fairbairn, the great Manchester engineer, was similarly interested in scientific–technical investigations, from motives of intellectual and practical curiosity and desire for renown, rather than for material gain, though they did lead to profitable engineering advances.[2] Such examples could be multiplied. At the same time, of course, one must beware of motives attributed to inventors by others, expecially after their deaths; an impressive quantity of evidence could easily be compiled, suggestive of the stimulus provided by competition and the profit motive. Nor is it correct to regard really able inventors as dilettante amateurs or tinkerers: most of them were actively engaged in industry, though not necessarily in the ones to which their inventions were applicable, and few appear to have been fanciful dreamers.

There is also a good deal of evidence to support the view of Hoselitz that technical knowledge and skills were possibly more important in the success of many industrial entrepreneurs than their financial and commercial abilities.[3] Many of the leading manufacturers of the Industrial Revolution came from humble social origins and acquired technical skills and experience while working as practical craftsmen. In the cotton industry, for example, outstanding figures such as McConnel and Kennedy, the Murrays, Ewart, Lee, and many others started in this way, and were notable for their technical capacity and improvements.[4] The same is true of engineering, as illustrated by Watt, Bramah, Maudslay, Roberts, Fairbairn, Nasmyth, Whitworth, etc. All these men began with very little capital, usually borrowing or securing credit initially from merchants, banks, etc., and it was their technical and managerial skills which formed the basis of their achievements. It is quite misleading to em-

---

[1] Musson and Robinson, op. cit., p. 100, quoting from Fairbairn's memoir of him.

[2] W. Pole (ed.), *The Life of Sir William Fairbairn, Bart.* (1877; new ed. 1970, with introduction by A. E. Musson), pp. 464–6, evidence by contemporary associates. See also below, p. 105.

[3] See above, p. 32.

[4] Even Arkwright, above all characterized as a business tycoon, appears to have acquired considerable technical skills and knowledge, which enabled him to develop the water-frame successfully. Owen similarly acquired knowledge of machine-making before becoming a factory manager.

E

phasize unduly their 'economic' characteristics, though, of course, technical ability alone was not a guarantee of business success. Their 'predominant orientation', to use Hoselitz's phrase, was 'in the direction of productivity, work, and creative integration', as distinct from mercantile personality characteristics.[1]

As to the factors which created this 'productive orientation', many explanations are possible. Some might say that it was a national or racial characteristic, somehow produced by geographical, ethnic, and other circumstances (the preponderance of Scots in the above list is not without significance); others might attribute it to a Puritan religious ethic, extolling the virtues of practical hard work, or to other socio-cultural or psychological factors, shaping personality traits favourable to technological innovation;[2] others might explain it as a development from traditional handicrafts, stimulated by expanding markets.

VII

The role of science in these technological changes is another enigma, which has not, until recently, been investigated with any thoroughness. Indeed, attention has tended to centre more on the preceding 'Scientific Revolution' of the sixteenth and seventeenth centuries, and on whether or not this was motivated by purely intellectual curiosity, or by the 'Puritan ethic' and other social forces, with the related question as to what extent, if any, science was applied in industry.[3] Much of the

[1] Hagen, op. cit., pp. 294–309, also stresses the manufacturing background of most of the leading innovators in the Industrial Revolution, though he points out that they 'were not typically poor men'.

[2] Following Hagen and McClelland. See also T. Burns and S. B. Saul (eds.), *Social Theory and Economic Change* (1967), especially the contributions by Flinn and Hagen. The Dissenters, both English and Scots, certainly played an immensely important role. See below, pp. 61–2.

[3] See, for example, A. Wolf, *A History of Science, Technology and Philosophy, in the Sixteenth and Seventeenth Centuries* (1935), and *in the Eighteenth Century* (1938); G. N. Clark, *Science and Social Welfare in the Age of Newton*, 2nd ed. (1949); H. S. Butterfield, *The Origins of Modern Science*, 1300–1800 (1949); A. R. Hall, *The Scientific Revolution, 1500–1800* (1954), and *From Galileo to Newton, 1630–1720* (1963); R. Taton (ed.), *The Beginnings of Modern Science from 1500–1800*, trans. by A. J. Pomerans (1944); H. F. Kearney, *Origins of the Scientific Revolution* (1964);

debate in this period, and later in the Industrial Revolution, hinges on what interpretations are given to the words 'science' and 'empiricism', or to 'pure' and 'applied' science. In the present writer's opinion, too strong and unrealistic a distinction is often drawn between them. The fundamental basis of modern science, 'pure' or 'applied', is the 'scientific method' of combining theory or hypothesis with practical experiment: modern science is 'experimental science'. The objects may be different: a 'pure' scientist may well have no utilitarian motives in his researches, whereas an 'applied' scientist is essentially concerned with practical objectives. But the distinction between them is often blurred: a 'pure' scientist may be interested in both furthering knowledge and putting such knowledge to use, while applied science may result in 'feed-back' of theoretically important ideas, as well as experimental information. It must also be remembered that science is not a set of immutable theories or laws, but of hypotheses, which have long been, and are still being altered with the progress of thought and experiment.[1] Science today is far more advanced than it was two or three centuries ago, so that by comparison the science (or 'natural philosophy') of the earlier period may appear crude, elementary, or even empirical. But since the 'Scientific Revolution' of the late medieval and early modern period, 'the scientific method' has been fundamentally the same. Moreover, in a more general way, the influence of the Renaissance, of rationalism and the 'scientific spirit', appears to have opened up vast possibilities of Man's controlling and exploiting his environment 'by reason and experiment'.[2] This greatly influenced the attitudes of entrepreneurs as well as scientists.

C. Hill, *Intellectual Origins of the English Revolution* (1965); M. Purver, *The Royal Society: Concept and Creation* (1967). The debate has also given rise to many articles: see, for example, those by Merton and Hall referred to above, p. 37. For further references and evidence, see Musson and Robinson, op. cit., chap. 1. See also D. S. Kemsley, 'Religious Influences in the Rise of Modern Science', *Annals of Science*, vol. 24 (1968).

[1] See T. S. Kuhn, *The Structure of Scientific Revolutions*, vol. II, no. 2, of the *International Encyclopedia of Unified Science* (Chicago, 1962). See also Musson and Robinson, op. cit., introduction.

[2] J. S. Duesenberry, 'Some Aspects of the Theory of Economic Development', *Explorations in Entrepreneurial History*, vol. III, no. 2 (December 1950), pp. 73-4. Duesenberry attaches more importance to this than to the 'Protestant ethic'.

Francis Bacon and his successors in the Royal Society, such as Boyle and Hooke, were passionately concerned with making science useful, and although the uses of applied science were limited in the seventeenth century, there is little doubt that there were some fruitful interactions between natural philosophy and industry. Usher, referring to the development of the suction pump and steam engine, and to the manufacture of scientific instruments, clocks and watches, has concluded: 'The sixteenth and seventeenth centuries mark the transition from complete empiricism to engineering techniques fully grounded in mathematics and applied science.'[1] Similarly, the late Dr Gibbs, who, before his death was the most knowledgeable authority on the early modern chemical industry, considered that by the first half of the eighteenth century 'the point had been reached where science, and particularly chemistry, could begin to give a lead to several manufactures'.[2] Professor Rees has also pointed out that, during the late sixteenth and seventeenth centuries, 'a more scientific attitude was being brought to bear on technical processes preparatory to the Revolution of the eighteenth century'.[3]

These developments continued during the Industrial Revolution, in which the role of science has, until recently, been considerably underestimated, or even ignored. The long-established view, still by no means defunct, has been that the inventors and innovators of that period were mostly practical, often illiterate men, whose achievements were almost entirely products of empiricism, or trial and error, practical experience, and native wit. Nor has this view been confined to economic historians. Some scientists, such as Dr Hardie, have continued to emphasize 'the empirical tradition'. While he admits, somewhat contradictorily, that the Renaissance witnessed 'the

[1] In Singer *et al.*, *History of Technology*, vol. III, p. 344. Professor Hall, however, while acknowledging that there were some significant advances, supports the 'empirical' viewpoint, e.g. 'Engineering and the Scientific Revolution', *Technology and Culture*, vol. II (1961).

[2] *History of Technology*, vol. III, p. 706. See also his 'Essay Review – Prelude to Chemistry in Industry', *Annals of Science*, vol. 8 (1952), in which he shows 'that applied chemistry in England has a long background history', and that by the early eighteenth century there was fruitful collaboration 'between chemists and the leading manufacturers in many parts of the country'.

[3] Rees, op. cit., foreword.

emergence of the scientific method and modern technologies', he considers that empiricism predominated in the chemical industry as late as the end of the nineteenth century.[1] It is now becoming clear, however, that this traditional view is inadequately based on historical research and that applied science played a considerably more important role than has been generally realized.

Bowden was one of the first historians to recognize this,[2] pointing out the growing spirit of rational inquiry, the increasing interest in 'experimental and applied science', expressed at the national level in the Royal Society and Society of Arts, and locally in such bodies as the Manchester Literary and Philosophical Society, the development of education, particularly in new colleges and schools where more attention was paid to 'the useful arts and sciences', and the growing numbers of periodicals, encyclopedias, dictionaries of arts and sciences, etc., containing scientific and technical information. Ashton also appreciated the significance of these developments:[3]

> The stream of English scientific thought, issuing from the teaching of Francis Bacon, and enlarged by the genius of Boyle and Newton, was one of the main tributaries of the industrial revolution. . . . Physicists and chemists, such as Franklin, Black, Priestley, Dalton, and Davy, were in intimate contact with the leading figures in British industry; there was much coming and going between the laboratory and the workshop, and men like James Watt, Josiah Wedgwood, William Reynolds, and James Keir were at home in the one as in the other. The names of engineers, ironmasters, industrial chemists, and instrument-makers on the list of Fellows of the Royal Society show how close were the relations between science and practice at this time.

[1] D. W. F. Hardie, 'The Empirical Tradition in Chemical Technology', the first Davis-Swindin Memorial Lecture, Loughborough, 1962. Dr Hardie, however, appears almost to equate 'applied science' with 'empiricism', in distinguishing it from 'pure' science. Moreover, some of his own researches hardly support this view. See below, chap. 7, for his article on the Macintoshes and the early chemical industry.

[2] Bowden, op. cit., chap. 1.

[3] T. S. Ashton, *The Industrial Revolution 1760–1830* (1948), pp. 16, 19–21.

More recent studies have confirmed the importance of the links between science and industry in that period.[1] The general background of knowledge, education, and training, now being stressed by economists in regard to modern technological progress, has been shown to have been vitally significant during the Industrial Revolution. The work of educational historians, especially Dr Hans,[2] has been followed by further research which has demonstrated in considerable detail the profusion of schools, colleges, libraries, books, periodicals, encyclopedias, philosophical societies, itinerant lecturers, etc. during the late eighteenth and early nineteenth centuries – with growing emphasis on mathematics, science, and technology – and how much more widespread was scientific–technical education, both formal and informal, than has hitherto been realized.[3] It is clear that the diffusion of such knowledge took place at all levels, ranging from the highest scientific advances down to elementary instruction in mathematics, mechanics, etc. for humble artisans and craftsmen. In the Royal Society and Society of Arts, scientifically-minded industrialists mingled with eminent philosophers; there was a similar community of interests in local societies such as the Birmingham Lunar Society,[4] the Manchester Literary and Philosophical Society, and innumerable similar, but less famous, bodies established in

[1] See, for example, in addition to the previously cited works by Musson and Robinson, A. and N. L. Clow, *The Chemical Revolution* (1952); R. E. Schofield, *The Lunar Society of Birmingham* (1963); S. Pollard, *The Genesis of Modern Management* (1965), chap. IV.

[2] N. Hans, *New Trends in Eighteenth-Century Education* (1951).

[3] Musson and Robinson, op. cit., especially chap. III. Professor D. C. Coleman has, with evident prejudice, accused us of exaggerated pretensions to originality, referring particularly to Ashton's earlier work (*Economic History Review*, 2nd ser., vol. XXIII, no. 3, December 1970, pp. 575–6). In fact, however, we explicitly acknowledged that we were 'not, of course, the first to explore this territory' (op. cit., p. 7); we fully acknowledged Ashton's prior discernment (pp. vii and 88), though he devoted only a few paragraphs to scientific–technological aspects of the Industrial Revolution; and we clearly recognized the earlier work of other scholars, such as Wolf, Clark, Singer, Hall, Clow, Schofield, Hans, etc. (see pp. 7, 87–8, and innumerable other references). At the same time we can justifiably claim to have produced a great deal of entirely new material, and to have brought about 'some modification of the traditional view of the Industrial Revolution' (p. 189), as other well-informed reviewers, such as Landes, Schofield, Pollard, etc., have fully recognized.

[4] See below, chap. 5, by Professor Schofield.

provincial towns throughout the country; while ordinary mill-wrights, builders, weavers, etc. sometimes belonged to the smaller local clubs, foreshadowing the later mechanics' insti-tutes. Some leading industrialists were educated either at the universities, especially in Scotland, or in Dissenting academies, while many others achieved remarkable feats of 'self-education', with the aid of books and libraries, and courses by itinerant lecturers, whose audiences, often very large and varied, could see numerous practical models of machinery, etc. The impor-tance of an educated, knowledgeable, and experienced class of managers has also been demonstrated: the 'managerial revolu-tion' is not as recent a phenomenon as has usually been imagined.[1] There seems, indeed, little doubt that in the Indus-trial Revolution, as in modern economic growth, the impor-tance of the 'capital stock of knowledge', of 'human capital' and 'investment in human beings', in improved education and training, has hitherto been seriously neglected, together with associated developments in applied science and technology. These developments were important not only in major applica-tions of scientific knowledge to industrial problems, but also less dramatically, though more extensively, in innumerable piecemeal improvements resulting from the improving literacy and numeracy of the mass of entrepreneurs, managers, and skilled workers, among whom technical knowledge was being diffused through an increasing multiplicity of channels.

In all these educational developments, as well as in the related industrial changes, there is no doubt that Noncon-formists, especially certain groups such as the Quakers and Unitarians, played a major role, out of all proportion to their numbers in the population. The emphasis by Merton and others on the scientific–technological significance of the 'Puritan ethic' in the earlier period receives considerable support from researches into the Industrial Revolution. Raistrick and others have revealed the multifarious activities of Nonconformists in industry, trade, and banking;[2] the Clows have shown the links

[1] Pollard, op. cit.
[2] A. Raistrick, *Quakers in Science and Industry* (1950); I. Grubb, *Quakerism and Industry before 1800* (1930); E. D. Bebb, *Nonconformity and Social and Economic Life, 1660–1800* (1934); R. V. Holt, *The Unitarian Contribution to Social Progress in England*, 2nd ed. (1952).

between Scottish universities, Dissenting academies, and scientific–industrial innovations;[1] McClelland has also emphasized the superiority of Dissenting education and childhood training in 'achievement motivation', leading to entrepreneurial enterprise and technological innovation;[2] and Hagen has similarly stressed the psychological drives of these 'alienated' or 'disparaged' groups, who were impelled to strive for improved status in scientific or industrial achievement.[3]

There is no doubt of the immense importance of these socio-psychological forces, and of the associated educational–scientific–technological factors, in the Industrial Revolution, which cannot, therefore, any longer be explained simply in economic terms of supply and demand. There is now plentiful evidence of fruitful collaboration between industrialists and scientists, and of applications of science in various fields. A few examples only must suffice here. The early steam engine, it is now clear, owed much to the scientific researches of philosophers such as Boyle and Huygens in the seventeenth century and was not just a product of empiricists such as Savery and Newcomen.[4] Watt's improvements were similarly based on scientific knowledge and careful experimental researches, while he benefited considerably from contact not only with Professor Black, discoverer of the principle of latent heat, but also with other scientists at Glasgow University, particularly Anderson and Robison.[5] Trevithick was likewise aided in his development of the high-pressure engine by scientific advice from Davies Gilbert (or Giddy).[6] Water-wheels, moreover, which have generally been regarded, by comparison with steam engines, as a part of 'traditional' technology,[7] were, in fact, enormously improved in efficiency and power as a result of practical–scientific experiments, particularly by John

[1] Clow, op. cit., *passim*. On the role of the Dissenting academies, see also Irene Parker, *Dissenting Academies in England* (1914), and H. McLachlan, *English Education under the Test Acts* (Manchester, 1931).
[2] McClelland, op. cit., pp. 46–57, 132–49.   [3] Hagen, op. cit., chap. XIII.
[4] See the introduction by A. E. Musson to H. W. Dickinson, *Short History of the Steam Engine*, 2nd ed. (1963).
[5] Musson and Robinson, *Science and Technology*, pp. 79–80, and *James Watt and the Steam Revolution*. See below, pp. 108–9.
[6] Musson and Robinson, *Science and Technology*, pp, 80–1. See below, p. 109.
[7] See, for example, Lilley, *Technical Progress*, pp. 8–9.

Smeaton, and by other scientifically-minded hydraulic engineers including Hewes, Rennie, and Fairbairn.[1] As Cardwell has demonstrated, there were also close links between science and technology in the development of water as well as of steam power.[2] Even the ordinary millwright, as Fairbairn emphasized, usually had a good knowledge of arithmetic, geometry, machine-drawing, and mechanics, as well as wide constructional experience,[3] while leading engineers such as those mentioned were generally as able in 'practical science' as the philosophers with whom they associated, sometimes more so.[4]

Similarly, in applied chemistry there is accumulating evidence not only from the chemical manufactures themselves, producing acids, alkalis, etc.,[5] but also from allied trades such as glass, pottery, and soap. Josiah Wedgwood, for instance, has been revealed as an able research chemist, employing Alexander Chisholm, a Scottish graduate and previously laboratory assistant to the then-famous industrial chemist Dr William Lewis.[6] James Keir, like Wedgwood a Fellow of the Royal Society and member of the philosophical society meeting at the Chapter Coffee House in London, as well as of the Birmingham Lunar Society, was another product of the Scottish universities, who not only applied his chemical knowledge in the manufacture of glass, soap, etc., at his famous works at Tipton in Staffordshire, but also wrote a *Dictionary of Chemistry* (1789), in which he referred to the 'diffusion of a general knowledge, and of a taste for science' as being 'the characteristic feature of the present age'.[7] In textile chemistry, the introduc-

[1] Musson and Robinson, *Science and Technology*, pp. 67–71, 73–4, 76, 98, 445–6, 481–2.

[2] D. S. L. Cardwell, 'Power Technologies and the Advancement of Science, 1700–1825', *Technology and Culture*, vol. VI, no. 2 (Spring 1965), and 'Some Factors in the Early Development of the Concepts of Power, Work and Energy', *British Journal for the History of Science*, vol. III (1966–7).

[3] W. Fairbairn, *Treatise on Mills and Millwork* (1861–3), vol. I, pp. v–vi. See below, p. 100.

[4] As Professor Robison acknowledged in the case of Watt.

[5] See below, chaps. 6, 7, and 8, by Clow, Hardie, and Gibbs.

[6] R. E. Schofield, 'Josiah Wedgwood, Industrial Chemist', *Chymia*, vol. 5 (1959); Musson and Robinson, op. cit., p. 78. See below, p. 106.

[7] Musson and Robinson, op. cit., *passim*; J. L. Moilliet, 'James Keir of the Lunar Society', *Notes and Records of the Royal Society of London*, vol. 22, nos. 1 and 2 (September 1967).

tion of vitriol sours and chlorine bleach not only resulted from researches by scientists such as Home, Scheele, and Berthollet, but was also considerably aided by industrial chemists in its development and diffusion. In Manchester, enterprising manufacturers such as Henry, Cooper, Taylor, and others who were outstanding in their chemical knowledge, played leading roles in the scientific–technical advances made in bleaching, dyeing, and calico-printing.[1] In Scotland, Charles Macintosh, who had studied at Glasgow and Edinburgh universities and was 'equipped with the best training that the "pure" chemistry of his day afforded', played a similar pioneering role in textile-chemical manufactures as well as in later founding the rubber industry in Manchester.[2]

In Manchester, as in Birmingham, many of the leading cotton-spinners and engineers, including Lee, Ewart, Kennedy, Hewes, Fairbairn, and Nasmyth, were well versed in theory as well as practice; they collaborated with men of science, and put their theoretical knowledge to industrial use in the construction of improved machinery.[3] Similar links between science and industry have been discovered in other industries and in other areas. Thus we find Thomas Telford, the famous road and bridge builder, going 'chemistry mad', avidly reading the works of Black, Fourcroy, and other chemists, to find out more about building materials, cramming mechanics, hydrostatics, and other scientific information into his working notebook, and collaborating with scientists in practical scientific publications and experiments;[4] John Rennie, the famous London engineer, another Scottish graduate, applying his scientific knowledge in construction of water-wheels, mills, and bridges;[5] John Southern, Boulton and Watt's manager, experimenting on heavy machinery to elucidate the theory of mechanics, reading papers on the subject to the Royal Society

[1] Musson and Robinson, op. cit., especially chaps. VII, VIII, and IX.

[2] D. W. F. Hardie, 'The Macintoshes and the Origins of the Chemical Industry', *Chemistry and Industry* (June 1952), reproduced below, chap. 7. Musson and Robinson, op. cit., pp. 293–5, 322–6; Clow, op. cit., *passim*.

[3] Musson and Robinson, op. cit., *passim*.

[4] Ibid., pp. 74–6. See below, pp. 102–4.

[5] C. T. G. Boucher, *John Rennie 1761–1821* (Manchester, 1963); Musson and Robinson, op. cit., pp. 76–7. See below, pp. 104–5.

(like Smeaton and other engineers), and holding his own with university professors in applied mathematics (in bridge-building, for example);[1] David Mushet, the famous Scottish ironmaster, writing a remarkable series of papers in the *Philosophical Magazine*, based on brilliant applications of chemistry and mineralogy to iron smelting and forging;[2] John Marshall, the great Leeds flax-spinner, carrying out prolonged experiments in chlorine bleaching, with the aid of the latest chemical publications and skilled French chemists.[3] So one could go on, almost endlessly.

At the same time, of course, traditional crafts and skills continued to be extremely important. Many trades and processes, in fact, remained largely if not entirely empirical, and even in those where science was applied, it had to be combined with much empirical trial-and-error. It is interesting to find one of the leading textile engineers in Manchester unconsciously confirming from his own practical experience the truth of Adam Smith's observation on the importance simply of subdivision and specialization of labour.[4] Where scientific theory was utilized, it was often rudimentary. For this and other reasons some scholars, such as Professor Mathias and Dr Gillispie, continue to be somewhat sceptical.[5] Gillispie, for instance, to some extent shares Hardie's view as to the long-continued importance of empiricism in the manufacture of soda.[6] He points out that the chemical reactions in the Leblanc process were not properly understood scientifically until nearly a century later, and considers, therefore, that Leblanc cannot be said to have applied chemical theory in inventing the process. But Gillispie does not take proper account of the evolution of scientific theory: it would seem that, by his view of science, nothing can be called scientific until complete and pure scientific truth has been established. (Has it even yet?)

---

[1] Musson and Robinson, op. cit., p. 172 n. 5.

[2] Ibid., pp. 184–5.

[3] Ibid., pp. 329–32; W. G. Rimmer, *Marshall's of Leeds, Flax-Spinners. 1788–1886* (1960), pp. 50–3. See below, pp. 106–7.

[4] Musson and Robinson, op. cit., p. 64.

[5] See below, chaps. 1 and 4.

[6] In addition to chap. 4, below, see C. C. Gillispie, 'The Discovery of the Leblanc Process', *Isis*, vol. 48 (1957).

Many chemical theories of the late eighteenth century may appear to some modern scientific minds as crude and 'wrong', but Leblanc, Berthollet, and others were among the leading scientists of their day, and were applying the best scientific knowledge then available, in fields such as soda manufacture and bleaching. What is significant and truly scientific is their rational, controlled experimental procedure.

S. D. Chapman, reviewing *Science and Technology*, accuses us of almost entirely ignoring empirical techniques and of exaggerating the importance of scientific technology; he quotes from the millwright, John Sutcliffe, to indicate the inadequacies of contemporary scientific theory.[1] Regrettably, however, he does not appear to have read our book very carefully, otherwise he could hardly have failed to notice the innumerable passages where, in fact, we emphasize 'the continued importance of practical craftsmanship'; indeed we point out that such empiricism was of 'immense and probably predominant importance'.[2] We repeatedly stress that

> we do not wish to exaggerate the extent to which natural philosophy contributed to 'arts and manufactures' in the Industrial Revolution. This period was, of course, a transitional one, and traditional handicrafts, with their rule-of-thumb procedures, proved remarkably long-lasting in many industries, while even in those industries which were being most rapidly 'revolutionized' it is clear that practical empiricism was largely responsible for technical advance. Several of our studies, in engineering and dyeing, for example, ... demonstrate its continued importance.[3]

We ourselves quoted contemporary opinion as to the limited applicability and sometimes erroneous principles of eighteenth-

[1] *Textile History*, vol. 1, no. 3 (December 1970), pp. 373-5.

[2] *Science and Technology*, pp. vii-viii and 65. See also pp. 7-8, 27, 38, 49-50, 56, 67, 81-4, 189, etc. It is remarkable that in a journal concerned specifically with textiles, this reviewer should make no reference whatever either to our extensive researches into early textile engineering in Lancashire, with its heavy reliance on traditional crafts, or (on the other hand) to the abundant evidence we have produced on the applications of chemistry in bleaching and dyeing (in which, however, empirical techniques also remained extremely important).

[3] Ibid., pp. 7-8. See also below, pp. 97-9, and 109-13.

century 'natural philosophy'.[1] In fact, we made the very point which Chapman imagines he has discovered, that philosophers such as Desaguliers and Banks were wrong in some of their theorizing on water-wheels, etc.,[2] and we also demonstrated repeatedly the importance of traditional millwrights (including Sutcliffe, incidentally).[3] On the other hand, what Chapman also overlooks is the fact that the three most outstanding hydraulic engineers of the age – Smeaton, Hewes, and Fairbairn – were all notable for their applied scientific achievements, and that many ordinary millwrights acquired knowledge of mathematics, mechanics, etc. for utilitarian purposes.

Cardwell has similarly shown how engineering theory gradually evolved, how it was applied to practical problems, and how practical experiment modified theory.[4] He also demonstrates that in mechanical engineering, as in chemistry, French scientists led the way. This French scientific predominance (though perhaps exaggerated) has led to the questioning of the significance of applied science in Britain during the Industrial Revolution, for if science were of fundamental importance to industrial development, one would have expected France to have achieved industrial leadership. This, however, is perhaps taking too narrowly national a view of the interconnexions between science and technology. Scientific ideas were not confined within national boundaries, as Sir Gavin de Beer has emphasized,[5] and there were many fruitful contacts not only between British, French, and other scientists, but also between the latter and British industrialists, who in some cases met or corresponded with foreign philosophers, and in many more cases studied their published works (either in the foreign language or in translations, which were very quickly made), and applied this knowledge in engineering, chemical manufactures, bleaching and dyeing, etc. While France was ahead in many branches of scientific theory, the reverse appears to have been the case in applied or industrial science, and practical-

---

[1] See, for example, ibid., pp. 82–4. See also below, pp. 110–13.
[2] Ibid., pp. 37, 73 n. 7, 83–4, and 107 n. 9.
[3] See, for example, ibid., pp. 443–5, in addition to previous references. See also below, pp. 97–9.
[4] See above, p. 63 n.2
[5] Sir Gavin de Beer, *The Sciences were never at War* (1960).

scientific knowledge seems to have been more widely and deeply diffused in Britain than in France. At the same time, of course, Britain had certain economic advantages over France, in natural resources (especially coal) and wider overseas trade and empire, as well as institutional advantages such as freedom from internal tolls and fewer Government restrictions, together with social advantages such as a more developed and enterprising middle class and greater social mobility.[1]

In the end, then, one has to recognize the existence of a multiplicity of interacting factors – economic, social, political, and psychological, as well as scientific and technical – among which there is not much possibility of indicating preponderance. Certainly there is no possibility whatever of *measuring* the percentage contribution of science and technology to economic growth in this period, either at the national level or even at that of the individual firm. A 'disaggregated', qualitative approach is the only feasible one, while bearing in mind the general concepts now emerging from economic, sociological, and psychological analysis in this field.[2]

[1] See F. Crouzet, 'Angleterre et France au XVIIIᵉ Siècle. Essai d'Analyse Comparée de Deux Croissances Economiques', *Annales* (1966), trans. in Hartwell, op. cit.

[2] Professor Coleman has made some absurdly distorting comments on what he alleges to be our exaggerated claims to have reinterpreted the whole Industrial Revolution in scientific–technological terms, without reference to economic and social factors (*Economic History Review*, vol. XXIII, no. 3, December 1970, pp. 575–6). If, however, he had read our Preface and Introduction, instead of quoting misleadingly from the publisher's 'blurb', he would have found our claims to be modest and cautious, combined with a clear warning statement, strongly emphasized in italics (Musson and Robinson, op. cit., p. 8), '*that scientific and technological factors were by no means entirely responsible for the Industrial Revolution, and that they were closely related to the economic and social changes of the time. But we do not propose in this book to deal explicitly with these complex interrelationships.*' While we recognized the importance of population growth, trade expansion, transport developments, capital investment, etc., we emphasized that our researches were more narrowly concerned with producing new evidence on the scientific–technological changes.

1 Who Unbound Prometheus? Science and Technical Change, 1600–1800[1]

PETER MATHIAS

This article is from Peter Mathias (ed.), *Science and Society*, *1600–1900*, Cambridge University Press, 1972,

I

An economic historian is interested in science not for its own sake (which for a historian of science is doubtless the only academically respectable way of looking at it) but for his own utilitarian purposes. He asks the questions: how was science related to technology at this time? how far did scientific change influence the process of technological change? to what extent was the Industrial Revolution associated with scientific advance? Taking the very long view from medieval times to the present day is to see a dramatic change in these relationships. Broadly, we may postulate the earlier position as a context where empirical discoveries and the development of industrial processes in such industries as metals, textiles, brewing, dyeing took place and advanced without being directly consequential upon knowledge of fundamental scientific relationships in the materials concerned. The chemistry of what happened inside a blast furnace was not known until the mid-decades of the nineteenth century. The secrets of fermentation were first revealed by Pasteur. There might be close links between science and technology in other ways, but this was none the less a world very different from our own where industrial advance becomes more directly consequential upon the advancing frontier of scientific and technological knowledge, with a developing institutional relationship between science and industry to consolidate the connexion.

[1] © 1972 Cambridge University Press. An early version of this article appeared in the *Yorkshire Bulletin of Economic and Social Research*, vol. XXI (I), 1969.

For the pivotal period of the seventeenth and eighteenth centuries, however, which saw dramatic advances in both scientific knowledge and industrial techniques, varying answers have been offered to these questions by economic historians and scholars generalizing about the relationships from the side of science. Professor A. R. Hall summed up for the earlier period 1660–1760 ' . . . we have not much reason to believe that in the early stages, at any rate, learning or literacy had anything to do with it [technological change]; on the contrary, it seems likely that virtually all the techniques of civilization up to a couple of hundred years ago were the work of men as uneducated as they were anonymous'.[1] Sir Eric Ashby concludes for the period 1760–1860: 'There were a few "cultivators of science" (as they were called) engaged in research, but their work was not regarded as having much bearing on education and still less on technology. There was practically no exchange of ideas between the scientists and the designers of industrial processes.'[2] Professor Landes is equally firm in this opinion to as late as 1850.[3] A. P. Usher is in the same tradition.[4]

Equally forthright assertions crowd the other side of the stage. 'The stream of English scientific thought,' writes Professor Ashton, 'was one of the main tributaries of the Industrial Revolution. . . . The names of engineers, iron-masters, industrial chemists, and instrument makers on the list of Fellows of the Royal Society show how close were the relations between science and practice at this time.'[5] Professor Rostow, considering the whole sweep of economic change in western Europe, gives the two essential features of post-medieval Europe as 'the discovery and re-discovery of regions beyond western Europe, and the initially slow but then accelerating development of modern scientific knowledge and

[1] A. R. Hall, *The Historical Relations of Science and Technology* (inaugural lecture) (London, 1963). J. D. Bernal, *Science in History* (London, 1954), pp. 345–6, 352, 354–5, 365–6, 370 argues in a similar vein.

[2] Sir E. Ashby, *Technology and the Academics* (London, 1958), pp. 50–1.

[3] D. Landes in *Cambridge Economic History of Europe*, vol. VI, pt. 1 (Cambridge, 1965), pp. 333, 343, 550–1; also *The Unbound Prometheus* (1969), pp. 104, 113–4, 323.

[4] A. P. Usher, *A History of Mechanical Invention* (Boston, 1954 ed.) contains very little reference to the role of science in this period.

[5] T. S. Ashton, *The Industrial Revolution* (London, 1948), pp. 15–16.

attitudes'.[1] When considering the essential propensies for economic growth (relationships that he does not specifically limit in time or place) the first two on his list are: 'the propensity to develop fundamental science and to apply science to economic ends'.[2] For the English case A. E. Musson and E. Robinson have recently sought to demonstrate how extensive the linkages were between innovation and science, between scientists and entrepreneurs.[3] They see this co-operation assisting England to 'retain that scientific lead over the Continent upon which she established her industrial supremacy'.[4] The Lunar Society, now documented at great length, has been called 'a pilot project or advance guard of the Industrial Revolution' on the argument that 'strong currents of scientific research underlie critical parts of this movement'.[5]

Many more such summary assertions could be deployed on either side. It seems likely that, as historians explore more systematically and in more local detail the development of different branches of the chemical industry and other industrial processes involving chemistry (following up the seminal work on the Chemical Revolution by A. and A. N. Clow, published in 1952); as they find out more about the various local societies of gentlemen meeting in small towns up and down the country in the eighteenth century on the lines of the Lunar Society of Birmingham, the balance will tip heavily towards the positive equation. This theme is captured in the remark: '. . . science is the mother of invention; finance is its father'.[6]

The question, therefore, invites discussion. The arguments, however, should be prefaced with one or two comments.

[1] W. W. Rostow, *The Stages of Economic Growth* (Cambridge, 1960), p. 31.

[2] W. W. Rostow, *The Process of Economic Growth* (New York, 1952), p. 23.

[3] A. E. Musson and E. Robinson, 'Science and Industry in the late Eighteenth Century', *Economic History Review*, vol. XIII (1960), pp. 222–4; *Science and Technology in the Industrial Revolution* (Manchester, 1969).

[4] E. Robinson, 'The Lunar Society and the Improvement of Scientific Instruments II', *Annals of Science*, vol. XIII (1957).

[5] R. E. Schofield, *The Lunar Society of Birmingham* (Oxford, 1963), pp. 410, 437. The argument is summed up on pp. 436–40. See also the special issue of the *University of Birmingham Historical Journal* (vol. XI, no. 1, 1967) devoted to the Lunar Society, particularly the articles by E. Robinson, M. J. Wise and R. E. Schofield; E. Robinson, 'The Lunar Society, Its Membership and Organization', *Newcomen Society Transactions*, vol. XXXV (1962–3).

[6] T. H. Marshall, *James Watt* (London, 1925), p. 84.

F

Without the assumption that a simple, linear, cause-and-effect relationship exists between phenomena like scientific knowledge and innovations in technique, multi-dimensional historical developments such as the Renaissance or the French Revolution or the Fall of the Roman Empire or the Industrial Revolution, cease to be analysable in terms of single-cause, single-variable phenomena. In the last analysis, quantification of contributory causes of them is impossible, given the intractable nature of the evidence and the subtlety of the inter-relationships, direct and indirect, involved. Therefore, no intellectually satisfying proof becomes possible that one answer is demonstrably 'correct' in a scientifically provable way. Quantification does not offer any obvious solution either. One might hope that, taking a defined population of innovations, it would be possible to determine the percentage which depended upon scientific knowledge, or to allocate degrees of such dependence upon some quantified scale. But establishing the criteria of such a scale would be subjective enough, while yet greater discretion would remain in allocating most innovations to the different boxes. Moreover, innovations form a most heterogeneous collection, differing very greatly in relative importance. Bringing qualitative considerations into the argument would imply further discretionary allocation of innovations into a scale of importance so that the degree of dependence of innovations upon scientific knowledge could be construed against some norm of economic significance. Were the scientifically-orientated innovations in the 'population' more, or less, important than their arithmetical proportion suggests?

The question of the *strategic* importance of innovations raises a further issue. For example, despite the percentage of total technical change subject to the linkage with science being small, a strategic blockage on a narrow front at the frontier of technical possibilities might hold up innovation in a wider span behind it. One strategic science-linked innovation could make possible a large number of empirically-based innovations which were, to a degree, dependent upon that initial advance, and vice versa. Moreover, it is impossible to demonstrate the potential quantitative importance of this by being able to indicate what would have happened if an absolute blockage at the frontier had occurred without substitute arrangements bypassing the obstruction. Perhaps detailed analysis can be applied in the micro-study of particular innovations (carefully chosen), but it is difficult to see how a quantified assessment can be made for the wide sweep of innovations under discussion here. History is a depressingly inexact science as economists – let alone natural scientists – discover to their frustration.

Conclusions in this field are also much influenced by methodological or definitional problems. Controversies on such general themes characteristically sink under the weight of semantic disagreement and pleas for more systematic research. What do we include in (or exclude from) the concept 'innovation'? Were the activities of these seventeenth and eighteenth-century people, properly speaking 'scientific'? Was it *real* science, identified by some later, designated, objective norm – in the 'Baconian' or mechanistic tradition – or was it bogus, mistaken, irrational – and following a magical, alchemical, or Hermetical tradition?[1] How much, for example, can one claim for Jethro Tull, eagerly pursuing 'scientific' technique in agriculture on the assumption that air was the greatest of all manures and that the fertility of soil consequently varied in direct correlation with the amount of ploughing and pulverizing that it received, to the exclusion of all else. Bogus science, quasi science, mistaken science, amateur science which was so very prominent in the seventeenth and eighteenth centuries, particularly in the field of chemistry (where the direct linkage between science and industry are probably most diffused) does raise interesting issues. Does one judge these practitioners by their intentions, their motivations, or by their results, however mistaken their assumptions, looked at *ex post facto* with hindsight? Arguments about distinctions between 'pure' and 'applied' science relate to these controversies, for the seventeenth and eighteenth centuries no less than the nineteenth and twentieth.[2]

---

[1] P. Rattansi, 'The Social Interpretation of Seventeenth Century Science', in P. Mathias (ed.), *Sciene and Society, 1600–1900* (Cambridge, 1972).

[2] R. K. Merton, 'Science, Technology and Society in Seventeenth-Century England', *Osiris*, vol. IV (1938); A. R. Hall, 'Merton revisited: Science and

This paper will first explore the positive case and then consider its qualifications.[1] The key question to be answered is not what examples can be found of links between science and industry in the period but rather how important relative to other sources of impetus was scientific knowledge to industrial progress? Can it be judged 'an engine of growth' for innovation, or a pre-condition? In short, how extensive were the linkages, how strategic, how direct?

II

If economic history is written from the evidence of intention, of aspiration and endeavour, rather than the evidence of results (which is often less accessible), then these connexions appear very intimate indeed. In the first place, a very large number of persons – scientists, industrialists, publicists, and government servants – said loudly in the seventeenth century and have gone on saying ever since then, even more loudly, that the linkage was important and ought to be encouraged. For most of the 'professional' scientists of the Restoration the improvement of techniques in the material world, science in the service of a technological utopia, was a subordinate quest, a relatively low priority. But, even so, many such as Robert Boyle, were active on both sides of the watershed between searching for knowledge and applying knowledge to practice, and certainly acknowledged that *one* of the roles of science was to help where it could. Boyle's *Usefulness of Natural Philosophy* (1664) was a systematic survey of the methods then used in industry and

Society in the Seventeenth Century', *History of Science*, vol. II (1963); C. C. Gillespie, 'The Natural History of Industry', *Isis*, vol. *XLVIII* (1957).

[1] An equivalent, and connected debate, which will not be considered here, is in progress over these relationships, and that of religion, in the seventeenth century. See H. K. Kearney, *Origins of the Scientific Revolution* (London, 1964); C. Hill, *The Intellectual Origins of the English Revolution* (Oxford, 1965), C. Hill, H. F. Kearney, and T. K. Rabb in *Past and Present*. vols. XXVIII (p. 81), XXIX (p. 88), XXXI (pp. 104, 111), XXXII (p. 110). The thesis was formulated by R. K. Merton, 'Science, Technology, and Society in Seventeenth-Century England', *Osiris* (1938). See also S. F. Mason, 'The Scientific Revolution and the Protestant Revolution', *Annals of Science*, vol. IX (1953); D. S. Kemsley, 'Religious Influences in the Rise of Modern Science', *Annals of Science*, vol. XXIV (1968). This, in turn, is an extension of the much older debate about the links between Protestantism and Capitalism, from Max Weber.

of the ways in which science was improving them and would continue to do so. 'These [mechanical] arts', he wrote, 'ought to be looked upon as really belonging to the history of nature in its full and due extent.'[1] 'There is much real benefit to be learned [from mathematical or philosophical inquiries],' wrote Dr J. Wilkins in 1648, 'particularly for such gentlemen as employ their estates in those chargeable adventures of Drayning, Mines, Cole-pits, etc. . . . And also for such *common artificers* as are well skilled in the *practise* of the arts. . . .'[2] Boyle was himself active particularly in investigating the techniques of mining, assaying, and agriculture. In evidence of intention, if not of result, John Richardson changed the title of his book on *Philosophical Principles of the Art of Brewing*, much taken up by the largest brewers in London, to *Philosophical Principles of the Science of Brewing*.[3] R. Shannon's more empirically titled work *Practical Treatise on Brewing* was primarily a plea that brewers and distillers should profit from contact with 'men of reflection acquainted with first principles who have more methodically considered the subject'. 'Chemistry', he remarked, 'is as much the basis of arts and manufactures, as mathematics is the fundamental principle of mechanics.'[4] They were echoing a traditional sentiment which continued to reverberate until scientific discoveries with major implications for technology in the industry really were made by Pasteur and others in the mid-nineteenth century.

Two eminent Victorians, out of many, may be quoted to show the canon during the nineteenth century. Charles Babbage, writing *On the Economy of Machinery and Manufactures* (1835) concluded: '. . . it is impossible not to perceive that the arts and manufactures of the country are intimately connected with the progress of the severer sciences; and that, as we advance in the career of improvement, every step requires, for its success, that this connexion should be rendered more

[1] Cf. A. R. Hall, *Ballistics in the Seventeenth Century* (Cambridge, 1952), p. 3; also G. N. Clark, *Science and Social Welfare in the Age of Newton* (Oxford, 1937), p. 14.

[2] J. Wilkins, *Mathematicall Magick* . . . (London, 1649), p. vi.

[3] J. Richardson, *Philosophical Principles of the Art of Brewing* (Hull, 1788); *Philosophical Principles of the Science of Brewing* (Hull, 1798).

[4] R. Shannon, *Practical Treatise on Brewing* (1804), pp. 48–9.

intimate.'[1] Dr Lyon Playfair, the forward-looking Scot who helped to organize the Great Exhibition of 1851 wrote, with justly famous perception: 'Raw material, formerly our capital advantage over other nations, is gradually being equalized in price, and made available to all by improvements in loco-motion, and Industry must in future be supported, not by a competition of local advantages, but by a competition of intellects.'[2] The assertion of the linkage has formed a con-tinuum; and still does.

Apart from such aspirations look also at what endeavours actually took place. The State actively sought to press scientists into utilitarian endeavour. A long list of instances can be drawn up. Typical examples are ballistics and navigation (improve-ments in cartography, scientific instruments, astronomy, mathematical tables, accurate time-keeping lay behind this). Much medical experimentation went on sponsored by the Admiralty, facing particular problems of maintaining efficiency in fleets, long on foreign station, from scurvy and other diseases. Standardization in production, in dockyards, of inter-changeable parts, exact measurement techniques were much encouraged by this. Industrial and scientific skills likely to be useful in war received particular attention. More widely, national rivalries became important in the seventeenth century for stimulating inventions in many industries where there was most technical progress – export industries, sugar refining, distilling, glass blowing, silk, tobacco, book printing, paper making, and others.[3]

The Royal Society in England of 1662, as the French *Académie* of 1666, personified such state patronage (although in England with virtually no public resources) for utilitarian ends, an intention explicitly stated in its first charter. The draft preamble of the statutes of the Royal Society ran: 'The business of the Royal Society is: to improve the knowledge of natural

---

[1] C. Babbage, *On the Economy of Manufactures* (London, 1835), p. 379, para. 453.

[2] Lyon Playfair, *Lectures on the Results of the Great Exhibition of 1851* (London, 1852). Royal Commissions joined the chorus in 1864 with the publication of the Taunton Commission report on technical and scientific education. Mark Pattison made the same plea in *Suggestions on Academical Organization* ... (Edinburgh, 1868).

[3] G. N. Clark, op. cit., p. 51 et seq.

things, and all useful arts, Manufactures, Mechanic practices, Engynes and Inventions by experiment. . . .'[1] Nothing could be more explicit. Its first historian stressed this need to focus the work of scientists upon technology; in the words of Thomas Sprat in 1667 its work was intended 'for the use of cities and not for the retirements of Schools'.[2] Pepys urged its members to 'principally aim at such experiments or observations as might prove of great and immediate use', and had the record searched for helps to navigation. The King, petitioned by 'projectors' with secret weapons to save an industry or confound the French, referred such proposals to the Society for vetting and report. Members divided themselves into special committees for this purpose. The *Philosophical Transactions* in the seventeenth century exemplify the common concern; experiments and reports intended to have practical applications, to agriculture as well as industry, had as much space or more devoted to them as any other. This, surely, is the breeding ground for innovation. The spark then jumps from the metropolitan scene of the Royal Society in its early days to the many provincial societies linking amateur scientists with gentlemen-manufacturers in the Lunar Society of Birmingham and very many others of lesser renown. Relatively obscure towns like Spalding, Northampton, Peterborough, and Maidstone for example, boasted such gatherings. Almost thirty are known to have existed.[3]

William Shipley called the Northampton Philosophical Society specifically a 'Royal Society in Miniature' – 'a Society of Gentlemen that are much addicted to all manner of natural knowledge'.[4] Most of these local societies had the specific aim

[1] See also M. Ornstein, *The Role of Scientific Societies in the Seventeenth Century* (Chicago, 1928), pp. 108–9. For details of the utilitarian aims of the French *Académie des Sciences* see chap. 5.

[2] T. Sprat, *History of the Royal Society* (London, 1667). See also J. G. Crowther, *The Social Relations of Science* (1967 ed.), pp. 274–87; C. R. Weld, *A History of the Royal Society* . . . (London, 1848), vol. I. pp. 146 et seq; vol. IV, section V; M. Purver, *The Royal Society: Concept and Creation* (London, 1967).

[3] D. McKie, 'Scientific Societies to the end of the Eighteenth Century' in A. Ferguson (ed.), *Natural Philosophy Through the Eighteenth Century* (1948); E Robinson, 'The Derby Philosophical Society', *Annals of Science*, vol. IX (1953); R. E. Schofield, *The Lunar Society* (Oxford, 1963); D. Hudson and K. W. Luckhurst, *The Royal Society of Arts* (London, 1954).

[4] D. G. C. Allan, *William Shipley* (London, 1968), p. 169.

of popularizing science and using scientific knowledge for practical ends in the improvement of practical skills in industry and agriculture – as with the national institutions of the Society of Arts (1754), founded by William Shipley, and the Royal Institution (1799), founded by Count Rumford, both of whom were passionate advocates of the application of science.

Next look at a growing list of examples of innovations which sprang, or appeared to spring, from this fertile soil of scientific discourse and social nexus between the men of science and industry. Steam-power above all; but also the adolescent chemical industry with chlorine-bleaching, sulphuric acid production, soda making, coal distillation.[1] James Watt, Dr John Roebuck, Josiah Wedgwood, Lord Dundonald, George and Charles Macintosh are the most well-known individuals who personify these connexions. The *extent* of interest in 'amateur science' coupled with the extent of endeavour in relating science to industry is remarkable, and in this, England is certainly unique in Europe. The important research of A. E. Musson and E. Robinson has placed all economic historians in their debt by revealing how extensive these interests were – almost, one might say, a 'sub-culture' of interest in science, faith in the possibilities of applying science and enthusiastic advocacy.

In fact, mathematics may well have played a wider role in these relationships than science until the end of the eighteenth century. Navigation techniques and improvements at sea (not alone sponsored by the navy), land-surveying techniques for estates, accountancy for business assaying, architectural drawing, spectacle-making are examples of practical skills that gained and were seen to gain, from mathematical knowledge. The Nonconformist and Quaker groups gave a prominent place to modern studies, particularly mathematics, that had a greater presence in new educational movements than science.[2]

---

[1] A long bibliography is contained in A. E. Musson and E. Robinson, *Science and Technology in the Industrial Revolution* (Manchester, 1969).

[2] S. Pollard, *The Genesis of Modern Management* (London, 1965), chap. 4; J. D. Bernal, *Science in History* (London, 1954), p. 346; N. Hans, *New Trends in Education in the Eighteenth Century* (London, 1951). A Mathematical Society was established in Spitalfields in 1717, and another at Manchester in 1718 (T. Kelly, *G. Birkbeck – Pioneer of Adult Education*, Liverpool, 1957, p. 66).

The observations of a distinguished user of the new mathematical knowledge for practical purposes underline this truth: 'We are sure of finding a Ship's place at Sea to a Degree and a half and generally to less than half a Degree,' wrote Captain James Cook, 'such are the improvements Navigation has received from the Astronomers of the Age by the Valuable Table they have communicated to the Publick under the direction of the Board of Longitude . . . [By] these Tables the Calculations are rendered short beyond conception and easy to the meanest capacity and can never be enough recommended to the Attention of all Sea Officers. . . . Much credit is also due to the Mathematical Instrument Makers for the improvements and accuracy with which their instruments are made for without good instruments the Tables would lose part of their use.'[1] The utility of such mathematical expertise coupled with precision measurement by new instruments for a trading, industrial, seafaring nation was sufficient for it to become institutionalized in schools on a fairly wide scale in eighteenth-century England. Rather than enlarge the catalogue of instances, however, let us now move to looking at some of the problems – acknowledging that a long list of such individual instances exists. It is the nature of the connexions between science and technical change, no less than the extent of the association between them which is in question.

III

The first complication is, perhaps, not a fundamental one within the European scene, although it raises important questions when relating science to innovation within a single country; or perhaps even more fundamentally when one compares scientific knowledge and its relation to technique (the general level of diffused technique rather than individual instances of 'best practice' technology) in Europe and beyond – say in China. The point is, simply, that we are much concerned with differences between national performances in industrial growth and innovation, in striving to explain the fact that the

[1] *Journals of Captain James Cook* (1768–79), ed. A. Grenfell Price (New York, Heritage Press, n.d.), pp. 112–13 (for 14 January 1773).

British economy advanced more extensively than others in this way, and became *relatively* so much more forward in adopting new techniques and developing new industries in 1750–1850 than other economies. This is particularly true of the general level of technique, productivity, and output characterizing growth industries (textiles, metal production, metal-using techniques, machine tools, machine making, particularly power engineering, chemicals, pottery, glass).

Scientific knowledge does not show, at all, the same concentration within Britain, particularly in the case of chemistry where the linkage between scientific knowledge and industrial innovation was probably most intimate. The advance of scientific knowledge was a European phenomenon. There was, in France, much greater state patronage for science through the *Académie des Sciences*, by military sponsorship, and direct industrial sponsorship, as with the research department attached to the Sèvres porcelain factory working on glazes, enamels, and paints. Provincial academies also flourished in the main regional cities.[1] In the *Description des Arts et Métiers* of Réamur 1761 one had a more elaborate schema published than any known in Britain. On balance, more systematic work was carried out in technology by scientists in France than on this side of the Channel. Countries innocent of industrialization (but with pressing military needs) also established equivalent academies, with state patronage for the useful arts – especially arts useful for military success – and much private interest in Sweden, Russia, Prussia, and Italy for example.[2] A Royal Irish Academy also flourished. The 'Dublin Society for Improving Husbandry, Manufactures and other Useful Arts' was the first of the 'popularizing' associations, established in 1731. The Welsh Society of Cymmrodorian followed in 1751. One of the earlier agricultural improvement societies was that of Brecknockshire, founded in 1753.[3] Evidence of motivation the

[1] F. A. Yates, *The French Academies of the Sixteenth Century* (London, 1947); H. Brown, *Scientific Organizations in Seventeenth-Century France* (New York, 1934).

[2] R. Hahn, 'The application of Science to Society: the Societies of Arts', *Studies on Voltaire and the Eighteenth Century*, vols. XXIV–XXVII (Geneva, 1963), pp. 829–36. This article lists a dozen such societies in different countries.

[3] H. F. Berry, *A History of the Royal Dublin Society* (London, 1915); D. G. C. Allan, op. cit., p. 61.

institutionalizing of practical science in these societies clearly was; but it may well have come, in such instances, where the need was greatest, rather than where the links were closest. It should also be said that the English societies flourished with very tiny material resources indeed, being amateur and self-financing. The very small cash premiums or medals they offered as inducements to inventors cannot be seen as 'research and development' costs in the modern sense of capital investment in innovation. The fact that endeavour was stimulated by the chance of winning a medal offered by such a private society or appearing in its transactions, says much for the prestige attached to science and to the quest for 'improvement' in practical matters. But clearly these investments and endeavours could be made on a scale more extensive absolutely than England (in the case of France) and on a scale relatively greater (judged against the resources of the country) without much of a 'fall out' giving a boost to industrial growth.

The French record of scientific growth and invention in the eighteenth century was a formidable one.[1] Berthollet first revealed to the world the bleaching possibilities of chlorine, first isolated as a gas in 1774 by a Swedish chemist Scheele, which was followed by energetic efforts to promote its manufacture in France. A similar sequence followed with Leblanc making soda from salt and sulphuric acid.[2] Very sophisticated work was done in the production of dyestuffs in France; with varnishes, enamels, and many other techniques and materials. Yet the difference in the rate of industrial growth based on these advances in chemistry between France and Britain in the period 1780 to 1850 was remarkable. Almost all the theoretical work on structures, stresses, and the mechanics of design in civil engineering was French. This did not appear to have much relationship to the speed of development, or even innovations in these fields, as far as economic progress was concerned. The same was true of power engineering and hydrodynamics.[3]

[1] See, in illustration, S. T. McCloy, *French Inventions of the Eighteenth Century* (Lexington, Ky., 1952) and *Government Assistance in Eighteenth-Century France* (Durham, N.C., 1946).

[2] C. C. Gillespie, 'The Discovery of the Leblanc Process', *Isis*, vol. XLVIII (1957).

[3] D. S. L. Cardwell, 'Power Technologies and the Advancement of Science,

The record of development and implementation was also significantly different from the record of invention.

The wider question, not to be pursued here, is even more interesting. The sophisticated scientific mechanical knowledge in China produced even less impetus to the general levels of industrial technique representative of that vast region or to industrial growth. It remained more sealed up in a small enclave of scholars, civil servants, and isolated groups under noble and royal patronage than in – say – St Petersburg. By itself, therefore, it becomes difficult to argue that a flow of new scientific knowledge and applied science was a key variable; it may be a pre-condition for advance, but it does not necessarily give the operational impetus.

Secondly, the problem of time-lags between knowledge and action raises awkward problems for the 'positive' one-to-one equation in its simple form. The economic historian is more interested in innovation and the diffusion of innovations than in invention for its own sake. Putting inventions to productive use involves all the costs and problems of translation from laboratory technique into industrial production, from the largely non-commercial context of the pursuit of knowledge to profitability as a condition of existence. One is not even very interested in isolated examples of new industrial techniques but rather in their diffusion to the point when innovations begin to affect general levels of output, costs, productivity in an industry; when their adoption is on a sufficient scale to affect the performance of the industry significantly. To mention a few of these astonishing time-lags. The screw-cutting lathe, foundation of the precision engineering skills which made an efficient machine-making industry possible, was clearly documented by Leonardo da Vinci in the *Note-Books*, laid out again in the section on watch-making tools in the *Description des Arts et Métiers* in mid-eighteenth century France and developed, spontaneously, again by Maudslay, to become – from that

1700–1825', *Technology and Culture*, vol. VI (1965); 'Some Factors in the Early Development of the Concept of Power, Work and Energy', *British Journal for the History of Science*, vol. III (1966–7); R. Hahn, L'hyrodynamique au XVIIIe siècle (Paris, 1965); D. Landes, *Cambridge Economic History of Europe*, vol. VI (Cambridge, 1965), p. 333.

innovation – the basis of a progeny of machine tools. Sir T. Lombe's silk-throwing machine, which was used for the first time in a factory in England in 1709, had been used and known in Italy since 1607 – with an accurate engraving in a book on the open shelves of the Bodleian Library by 1620.[1] The same is true of gearing and the design of gear wheels, bridge design, pumps, Archimedian screws, the 'pound' lock, mass production needle-grinding machines and a host of others (all to be found in Leonardo's work).[2] In certain respects, steam power is another example. The pound lock – being the basic technology of a dry dock – was known in Dutch shipyards in the fifteenth century, perhaps much earlier, and appeared in England in the sixteenth century. But a still-water canal system of which this is the only important piece of technology was an eighteenth-century phenomenon in Britain.[3] Equally dramatic time-lags exist in the opposite direction – between empirical improvements in technique and the beginning of scientific interest in explaining them.[4]

Bound up with this problem of time-lags between knowledge and invention, invention and adoption, adoption and diffusion are correlated phenomena such as simultaneous inventions (developed spontaneously and independently in different places at about the same time), re-inventions of lost techniques, 'alternative' inventions coming very close together in time for providing different ways of getting the same thing done.[5]

The 'profile' of technical change usually shows an evolutionary curve as well as revolutionary discontinuities. The interstices between the discrete advances made by identifiable

[1] Quoted G. N. Clark, op. cit.

[2] I. B. Hart, *The World of Leonardo da Vinci* (London, 1961).

[3] Surveying techniques were certainly advanced enough in the late sixteenth century to facilitate canal cutting. The New River project bringing water from Hertfordshire to North London involved very sophisticated routing and exactness in calculating levels.

[4] A. R. Hall and T. S. Kuhn in M. Clagett, *Critical Problems in the History of Science* (Madison, Wisc., 1959), pp. 16–17.

[5] R. K. Merton, 'Singletons and Multiples in Scientific Discovery', *Proceedings of the American Philosophical Society*, vol. CV (1961); W. R. Maclaurin, 'The Sequence from Invention to Innovation . . .', *Quarterly Journal of Economics*, vol. LXVII (1953).

individuals are filled by 'continuum' improvements made on the job by countless improvements without known, or identifiable and published authorship. Collectively the latter may yield a cumulative advance in productivity greater than the identifiable discrete innovations. This has been likened to biological change; improvement and survival by the techniques most efficiently and economically adapted to their function – a kind of technological Darwinism.[1] The burden of all this is, of course, that invention waits upon economic opportunity before it can come to fruition in innovation and the diffusion of new techniques. The determinants of timing are usually set – in the long run – by non-technical criteria. These determinants may be economic criteria of different sorts – the widening of the market giving inducement for larger production and hence new methods, greater facility in the supply of capital, a change in factor prices[2] (for example, labour becoming relatively more expensive or intractable, raising the incentives to cut labour costs). Boom conditions, creating bottle-necks in supply, higher profits, and greater incentives to expand may create the operational incentives. In a dynamic sequence, when an economy is on the move with innovations flowing, a depression may equally induce further innovation by creating pressures to cut costs. The process of innovation itself creates a dis-equilibrium in various ways – that dis-equilibrium, to be resolved, creating the need for further changes, which become self-reinforcing. These may indeed be technical in nature, but they are need-creating in the way they operate. The causal arrows flow from industrial demand towards the absorption of new knowledge. The timing is set from within the industrial rhythm and the economic context rather than given to it exogenously by new acquisitions of knowledge.[3] There are

[1] S. C. Gilfillan, *The Sociology of Invention* (Chicago, 1935); 'Invention as a Factor in Economic History', *Journal of Economic History*, Supplement (1945).

[2] '. . . every price change, by creating cost difficulties in certain fields and opportunities for profit-making in others, provides a double stimulus to invention' (A. Plant in *Economica*, 1934, p. 38, quoted Clark, op. cit.).

[3] J. Schmookler, *Invention and Economic Growth* (Cambridge, Mass., 1966); 'Economic Sources of Inventive Activity', *Journal of Economic History*, vol. XXII (1962); W. F. Ogburn and D. Thomas, 'Are Inventions Inevitable?', *Political Science Quarterly*, vol. XXXVII (1922); R. C. Epstein, 'Industrial Inventions: Heroic or Systematic?', *Quarterly Journal of Economics*, vol. XL

other determinants – social, political, and legal affecting the conditions of risk. 'Entrepreneurship' may also prove to be greater than the sum of these other criteria.

These sorts of motivations tend to be the operational criteria in this period, I believe, determining which bits of scientific knowledge were taken up, developed, applied, and which lay unused; which inventions remained known, but sterile, and which quickly became adopted, perhaps outside the country which gave them birth. Clearly, this is the style of explanation behind the very rapid adoption of 'chemical' bleaching in the cotton industry in Britain more than in France: the enormous expansion in the output of cloth made a more rapid means of bleaching imperative. Great stress has recently been placed by historians of science on the ways in which empirical processes and skilled artisan technology in the mechanical arts stimulated scientific advance in these centuries.[1]

However, this does not necessarily subvert the core of the 'positive' equation. It can be argued that applied science needs to build up a capital 'stock' or a 'library' of knowledge, so to speak, which is thereupon available for industrialists to draw upon in innovation – across national frontiers, no doubt, for science now enjoyed, in printing, a very effective means of diffusing knowledge in the seventeenth century and after; and

---

(1926); R. K. Merton, 'Fluctuations in the Rate of Industrial Invention', *Quarterly Journal of Economics*, vol. XLIX (1934–5).

The very large literature about technical change and innovation now developing is seeking to establish criteria for measuring and evaluating this phenomenon in economic theory. Almost all of it relates to twentieth-century examples and assumptions, particularly that concerned with research costs and applied science. Conclusions are therefore not *ipso facto* applicable to innovation as a phenomenon in the seventeenth and eighteenth centuries.

[1] E. G. P. Rossi, *Francis Bacon* (London, 1968), p. 9; E. J. Dijksterhuis, *The Mechanization of the World Picture* (Oxford, 1961), pp. 243–4; T. S. Kuhn, 'Energy Conservation . . .' in M. Clagett, op. cit.; A. R. Hall, *From Galileo to Newton, 1630–1720* (London, 1963), pp. 329–43; A. R. Hall, *The Scientific Revolution*, 2nd ed. (London, 1962), pp. 221, 225, 236; J. D. Bernal, *Science in History* (London, 1954), pp. 345–6, 371. At its extreme, this case becomes the doctrinaire Marxist position that advances in scientific knowledge were determined purely by the bourgeoisie's commercial and industrial needs. See B. Hessen, *Science at the Cross-Roads* and the debate given in condensed form in G. Basalla (ed.), *The Rise of Modern Science* (Boston, D. C. Heath, 1968).

with a timing doubtless profoundly influenced by conditions and incentives within industry. But, without that capital stock produced by the advance of scientific knowledge, runs the argument, a limit would have been placed upon the range of advance.

This begs the question as to how far the impetus deriving from industry was able to produce the conditions – of innovation as well as other things – needed to sustain its own progress. To what extent was the flow of innovations produced from within the empirical world of industry and not given to it from an 'exogenous' world of science, advancing under its own complex of stimuli? That in turn begs the question as to how far industrial demand, with the needs of the 'empirical' world, was itself the stimulus for creating new scientific knowledge in this period, of what 'feeds-back' or 'feeds-forward' there were?

Judging the effectiveness of the contributions of science by results, *ex post facto*, rather than by endeavour, is to greatly reduce their importance. Little of the mass of experimentation in agricultural projects of the Royal Society in its early years, for example, seems to have had much direct effect upon improving the efficiency of farming.[1] Most of the more direct links between advancing knowledge of chemistry and the expanding chemical industry came only at the end of the eighteenth century. This disconnects the timing of much of the new knowledge, particularly in chemistry, from the initial phases of industrial growth. The great advances in mechanics in the seventeenth century – then one of the most advanced of the sciences – had given birth to very sophisticated theoretical schema about ballistics, which do not appear to have significantly affected the processes of innovation in making metals or working metals, of gunfounding or of gunnery, again judging by result, until after the Crimean War. The 'science' remained almost purely abstract. Each cannon cast and bored remained slightly different from each other; each shot and each charge of powder were equally 'unique', which kept techniques of gunnery strictly empirical. A precision engineering industry to produce the guns, and a precision

[1] See below, pp. 89–91.

chemical industry to produce the propellants, were required before this theoretical knowledge could become operational.[1]

The empirical stimulus creating response within the immediate context of production accounts for a very high proportion of the advance in productivity, even in those industries most exposed to the impact of science, and a great determinant of timing and the rate of diffusion of new techniques. Great areas of advance were relatively untouched by scientific knowledge, judging by result rather than by intention or endeavour, until the nineteenth century: agriculture, canals, machine-making, the mechanization of cloth-making (as distinct from bleaching and dyeing), iron- and steel-making. Taking the occupational census of 1851, a very small percentage indeed of the labour-force was engaged in trades where the linkages were – superficially at any rate – high, as in chemicals.

IV

Steam power is important enough to merit separate attention. Here was the greatest gift from science to industry, it has often been claimed, born exactly from the world of the Royal Society, of noblemen's laboratories, from an international competition among scientists and their leisured patrons in the seventeenth century. Watt, in his generation, carried on this precise linkage between scientific knowledge and commercial application in the series of formal experiments to analyse the properties of steam and the conductivity of metals which lay behind his own inventions of the separate condenser and steam power proper (as distinct from 'atmospheric' power). This can be called the classical example of science in alliance with practice.[2] But other factors also conditioned the rates of advance of efficiency in steam power and the timing of stages of growth of this innovation. Thomas Newcomen and Savery were not so directly within this educated scientific tradition. And historians of science continue to push back the genealogy of the basic scientific awareness of steam power – knowledge

---

[1] A. R. Hall, *Ballistics in the Seventeenth Century* (Cambridge, 1952).
[2] G. N. Clark, op. cit., p. 21.

G

as distinct from laboratory experiments that worked.[1] The jump to the world of Thomas Newcomen, who had no personal contacts with the leading scientists of the day,[2] fashioning an effective commercial device, meant problems of manufacture, of standards of accuracy in metalworking, that alone made effective use possible on a commercial basis. This, it can be argued, more than anything else set the limits of efficiency. And this, as a blacksmith, was Newcomen's world, not that of the Royal Society. Once again, the context within which Watt's inventions had to become operational meant that the accuracy of working metal, of fitting a piston to a cylinder throughout its length, of getting steamproof valves and joints set the limits to the rise in the degree of efficiency which potentially resulted from the new inventions. These efficiencies came from the empirical world of John Wilkinson and Matthew Boulton, with rising standards of its own, a world increasingly working to rule, but still mainly innocent of formal scientific thought.

And, subsequent to Watt, most of the pioneering of 'high-pressure steam', the adaptation of steam to traction, to small-bench engines, to ships and the continuum of improvement to the Watt-style engine itself, belonged, for the most part, to the empirical world of the obscure colliery engineers, the captains of Cornish mines, the brilliant mechanics such as Murdock. Some of them were trained in the best precision workshops of the country, such as Maudslay's, but remained nevertheless innocent of scientific fundamentals and were not seeking to create their improvements in the light of awareness of such fundamentals. Yet the cumulative total of 'continuum' innovation, effected on the job, at the work bench, bit by bit, were profound. Taking steam-power efficiency again as one example, the first Newcomen engine had a duty[3] of *c.* 4·5 m, it has been

---

[1] A. R. Hall has gone so far as to state: 'No scientific revolution was needed to bring the steam engine into existence. What Newcomen did could have been done by Hero of Alexandria seventeen hundred years before, who understood all the essential principles' (*From Galileo to Newton, 1630–1720*, London, 1963, p. 333).

[2] D. S. L. Cardwell, *Steampower in the Eighteenth Century* (London, 1963) p. 18.

[3] The number of pounds of water raised 1 foot by the consumption of 1 bushel of coal.

calculated.[1] This had been raised to 12·5 m by the time of Smeaton's improvements in 1770. The initial Watt separate condenser engine raised this duty to *c.* 22 m. By 1792 it had been raised by continuing improvement to over 30 m. The best recorded Watt-type engine in 1811, working in Cornwall, had a duty of 22·3 m. In 1842–3, under continuous gradual improvement, the best duty was recorded at 100 m. Average duty rates recorded on Cornish engines quadrupled between 1811 and 1850 as a result of this continuum-type improvement.

V

Although this paper is primarily concerned with sources of innovation in industrial techniques, improvements in agriculture are relevant to the issue, both because agriculture potentially stood to gain from the application of science, comparably to industry (and has gained as dramatically from its connexion with science as has industry in the twentieth century), and because contemporaries certainly gave agricultural improvement at least as high a priority as industrial advance. Agricultural improvement also had a more general appeal to the upper and middle classes of English society than any other branch of production, if only because larger and more influential social groups were concerned with the land. Agricultural innovations and scientific experiments in agriculture featured in virtually all the scientific and philosophical societies mentioned above; while other societies were specifically agricultural in their terms of reference. The Georgical Committee of the Royal Society was established in 1665 (as one of eight sectoral groups). Many experiments in husbandry found a place in the *Philosophical Transactions* over the years; and eleven reports are known to have been made about agricultural practices, produced from national inquiries.[2] A 'Society of Improvers in the Knowledge of Agriculture in Scotland' was founded in 1723 (forty years before that in

---

[1] D. B. Barton, *The Cornish Beam Engine* (Truro, 1966), pp. 28, 32, 58. These figures are suspect, but there is no reason to suppose that the degree of suspicion advanced with time – rather the reverse. Other factors went into these duty counts as well as the intrinsic technical potentiality of the engines.

[2] R. L. Lennard, 'Agriculture under Charles II', *Economic History Review* (1932).

Brecknockshire) and many local agricultural societies followed, particularly in the 1790s.[1]

Scientists concerned themselves with agricultural experiments, advocating the experimental method and lauding the claims of science in farming no less than in industry. Francis Bacon's *Sylva Sylvarum* (1651) included a comparative study of different modes of fertilizing. In 1671, Boyle urged farmers to experiment: 'Chymical experiments . . .' he wrote, 'may probably afford useful direction to the Husbandman towards the melioration of his land, both for Corn, Trees, Grass and consequently Cattell.'[2] John Evelyn's various works contained a curious – if typical – mixture of magic and shrewd common-sense, in circumstances where virtually anything organic, and much inorganic, could be thrown on to the land with advantage.[3] Hale's *Vegetable Statics* (1727) continued the line, for the first time challenging the view that plants were composed simply of water. Francis Home, both a doctor and subsequently a professor in Edinburgh, also deliberately set out to apply science to agriculture to see 'how far Chymistry could go in settling the Principles of Agriculture'.[4] Lavoisier set up agricultural experiments and ran a model farm.[5]

Thus, by intention and endeavour, agricultural innovation shares with industry a common link with science in the seventeenth and eighteenth centuries. The problems about concluding from these aspirations and associations that applied science was the prime source of such innovation in agriculture as actually occurred are even greater, if anything, than with industry. There, at least, in the specialized sector of the chemical industry and immediately related fields there is solid evidence for the connexion in a direct way (though causal links could flow in both directions). Much theorizing was

[1] These include the Canterbury Agricultural Society, Odiham Society, London Veterinary College, Bath and West and Southern Counties, Norfolk Agricultural Society.

[2] R. Boyle, *Some Considerations Touching the Usefulness of . . . Natural Philosophy* (Oxford, 1671).

[3] J. Evelyn, *Sylva* (London, 1664); *Kalendarium Hortense* (London, 1664); *A Philosophical discourse of earth . . .* (London, 1676).

[4] F. Home, *Principles of Agriculture and Vegetation* (Edinburgh, 1757).

[5] E. J. Russell, *A History of Agricultural Science in Great Britain, 1620–1954* (London, 1966), p. 53.

plainly mistaken, based on quite irrational premisses. The innovations which characterized progressive farming did not owe much, if anything, to such science; while only the very exceptional farmer or landowner was directly influenced by the scientists. Russell, as a leading present-day agricultural scientist, is profoundly sceptical of the relevance of chemistry to agricultural advance before the generation of Leibig, Davy's *Elements of Agricultural Chemistry* (1813), and the Rothamsted experiments of Lawes and Gilbert in the 1840s.[1]

But scepticism about the significance of the direct application of formal scientific knowledge to agrarian improvement in these two centuries does not end the story of the relevance of this evidence. To anticipate a tentative conclusion drawn below, one can certainly take this large body of data as strong evidence of *motivation* for agrarian advance. Coupled with false premisses about chemical reactions were urgent pleas for experimentation, shrewd observation and recording, the comparative method, seeking alternative ways of doing things which could be measured and tested to see if they were superior to the old. This was a programme for rejecting traditional methods justifiable only because things had always been done in that way (even though such customs, hallowed by the passing of time, often did embody strict rationality, even if unself-conscious and inarticulate on the lips of their practitioners). Scientific procedures and attitudes encouraged by the scientists may have been more influential than the scientific knowledge they dispensed. 'I should not, therefore, proceed a single step', wrote Francis Home, 'without facts and experiments.'[2]

The publicity given to new methods, new crops, rotations, and implements by these same groups may also have increased the pace of diffusion of innovations in agriculture. Certainly the flood of writing, at all different levels, is evidence of an intellectual world where progress was written into the assumptions of the age.

---

[1] E. J. Russell, op. cit., pp. 25, 37, 46. See also G. E. Fussell, 'Science and Practice in Eighteenth-Century British Agriculture', *Agricultural History*, vol. XLIII (1969). But see the comments of D. J. Brandenburg.

[2] F. Home, *Principles of Agriculture and Vegetation* (Edinburgh, 1757). He urged the Edinburgh Society to raise 'a spirit of experimental farming over the country'.

VI

The institutional development of science creates certain problems, because the patterns of development in science do not always fit sequences of innovation and development in industry. The foundation of the Royal Society and the Lunar Society are always quoted in evidence of the developing nexus between science and industry. But one must then face the issue of the decline in the utilitarian orientation towards applied science of the Royal Society after 1670, its decline during the first half of the eighteenth century and in parts of the nineteenth century, and its great weaknesses compared with the equivalent academy in France. The Lunar Society also withered into a state of collapse after the 1790s. In some fields, also, it seems perfectly possible – even in that most applied of sciences, medicine – for the accumulated advances of several generations, well institutionalized, not to result in any major impact upon national demographic trends in death-rates or disease-rates. Medicine, we are told, did not begin to have such a major impact – that is, upon a statistically significant proportion of the population – until the second half of the nineteenth century, apart, perhaps, from the effects of innoculation and vaccination on smallpox. And this was in a field where there was very great interest, considerable advances in scientific knowledge, a greater flow of money, and probably more scientifically trained persons than in all other branches of science put together.[1]

The problem of numbers is also relevant. Persons professionally trained in medicine, in chemistry, the 'scientific' members of the Royal Society (as distinct from the much larger number of 'gentlemen' innocent of professional commitment) remained the merest handful. The average number of elections to the Royal Society in the early eighteenth century was about ten. The average number elected in each year to the College of Physicians was five or six before 1700, supplemented only marginally with those with degrees from foreign universities. These numbers did rise after 1700 but remained

---

[1] This conclusion may need to be modified in the light of research being currently undertaken by Dr E. Sigsworth of York.

very tiny. This may be taken as an index of the professional-ization of science to the extent that this term possessed its modern connotation in the eighteenth century. Beyond this there were, of course, much larger numbers of amateurs and people in business, such as opticians and distillers, who practised empirical science in a commercial way. As Professor Hall has said: '. . . the impact of any question of abstract science upon a human brain was exceptionally infrequent – it could only happen to, say, one individual in a hundred thousand. But, in the history of technology the situation is very different; the proportion of human beings who could have been very well acquainted with handmills and ploughs and textile-and horsegear has always been very large indeed, until the last century or so in the West. Very few of these ever effected the slightest variation in any technique; but the potentiality for effecting a variation was virtually universal. It is only when the use of relatively uncommon machines or techniques is intro-duced that the potentiality for innovation becomes restricted.'[1]

In England no great expansion of institutions in 'profes-sional' science developed in this period outside the Royal Society, either within the universities or outside them, apart from the amateur groups and the popularizers. Science did not become an established part of the educational system, either within the traditional institutional hierarchy or beyond it in special organizations of its own. The Mechanics' Institutes subsequently became the only widespread response to be institutionalized in this way in the first half of the nineteenth century, and they trained the aspiring literate artisan, not the research chemist. The greatest contrast existed between the English experience and French and German developments in the *École Polytechnique* and the *Technische Hochschule*. The School of Mines and the Royal College of Chemistry in London were the two institutions that challenged this generalization. They remained very small, isolated geographically, socially, and technically from having any significant impact upon mining or industry in Britain as a whole during the greater part of the nineteenth century.

[1] A. R. Hall, *The Historical Relations of Science and Technology* (London, 1963).

VII

In conclusion: it was the same western European society which saw both great advances in science and in technological change in the great sweep of time and region across the fifteenth to the nineteenth centuries. It would be carrying nihilism to the point of dogma to write this off as a mere accident, even though the case of China suggests that it is perfectly possible for sophisticated scientific and technological knowledge in some fields to produce a very small impetus towards lifting general levels of industrial technique. The simplest assumptions of causation flowing directly and in one direction need to be questioned; the presumption that connexions between science and industry were direct, unitary, simple. Negatively it can be argued that the many other conditioning factors in technical change were collectively of much greater importance during the first century of industrialization and that, in the immediate context of manufacture, formal scientific knowledge was much less strategic in determining commercial success than some modern studies have suggested. In longer perspective we may see that the main impetus from formal applied science to innovation came after 1850 on an over-widening front, but in a context which was highly favourable for many other reasons. That this was the real pivot in the connexions between science and industry was shown by default, to a large extent, in the case of Britain lagging most in exactly those fields of innovation where the connexion was becoming most intimate.

But much depends upon whether we are looking at the immediate context of innovation or at the general nature of the society, and its intellectual parameters, within which industrial advances were burgeoning. 'We have to see,' as G. N. Clark concluded long ago, 'not a gradual and general mutual approach of these elements in society, but the joining of contact, first at isolated points, then at more points; finally almost everywhere.'[1] Until the end of the eighteenth century – that is, until long after systematic, cumulative change on a scale quite uncharacteristic of medieval technical change was under

[1] G. N. Clark, op. cit., p. 22.

way – that inter-penetration was confined to fairly small areas, even if some of them were strategic.

It should also be acknowledged that scientific attitudes were much more widespread and diffused than scientific knowledge. Attitudes of challenging traditional intellectual authority, declining lines of development by observation, testing, experimentation, and adopting – indeed, actively stimulating the development of – scientific devices such as the thermometer and hydrometer, which enabled industrialists to reduce their empirical practices to rule wherever possible, were certainly being strengthened.[1] The quest for more exact measurement and research for the means to fulfil it was certainly characteristic of these linkages, even where the object was not to subvert empirical techniques, of which the chemistry remained unknown, but to standardize best practice within them. Scientific devices and techniques were thus often used to buttress empirical techniques rather than to challenge them. In this sense, the developing Baconian tradition of the experimental sciences, the tradition of research based upon systematic experimentation (as in late eighteenth-century chemistry) had closer links with the process of innovation than did advances in cosmology, mechanics, or physics in the seventeenth century. And in such linkages science probably learned as much from technology as technology from science until the nineteenth century: scientists were much concerned with trying to answer questions suggested from industrial techniques. 'Technological progress implied the idea of intellectual progress, just as chance discoveries implied the possibility of systematic ones.'[2]

We may conclude that together both science and technology give evidence of a society increasingly curious, increasingly questing, increasingly on the move, on the make, having a go, increasingly seeking to experiment, wanting to improve. This may be the prime significance of the new popularizers of science and technology, the encyclopedias, the institutions like the

[1] The brewing and distilling industries, with the excise authorities anxious to have more precise calculations in gauging for taxation, offer a good example of such a sequence. See P. Mathias, *The Brewing Industry in England, 1700–1830* (Cambridge, 1959), pp. 63–78.

[2] A. R. Hall, *The Scientific Revolution* (London, 1962), p. 369.

Society of Arts, the Royal Institution, the Lunar Society and the various local philosophical and scientific societies, the new educational movements, the intriguing links between radical nonconformist scientific and business groups in the eighteenth century or between Puritans and the founders of the Royal Society in the seventeenth century. So much of the significance, that is to say, impinges at a more diffused level, affecting motivations, values, assumptions, the mode of approach to problem-solving, the intellectual milieu, rather than a direct transference of knowledge. In this sense, of course, the conclusion is banal, that the advances in science and in technical change should both be seen as characteristics of that society, not one being simply consequential upon the other.

2 The Diffusion of Technology in Great Britain during the Industrial Revolution

A. E. MUSSON

The following extracts are taken from chapter II of A. E. Musson and E. Robinson, *Science and Technology, in the Industrial Revolution*, Manchester University Press, 1969.]

Was it [the Industrial Revolution], as Professor Landes has said, achieved through the efforts of 'practical tinkerers',[1] or did it have some scientific basis? There is no doubt that native empiricism was of immense and probably predominant importance. It was strongly evident, for instance, in the development of engineering and industrial motive power – the bases of modern mechanized mass-production. Mr Robinson and I have investigated the origins of engineering in Lancashire, where the early factory system had its most striking developments.[2] We have traced how early engineering workers were recruited from a wide range of traditional skilled craftsmen; smiths, wheelwrights, millwrights, carpenters, turners, clockmakers, etc., in fact from all kinds of workers in metal and wood. The millwright – the jack-of-all-trades described by Fairbairn[3] – was especially important. So, too, as we have demonstrated, was the clock-maker, whose skills and tools

[1] D. S. Landes, 'Entrepreneurship in Advanced Industrial Countries: The Anglo-German Rivalry', *Entrepreneurship and Economic Growth*, papers presented at a conference in Cambridge, Massachusetts (November 1954), p. 8. He has somewhat revised this view, however, in the *Cambridge Economic History of Europe*, vol. VI (1965), part I, pp. 293–6, in the light of the evidence we have produced.

[2] A. E. Musson and E. Robinson, 'The Origins of Engineering in Lancashire', *Journal of Economic History* (June 1959); also chap. XIII in *Science and Technology*.

[3] W. Fairbairn, *Treatise on Mills and Millwork* (2 vols., 1861–3), vol. I, pp. v-vi; Musson and Robinson, *Science and Technology*, pp. 73, 429, 481.

were turned to cutting gear-wheels, etc. for the 'clockwork' of early textile machinery. A similar transition is uniquely illustrated in Pyne's *Microcosm* of 1808,[1] where we see how the making of wooden cart wheels metamorphosed into the construction of wooden 'wheel machinery' (spur wheels, crown wheels, pinions, etc.) for the early mills. Brindley was such a wheelwright and millwright. Similarly, craftsmen from other trades – notably Smeaton (instrument-maker) and Rennie (millwright) – developed the use of cast-iron gears and other mechanical improvements; Rennie, for example, appears to have brought the centrifugal governor for steam engines – the invention of which is often attributed to James Watt – from his millwright practice in windmills.[2] In the same way, turners in wood changed easily into turners in metal. . . . Iron-founders, of course, were especially important in this development of engineering. . . .

Traditional empirical skills were undoubtedly important. . . . It should also be emphasized that traditional forms of power remained far more important in the industrial revolution than is generally realized. Water power was especially important. We know, of course, that water-wheels had long been used for grinding corn and fulling cloth, and increasingly, from the sixteenth century onwards, for working mine-drainage pumps and winding engines, for operating furnace-bellows, hammers, and rollers in iron-works, for driving saw-mills and paper mills, and for many other industrial purposes. We know, too, that early textile factories, such as Lombe's silk mill and Arkwright's cotton mills, were powered by water-wheels. But the enormous number and wide variety of uses of such wheels have never been fully appreciated, nor have the improvements in their design and their increasing size during the Industrial Revolution. . . .

These advances in water power deserve stressing because they have been unduly overshadowed by the early develop-

[1] W. H. Pyne, *Microcosm*, vol. II (1808), plate 69, reproduced in W. H. Chaloner and A. E. Musson, *Industry and Technology* (1963), plate 64.

[2] C. T. G. Boucher, *John Rennie 1761–1821* (1963), pp. 11, 81–4. Mr Robinson, however, considers that Watt developed the use of this device independently, though also from windmills.

ment of steam engines. In the long run, of course, steam power was to be of far greater importance, but it was a longer run than is generally realized. . . .

The early steam-engine makers [also] came from the ranks of ironfounders, millwrights, and other traditional trades, as previously mentioned. Watt himself was originally an instrument-maker, like Smeaton. They were able to apply their practical skills to the solution of new engineering problems. Probably most of the achievements of the early Industrial Revolution were similarly products of practical empiricism. But during the past decade or so an increasing amount of evidence has been accumulating to show that scientific technology was also developing at this time and assisting in these achievements. Dr and Mrs Clow, for example, have shown how the Scottish universities contributed to advancements in chemical technology in a wide range of industries, such as the alkali, soap, glass, bleaching, dyeing, and other trades.[1] Many similar examples can be culled from the pages of *Isis*, the *Annals of Science*, and the growing number of similar journals. Mr Robinson and I have also tried to show the industrial significance of philosophical societies in Birmingham, Manchester, and other towns, of dissenting academies, embryo technical colleges and schools, of books, encyclopedias, periodicals, and libraries, and of itinerant lecturers – all of which helped to spread scientific–technological knowledge and interests more widely.[2] Dr Schofield has more recently demonstrated in copious detail the links between science and industry in the Birmingham Lunar Society.[3]

Professor Jewkes and his collaborators have suggested that 'the disposition of modern writers to regard nineteenth- [and eighteenth-] century inventors as uneducated and empirical in their methods is a direct outcome of the difficulty which academically educated people often have in understanding the possibilities of self-education'.[4] As they briefly observe,

[1] A. N. and N. Clow, *The Chemical Revolution* (1952).

[2] Musson and Robinson, 'Science and Industry in the Late Eighteenth Century', *Economic History Review*, vol. XIII, no. 2 (December 1960), and *Science and Technology in the Industrial Revolution*, chap. III.

[3] R. E. Schofield, *The Lunar Society of Birmingham* (1963).

[4] Jewkes, op. cit., pp. 63–4.

facilities for self-education certainly existed, and some of the
most notable scientists and industrialists were self-educated.[1]
Many of the early engineers, for example, combined scientific
knowledge with practical experience. Even the ordinary
eighteenth-century millwright, according to Fairbairn, was
generally 'a fair arithmetician, knew something of geometry,
levelling, and mensuration, and in some cases possessed a very
competent knowledge of practical mechanics. He could cal-
culate the velocities, strength and power of machines; could
draw in plan and in section . . .': indeed they were commonly
regarded as men of 'superior attainments and intellectual
power'.[2] The truth of this statement is clearly evident, not only
in Fairbairn's own works, but in those of earlier engineers such
as Smeaton, Telford, and Rennie. Smeaton's high abilities in
surveying, designing, mechanics, etc. are revealed in the four
volumes of his *Reports*, published by the Smeatonian Society
of Engineers in 1812, and also in his drawings,[3] while his
capacity for scientific–technological experiment is brilliantly
demonstrated in 'An Experimental Inquiry concerning the
natural Powers of Water and Wind to turn Mills, and other
Machines',[4] and by his similar investigations into the atmospheric steam engine, all scientifically controlled, with results
tabulated mathematically.[5] Hence his election as a Fellow of the
Royal Society, to which he read numerous other papers on

[1] Faraday, Davy, Sturgeon, and Wheatstone are among the 'self-educated'
scientists mentioned by Jewkes; Young, Hodgkinson, and others could be added.
We shall be referring to numerous industrialists who similarly acquired scientific
knowledge.

[2] W. Fairbairn, *Treatise on Mills and Millwork* (1861–3), vol. I, pp.
v–vi.

[3] See *A Catalogue of the Civil and Mechanical Engineering Designs, 1741–92, of
John Smeaton, FRS, preserved in the Library of the Royal Society* (Newcomen Society
Extra Publication no. 5, 1950).

[4] Smeaton made his experiments in 1752–3. The results formed the subject of
papers read to the Royal Society in May and June 1759 (*Philosophical Transactions*,
vol. LI, 1759, pp. 100–74), for which he was awarded the Society's Copley Medal.
These papers were republished in 1794. These and his other papers on mechanics
were frequently referred to by later engineers.

[5] These experiments, made in the early 1770s, are explained and analysed in
detail by J. Farey, *A Treatise on the Steam Engine* (1827), pp. 134, 158, 166 ff.
The experiments, of which he recorded over 130, were spread over four
years.

mechanics,[1] scientific instruments,[2] and astronomy. During his visits to London, 'it was a source of great pleasure to him to attend the meetings of the Royal Society, as well as to cultivate a friendship with the distinguished members of the Royal Society Club'.[3] He was one of the leading figures in the earliest society of engineers, founded in 1771, which, after his death, became the Smeatonian Society in 1793 and was the forerunner of the Institution of Civil Engineers, founded in 1818.[4] The members, who included most of the leading engineers of that day, discussed engineering theory as well as practice. One of their meetings in 1778, for example, was spent 'canallically, hydraulically, mathematically, philosophically, mechanically, naturally, and socially'.[5]

Smeaton, so Smiles tells us, deliberately 'limited his professional employment, that he might be enabled to devote a certain portion of his time to self-improvement and scientific investigation'; he was frequently engaged in study and experiment in the specially erected tower, combining workshop, study, and observatory, at his home at Austhorpe, near Leeds.[6] He was also a member of the scientific coterie in Leeds, including Joseph Priestley and others.[7] George Stephenson later referred to Smeaton as

> the greatest philosopher in our profession that this country has yet produced. He was indeed a great man, possessing a truly Baconian mind, for he was an incessant experimenter. The principles of mechanics were never so clearly exhibited as in his writings, more especially with respect to resistance, gravity, and the power of water and wind to turn mills.

[1] Notably 'An Experimental Examination of the Quantity and Proportion of Mechanic Power necessary to be employed in giving different Degrees of Velocity to Heavy Bodies from a State of Rest', read 25 April 1776, *Philosophical Transactions*, vol. LXVI (1776), pp. 450–75, and 'New Fundamental Experiments upon the Collision of Bodies', read 18 April 1782, ibid., vol. LXXII (1782), pp. 337–54. Smeaton refuted the theoretical opinions of earlier philosophers such as Belidor, Parent, Desaguliers, Maclaurin, etc. on these matters, especially in regard to the operation of water-wheels.

[2] See, for example, Musson and Robinson, *Science and Technology*, p. 50, n. 4.

[3] Smiles, *Lives of the Engineers* (1874), vol. II, p. 169.

[4] S. B. Donkin, 'The Society of Civil Engineers (Smeatonians)', *Newcomen Society Transactions*, vol. XVII (1936–7).

[5] Ibid., p. 58.   [6] Smiles, op. cit., chap. VI.

[7] See Musson and Robinson, *Science and Technology*, pp. 157–8.

His mind was as clear as crystal, and his demonstrations will be found mathematically conclusive. To this day there are no writings so valuable as his in the highest walks of scientific engineering . . .[1]

Telford, originally a stonemason, is often regarded, like Brindley before him, as a purely practical engineer, devoid of, and even hostile to, scientific theory.[2] There is no doubt, as Sir Alexander Gibb has shown,[3] that Telford emphasized above all the value of practical experience, but he was 'no enemy to either mathematics or theory'. Indeed, he acquired a considerable fund of theoretical knowledge. His early letters reveal him reading very widely on architecture, mathematics, chemistry, mechanics, hydrostatics, etc., on which he made copious notes. Thus on 1 February 1796 he wrote to his friend, David Little:[4]

> Knowledge is my most ardent pursuit . . . I am now deep in Chemistry – the manner of making Mortar led me to inquire into the Nature of Lime and in pursuit of this, having look'd into some books on Chemistry I perceived the field was boundless – and that to assign reasons for many Mechanical processes it required a general knowledge of that Science. I have therefore had the loan of a MSS Copy of Dr Black's Lectures. I have bought his Experiments on Magnesia and Quick Lime and likewise Fourcroy's Lectures translated from the French by a Mr Elliott. And I am determined to study with unwearied attention until I attain some general knowledge of Chemistry as it is of Universal use in the [practical] Arts as in Medicine.

A year later, he was still 'Chemistry mad' and especially interested in 'Calcareous matters', with the practical objective of securing the best type of cement for building bridges, etc.,

---

[1] Quoted by Smiles, op. cit., p. 177. Smiles rightly emphasized, however, Smeaton's distrust of pure theory unsupported by practical experiment.

[2] This view appears to have been based on the statement by Sir David Brewster in the *Edinburgh Review*, October 1839, that 'Telford had a singular distaste for mathematical studies, and never even made himself acquainted with the elements of geometry'; he is even said to have considered that mathematical acquirements unfitted a man for practical engineering. Dr Boucher has recently repeated this view uncritically, in an unfavourable comparison with Rennie (op. cit., p. 30).   [3] In *The Story of Telford* (1935).

[4] Quoted in S. Smiles, *The Life of Thomas Telford* (1867), pp. 128–9, and Gibb, op. cit., p. 10.

both above and below water. But his interests were 'not . . . confined to that alone', and in addition to the works of Black and Fourcroy, previously mentioned, he had read Scheele's *Essays*, Macquer's *Dictionary*, Watson's *Essays*, and writings by his friend Dr Irving [Irvine?]. From these he had taken notes in a pocket-book, 'which I always carry with me,' and into which he had also 'cramm'd Mechanics, Hydrostatics, Pneumatics, and all manner of Stuff, and to which I keep continually adding'.[1]

Telford became friendly with various professors at Edinburgh University, such as Professors Stewart, Gregory, Playfair, and Robison, who secured his election to the Royal Society of Edinburgh. Towards the end of his life, in 1827, he was elected FRS, in recognition of his experimental research as well as of his civil engineering achievements. His researches generally had a strong practical bias, such as those on the strength of iron chains and rods for bridge-building, or on the movement of canal boats through water, but, as Sir Alexander Gibb has remarked, they were 'always carried out scrupulously, in logical order and with real scientific care'. Moreover, though he himself lacked a thorough scientific education, he could draw on the scientific help of others, as in 1814 when he carried out experiments on the strength of iron with the assistance of Peter Barlow, Professor of Mathematics at Woolwich Military Academy, who published the results in his book on *The Strength of Materials*.[2] Telford himself contributed long articles on architecture, bridge-building, and canals to the *Edinburgh Encyclopaedia*. He also wrote a treatise *On Mills* (1798).[3] He accumulated a large collection of scientific and technological

[1] Letter to David Little, 27 January 1797, quoted in Smiles, op. cit., p. 134, and Gibb, op. cit., pp. 266–7. This practice of noting down information, gained from reading and observation, in a pocket memorandum book, 'a sort of engineer's vade-mecum', was continued by Telford throughout his life.

[2] For Barlow, see the *Dictionary of National Biography* (hereafter *DNB*) and also E. G. R. Taylor, *Mathematical Practitioners of Hanoverian England* (1966), pp. 330–1. Fairbairn later carried out similar experiments with the scientific aid of Eaton Hodgkinson. See Musson and Robinson, *Science and Technology*, pp. 77, 117–18, 481, 487. See also ibid., p. 79, and below p. 107, for the earlier experiments of Charles Bage.

[3] E. L. Burne (ed.), 'On Mills', by Thomas Telford, *Newcomen Society Transactions*, vol. XVII (1936–7).

H

books, many of which he donated to the Institution of Civil Engineers when he was elected its first President in 1820. But he always stressed the practical side of engineering, and was scornful of engineering theories untested by experience.

John Rennie's career, as Dr Boucher has emphasized, provides 'a happy blend of theory and practice'.[1] He was educated at Dunbar High School, where he displayed remarkable ability in mathematics and in natural and experimental philosophy, before proceeding to Edinburgh University, where he developed a lifelong friendship with John Robison, the famous Professor of Natural Philosophy. In his youth he is said to have read 'the treatises of Belidor, Parent, and Lambert; Emmerson's *Fluxions and Mechanics*, Switzer's *Hydraulics*, Smeaton's *Experimental Inquiry*, and others'. At the same time he had a thorough practical training under the celebrated millwright, Andrew Meikle, inventor of the threshing machine and the spring sail for windmills. In his subsequent civil and mechanical engineering structures, 'he applied scientific theory, as well as practical experience . . . and used his university training to seek out the root causes of problems which he encountered'. In regard to his water-wheel constructions, for example, Dr Boucher remarks:

> It should not be thought that Rennie's application of water power was based on a mere rule of thumb and tradition. He was a practical student of the science of hydraulics, as has been shown by reference to the textbooks he studied. Among his possessions is a handbook on hydraulics in his own writing compiled by himself. Along with the principal formulae are tables incorporating their application.

Rennie also helped John Robison with articles published by the latter in 1797 under the title *Outlines of a Course of Lectures in Mechanical Philosophy*, which then appeared in the third edition of the *Encyclopaedia Britannica*, and were afterwards published separately in four volumes on *Mechanical Philosophy*. It is evident that Rennie had a very good knowledge of structural theory, and Dr Boucher has demonstrated in detail how

[1] In addition to Dr Boucher's recent book on Rennie, previously cited, see also the older life by Smiles, *Lives of the Engineers* (1874), vol. II, in which Rennie's successful combination of theory and practice is similarly emphasized.

he applied this to bridge-building, etc. Rennie was one of the founders of the London Literary and Philosophical Institution, which he attended whenever possible, and he was also a member of the Smeatonian Society. Like Telford, he built up a library rich in works on engineering and other subjects.

Other engineers of this period, such as Thomas Hewes, Peter Ewart, and George Lee in Manchester, were similarly knowledgeable in science and technology.[1] Henry Maudslay, although he started work at twelve years of age, was another remarkable example of 'self-education'. 'He was not merely a mechanical genius wholly ignorant of science; astronomy and the manufacture of telescopes for his own use was his chief hobby. Faraday was his close friend and a frequent visitor to his works. Like many inventors of this period, scientific discoveries were of as much interest to Maudslay as his practical achievements were to the scientist.'[2]

William Fairbairn, another great self-educated engineer, has left his own account of how he spent his youthful evenings studying arithmetic, algebra, geometry, trigonometry, etc.[3] After starting his own engineering business in Manchester, he became a member of the Literary and Philosophical Society, carried out important scientific experiments with Eaton Hodgkinson, the mathematician, on the strength of iron beams and pillars,[4] was eventually elected a Fellow of the Royal Society, and wrote a considerable number of books on engineering and industrial development.[5] Other leading engineers

[1] See Musson and Robinson, *Science and Technology*, pp. 98–101.

[2] Jewkes, op. cit., pp. 46–7. Similar examples of the relationships between scientists such as Faraday, metallurgists, and engineers in the early nineteenth century are provided in the diaries of the Swiss industrialist, J. C. Fischer. See W. O. Henderson, *J. C. Fischer and his Diary of Industrial England 1814–51* (1966), pp. 5, 12, 13, 33, 36–7, 65, 106, 117, 160.

[3] W. Pole (ed.), *The Life of Sir William Fairbairn . . . Partly written by himself* (1877), pp. 72–80, 101, 103. See Musson and Robinson, *Science and Technology*, pp. 480–1.

[4] See *Manchester Literary and Philosophical Society Memoirs*, 3rd ser., vol. V (1831); *British Association, Third Report* (1833), *Fourth Report* (1835), *Fifth Report* (1835), *Seventh Report* (1837); *Royal Society Transactions*, 14 May 1840. See Musson and Robinson *Science and Technology*, pp. 117–18, 481, 487.

[5] See, for example, his *Useful Information for Engineers* (1856), *The Rise and Progress of Civil and Mechanical Engineering* (1859), *Iron: Its History, Properties and Process of Manufacture* (1861), and *Treatise on Mills and Millwork* (2 vols., 1861–3).

acquired scientific knowledge in much the same way, but they were not all 'self-educated'; Nasmyth, for example, like Rennie, had the benefit of a good academic education.[1] Charles Holtzappfel also appears to have been well educated and 'devoted himself assiduously to the acquirement of scientific and practical knowledge'.[2]

It was not only in engineering that science was applied. The famous potter, Josiah Wedgwood, was greatly interested in experimental scientific research into clays, glazes, colouring, and temperature control.[3] Together with Watt, Boulton, and other industrialists, he associated with scientists such as Darwin, Priestley, and Withering, and was elected a Fellow of the Royal Society. Moreover, in his factory at Etruria, he introduced men who could apply scientific knowledge to pottery manufacture:

> Scientific men were engaged, at liberal salaries, in the various departments of the business – in chemistry, in design, in modelling, in painting, etc. The ingenious Mr Alexander Chisholme, who had been employed in experimental chemistry by Dr William Lewis, the celebrated author of the 'Commercium Philosophico-Technicum', was taken into Wedgwood and Bentley's service in 1781, and for many years . . . up to the period of his death, enjoyed the bounty of Mr Wedgwood.[4]

John Marshall, the great Leeds flax-spinner, also had an enthusiasm for natural philosophy, attending scientific lectures and putting his knowledge to practical use:

> Before the age of forty his intellectual interests had revolved around the mills and new scientific techniques.

---

[1] See Musson and Robinson, *Science and Technology*, pp. 489–90.

[2] *Proceedings of the Institution of Civil Engineers*, 1848, p. 14. Holtzappfel's book on *Turning and Mechanical Manipulation* (3 vols., 1843) 'displays a masterly knowledge of technical art and of the scientific principles underlying it'. *DNB*.

[3] R. E. Schofield, 'Josiah Wedgwood and a Proposed Eighteenth-Century Industrial Research Organization', *Isis*, vol. 47 (1956), pp. 16–19; 'Josiah Wedgwood, Industrial Chemist', *Chymia*, vol. 5 (1959), pp. 180–92.

[4] J. Ward [and S. Shaw], *The Borough of Stoke-upon-Trent* (1843), pp. 433–4. See also S. Parkes, *Chemical Essays* (1815), vol. I, pp. 48–9. For Lewis and Chisholm, see Musson and Robinson, *Science and Technology*, pp. 53–4.

He studied science because it helped him: a knowledge of chemistry was useful in bleaching, the theory of machines in providing power, the properties of materials in construction. Beyond this, he took lecture-notes on optics, electricity, and astronomy. He studied and talked about geology . . . In short he wanted to keep up with the rush of modern knowledge because it could be useful.[1]

He was a member of the Literary and Philosophical Society of Leeds, and participated in the founding of a Lancastrian school and Mechanics' Institute in that town; later he proposed the establishment of a university there, and subscribed towards the new university in London, becoming a member of its council.

Professor Rimmer has also shown how Charles Bage, who was associated in business with Marshall, made similar use of applied science. Thus in designing the Castle Foregate mill at Shrewsbury, 'Bage calculated the strength of his mill beams and proved them by full-scale tests. In this, and in other fields like bleaching, he was abreast if not ahead of current developments in science and engineering.'[2]

Bleaching provides a particularly good example of applied science. The discoveries of the scientists Scheele and Berthollet have already been mentioned. We have found abundant evidence of applied chemistry in the correspondence of James Watt, Thomas Henry (of Manchester), and others, who utilized their chemical knowledge in bleaching, dyeing, and calico-printing experiments.[3] As early as the mid-eighteenth century one comes across a reference to chemical analysis of water-supplies preparatory to location of a bleachworks,[4] while later

[1] W. G. Rimmer, *Marshall's of Leeds, Flax Spinners 1788–1886* (1960), p. 103. See also Musson and Robinson, *Science and Technology*, pp. 153–5, 329–32.

[2] Rimmer, op. cit., p. 59. Bage combined mathematical theory with experimental testing in ascertaining the strength of iron beams and columns for mill construction. T. C. Bannister, 'The First Iron-framed Buildings', *Architectural Review*, vol. 108 (April 1950), pp. 231–46; A. W. Skempton, 'The Origin of Iron Beams', *Actes VIII International Conference History of Science* (Florence, 1956), vol. 3, pp. 1029–39; H. R. Johnson and A. W. Skempton, 'William Strutt's Cotton Mills, 1793–1812', *Newcomen Society Transactions*, vol. XXX (1955–7), pp. 179–205.

[3] See Musson and Robinson, *Science and Technology*, chaps. VII, VIII, IX.

[4] F. Home, *Experiments on Bleaching* (1756), pp. 281–8; S. Parkes, *Chemical Essays* (1815), vol. IV, pp. 211–12.

on, in the early nineteenth century, one finds the scientist John Dalton providing similar services to industry.[1] A great deal of evidence has also come to light regarding James Watt's collaboration with Dr Joseph Black in the development of synthetic soda manufacture.[2]

In the development of the steam engine, science also played a considerable role.[3] Papin, Savery, and Newcomen owed much to the earlier scientific investigations of such men as Boyle and Huygens. Watt's relations with Black – discoverer of the principle of latent heat – at the time of his development of the steam engine have often been referred to, but Watt's own scientific abilities have been inadequately appreciated. It is abundantly clear, however, that, in the words of his intimate friend, Professor John Robison, he 'was a person of truly philosophical mind, eminently conversant in all branches of natural knowledge'.[4] He was on very friendly terms, not only with Robison, but with Black, Anderson, and other professors at Glasgow and Edinburgh universities,[5] and later with Priestley, Darwin, and most other eminent philosophers in England, and also with many French, German, and other continental scientists. He was not merely a brilliant mechanic, but a truly scientific engineer and chemist, well versed in contemporary scientific knowledge and constantly engaged in scientific experiments. He inherited the abilities of his grandfather, a teacher of mathematics, and of his father, a shipwright;

[1] Sir A. J. Sykes, *Concerning the Bleaching Industry* (1925), p. 91. Sykes, of Edgeley, Stockport, 'employed John Dalton, the famous scientist, as consultant on the quality of their water supply'. Parkes, op. cit., vol. IV, pp. 181 ff., strongly emphasized the necessity of chemical analysis of water supplies for bleaching, dyeing, and calico-printing.

[2] See Musson and Robinson, *Science and Technology*, chap X.

[3] See M. Kerker, 'Science and the Steam Engine', *Technology and Culture*, vol. 2 (1961), pp. 381–90; the introduction by A. E. Musson to the new edition of H. W. Dickinson, *Short History of the Steam Engine* (1963); D. S. L. Cardwell, *Steam Power in the Eighteenth Century* (1963).

[4] Article on 'Steam Engine', *Encyclopaedia Britannica*, 3rd ed. (1797). Robison's articles on steam and steam engines were later reprinted, with notes and additions by Watt (Edinburgh, 1818). See also F. Arago, 'James Watt', in *Biographies of Distinguished Scientific Men* (English trans., 1857); J. P. Muirhead, *The Life of James Watt*, 2nd ed. (1859); G. Williamson, *Memorials of . . . James Watt* (1856).

[5] See Musson and Robinson, *Science and Technology*, pp. 179–80, for Watt's relations with Anderson.

educated at Greenock Academy and trained as an instrument-maker, he early exhibited strong interests in mathematics, mechanics, and chemistry – before he was fifteen he had read Gravesande's *Mathematical Elements of Natural Philosophy*, translated by Desaguliers. Later, when appointed instrument-maker to Glasgow University, he started learning German so that he might read Leupold's *Theatrum Machinarum*, and Italian for a similar purpose; to construct an organ, he read the *Harmonics* of Dr Robert Smith, of Cambridge. Before his famous improvements on the steam engine, he had read Desaguliers and Belidor on this subject, and these improve-ments were the outcome of careful experiments on steam and on models of Savery and Newcomen engines, in which he con-sulted with Professor Black. His famous tea-kettle, usually dismissed nowadays as mythical, was in fact, as his diary reveals, used as a miniature boiler in a series of laboratory experi-ments, and he produced tables on the thermal efficiency of steam engines, based on mathematical theory as well as prac-tical experiment. He also appears to have rediscovered the principle of latent heat, independently of Black.[1] Watt himself, of course, like Boulton, Wedgwood, Keir, and other indus-trialists, was made a Fellow of the Royal Society.

That science could make useful contributions to early steam engineering is also shown by other evidence. The scientist Davies Gilbert (or Giddy), for example, provided Jonathan Hornblower, the practical engineer, with a great deal of advice in regard to the latter's attempts to develop his compound and 'rotary' (turbine) engines.[2] Similarly, he rendered valuable assistance to Richard Trevithick, inventor of the high-pressure, non-condensing steam engine.[3]

In many ways, then, applied science was helping to bring about the Industrial Revolution. On the other hand, one must not fall into the error of supposing that the latter was simply

[1] On this latter point, see D. Fleming, 'Latent Heat and the Invention of the Watt Engine', *Isis* vol. 43 (1952), pp. 3–5.

[2] A. C. Todd, 'Davies Gilbert – Patron of Engineers (1767–1839) and Jonathan Hornblower (1753–1815)', *Newcomen Society Transactions*, vol. XXXII (1959–60), pp. 1–13.

[3] H. W. Dickinson and A. Titley, *Richard Trevithick, the Engineer and the Man* (1934), p. 36 *et passim*.

a product of the Scientific Revolution. . . . In the early mechanization of the cotton industry, applied science appears to
have played a very minor role.[1] Inventors such as Kay, Paul,
Wyatt, Hargreaves, Arkwright, Crompton, and Cartwright
appear to have had little or no scientific training, though they
often utilized the knowledge and skills of clock- and instru-
ment-makers. They have fairly recently been described as
'mostly . . . men of some social standing and good education',[2]
but this is questionable. Kay, Hargreaves, and Arkwright, for
instance, appear to have had a very limited and rudimentary
schooling before being put to a trade, and Wyatt, though
educated at Lichfield Grammar School, became a carpenter.
Cartwright, it is true, was a Fellow of Magdalen College,
Oxford, but he was a Doctor of Divinity and was apparently
unacquainted with mechanical matters prior to his invention of
the power-loom. Crompton, however, is an interesting case.
He had a good schooling in writing, arithmetic, book-keeping,
geometry, mensuration, and mathematics, under an outstanding
master, William Barlow of Little Bolton, and during his later
'teens he continued his education by attending evening-school,
improving his knowledge of algebra, trigonometry, and
mathematics generally.[3] According to French, his biographer,
his invention of the mule 'appears to have been the result of
pure inductive philosophy, followed out step by step with a
mathematical precision for which his mind had been duly
prepared by previous education'.[4]

Sometimes one comes across contemporary scientists and
industrialists deploring the general lack of applied science in
industry. Theophilus L. Rupp, for instance, a German who

---

[1] As was pointed out by Arkwright's Counsel during the great patent case of
1785, in oft-quoted words: 'It is well known that the most useful discoveries
that have been made in every branch of art and manufacture have not been made
by speculative philosophers in their closets but by ingenious mechanics, practically acquainted with the subject matter of their discoveries.'

This statement may be contrasted, however, with that of defending Counsel
in the Tennant bleaching patent case of 1802, that 'most of these discoveries arise
from scientific men engaging in them, for the purpose of science and speculation
in their closet'.

[2] Jewkes, op. cit., pp. 44–5.
[3] G. J. French, *The Life and Times of Samuel Crompton* (1859), pp. 30, 32.
[4] Ibid., p. 53.

settled in Manchester as a cotton manufacturer in the late eighteenth century, wrote as follows.[1]

The arts [manufactures], which supply the luxuries, conveniences, and necessaries of life, have derived but little advantage from philosophers. . . . In mechanics, for instance, we find that the most important inventions and improvements have been made, not through the reasonings of philosophers, but through the ingenuity of artists [craftsmen], and not unfrequently by common workmen. The chemist, in particular, if we except the pharmaceutical laboratory, has but little claim on the arts: on the contrary, he is indebted to them for the greatest discoveries and a prodigious number of facts, which form the basis of his science. In the discovery of the art of making bread, of the vinous and acetous fermentations, of tanning, of working ores and metals, of making glass and soap, of the action and applications of manures, and in numberless other discoveries of the highest importance, though they are all chemical processes, the chemist has no share. . . . The art of dyeing has attained a high degree of perfection without the aid of the chemist, who is totally ignorant of the rationale of many of its processes, and the little he knows of this subject is of late date.

It is significant, however, that Rupp went on to refer warmly to the recent experimental and theoretical work of Thomas Henry of Manchester, in dyeing, and of the French chemist, Berthollet, in bleaching. And it is also significant that Rupp himself was described by his fellow-countryman, P. A. Nemnich as

a German, who possesses great knowledge of chemistry, and who at the same time, as a manufacturer, can carry out most splendid experimental applications for the benefit of scientific knowledge . . . Mr Rupp at the time of my visit to Manchester was very busy with the building of a big

[1] T. L. Rupp, 'On the Process of Bleaching with the Oxygenated Muriatic Acid', *Manchester Literary and Philosophical Society Memoirs*, vol. V, part i (1798).

spinning mill to be erected according to his own ideas, and many improvements are expected from him.[1]

Rupp was a member of the Manchester Literary and Philosophical Society, to which he read several papers, including a notable one on chlorine bleaching and another making an anti-phlogiston attack on Priestley and defending 'the new chemical theory', with numerous references to the works of foreign chemists such as Lavoisier, Bergman, etc.[2] William Henry, second only to John Dalton as a scientific chemist in Manchester in this period,[3] referred to some of his experiments having been witnessed by 'my friend Mr Rupp . . . who is much conversant in the observation of chemical facts'.[4]

Like Rupp, however, William Nicholson also referred to the many matters on which chemists were ignorant, or which they could not adequately explain.[5] The great controversy over phlogiston and the new chemical theory, he said, 'amounts to a confession of ignorance in our theoretical explanation'. But he pointed out that continuous experimental investigation was leading to the discovery of the laws of nature, and that one must expect the 'successive emendation' of scientific theories, and 'the rejection of principles formerly held to be essential to the science' of chemistry. Nicholson himself did much to spread a knowledge of chemical theories and facts, by his own works and by his translations of those of foreign chemists.

In engineering, too, one comes across similar remarks emphasizing the role of empiricism. George Atwood, for instance, Fellow of Trinity College, Cambridge, and lecturer in natural philosophy, pointed out inconsistencies in the theory

---

[1] P. A. Nemnich, *Beschreibung einer in Sommer 1799 von Hamburg nach und durch England geschehenen Reise* (1800), p. 324.

[2] *Manchester Literary and Philosophical Society Memoirs*, vol. V, part i (1798).

[3] See Musson and Robinson, *Science and Technology*, pp. 246–50.

[4] *Philosophical Transactions* (1797), p. 410. Manchester Central Reference Library possesses a copy of Henry's *General View of the Nature and Objects of Chemistry* (1799) inscribed to 'Mr Rupp from the Author'.

[5] See, for example, his remarks in his *Dictionary of Chemistry* (1795), pp. iii–v and 1–2. He had previously published *An Introduction to Natural Philosophy* (1782) and *The First Principles of Chemistry* (1790), both of which ran into several editions. Later he started *Nicholson's Journal of Natural Philosophy, Chemistry and Arts*, an important scientific periodical. See *DNB* and Hans, op. cit., pp. 115 and 158.

of motion and doubted whether it could provide any assistance to the practical mechanic in constructing power-driven machinery. 'Machines of this sort owe their origin and improvement to other sources: it is from long experience of repeated trials, errors, deliberations, [and] corrections, continued through the lives of individuals, and by successive generations of them, that sciences, strictly called practical, derive their gradual advancement . . .'[1]

Peter Ewart, however, an outstanding Manchester engineer of that day, well versed in engineering science,[2] though regretting 'that theory should appear to be at variance with practice', thought that Atwood had 'pressed his argument too far'.[3] There was no doubt 'that ingenious men, of rare natural endowments, have, without any scientific aid, accomplished wonders in the invention and improvement of machinery', but there were also some notable examples to the contrary in 'the history of useful discoveries in mechanics'.

> If Huygens and Hooke had not been scientific as well as ingenious men, we might possibly have been still ignorant of the properties of the balance regulated by springs. If Smeaton had not availed himself of just theory, as well as experiment, we might still have had to learn the principles by which we must be guided in applying water to the best advantage as a moving power. If a clear and strong understanding, and a mind richly stored with scientific attainments, had not been combined with wonderful fertility of invention in the justly celebrated improver of the steam engine [Watt]; incalculable labour might still have been wasted in performing operations which are now accomplished with as much ease and regularity as the gentle motions of a time-piece.

Similarly, in regard to the application of chemical science, one frequently comes across contemporary statements of its importance. Thus we find William Henry putting forward

---

[1] G. Atwood, *A Treatise on the Rectilinear Motion and Rotation of Bodies* (1784), p. 381, quoted by P. Ewart, 'On the Measure of Moving Force', *Manchester Literary and Philosophical Society Memoirs*, 2nd ser., vol. II (1813), p. 111.

[2] See Musson and Robinson, *Science and Technology*, p. 99.

[3] Ewart, op. cit., pp. 112–14.

A General View of the Nature and Objects of Chemistry, and of its Application to Arts and Manufactures (Manchester, 1799), in which, after quoting Bacon in support of 'the union of theory with practice', he referred to the illustrious example of Watt and Wedgwood, 'both of whom have been not less benefactors of philosophy, than eminent for practical skill', and went on to demonstrate the utility of chemistry in a wide range of industries – in metallurgy, in the production of alkalis, acids, etc., in the glass and pottery manufactures, in brewing, in bleaching, dyeing, and calico-printing.

Some parts of the natural philosophy of the eighteenth century, as of the seventeenth, had no immediate practical application. Though in some cases they were ultimately to have revolutionary industrial consequences, they were originally developed mainly out of intellectual curiosity, out of a desire to unravel the mysteries of nature. Electricity and magnetism, for instance, which were very popular subjects in contemporary lecture courses, played little or no part in the early Industrial Revolution. 'Electricity,' said the German traveller, C. P. Moritz, 'is the plaything of the English.'[1] But other subjects, such as chemistry, mathematics, mechanics, hydraulics, and hydrostatics. . . . certainly were studied for utilitarian as well as scientific reasons. Even the most purely philosophical investigations sometimes had very practical connexions and consequences. Priestley, for example, says that he began his researches into 'airs' or gases as a result of living in Leeds next to a brewery, where he noticed that 'fixed air' (carbon dioxide) was evolved in the fermentation vats;[2] his investigations led immediately to the manufacture of artificial mineral waters,[3] while their long-term consequences were of far wider importance.

[1] C. P. Moritz, *Journeys of a German in England in 1782* (trans. and ed. by R. Nettel, London, 1965), p. 70.

[2] J. Priestley, *Experiments and Observations on Different Kinds of Air*, vol. II (1775), pp. 269–70; F. W. Gibbs, *Joseph Priestley* (1965), pp. 57–60.

[3] See Musson and Robinson, *Science and Technology*, pp. 234–9.

3 Some Statistics of the Industrial Revolution in Britain

T. S. ASHTON

[The following extracts are taken from the article by T. S. Ashton in *The Manchester School*, vol. XVI, 1948, pp. 214–34.]

The years between 1760 and 1830 saw a series of changes in British life so spectacular as to lead historians to attach to the period the somewhat misleading title of the Industrial Revolution. Early observers, impressed by the developments associated with the names of Arkwright, Crompton, Watt, Cort, Stephenson, and many others, tended to regard the technical innovations as the hinge on which all else turned. It was only later that scholars began to ask why these men of invention appeared just when they did. Historians, obsessed as most of them are with the affairs of government, were at first disposed to give the answer in terms of policy. Some attributed the outbursts of invention and enterprise to the action of enlightened rulers who, they believed, had built up a powerful mercantilist society in England, with widespread connexions overseas: the inventions and the new methods of organization were the response of industry to the demands of trade. Others argued that it was not positive measures of statecraft, but the gradual decline of attempts at regulation and stimulus that threw open the door to innovation. One group of writers, looking at the social and religious affiliations of the industrialists, finds the source of the technical changes – and much else besides – in seventeenth-century puritanism and eighteenth-century nonconformity. Another, pointing out that the changes in technique were, in fact, less sudden than had been imagined, presents them as the fruit of a tree springing from the work of Newton, Bacon, and still earlier scientists. And yet another school of writers treats the whole movement as a product of the new systems of speculative thought and political theory to which the eighteenth century gave rise.

It is not my purpose to pass judgement on these interpretations of the Industrial Revolution. Every historical event is the result of everything that happened before; and there is, no doubt, some measure of truth in all of them. But historical relationships may be either close or remote – in space, in time, and in logic. If we wish to ascertain the degree of relationship between changes of one kind and those of another we must make use of statistical methods: today almost every branch of historical studies is becoming increasingly statistical. There is, let it be admitted, some danger in this development. For since economic phenomena are more susceptible of measurement than political or social or intellectual phenomena there may be a tendency to overstress their importance. Some recent writers – not all of them Marxists – have gone so far as to attribute the changes in politics, art, and religion, to the development of industrial technique or of 'production functions'. Schumpeter (who professes to see capitalism alike in the canvases of El Greco and in the evolution of the lounge suit) treats the Industrial Revolution as one of the long waves which he believes to be a characteristic of capitalistic progress; and Kondratieff, who has expressed this determinist doctrine in extreme form, suggests, not merely that the wars and revolutions of the period had economic aspects, but that they were the direct and inevitable result of pressures generated by the long wave.

I have no wish to enter these regions of speculation [in this paper]. I am content to express the not very original opinion that the *proximate* causes of the Industrial Revolution were economic. Under whatever favouring conditions of policy, creed, or scientific thought, there took place in the eighteenth century a vast increase of natural resources, labour, capital and enterprise – of what the economist calls the factors of production. In the early stages it was the growth of capital that was of chief significance. At the beginning of the century the Government itself had been obliged to pay 7 or 8 per cent for money, and but for the operation of the usury laws industrialists would have had to pay considerably more than this. Since, however, people were prohibited from offering more than 5 per cent, and evasion of the law was expensive, some of them, it appears, had to go without the resources they needed. When, fifty years later, the yield on Consols was down to 3 or less, and 4 per cent was the accepted long-term rate over a wide field of business, all sorts of projects that had been previously impossible came into the open. It would, no doubt, be a mistake to interpret the financial trends of the eighteenth century in terms of twentieth-century conditions. There was, of course, no organized capital market. The typical firm was a partnership which obtained its resources largely by the reinvestment of profits; and the amount ploughed back, it seems likely, was influenced very little by changes in the rate of interest. Outside ordinary industry, however, were the chartered companies, the turnpike trusts, the river and canal and dock undertakings and other public utilities. When money was cheap these tended to increase the scope of their operations; investment here, we may assume, increased incomes in the community in general, and so increased the demand for the products of industry in the narrow sense. In this way the fall in the rate of interest played a part (the importance of which has not, I think, been properly appreciated) in the industrial expansion.

Innovations means much more than technical invention: it includes (as Schumpeter says) changes in markets, in methods, and in the proportions in which factors are combined to attain a given end. It is not possible to measure such changes precisely, and even the course of invention in the narrow sense is not easy to chart. Much technical improvement takes place behind the scenes: in the eighteenth century, in particular, there was some reluctance to make public even such a hazy sketch of the nature of a device as was necessary for a specification. Nevertheless, the number of patents taken out may serve perhaps as a rough index of innovation. The figures in Table I show, as we should expect, a strong upward trend, but they show also the cyclical variations typical of most economic data. There are significant peaks in the figures for 1766, 1769, 1783, 1792, 1801–2, 1813, 1818 and 1824–5 – nearly all of them years when the rate of interest was low, and when, as we have evidence, industry and trade were active. (1813 is the only one of the series which cannot be described as a year of boom.) It may reasonably be objected that many of the discoveries may possibly have been made earlier but were held back until times were more propitious. Kondratieff has argued (though without much supporting evidence) that most major inventions are made during periods of recession and applied during the ensuing periods of recovery. But at least, the fact that so many patents were taken out in years of prosperity, and so few in years of depression (such as 1775, 1788, 1793, 1797, 1804, 1817, 1820, and 1826), suggests that it was the hope of gain, rather than of avoiding loss, that gave the impulse. It may also be objected that many patents were taken out by men whose hopes outran their ingenuity or practical sense, and that the high figures of the booms represent not solid progress but the mere blowing of bubbles. A glance at the names of the patentees in each of the years of high activity suggests, however, that there is something more in it than that. The list includes, for 1769, Arkwright, Watt, and Wedgwood; for 1783, Cort, Onions, and Bramah; for 1792, Wilkinson, Cartwright, and Curr; for 1801–2, the Earl of Dundonald, Trevithick, and Symington; for 1813, Horrocks; for 1818, Brunel and Mushet; and for 1824–5, Maudslay, Roberts, and Biddle. One could write a fairly complete history of technology for this period without mention of any other names than these.

The chronology of patents is a field that would repay further study. Sir Arnold Plant, who has surveyed the later history of patents (from 1854) makes the interesting suggestion that the inventive faculty is aroused by any sudden change in the trends of prices, wages, or costs.[1] On such matters we have for the period of the Industrial Revolution only very scanty data. But it may be noticed that the peaks in the figures of patents in 1766, 1783, 1802, and 1818 came (at varying intervals, it is true) after the transition from conditions of war to those of peace, with, in each case, some disturbance of relative prices. And the outstanding booms in patents of 1792, 1802, and 1824–5 came at the end of periods when the rate of interest had been falling significantly. It may be, indeed, that both the

[1] 'The Economic Theory Concerning Patents for Inventions', *Economica*, N.S., vol. I, no. 1 (1934).

TABLE I

Year	Number of Patents	Yield on Consols	Year	Number of Patents	Yield on Consols
1756	3	3·4	1794	55	4·4
7	9	3·4	5	51	4·5
8	14	3·2	6	75	4·8
9	10	3·6	7	54	5·9
60	14	3·8	8	77	5·9
1	9	3·9	9	82	5·1
2	17	4·3	1800	96	4·7
3	20	3·4	1	104	4·9
4	18	3·6	2	107	4·2
5	14	3·4	3	73	5·0
6	31	3·4	4	60	5·3
7	23	3·4	5	95	5·0
8	23	3·3	6	99	4·9
9	36	3·5	7	94	4·9
70	30	3·6	8	95	4·6
1	22	3·5	9	101	4·6
2	29	3·3	10	108	4·5
3	29	3·5	1	115	4·7
4	35	3·4	2	118	5·1
5	20	3·4	3	131	4·9
6	29	3·5	4	96	4·9
7	33	3·8	5	102	4·5
8	30	4·5	6	118	5·0
9	37	4·9	7	103	4·1
80	33	4·9	8	132	3·9
1	34	5·2	9	101	4·2
2	39	5·3	20	97	4·4
3	64	4·8	1	109	4·1
4	46	5·4	2	113	3·8
5	61	4·8	3	138	3·8
6	60	4·1	4	180	3·3
7	55	4·1	5	250	3·5
8	42	4·0	6	141	3·8
9	43	3·9	7	150	3·6
90	68	3·9	8	154	3·5
1	57	3·6	9	130	3·3
2	85	3·3	30	180	3·5
3	43	4·0			

secular and cyclical falls of interest rates explain why most of the inventions of the period were directed to the economy of labour rather than of natural resources or of capital. But this is speculation. It is at least clear that, whatever the nature of the connecting thread, the inventions were not a force operating more or less casually from outside the system, but were an integral part of the economic process.

The record of patents tells only a part of the story. Innovation was not simply a matter of the introduction of a number of devices at particular points of time: it was a continuous process. Details of the day-to-day adjustments of machinery, of the innumerable petty economies of materials, of the gradual training of labour, and so on, are hidden from us. But their results can be read in the statistics of output. . . .

4 The Natural History of Industry

CHARLES C. GILLISPIE

[This article was first published in *Isis*, vol. 48, 1957, pp. 398–407.]

I

In a previous paper, the problem of science and industrialization was pursued in some detail through an account of the discovery of the Leblanc process. The present paper approaches the question on a broader plane and ventures to offer some general considerations. Both articles are a result of investigations pursued in France, and refer specially, therefore, to the pattern of French scientific and industrial development. This was necessarily affected by certain factors peculiar to French history, notably the ever-growing centralization of cultural development in Paris and its learned bodies and the profound instinct of everyone concerned – scientist and statesman, industrialist and artisan – to expect of a paternalistic state the impetus which their British counterparts drew from private venture and expected only of themselves. But these are only social influences. Neither science nor industrialization has ever been national in scope, and to consider a question related to the Industrial Revolution in a framework other than British may have the merit of modifying the tendency to see this great event in the exclusive perspective of the Midlands of England and the Lowlands of Scotland.

In histories of eighteenth-century and imperial France, the assertion is often encountered that science was revolutionizing manufacturing, and Napoleon's encouragement of this process is frequently described as a major reason for the success of his industrial policy until the crisis of 1810. Historians have obviously drawn this judgement from contemporary writings by scientists themselves. That science ought to receive public credit for the unprecedented progress of the arts since the 1770s or 1780s is perhaps the most protean reflection in the technological literature of the time. Of chemistry, for example, Chaptal writes:

> On l'a vue donner de nouvelles méthodes pour le blanchissage des toiles; fabriquer, de toutes pièces, le sel ammoniaque, l'alun et les couperoses; décomposer le sel marin pour en extraire la soude; enricher la teinture de nouveaux mordans; former le salpêtre et le raffiner, par des procédés plus simples; composer la poudre par des méthodes plus promptes et plus sûres; réduire le tannage des peaux à ses vrais principes, et en abréger l'opération; perfectionner l'extraction et le travail des métaux; simplifier la distillation des vins; rendre les moyens de chauffage plus économiques; établir la combustion de l'huile et l'éclairage de nos habitations sur de nouveaux principes, et nous fournir les moyens de nous élever dans les airs et d'aller consulter la nature à trois ou quatre mille toises audessus de nos têtes.[1]

No one, it is true, specifies exactly how science was changing the face of industry. But knowledge is power; yesterday's banality is today's source material; and on the basis of all this authoritative testimony, the modern historian has very naturally supposed that theoretical science exerted a fructifying and even a causative influence in industrialization. The proposition is inherently persuasive, and there must be something in it.

II

The problem, however, is to know what there is in it. For if the question be approached in detail – as for example in my study of the origin of the Leblanc process – it proves extraordinarily difficult to trace the course of any significant theoretical concept from abstract formulation to actual use in industrial operations. The objection might be raised that such an approach loses sight of the forest for the trees. But in this case no coherent pattern emerges from the widest perspective or the most distant focus. Consider the more significant achieve-

[1] J. A. C. Chaptal, *Chimie appliquée aux arts* (3 vols.; Paris, 1807), vol. I, p. xiv.

ments in basic science – the progress of taxonomy in botany and zoology, the theory of combustion, the foundation of exact crystallography, the discovery of the electric current, the extension of the inverse-square relationship to magnetic and electrostatic forces, the analytical formulation of mechanics, the resolution of the planetary inequalities – and range these accomplishments side by side in the mind's eye with the crucial points of technological advance in the Industrial Revolution – deep ploughing and crop rotation, the development of power-driven textile machinery and factory production, the discovery of coke and its substitution for charcoal in smelting ores, the improvement of the steam engine by the separate condenser and the sun-and-planet linkage, the puddling process for the conversion of iron to steel – and it is immediately evident that no apparent relationship existed between these two sets of achievements except the vague and uninteresting one that both occurred in a technical nexus. In a recent book Mr and Mrs Clow have demonstrated with great force that the rapid expansion of chemical industry must henceforth be numbered among the basic factors in industrialization.[1] But although the chemical industry was no doubt closer to science than any other, their discussion does not suffer in the slightest from the fact that its references to the revolution in theoretical chemistry are fleeting – to have brought this into an account of Scottish industry would have been to introduce an extraneous element. And this excellent work does not illuminate the question, therefore, as indeed it was not intended to do; in fact the authors fall into the altogether trifling error of repeating the legend about Watt's invention of the separate condenser having been a practical outcome of Black's formulation of the principle of latent heat.[2] Ultimately, then, one is tempted to fall back upon a generalization of L. J. Henderson's much quoted dictum to the effect that science is infinitely more indebted to the steam engine than is the steam engine to science. But this is too easy a way out, for repeating this famous remark does not conjure away the sources. It cannot very well

[1] A. and N. Clow, *The Chemical Revolution* (London, 1952).
[2] Ibid., p. 590; cf., Donald Fleming, 'Latent Heat and the Invention of the Watt Engine', *Isis*, vol. 43 (1952), pp. 3–6.

be supposed that men of the eminence of Chaptel, Lavoisier, Cuvier, and many others had no more in mind, in their frequent references to the utility of science, than to win for it public esteem, and that no real substance lay behind their belief in its practical contribution to the arts.[1]

Neither does it clarify the issue to turn to economic history. For, on the one hand, the sources do not exhibit a steady movement forward in French industry, and on the other hand, except in the case of chemistry, no correlation is to be discerned between the areas of greatest progress in industry and in science. More intensive scientific attention was devoted, for example, to the extractive and metallurgical industries than to any other. To cite only the most obvious illustrations, Gabriel Jars's splendid *Voyages métallurgiques* was published between 1774 and 1781;[2] in 1788, Berthollet, Vandermonde, and Monge printed a very lucid memoir on iron and steel;[3] and in 1794, a further treatise by Monge was the most solid contribution to the technological series commissioned by the Committee of Public Safety in order to stimulate war production.[4] But what practical effect all this study had is far from

[1] Though outdated, the most comprehensive account of technological history is still Charles Ballot, *L'Introduction du machinisme dans l'industrie française* (Paris, 1923). To mention only the most obvious printed materials, Ballot may be supplemented with G. and H. Bourgin, *L'industrie sidérurgique en France au début de la Révolution* (Paris, 1920); Odette Viennet, *Napoléon et l'industrie française* (Paris, 1947); A. L. Dunham, *La Révolution industrielle en France* (Paris, 1953); Henri Sée, *Histoire économique de la France*, vol. II (Paris, 1951); *Documents relatifs à la vie économique de la Révolution* (5 vols., Paris 1906–10), a series which in 1911 became *Bulletin D'histoire économique de la Revolution* (5 vols., 1912–19); and among older works: J. A. C. Chaptal, *De l'industrie française* (2 vols., Paris, 1819); C. A. Costaz, *Essai sur l'administration de l'agriculture, du commerce, des manufactures, et des subsistances* (Paris, 1818); the *Bulletin de la Sociétié d'Encouragement* (from 1801); the *Journal des Mines* (from 1794); and the *Annales de Chimie* (from 1789).

[2] (3 vols.; Lyon, 1774–81). Published posthumously, these memoirs describe the iron industries of Germany, Sweden, Norway, England, and Scotland which Jars had studied between 1757 and 1769 in a series of expeditions originally undertaken at the instance of Trudaine.

[3] 'Mémoire sur le Fer', *Mémoires de l'Académie royale des sciences* (1786), pp. 132–200.

[4] *Description de l'art de fabriquer les canons* (Paris, 1794). Monge begins this treatise with a little disquisition on the composition of the atmosphere and the occurrence of iron as the oxide, but his description of smelting procedures does not, of course, differ in any essential from that given in the 1786 *Mémoire* (note 3), in which what iron ore is deprived of is its dephlogisticated air (loc. cit., p. 133).

clear. The metal trades proved the least resilient in recovering from the drastic technological setbacks dealt to French industry by the revolutionary disturbances. There is some doubt whether rehabilitation was complete even by 1815.[1] All through this period, inspectors of the *Agence des mines* were very fretful about the reluctance of iron masters to disturb themselves by shifting to coke; and with good reason, for at the end of the Napoleonic wars the only foundry in all France using coke was the furnace established at Le Creusot, which had gone into operation in 1782.[2] In any case, if it be agreed that the central feature of industrialization was the development of factory production, the crucial role must clearly be ascribed to the textile industries, and one searches their history in vain for any trace of scientific influence, except in the bleaching or dyeing of the finished product. In textile manufacturing – and even in metallurgy – French entrepreneurs were shown the way, not by scientific research, but by Englishmen and Scotsmen. John Holker's establishment at Rouen is the most famous example, but judging from the number of traces which his compatriots have left behind them in the commercial sources at the *Archives nationales*, there must have been literally hundreds of British artisans selling eagerly sought skills and ingenuity in France in the latter part of the eighteenth century.[3] Many remained even through the 1790s. Yet despite the ambiguities just discussed, and notwithstanding the economic disarray of the 1790s, this is precisely the decade from which Cuvier, for example, illustrated the benefits conferred by science on the arts.[4] The literature, therefore, exhibits real contradictions, and it is with this in view as the problem to resolve that the remainder of this paper is addressed to the question of what sort of influence science actually did exert in manufacturing.

[1] Ballot, op. cit. pp. 494–527.

[2] Dunham, op. cit. p. 78.

[3] André Rémond, *John Holker* (Paris, 1946).

[4] Georges Cuvier, *Rapport historique sur les progrès des sciences naturelles* (Paris, 1808).

III

In approaching the problem, it will be convenient to recall the history of the Leblanc discovery, which resists with great firmness being fitted into either of the extreme views that are sometimes expressed about the historical relations between science and invention. It cannot be used as an illustration of the austere doctrine that there was no real connexion – Leblanc was closely associated with leading members of the scientific community, and it is a revealing fact that every one of the processes for making soda invented in France between 1775 and 1800 was verified and evaluated by one of a succession of three scientists, Macquer, Berthollet, and Darcet, who among them were informed about every development and exercised, therefore, a measure of control over the field. (This indeed was typical of the relationship, if not between science and the arts, at least between scientists and artisans, which obtained in eighteenth-century France and which lends to the phrase 'Science governs the Arts' a literal sense not always appreciated, one that goes far to explain the rebellion of the artisans' societies against the *Académie des sciences* at the time of the Revolution and the enmity of the popular clubs for science.)

On the other hand, neither does the Leblanc invention bear out the contention that there is no essential difference between science and applied science. Leblanc seems to have found his process, not through some flashing theoretical insight, but by means of a fallacious analogy with the smelting of iron ore. Not only so, but after he had worked it out, neither he nor any of the other artisans interested in alkali production made any attempt to investigate or explain the nature of the reactions involved. They concentrated their efforts – though for a long time with no success – on trying to make money by one method or another – in Leblanc's case by first persuading the Government to subsidize him.

Instead, therefore, of substantiating a doctrinaire interpretation of the relations between science and industry, the history of the Leblanc discovery suggests rather that the two main departments of technical activity are distinct but related. It is a relationship which may, perhaps, be observed quite

generally throughout the technical history of industrialization
– it could equally well be illustrated by a detailed history of
any of the innovations credited to chemical science by Chaptal
in the passage quoted in the second paragraph of this paper, as
well as in many others of those eighteenth-century inventions
which owed anything at all to scientific activity.[1] And there
may even be discerned a certain structure in the relationship.
For schematically there were two phases through which
science moved in becoming effective in industry; first, the exploitation of science by inventors, artisans, and industrialists,
and second (often simultaneously), the conscious application
of science to practical problems.

IV

The first phase is precisely illustrated in the activities of Carny,
Malherbe, Guyton de Morveau, and Leblanc's other fore-
runners, whose processes for making soda were more scientific
and ultimately less successful than his – more scientific in that
instead of being discoveries, they were attempts to draw
advantage from reactions already known to chemical science.
This practical exploitation of scientific knowledge may also be
exemplified by the telegraph, the origins of military aviation,
the emergency production of saltpetre, and indeed by most of
the items which, like these, are cited by Pouchet, Despois,
and even Mathiez in their jejune portrayals of the great
revolution as favourable to scientific activity.[2] Actually, of
course, these accounts simply adopt the Jacobin view which
found value in science only in so far as its utility could be
demonstrated. In fact, however, the distinction between this
sort of thing and science is obvious and elementary. It can
even be brought down to the level of persons, where the
difference between the scientist and the practical man is
basically a matter of temperament.

The point was discussed by Lavoisier, when in his forlorn

[1] See, for example, Cuvier, pp. 345–58, for an enumeration of innovations
attributed to scientific progress.

[2] G. Pouchet, *Les sciences pendant la terreur* (Paris, 1896); Eugéne Despois, *Le
Vandalisme révolutionnaire* (Paris, 1868); Albert Mathiez, 'La mobilisation des
savants en l'an II', *Revue de Paris* (November–December 1917), pp. 542–65.

defence of the *Académie des sciences*, he was trying desperately to preserve the independence of science, of free inquiry, from the Jacobin passion for assimilating it to the useful arts. However useful to industry science may be, wrote Lavoisier – and he thought it very useful indeed – the spirit which moves the scientist is fundamentally unlike that which animates the artisan. The scientist works for love of science and to increase his own reputation. When he makes a discovery, he is eager to publish it, and his object is only to secure his intellectual property in his achievement. The artisan on the other hand, whether in his own research or in using the research of others, is always thinking of his economic advantage. He publicizes only what he cannot keep secret and tells only what he cannot hide. Society benefits both from the disinterested investigation of the *savant* and the interested speculation of the artisan. Confound the two, however, and both will lose the spirit distinctive to them.[1]

Already in the eighteenth century, France was playing Greece to the modern world, and men of learning clearly and instinctively distinguished between the domains of science and practice. Throughout its history, the *Académie des sciences* had had two duties: to advance the sciences and to act as a panel of experts who evaluated the projects of aspirants for the favour offered by the state in its perennial effort to encourage French industry. And the very procedures of the *Académie* as recorded in its *registres* make it evident that disinterested research was the main interest of the foremost members, and that technological *expertise* was at best their corporate duty.[2] To say that they despised the latter would strain the classical analogy. On the contrary, they regarded it as a just and important obligation, if sometimes an onerous and tiresome one; but however important to society, the realm of practice belonged to a different and a lower order of consideration than the realm of theory and abstraction and advancement of the understanding of nature.

In this attitude, French scientists were more severe, perhaps,

[1] Lavoisier to Lakanal, *Œuvres de Lavoisier*, (6 vols.; Paris, 1864–93), vol. IV, p. 623.

[2] Unfortunately the *procès-verbaux* of the academy remain unpublished. They may be consulted, however, at the *Archives de l'académie des sciences*, at the *Institut de France*.

than their colleagues in other countries and particularly in Great Britain. Accompanying this paper, there is another by Dr Robert E. Schofield, who offers an account of his most meticulous researches into the industrial orientation of science in the Lunar Society circle. And in a large sense Dr Schofield's subject would appear to be a further illustration of that mutual stimulation of science, commercial enterprise, and Puritan influence (now softened into Nonconformity or Unitarianism), successive manifestations of which so forcibly strike students of British social, intellectual, and scientific history from the seventeenth through the nineteenth centuries. But there is perhaps an underside to the coin of this famous correlation. For technical activity is one thing, but power of abstract thought is another; and it may well be wondered whether a certain vulgarity in this British utilitarianism – thoroughly evident, for example, in Bacon – was not responsible for the relative poverty of British achievement over the centuries in the abstract reaches of scientific thought; and further whether the French instinct to separate thought and practice, while giving each its due, was not by the same token responsible for the formal elegance and intellectual eminence of French scientific leadership in its great days.

But however that may be in general, it is at least notable that after the mobilization of talent in the year II, the men who were truly scientists – Berthollet, Monge, Fourcroy, and Vauquelin, for example – moved back from war service to science, whereas those whose instincts and interests lay in production and enterprise – Carny, Deyeux, Pelletoer, Chaptal, and many others – moved outwards in the favourable climate of Thermidor towards the exploitation of whatever opportunities their war service had suggested to them. It is true that, on the whole, the scientists had served the State in a higher advisory capacity. They saw the problems and possibilities more clearly and steadily, and they had prestige. But it is an illusion that theoretical science was applied to war production, even in the terrible emergency of the year II. Science was only exploited. What was applied was scientists.

V

Turning then to the second phase, the phase of science consciously applied, it is in general an illusion to suppose that it consisted in any utilization of the latest theory. The literature of chemical manufacturing makes frequent reference to the guidance offered by chemical theory to those well versed in it. But the theory in question was the theory of affinities, not the theory of combustion, and the theory of affinities was devoid of abstract interest. It did not in fact amount to much more than a tentative classification of substances according to their relative activity. If one read only the memoirs on the soda industry, one would suppose that the great chemist of the century was Richard Kirwan.[1] Lavoisier is never even mentioned. Leblanc and his kind needed knowledge of the chemical properties of substances. They did not need to understand combustion. Similarly in the dyeing industry, the line from Dufay to Berthollet does not pass through Lavoisier. In basic chemistry, on the other hand, neither does the line from Lavoisier to Gay-Lussac and Dalton pass through Berthollet. It was, indeed, the attempt to make it do so, misguided by the current fashion in scientific explanation, which led Berthollet to expand an excellent memoir on mass action into that curious and shapeless book, *Essai de statique chimique*,[2] quite unworthy of his real abilities, in which he tried to fix the elements of chemical science in the circumstances instead of the materials of reactions.

The true mode in which science was actively applied to industry has been obscured by the tendency of modern historical writers to suppose that the framing of basic theories is the main business of science, and that if science was related to industry, it must have been through the medium of advancing theory. They have failed to pay attention to the language of their texts, where the relationship of science to industry is not only clear but so clearly a corollary of the eighteenth-century

[1] See, for example, the translation of Kirwan's procedure for the analysis of soda, *Annales de chimie*, vol. 18 (1793), pp. 163–220.

[2] (2 vols.; Paris, 1803); Berthollet's adumbration of the law of mass action, 'Recherches sur les lois de l'affinité', was published in the *Mémoires de la Classe des Sciences . . . de l'Institut*, vol. III, pp. 1–96.

conception of scientific explanation that it required no explicit formulation. For the eighteenth-century scientists do not write of the application of theory. What they say is that science illuminates the arts, that it enlightens the artisans, and that this process honours the century, and in holding this language they are simply considering industry in the light of that pervasive notion of the function of scientific explanation which (after Locke) is to be found in Condillac and Condorcet, in Jussieu and Carnot, in Lavoisier, Lamarck, and Laplace, in the physiocrats, the *idéologues* and the first *École normale*. In this light, science itself is positive knowledge, of course. Its function in the world is essentially an educational one, however, and its mode of procedure is analytical. First, it seeks to discern the essential elements of a complex subject. These once found, it ranges and classifies them according to the logical connexions which subsist underneath all the welter of phenomena. Next, it establishes a systematic nomenclature designed to fix the thing in the name, fasten the idea to its object, and cement the memory to nature. In this fashion, the human understanding will be led descriptively towards a rational command over every department of nature by following its inherent order. Scientific explanation, then, consists in resolving a subject into its elements in the objective world in order that it may be reassembled in the mind according to the principles of the associationist psychology. The inspiration was algebra. But the model was botany.

It is consistent, therefore, that when scientists turned to industry, it was to describe the trades, to study the processes, and to classify the principles. In this taxonomic fashion science was indeed applied to industry, and very widely. What were those enormous ventures, the Academy's *Description des arts et métiers*, the *Encyclopédie* itself, the *Encyclopédie méthodique*, if not attempts to lift the arts and trades out of the slough of ignorant tradition and by rational description and classification to find them their rightful place within the great unity of human knowledge? The eighteenth-century application of science to industry, then, was little more and nothing less than the attempt to develop a natural history of industry. In this sense, the scientific development of an industry is measured, not by the degree to which new theory is used to change it, but by the extent to which science can explain it theoretically. 'We are frequently able', writes Berthollet (the quotation is from the first translation of his *Éléments de l'art de la teinture*), 'to explain the circumstances of an operation which we owe entirely to a blind practice, improved by the trials of many ages; we separate from it everything superfluous; we simplify what is complicated; and we employ analogy in transferring to one process what has been found useful in another. But there are still a great number of facts which we cannot explain, and which elude all theory: we must then content ourselves with detailing the processes of the art; not attempting idle explanations, but waiting till experience throws greater light upon the subject.'[1] Similarly, the metal industries were not at first much changed by the development of the science of metallurgy; they simply began to be understood. But that processes will be altered for the better if their principles are understood, that artisans will improve their manipulations if they know the reasons for them, are simply illustrations of the eighteenth-century faith in progress through classification and industrial examples of the eighteenth-century belief in scientific explanation as a kind of cosmic education.

Accordingly, the revolutionary manufacture of saltpetre consisted essentially in subjecting the French people to mass instruction in a simple technical process. What Monge, Fourcroy, Guyton, Berthollet, and the others did when they were brought into this enterprise, was to give popular courses.[2] The military crisis of 1793–4 created the greatest practical incentive ever experienced for the application of science to production in general. The Committee of Public Safety urged it forward with all its fearful authority. And inevitably the project assumed an educational form; science was mobilized in defence of the Republic, and at great speed scientists produced a series of textbooks, instructing practitioners, not so much in

---

[1] *Elements of the Art of Dyeing* (Edinburgh, 1792), p. 17.
[2] On the *cours révolutionnaires*, see C. Richard, *Le comité de salut public et les fabrications de guerre sous la Terreur* (Paris, 1922), pp. 469–86; *Procés-Verbaux du comité d'instruction publique* (Paris, 1901), vol. IV, pp. xxi–xxviii; the text of the courses is at the *Archives nationales*, AD VI, 79, pièce 69.

new methods, as in the best methods.[1] Finally (not to labour illustrations), it may perhaps be consistent with the nature of the mathematical achievements of Monge in descriptive geometry that he should have been the one important mathematician who consistently expressed the utilitarian valuation even of mathematics and that he should also have been the moving spirit in the foundation of the *École polytechnique*, that portentous institution.[2]

Nor was the faith in science as the educator of industry simply abstract, for their relations can be brought down to a question of what people actually did. Chaptal's testimony may again be quoted:

> Mais du moment que la chimie est devenue une science positive; surtout lorsqu'on a vu des chimistes à la tête des plus grandes entreprises, et faire prospérer dans leurs mains plusieurs genres d'industrie, le mur de séparation est tombé, la porte des ateliers leur a été ouverte, on a invoqué leurs lumières; la science et la pratique, se sont éclairées réciproquement, et l'on a marché à grands pas vers la perfection.[3]

Chaptal dates this change from the Revolution when the government 'pressé par le besoin, a successivement tiré plusieurs savans de leur cabinet pour les placer dans les ateliers, et la plupart y ont fait des prodiges en très-peu de temps'. And there

---

[1] For the present purpose, it would burden this note unnecessarily to cite full titles. Suffice it to say that treatises by leading scientists were published on the following trades or processes: iron-working; small-arms; the casting and boring of artillery pieces; the incineration of plants (for potash); the soda industry; the soap industry; tanning; the separation of copper from bell metal; etc. Most of these treatises are gathered together in the *Archives nationales*, AD VIII, 40. But relatively little was attempted in the way of innovation. Perhaps the most interesting exception was the establishment in the year II of the *Atelier de perfectionnement*, an embryonic technological development laboratory, under the direction of Vandermonde, where experiments were made looking towards standardized and rationalized production, including the introduction, where appropriate, of interchangeable parts. But little came of this hopeful venture, which was eventually absorbed in the *Conservatoire des arts et métiers*. For documents concerning this project, see *Archives nationales*, F^{12} 233, 234, 1310; F^{13} 288.

[2] Besides the excellent study of Monge's work by René Taton, *L'oeuvre scientifique de Monge* (Paris, 1951), there is also available a rather inferior recent biography, Paul V. Aubry, *Monge, le savant ami de Napoléon Bonaparte* (Paris, 1954). For the caution with which this must be used, see my review in *Scripta Mathematica*, vol. 22 (1956), pp. 245–6.

[3] *De l'industrie française* (2 vols.; Paris, 1819), vol. II, pp. 38–9.

is ample confirming evidence that a new generation of scientifically instructed entrepreneurs and managers came into control of industrial operations during the Revolutionary period, and that the Revolution saw the culmination and the end of the very real hostility between scientists and artisans.[1] As a result, it was no longer necessary to complain constantly of the obstruction of rational procedures by the ignorance and traditionalism of the ordinary artisan, always singled out as the greatest barrier to progress. Popular superstition was the *bête noire* of the rational writer, and whether he looked to religion or technology, he found it flourishing in ignorance and secrecy. To publicize processes, therefore, to get them out in the light of day, must be the business of science, and the importance attached to this is evident in the condition of publicity attaching to the prize programme of the *Académie des sciences* and the grants of the *Bureau de consultation*. That such was also the policy of the English Society of Arts is an indication that the apparent differences in the relations of science and industry in France and Britain were more verbal than real.[2] There is no contesting the reality of British industrial leadership in the eighteenth century, but it is conceivable that the industrial interests of British scientists were more a result than a cause of this pre-eminence. If they did not relate them to some general outlook, this circumstance may possibly be taken as another illustration of the historical law binding the two great western societies which prescribes that the French should formulate what the British only do.[3] In any case, it is, perhaps, not overly fanciful

[1] See, for example, C. A. Costaz, *et al.*, 'Rapport au Ier Consul', *Bulletin de la Société d'Encouragement*, vol. 1 (1802), pp. 45–8.

[2] See Derek Hudson and K. W. Luckhurst, *The Royal Society of Arts* (London, 1954).

[3] Far from regarding Dr Schofield's accompanying paper, 'The Industrial Orientation of Science in the Lunar Society of Birmingham', as calling for conclusions different from those which I base on a study of French developments, I think his material calls for a similar conclusion and could be better taken as a confirmation than a refutation of my point. The difference lies no doubt in what we mean by science. I mean abstract understanding of nature. Dr Schofield seems to mean technical activity. What is the relationship of any of the scientific work alluded to by Dr Schofield to basic theory? Indirect, at best – in fact this work was precisely the sort which led French writers sympathetic to the utilitarian or Jacobin tradition to describe the Revolution as favourable to science. But perhaps this question of interpretation had better be left to the reader.

to summarize the problem by contrasting the enterprising, bold manufacturer of the nineteenth century, the engineer, the industrialist, in whatever country, to the Gothic master-craftsman of olden times, protecting his secrets and his mysteries, bending over his cauldron and stirring some traditional receipt, some confidential brew. The application of science to industry takes on real meaning, then, if it is seen, not naïvely as the alteration of old practices by theoretical concepts, but rather as an intellectual process and a chapter in the history of the Enlightenment. 'Au tableau des sciences,' writes Condorcet of his century, 'doit s'unir celui des arts qui, s'appuyant sur elles, ont pris une marche plus sûre, et ont brisé les chaines où la routine les avait jusqu'alors retenus.'[1]

---

[1] *Esquisse d'un tableau historique des progrès de l'esprit humain* (Paris, 1795), p. 296.

K

5 The Industrial Orientation of Science in the Lunar Society of Birmingham

ROBERT E. SCHOFIELD

[This article was first published in *Isis*, vol. 48, 1957, pp. 408–15.]

The historical relationship of science with technology is a complicated one and conclusions as to the extent of that relationship vary depending on the country and the perspective in which the problem is studied. Dr C. C. Gillispie has presented us with his conclusions based on a study of France in the revolutionary period and the early years of the empire.[1] He suggests that the relationship for this period in France is, at best, an indirect one.

The same type of argument can be – and indeed has been – made for Great Britain for approximately the same period. It is suggested, however, that were the same conclusion drawn for this period in Great Britain a mistake would be made. The social patterns of scientists in late eighteenth-century England were quite different from those of France. Dr Gillispie refers to the 'mutual stimulation of science, commercial enterprise, and Puritan influence . . . [characteristic] of British social, intellectual, and scientific history from the seventeenth through the nineteenth centuries.'[2] He also points out the very evident connexion between the consequent utilitarianism and the relative poverty of British achievements in abstract science during the years of greatest dominance of this stimulation. Few would deny this latter observation, but that is not really the point here. For if one studies the activities of the scientists responding to this stimulation, one must conclude

[1] C. C. Gillispie, 'The National History of Industry', *Isis*, vol. 48 (1957), pp. 398–407. See above, chap. 4.

[2] Gillispie, op. cit., p. 403.

that science and industry were, by that very fact, more closely and more deliberately related in Great Britain than in France.

One cannot approach the problem of science and technology in late eighteenth-century England or Scotland by referring to the technological activities of the Royal Society, for the Royal Society was in its doldrums during this period. Nor can even the activities of the Society Instituted at London for the Promotion of Arts, Manufactures, and Commerce (i.e., the Society of Arts, later the Royal Society of Arts) be used as a standard. However influential the Society of Arts may have been in encouraging (and spreading information about) technological improvements, it cannot seriously be maintained that there was much of a scientific nature in its work. For many an eighteenth-century English scientist, membership in the Royal Society was a matter only of social prestige, while eighteenth-century English manufacturers were members of the Society of Arts on the off-chance that something useful might almost accidentally result from its endeavours. These two groups, the scientists and the manufacturers, combined however in one type of organization – the provincial scientific societies – a study of which enables us to draw rather different conclusions for England than Dr Gillispie could draw for France.

One of the most characteristic developments of eighteenth-century English science was the proliferation of provincial scientific societies. There was a Manchester Literary and Philosophical Society, a Derby Philosophical Society, a Literary and Philosophic Society of Newcastle-on-Tyne, and philosophic clubs in Liverpool, Bristol, Leeds, and many other places. It may not be significant that the most active and successful of these societies were founded in manufacturing centres in the North and Midlands of England. These were, after all, the growing population centres and might be assumed to be more likely places for this type of activity. Much more to the point, at any rate, is the fact that prominent manufacturers were themselves members of such societies – e.g., the Strutts of Derby, the Lloyds, Brandts, and Phillips of Manchester, and Thomas Bentley of Liverpool were all members of such societies.[1] Of all the provincial scientific societies, the one which most exemplifies the joining of interests of manufacturer and scientist is the Lunar Society of Birmingham and of all such societies this is perhaps the best known – in spite of the fact that less exact information has been published about the Lunar Society than about many of the other societies of the period. This is one of the reasons why an extensive study of this society has been undertaken.[2] The remainder of this paper is a report of some of the results of that study.

The Lunar Society left no formal records; the only published contemporary references to the society were those made by Joseph Priestley – chiefly in the dedication of his *Experiments on the Generation of Air from Water* (1793) and in his *Memoirs*, published posthumously in 1806. In these publications Priestley gives a list of some of the members, describes the origin of the name of the Society, and tells what the Society did not do. He fails to give much indication of what the Society did do. Not until Samuel Smiles investigated the papers of Matthew Boulton and James Watt did we get any serious recognition of the significance of the Lunar Society and Smiles's account[3] contains too many pure speculations for comfort. Nevertheless, directly or indirectly, Smiles's work has provided the source of all subsequent accounts of the Lunar Society, and his speculations were only the beginnings of what has developed into a Lunar Society legend of extraordinary proportions.

An investigation of original sources was needed to interrupt the perpetuation of this legend. With this in mind, a study was begun of the letters, manuscripts, and publications

[1] See Eric Robinson, 'The Derby Philosophical Society', *Annals of Science*, vol. 9 (1953), pp. 359–67. R. Angus Smith, *A Centenary of Science in Manchester* (London, Taylor and Francis, 1883), pp. 32–3; and R. B. (Richard Bentley), *Thomas Bentley, 1730–80, of Liverpool, Etruria and London* (Guildford, Richard Bentley, 1927).

[2] My research on the Lunar Society, a small part of the results of which are presented in this paper, was done chiefly from MSS in the collections of the Wedgwood Museum, The Royal Society, The Royal Society of Arts, The Assay Office, and the Reference Library of Birmingham, and the Darwin Museum, Down House, Downe, Kent. I take this opportunity to acknowledge the assistance of the librarians and the curators of these collections.

[3] Published in his *Lives of Boulton and Watt* (London, John Murray, 1865).

of the persons most commonly assumed to have been members of the Society. It was hoped that we might establish a more accurate membership list than had previously existed and that something reasonably definite could be learned about the activities of the Society. Both of these hopes have, to some extent, been justified. We can now give a credible list of those persons whose associations were of a sort entitling them to be named members of the Society. That list includes:

MATTHEW BOULTON (1728–1809), manufacturer of metal products and later partner with James Watt in the production of steam engines.

ERASMUS DARWIN (1731–1802), physician, poet, and dabbler in scientific speculation of all sorts; grandfather of Charles Robert Darwin and Francis Galton.

THOMAS DAY (1748–89), gentleman eccentric, philanthropist, interested chiefly in politics and metaphysics.

RICHARD LOVELL EDGEWORTH (1744–1817), Irish landowner, inventor of miscellaneous mechanical contrivances, interested in agriculture and education, father of Maria Edgeworth.

SAMUEL GALTON, JR. (1753–1832), Quaker gun-manufacturer, dilettante in many sciences – particularly ornithology and optics, grandfather of Francis Galton.

ROBERT AUGUSTUS JOHNSON (?–1799), Anglican clergyman, FRS, but otherwise unknown.

JAMES KEIR (1735–1820), chemist, geologist, chemical manufacturer and mine operator.

JOSEPH PRIESTLEY (1733–1804), Unitarian clergyman, experimenter in electricity and chemistry.

WILLIAM SMALL (1734–75), physician, metallurgist, onetime Professor of Natural Philosophy at the College of William and Mary, teacher of Thomas Jefferson.

JONATHAN STOKES (1755–1831), physician, botanist, chemist.

JAMES WATT (1736–1819), inventor, engineer, chemist.

JOSIAH WEDGWOOD (1730–95), potter and chemist.

JOHN WHITEHURST (1713–88), instrument maker, geologist.

WILLIAM WITHERING (1741–99), physician, botanist, chemist.[1]

This is an extraordinary collection of people. Only Robert Augustus Johnson left no record of his activities; all the rest made significant contributions to the culture of their period and many are still classed as among the more important individuals of eighteenth-century England. It is, of course, that fact that encouraged the interest in the Lunar Society. With some justice, it was felt that men of this calibre do not regularly associate with one another over trivialities.

We can arrive at some idea of the work of the Society by comparing the letters and published works of these members. It is assumed that the interest of more than two of these individuals in any subject at the same time may reasonably be claimed as an interest of the Society. Acting on that assumption, one arrives at two major conclusions. First: the meetings of the Society were comparatively unimportant. Members living in reasonably close proximity associated with one another almost daily; those living, or temporarily occupied, outside the Birmingham area were kept in constant touch with the other members through continual correspondence – usually averaging at least one letter per week from some one of the Birmingham residents. The meetings gave rise to the name of the Society, but otherwise they seem important only as a social cement for keeping the group together. Information was exchanged between members outside meetings as freely and more frequently than inside them. Second: the kind of problems most commonly considered demonstrates so clearly an industrial orientation of scientific interest that it is not unreasonable to claim the Lunar Society as an informal technological research organization.

The nucleus of that organization was created by the meeting of Boulton and Darwin sometime before 1760. These two, one living in Birmingham and the other in Lichfield, less than fifteen miles from Birmingham, were brought together by a common love of science and a shared admiration for Benjamin Franklin,

[1] The justification of this choice of members will be contained in a more extensive treatment of the Lunar Society now being prepared.

to whom they were introduced by a letter from John Michell. Franklin provided an early link between various members-to-be of the Lunar Society; he was already, or was to become, the friend of Priestley, Day, Small, and Whitehurst, and a patient of Withering. Franklin's interest in electricity encouraged Boulton and Darwin in their experiments on electricity. Darwin's first published scientific work was a paper, 'Remarks on the Opinion of Henry Eeles, Esq. . . . Concerning the Ascent of Vapour',[1] which discusses the behaviour of 'electric matter' and includes a practical query as to the possible substitution of that 'matter' for steam in steam engines. Boulton had more direct practical interests in electricity. He began the manufacture (for sale) of a small number of electrical machines and later added permanent magnets to his stock-in-trade. Priestley first entered the orbit of Lunar Society members when he referred to Darwin's work in his *History of Electricity*.[2] At about the same time, Wedgwood met Priestley and began to speculate about a possible application of Priestley's electrical experiments to the problem of gilding pottery.[3] From this time on, Priestley was to be in contact with Lunar Society members, although he did not become a member himself until late in 1780 or early in 1781.

An interest in the improvement of transportation is characteristic of the Industrial Revolution and could be found in most enlightened Englishmen of the eighteenth century. In the Lunar Society, this interest took many forms. Boulton, Darwin, Small, Watt, and Wedgwood concerned themselves in turnpike trusts and canal projects, Edgeworth considered the possibility of improving road design and is credited by some with having anticipated Macadam.[4] A common interest in the improvement of carriage design brought Edgeworth together with Boulton and Darwin. Boulton's work seems to have been

---

[1] *Philosophical Transactions*, vol. L (1757), p. 240.

[2] Joseph Priestley, *History and Present State of Electricity* (London, J. Dodsley, J. Johnson, B. Davenport, and T. Cadell, 1767), pp. 215, 264.

[3] E. Metayard, *Life of Josiah Wedgwood* (London, Hurst and Blackett, 1865), vol. I, p. 388.

[4] See, for example, Henry Law and D. K. Clarke, *The Construction of Roads and Streets*, 6th ed., revised with additional chapters by A. J. Wallis-Taylor (London, Crosby, Lockwood and Son, Ltd, 1901).

confined to empirical studies, but Darwin's Commonplace Book shows an application of theoretical considerations to the design of wheel mountings, while Edgeworth approached the problem as an experimental study in basic mechanics.[1] Both Darwin and Edgeworth communicated their designs to the Society of Arts[2] and both considered the idea of manufacturing carriages of their improved design – a project in which they interested Wedgwood – though nothing came of their plan.

Even before James Watt became part of the Lunar circle, members had been interested in steam engines. We have already referred to Darwin's paper of 1757 in which steam engines were mentioned; his correspondence with Boulton shows a continued interest in steam engines down to the date when Watt joined the group (about 1767). Edgeworth hoped to drive carriages and boats by steam. In 1768 he constructed a steam-engine model of his own design and submitted it to the Society of Arts.[3] Several years before he met Watt, Boulton had consulted Franklin about steam-engine design. He also constructed a model of an engine which was sent to Franklin for suggestions. Details of Edgeworth's and Boulton's work are unknown, but it is probable that both approached the problem empirically. The introduction of Watt's work naturally changed the situation. Darwin and Edgeworth turned their attention to other problems, Boulton enlisted the help of William Small and attention was given to making Watt's scheme operable on a large scale. One important consideration in this respect was the metallurgical problem involved – especially in the design of piston seals. Small began an intensive study of metallurgy, during which he obtained the assistance of Whitehurst and read all the current texts on metallurgy he could find – even-

[1] MS Commonplace Book, Darwin Museum, Down House, Downe, Kent; R. L. Edgeworth, 'On Wheel Carriages', *Transactions of the Royal Irish Academy*, vol. II (1788), pp. 73–80.

[2] Letters of Erasmus Darwin and Richard Lovell Edgeworth to Ralph Templeman, 8 March 1766 and 15 May 1766, respectively (Archives, Royal Society of Arts).

[3] Minutes of Committees 1768–9: Mechanics, 5 January 1769 (Archives, Royal Society of Arts). The model and description have since been lost. Edgeworth was not aware of Watt's work, since both he and Watt at that time were in contact with the Lunar Society only through correspondence with members of the society, who naturally did not divulge one another's secrets.

tually condemning all of them as inadequate. Boulton, as a manufacturer of metal products, had long been interested in metallurgy on a wider scale. He experimented with different metals and ores, worked with Keir in devising new alloys and new working technics, and had Withering translate the mineralogical treatise of Bergmann for his use.[1]

While we must agree that the discovery of the latent heat of vaporization was not a significant factor in Watt's invention of the separate condenser,[2] we must not be carried to the extreme of deciding that Watt's work was simply good empiricism. The best example of empiricism well applied to a study of steam engines is the work of John Smeaton.[3] One need only compare Smeaton's work with Watt's to recognize a decided difference in approach to the problem – a difference most adequately described by insisting that Watt was the more scientific of the two. He demonstrated his early recognition of the importance of more theoretical considerations in improving the design of steam engines by his assistance of Joseph Black in the investigation of the properties of heat and steam. He continued these investigations in Birmingham and obtained the assistance of Boulton, Wedgwood, Whitehurst, and Withering. Boulton and Wedgwood had other reasons to be interested in the question of heat. Boulton had manufactured thermometers for sale since early in the 1760s, while Wedgwood's manufacturing processes involved the use of high temperatures. Erasmus Darwin's son, Charles, sent both of them copies of his notes of Black's lectures. Wedgwood subsequently developed a ceramic pyrometer for use in measuring high temperatures and then produced the pyrometer for sale. Whitehurst performed experiments to determine whether heat had weight,[4] and Watt had Withering perform experiments on 'heating iron red-hot by hammering'.[5] Priestley was involved

---

[1] Torbern Bergmann, *Outlines of Mineralogy*, trans. W. Withering (Birmingham, for T. Cadell and G. Robinson, 1783).

[2] See, for example, D. Fleming, 'Latent Heat and the Invention of the Watt Engine', *Isis*, vol. 43 (1952), pp. 3–5.

[3] See Farey, *Treatise on the Steam Engine* (London, 1827).

[4] John Whitehurst, 'Experiments on Ignited Substances', *Philosophical Transactions*, vol. LXVI (1776), pp. 575–7.

[5] Letter from Watt to Black, 9 March 1780; quoted by J. P. Muirhead, *Origins*

in steam-engine research first when he inspected a steam-turbine design of Kempelen at the request of Watt and again when, at the request of Boulton, he investigated the possibilities of substituting the chemical reactions of gases for steam condensation as a source of energy for engines. He also investigated the properties of steam; his experiments led Watt to make suggestions about the composition of water.

Whitehurst's interest in geology gave him a connexion with industrial problems of Wedgwood and Boulton. Boulton's interest in geology stemmed from his financial operations in Cornwall, where he eventually established a research assay office to investigate the properties of the various ores found there. He and Whitehurst went on mineralogical expeditions together. Wedgwood supplied Whitehurst with specimens and descriptions of canal diggings, while Whitehurst sent Wedgwood samples of stone and clay which might be of use in ceramic experiments. Whitehurst was, for example, one of the sources from whom Wedgwood obtained the barium carbonate, or witherite, he used in his jasper-ware. The name 'witherite' was given to this substance because William Withering was the first person to perform a significant analysis of it.[1]

Priestley, Watt, and Keir were also involved in Wedgwood's ceramic investigations. Wedgwood called upon Priestley for experiments on ceramic materials, and sent him samples to experiment on. Wedgwood read Priestley's chemical works for insight into the theoretical interpretations of chemical–ceramic reactions. He reciprocated Priestley's services by supplying him with gifts of chemical apparatus. Similar apparatus was later sold to Boulton, Watt, Keir, Withering, and Johnson. Watt became involved in pottery problems because he owned part of a pottery works in Scotland and had assisted in directing its operation. Wedgwood obtained samples of clays from Watt and quoted Watt's interpretation of the behaviour of pipe-clay when subjected to high temperatures.[2]

and Progress of the Mechanical Inventions of James Watt (London, John Murray, 1854), vol. 2, p. 118.

[1] *Philosophical Transactions*, vol. LXXVII (1784), pp. 293–311.

[2] Wedgwood Commonplace Book: '. . . series extracted from experiment book: 21 June 1780' (Wedgwood Museum, Josiah Wedgwood and Sons, Ltd, Barlaston, Stoke-on-Trent).

Keir, who managed a glass-works for a time, shared Wedgwood's interest in annealing processes. Keir experimented on glazes for Wedgwood, and Wedgwood returned the favour by experimenting on the improvement of glass-making. Keir's glass-works involved him also in geological speculation, when he noticed that molten glass will crystallize if slowly cooled. He suggested that this observation might be extended to the case of basaltic crystals which could then be established as of volcanic origin.[1]

Keir shared with Priestley, Watt, Wedgwood, and Withering an interest in chemistry, but Keir made a career of it. He deliberately prepared himself for his chemical career by the translation of the best practical chemical treatise of the period – the chemical dictionary of Macquer – and then went into a chemical manufacturing business which rivalled Boulton and Watt's Soho operation in size and in the variety of materials produced. His chemical works at Tipton made red and white lead, soap, acids, and alkali, the latter from the waste products of other processes. He had previously experimented with the manufacture of alkali from salt, as had James Watt, in company with Joseph Black and John Roebuck. Wedgwood and Darwin were great admirers of Keir's translation of Macquer.

Some of Keir's notes to the translation refer to a theory of dyeing. According to Thomas Henry: 'Mr Keir . . . appears to have been the first who suspected that the earth of alum [used as a mordant] was precipitated, and in this form attracted to the material.'[2] Other Lunar Society members also gave some consideration to the cloth industries. Erasmus Darwin attempted improvements on stocking-frame design, Withering consulted friends about dyeing theory, while Watt invented steam drying-machinery and returned from a visit to Berthollet with the news of the bleaching properties of chlorine, a discovery which he was one of the first to introduce into England.

Priestley constantly emphasized the practical potentialities

---

[1] *Philosophical Transactions*, vol. LXVI (1776), pp. 530–42. This was twenty-two years earlier than the similar suggestion of Sir James Hall.

[2] Quoted by R. Angus Smith, *A Centenary of Science in Manchester* (London, Taylor and Francis, 1883), p. 112.

of his chemical discoveries. His first public chemical announcement dealt with the possible use of 'fixed air' or carbon dioxide as an anti-scorbutic; he also commented, at the time he announced his discovery of oxygen, on the possible medical application of this new 'air'. The investigation of the medicinal use of gases was carried out later at the Pneumatic Medical Institution of Thomas Beddoes, the son-in-law of Richard Lovell Edgeworth. Beddoes's work was partially supported by contributions from Wedgwood, Boulton, and Watt. Watt joined Beddoes in experimenting on this problem and Boulton and Watt manufactured and sold apparatus for the use of Beddoes's patients.

The Industrial Revolution also included an agricultural phase, and we find Lunar Society personnel participating in this 'agricultural revolution'. Priestley's discovery of the way plants make use of carbon dioxide involved him in a correspondence with Arthur Young about agriculture. William Withering's first published non-medical, scientific paper concerned the production of a chemical fertilizer,[1] and Erasmus Darwin wrote a book, the *Phytologia* (1800), about agriculture. Boulton, Wedgwood, Withering, Edgeworth, and even Day concerned themselves with improvements in agricultural operations.

This paper cites only briefly some of the attempts of the Lunar Society members to apply scientific knowledge and scientific processes to the technical problems of the Industrial Revolution. It is true that many of these attempts may also be described as the application of scientists and the exploitation of science,[2] but if the scientists were applied, it was their own idea, and it is not always easy to distinguish, even today, between the application and the exploitation of science. Then, as today, science was frequently used to explain a manufacturing process developed independently of the science, but these explanations were used by Lunar Society manufacturers in an attempt to improve those processes. Furthermore, the manufacturers

[1] 'Experiments upon the different kinds of Marl found in Staffordshire', *Philosophical Transactions*, vol. LXIII (1773), p. 161.

[2] See Gillispie, op. cit., p. 404, where these terms are suggested as a more adequate description of French practice than is 'applied science'.

themselves contributed, or attempted to contribute, to the development of the 'pure' science of their day. If their contributions in this line were rather minor, so also were the contributions of the majority of their 'purer-scientist' colleagues. If, like Boulton, a few were rather more inclined to make use of the scientific work of their fellow society members than to contribute by their own studies, still they were prepared to make financial grants to enable the continuation of research in pure science, if only in the hope that something useful might develop. In what way does this significantly differ from the motives behind the great industrial research laboratories of today where study of pure as well as applied science is supported?

The examples of Lunar Society activities cited here are only a few of those which touch on science and industry. These and the many others should, of course, be studied more intensively, but even so cursory an account should adequately have demonstrated the validity of our claim that the Lunar Society represented an eighteenth-century technological research organization. It would be hard to find a single activity, of either the science or the technology of the eighteenth century, in which more than one Lunar Society member cannot be found to have been involved – usually with an attempt to turn his knowledge to practical advantage. No consideration of the relationship between science and technology during the early years of the Industrial Revolution can afford to ignore the activities of the Lunar Society. It seems reasonable to suggest that a study of the activities of other provincial scientific societies might prove equally rewarding.

6 Vitriol in the Industrial Revolution

ARCHIBALD CLOW and NAN L. CLOW

[This article was first published in the *Economic History Review*, vol. XV, 1945, pp. 45–55.]

In 1843 Justus Liebig made the following generalization:

> We may fairly judge of the commercial prosperity of a country from the amount of sulphuric acid (oil of vitriol) it consumes.[1]

By 1843, oil of vitriol had been manufactured in Great Britain for over a century, during which time it brought about more than one revolution in social technology, yet even today it is impossible to find an extended account of the first century of this fundamental industrial chemical, which of all *materia chemica* had the greatest effect on the course of late eighteenth- and early nineteenth-century economic history.

Oil of vitriol was first used as an apothecaries' nostrum, and it is for use as such that we have our first account of its manufacture in England. In 1733 Joshua Ward (1685–1761) returned to England from France whence he had gone to evade justice in connexion with a parliamentary offence. Three years later, in partnership with John White, he set up a vitriol works at Twickenham where he proceeded to make vitriol, or sulphuric acid, in large glass vessels, or as it was then described, *per campanam*. Ward is variously described as a quack doctor, vendor of analeptic pills, and inventor of the noted white drops. In 1740 Ward and White removed from Twickenham to Richmond.[2] The important point about Ward and White's establishment is that it reduced the price of oil of vitriol or sulphuric acid from between 1s. 6d. and 2s. 6d. per oz to between 1s. 6d. and 2s. 6d. per lb, thus paving the way for it to

---

[1] *Familiar Letters on Chemistry*, p. 31.
[2] H. W. Dickinson, *Newcomen Society Transactions*, vol. XVIII (1937), p. 43.

become the particular substance which contributed a major part to the non-mechanical aspect of the Industrial Revolution. It is, therefore, to industrial rather than to pharmaceutical application that we must turn for the impetus that stimulated the subsequent rapid expansion in its production.

Throughout the literature of the early Industrial Revolution we find sporadic reference to the use of sulphuric acid; more often, however, all that is said is that the applications of sulphuric acid are so well known that they do not need enumeration. Of particular significance in view of the *locus* of the second vitriol works in England was its use by brass-founders, button-makers, japanners, gilders, refiners, tinplate-makers, tanners, hatters, and paper-makers, most of whom used it for metal-cleaning and pickling. That the second set of persons to take up the manufacture of sulphuric acid in England should be consulting chemists, refiners, and recoverers of silver and gold, and the site of their works Birmingham, need occasion no surprise.

The manufacturers were John Roebuck (1718–94) and Samuel Garbett (1717–1805), the former a doctor of medicine trained at Edinburgh and Leyden, the latter a Birmingham business-man. In 1746 they began making sulphuric acid as an adjunct to their refinery at Steelhouse Lane, Birmingham – a pivotal event in eighteenth-century economic history.

Sulphuric acid is a highly corrosive liquid and, considering the state of English roads at the middle of the eighteenth century, it must have been a load only transportable with considerable risk. The setting up of Roebuck and Garbett's factory brought the actual production of sulphuric acid into a district where it would be used in quantity. Furthermore, profiting by an observation of the alchemist Glauber that lead is not attacked by the corrosive liquid, they abandoned the glass vessels used by Ward and built their plant wholly of lead. This removed limits set by size and fragility of glass and made possible a further reduction in the cost of the acid.

In 1749 Roebuck and Garbett established a second vitriol works, this time at Prestonpans, on the Firth of Forth a few miles east of Edinburgh, in a district where manufacture of salt, pottery, and glass was already established. The reason behind the great change in locality is not known definitely, but our thesis is that Roebuck, who derived his interest in chemistry from Professor Plummer of Edinburgh, under whom he had studied, saw in Scotland a market for his sulphuric acid not offered by England.

Over a long period, during the earlier part of the eighteenth century, the Board of Trustees for Fisheries, Manufactures, and Improvements in Scotland did its utmost to effect improvement in the finishing of Scottish linen by subsidizing the laying down of bleachfields and by fostering research into new methods of bleaching. According to Andrew Brown's *History of Glasgow*, the bleachfields established in Scotland under the patronage of the Board of Trustees were supplied with what sulphuric acid they needed in the first instance (i.e. before 1750) by importation from England or Holland at a price of 1*s.* 4*d.* per lb.[1] This indicates that before 1750 some sulphuric acid was substituted for the acid formerly used in the primitive bleaching industry, viz., the acid in sour milk. The process of bleaching was then a simple process consisting of boiling alternately with ashes (alkali) and a *sour* (sour milk or sulphuric acid) with intervening exposure to the sun.

We know also that Roebuck himself had experimented with sulphuric acid, since his biographer Jardine says:

> It is well known to several of Dr Roebuck's chemical friends that he had tried it, found it effective, and had frequently recommended it to bleachers.[2]

The first official notice of the use of sulphuric acid was the publication in 1756 at the instigation of the Board of Trustees of a memoir, *The Art of Bleaching*, by Francis Home (1719–1813), professor of *materia medica* at Edinburgh. In his memoir Home describes the researches for which the Trustees awarded him a premium on 15 April 1756. According to Home,

> the milk takes five days to perform its task, but the vitriol sours do it in as many hours, nay, perhaps in as many minutes.

[1] Vol. II (1795), p. 250.
[2] *Transactions of the Royal Society Edinburgh*, vol. IV (1796), p. 65.

The increased *tempo* effected by substituting sulphuric acid for sour milk was early appreciated by the finishing trades. Other branches of the finishing trades also made use of the cheap acid, the dyers for dissolving indigo, calico-printers for making *sours* and in the preparation of citric acid, of which they used a great deal.

Roebuck and Garbett's sales throughout Great Britain are not now known, but we can follow the rise of their export trade from Customs House returns for Prestonpans preserved in the General Register House, Edinburgh. The first recorded export is:

14 March 1750-1: in the Huckster of Hamburgh, for Hamburgh, twenty large bottles containing 1990 pounds wt. of Oyle of Vitriol. British manufacture to be exported duty free.

Two months later:

14 May 1751: In the Buccleugh of Fisherrow for Dunkirk, sixteen large bottles containing 1665 pounds wt. of Oyl of Vitriol. Three large bottles containing 203 pounds wt. of Aqua Fortis.

Two years elapse before another export is recorded, but the quantity has greatly increased:

16 February 1753: in the Hope of Leith for Rotterdam, 100 bottles containing 11,179 pounds wt. oil of vitriol.

Cargoes follow to Bremen, Copenhagen, and Campvere, the average cargo being by 1756 about 25,000 lb weight contained in two hundred bottles:

Garbett's enterprising spirit and able management rewarded them well, providing them with considerable capital for their future projects. Articles were drawn up between the two, for carrying on the partnership at Prestonpans and Birmingham over a period of forty years.[1]

Following Roebuck and Garbett's two foundations, a third vitriol works was founded at Bradford. Although without

[1] P. S. Bebbington, *Samuel Garbett, 1717–1803* (Thesis, Birmingham University).

definite records before 1792, it is probable that Benjamin Rowson founded a works there in 1750. Of the founder personnel we know nothing, but it is said to have a continuous history and to be represented at the present day by the Leather Chemical Co. Ltd.

The amount of sulphuric acid made by these works was considerable, and its cheapness a direct impetus to extended application. The transition from ashes and sour milk as bleaching agents can be followed in orders placed with London drysalters by Messrs John and Nathaniel Philips and Co., tape-manufacturers of Tean, Staffs. In 1753-4 they ordered weed and wood-ashes, 'a cask of Danzig ashes to look at', alum, tartar, etc., while a decade later (1765-9) their orders were much more comprehensive, including, in addition to a big variety of ashes, sulphuric acid, probably bought from Roebuck and Garbett in Birmingham.[1]

For more than twenty years Roebuck and Garbett relied upon secrecy to protect them from rivals who wished to ascertain the details of their process so that they might exploit it for their own benefit. During those twenty years, however, Roebuck and Garbett were the unwitting suppliers of information to industrial rivals who bribed their workmen and offered jobs to dismissed or absconding workmen from both Birmingham and Prestonpans.

This was the origin of a sulphuric acid works at Bridgnorth on the Severn, established in 1756 by a Mr Rhodes, who was persuaded to do so by Sam Falconbridge, an employee of Roebuck's.[2] Some time later, the same workman appears to have moved to Mr Skey (1726-1800), a dry-salter of Bewdley, who had just begun to make vitriol at Dowles in chambers erected under the supervision of a workman from Prestonpans whom he had met by accident.[3]

In consequence of these developments and the periodic appearance of suspicious characters in the neighbourhood of Prestonpans, Roebuck and Garbett, on 9 August 1771, regis-

[1] A. P. Wadsworth and J. de L. Mann, *The Cotton Trade and Industrial Lancashire, 1600-1780* (1931), p. 296.

[2] Signet Library, Edinburgh, *Session Papers*, F. 166: 18.

[3] S. Parkes, *Chemical Essays*, vol. II, (1815), p. 399.

tered a patent in fulfilment of a promise in letters-patent granted by the King to work their process in Scotland for fourteen years, their particular invention being the use of lead vessels for all operations. The parchment recording the patent and signed by Roebuck is in the General Register House, Edinburgh.[1]

Roebuck tells how persons 'who kept their names and their business a profound secret' were apt to appear. One of these was Neil Macbrayne, who came in disguise to Prestonpans in June and July 1770 and entertained some of the vitriol works employees in his rooms. From one, whom he bribed with $4\frac{1}{2}$ guineas, he discovered that lead vessels were used by Roebuck and Garbett. Andrew Brown indicates that the said Neil Macbrayne, whom he describes as 'a true friend to the freedom of the arts', was again active in 1771. According to Brown he took a few workmen to Langlone, Prestonpans, 'and in the course of a summer's bathing the mystery came out in the process'. The stolen information was used by Mat. Machen to erect a small works near Govan coal works.[2] At first Roebuck and Garbett did not comprehend the purport of these visits, but when it became clear that they were the activities of rivals they applied for the protection of a patent. The need for a patent was evidently imperative, for in 1772 yet another firm took up the manufacture of sulphuric acid. This time it was a London firm, Messrs Kingscote and Walker, who began at Battersea in 1772 with seventy-one chambers, which they continued to operate for a number of years.

Towards the end of 1772 Roebuck and Garbett in terms of their patent brought an action against Messrs William and Andrew Stirling, merchants in Glasgow, who were known to be erecting buildings near Glasgow with the intention of making sulphuric acid in lead chambers. On being challenged, the validity of the patent was called to question by the Stirlings.[3]

According to the respondents, they carried on 'an extensive manufactory for printing and whitening linen, in the neighbourhood of Glasgow' and 'consumed great quantities of the

---

[1] *Specifications of Patents and Drawings, 1767–87.*
[2] Op. cit., vol. II, p. 251.
[3] *Session Papers*, F. 166: 18.

acid Spirit or Oil of Vitriol, in that manufacture'. They therefore decided to erect oil of vitriol works of their own. The
Stirlings brought forward various arguments and pointed out
that another manufactory, in addition to their own, had been
erected at great expense in the neighbourhood of the city of
Edinburgh by Messrs Steel, Gladstanes and Co.[1]

The Scottish Courts decided that the patent was bad, on the
ground that Roebuck and Garbett had practised the method
for twenty years and that in any case it was in general use elsewhere in Great Britain. The case was next taken to the House
of Lords, where it was argued (*a*) that the substitution of lead
for glass was no new discovery, but only a slight variation; (*b*)
that it was no *new* discovery, since it had been in use for twenty
years; and (*c*) that the use of lead vessels was known to various
people both in England and Scotland. Lastly it was pointed
out that while the patent was in favour of Roebuck and Garbett,
it was signed by Roebuck only, and therefore should be declared invalid. Witnesses from Bridgnorth and Bewdley were
called, one the wife of Sam Falconbridge mentioned above.
The Lords upheld the decision of the Scottish Court, declaring
that a patent obtained for an invention in Scotland was in-
validated by proof of previous use in England.[2]

Bereft of the protection of a patent, Roebuck and Garbett
continued to place what reliance they could on secrecy. When
the celebrated French traveller, B. Faujas de St Fond visited
Scotland in 1784 he found the Prestonpans vitriol works still
surrounded by high walls. All operations were kept secret and
no strangers admitted. It was, however, a trying period for
both Roebuck and Garbett. Within a decade of the loss of their
patent, but not directly attributable to that event, both were
overtaken by financial disaster. Roebuck, on account of his
greater commitments, was the first to feel the effects of the
financial crisis of 1772–3. As a result, Garbett acquired full
control of the Steelhouse Lane works in 1773. Then in 1776
he also acquired Prestonpans. What exactly was happening at
this period is still obscure, but it looks as if Roebuck and

[1] *Session Papers*, F. 31:20 and F. 166:18.
[2] *Session Papers*, F. 31:20; *Journals of the House of Lords* (1774), vol. XXXIV,
pp. 76, 217.

Garbett were not pulling together, as the following letter shows. Garbett is writing to his son-in-law.

> I have made a contract with K(ingscote) and W(alker)[1] and Coney and Gascoigne, for seven thousand bottles of oil of vitriol annually; and we are not to sell to any body else (not even in Scotland) after Christmas next, when the whole sales are to commence on their account at $3\frac{1}{2}d$. per lb, and six months credit as usual, for twenty-one years, expirable on two years' notice. I don't let Doctor Roebuck know this until I come to Scotland.[2]

At Birmingham, Garbett took in a partner in 1776 and the firm became Samuel Garbett and Co. In 1782 Prestonpans was sold to Pat Downey for £11,000, and the following year, on Garbett's failure, Steelhouse Lane passed to James Alston, under whose name it continued for many years. Both Downey and Alston were connected with their respective works for a number of years before becoming sole proprietors. Garbett later recovered sufficiently to start again at Birmingham Heath as an independent manufacturer.[3]

Change in ownership and reversal of private fortune did not react adversely on the prosperity of the Prestonpans vitriol works. When Faujas de St Fond visited Roebuck in 1784 the works was still the greatest manufactory of sulphuric acid in Great Britain. Sir John Sinclair spoke of it in the following terms:

> A manufactory of oil of vitriol, *aqua fortis*, and spirit of salt is carried on here. . . . of late it has extended to white ashes and Glauber salts. More than fifty men are employed, some by day and others by night. They are bound under indentures for twenty-one years, during which time they are paid weekly 6*s.* for stated wages, with a proportional allowance for extra work.[4]

[1] Garbett simply gives the initials K and W. We presume this was the firm of Kingscote and Walker mentioned above and founded in 1772.
[2] S. Garbett to C. Gascoigne, 2 November 1776, cited in Bebbington, p. 16.
[3] R. B. Prosser, *Birmingham Inventors and Inventions* (1881), p. 16; P. S. Bebbington, op. cit.; *Session Papers*, F. 29:31.
[4] *Statistical Account of Scotland* (1791–9), vol. XVII, p. 67.

Then follow details of raw materials consumed, prices of products, etc. Sulphur came from Leghorn, nitre from the East India Co.'s sales in London, while sixty tons of local coal were consumed per week. Oil of vitriol sold at $3\frac{1}{2}d$. per lb, *aqua fortis* at $7\frac{1}{2}d$. to $10d$., spirit of salt at $6d$., Glauber's salt at $12s$. per cwt, and white ashes at £1. $8s$. per cwt.

Following the failure of the partners in the Birmingham and Prestonpans vitriol works, expansion in the industry was rapid. As already mentioned, Garbett himself started again at Birmingham Heath, and in 1778 Thomas Farmer and Co., which continued to operate for over a century, was founded. In 1783 a nephew of Walker of Kingscote and Walker founded an offshoot of that concern, namely, Walker, Baker and Singleton, at Pitworth Moor near Manchester in Lancashire. Thereafter the pace of development is so rapid that detailed data for all individual firms cannot be given here.

To a second eighteenth-century revolution in the art of bleaching we attribute a further impetus to expansion in sulphuric acid manufacture. Increased *tempo* in textile production put considerable pressure on cloth finishers to accelerate their processes. Improvement was first effected by the substitution of sulphuric acid for sour milk, followed in 1787 by the introduction of an entirely new bleaching reagent, viz. chlorine. Chlorine required sulphuric acid to make it, so sulphuric acid production kept in step with the expanding textile industry. Further new vitriol works were opened in Scotland. That 'allowed to be the second of the kind in Scotland' and, therefore, next to Prestonpans, was at Burntisland. It was founded *c*. 1785 by William Muir, who later went to Leith, leaving Alexander Pitcairn and other partners to carry on. By Candlemas 1790, Pitcairn was in sole possession, the other partners having died or withdrawn their shares. This works was extensive, being reputed to contain three hundred and sixty chambers. The cess (tax) paid by Pitcairn alone amounted to one twenty-fourth of the cess paid by the whole town.[1]

By 1797 there were six to eight factories in the neighbourhood of Glasgow alone, probably those mentioned as at Woodside, Napier's Hall, Port Dundas, and Carntyne. Further

[1] *Session Papers*, F. 183:30; J. Sinclair, *General Report*, Appendix 2, p. 307.

expansion took place at the beginning of the nineteenth century.

The very intimate connexion between sulphuric acid and bleaching made progressive bleachers realize that they could with advantage make their own chemicals. The first to do so were Messrs Bealy of Radcliffe, Manchester, who erected six chambers in 1799. Bleaching reagents were still somewhat unruly servants, and rendering a bleaching agent transportable brought great fame and a considerable fortune to Messrs Tennant, Knox and Co. of St Rollox Chemical Works, Glasgow. Charles Tennant was originally a bleacher at Darnley near Glasgow. In his name the firm registered two important patents for bleaching with chlorine. Their dry, and therefore readily transportable, bleaching powder was patented in the name of Charles Tennant in 1798. To work the patent, ground for a factory was acquired at St Rollox, Glasgow, where in 1814 some twelve to twenty men were employed, and from this beginning one of the greatest chemical works in the mid-industrial-revolution period developed.[1] It covered no less than ten acres by 1830, with plant engaged in the production of sulphuric acid, bleaching powder, alkalis, soap, etc.

When he first set up on his own, Tennant bought sulphuric acid from the Prestonpans Vitriol Co. and from Messrs Norris and Sons, Halifax. In 1803 he erected his own chambers at a cost of about £50 per chamber. Each chamber burned a thousand pounds of sulphur per week. The rapid progress made by Tennant, Knox and Co. may be attributed to the rapidity with which its promoters adopted any new technological improvement. From the beginning they burned nitre (KNO_3) and sulphur external to the chambers proper, and four years later added a floor to burn sulphur residues which could be bought from less progressive manufactures at the low price of £5 per ton. De la Faille next suggested blowing steam into the chambers instead of using water, and by 1813–14 the innovation was adopted at St Rollox. Annual production of sulphuric acid was then in the region of three thousand tons.

Tennant in turn passed plans for sulphuric acid plant on to

[1] Ibid., p. 313.

Messrs Doubleday and Easterby, Newcastle, who erected the first lead chambers at Bill Quay on the Tyne. The same firm, at a cost of £700, erected the first platinum retort for rectifying acid. This was probably similar to a vessel referred to by Parkes in the *Chemical Catechism*:[1]

> Some years ago I saw a vessel of platina constructed for the purpose of rectifying sulphuric acid. It holds thirty-two gallons, and cost several hundred pounds; but the advantages which result from its employment are fully adequate to the expense.

Despite the large capital required for this single unit, Doubleday and Easterby soon added two further retorts.[2]

The cheapness of the abundant supply of sulphuric acid forthcoming began to lessen the cost of erecting lead chambers themselves, since hydrogen generated from sulphuric acid became correspondingly cheap, and was used by lead burners in jointing lead sheets from which chambers were made.

By 1820, in addition to the factories in Scotland which have been mentioned, there were twenty-four in England, distributed according to James Mactear, as follows: London 7, Staffordshire 2, Bristol 2, Birmingham 4, Leeds 1, Halifax 1, Rotherham 1, Newcastle 1, Bolton 2, Manchester 2, Whitehaven 1. The importance of Birmingham is noteworthy.[3] The rapid expansion which these figures illustrate is evidence of continually increasing pressure for larger and larger quantities of sulphuric acid, whose commercialization was in turn leading to the foundation of a more involved chemical industry.

Technological improvements brought about a gradual reduction in the price of sulphuric acid till the selling price remained fairly constant at $3\frac{1}{2}d$. per lb, or £33 per ton. Raw material costs varied somewhat in accordance with local conditions: sulphur from £7 to £16 per ton, nitre from £36 to £64 per ton. Although the ratio of nitre to sulphur used was small, being of the order of one to ten, its high price had a

---

[1] P. 371 n.

[2] T. Richardson, J. C. Stevenson, and R. Chapman, 'On the Chemical Manufactures of the Northern Districts', *British Association Report* (1863), p. 701.

[3] James Mactear, 'History of the Technology of Sulphuric Acid', *Proceedings of the Philosophical Society* (Glasgow, 1881), vol. XIII, p. 409.

marked effect upon the total production cost, which worked out on an average at $2\frac{1}{2}d.$ per lb or £22 per ton. Sulphuric acid manufacture, therefore, had an important influence on the production cost of bleached and printed cotton goods, on soap, glass, and alkalis, and, as Great Britain exchanged such commodities for colonial products like raw cotton, silk, indigo, etc., its fundamental position in early nineteenth-century economy cannot be overrated.

Frequent reference to the use of oil of vitriol by the bleaching industry at various stages of its evolution must not be taken to suggest that this was the only important influence that it had on the course of industrial evolution. Yet another industry, or perhaps trade, was revolutionized by Roebuck's pioneer works at Birmingham and Prestonpans. Successful commercialization of a process for the conversion of common salt (sodium chloride, $NaCl$) into soda (sodium carbonate, Na_2CO_3) signalizes what is usually termed the foundation of the heavy chemical industry. This was secondary to, and dependent on, supplies of cheap sulphuric acid which became available during the second half of the eighteenth century in quantities sufficient for commercial operation. By-products from the soda synthesis afforded new raw materials to revolutionize the bleaching industry.

The works of an alkali manufacturer tended to become larger and more complicated; he began to make soda, using common salt and sulphuric acid and other raw materials. After a time he started to make his own sulphuric acid by burning sulphur or pyrites; if he used pyrites it was probably a mixed sulphide of copper and iron, and it was comparatively easy to make copper sulphate and ferrous sulphate from roasted pyrites. The process of making sodium sulphate produced large quantities of hydrochloric acid, and, as nitric acid was required in the manufacture of sulphuric acid, the alkali manufacturer easily developed into a manufacturer of acids. . . . It was very common for the alkali manufacturer to use the chlorine he recovered so as to make bleaching-powder, and in these ways he became a maker of . . . bleaching powder. The manufacture of all these *heavy* chemicals became in this way an involved process, in which one part was dependent on the others and almost every effort to prevent waste involved the manufacture of some new product.[1]

The influence of these developments upon advancing industrial technology in the early nineteenth century was described by the illustrious Liebig in the following words:

> The manufacture of soda from common culinary salt may be regarded as the foundation of all our improvements in the domestic arts; and we may take it as affording an excellent illustration of the dependence of the various branches of human industry and commerce upon each other, and their relation to chemistry.[2]

The need to solve the salt-to-soda problem became increasingly pressing as the Industrial Revolution pattern developed. While earlier manufacturers' demands were met by importation of weed and wood-ashes, barilla (imported seaweed ash), and kelp (Scottish seaweed ash), demand far exceeded supply and for several decades towards the end of the eighteenth century Scottish kelpers enjoyed a boom in their product.

A detailed history of the multitude of attempts to solve the salt-to-soda problem during the latter half of the eighteenth century has yet to be written, and the function of the remainder of this paper, severely limited as it is by lack of space, is to sketch, particularly in relation to the use of sulphuric acid, some of the efforts that were made between the founding of the first sulphuric acid works in Great Britain and the usually accepted foundation of the alkali industry, i.e. the founding of a factory operating the patent of Nicholas Leblanc (1742–1806)[3] by James Muspratt (1793–1883) in the neighbourhood of Liverpool in 1823. It will be remarked how the pioneers in

---

[1] S. Miall, *History of British Chemical Industry* (1931), p. 5.

[2] *Familiar Letters on Chemistry*, p. 21.

[3] When the scarcity of ashes throughout Europe became so acute during the revolutionary wars, the *Académie des Sciences* in 1775 offered a prize of 2,400 *livres* for a method of making alkali from non-vegetable sources. This stimulated Nicholas Leblanc to submit about 1790 the process which now bears his name. His patent is dated 25 September 1791, but he was not awarded the prize. His works were confiscated in 1793, and he died in the workhouse by his own hand.

the vitriol field contributed to the solution of the co-extensive problem.

Roebuck himself while at Prestonpans was probably interested in soda production. Associated with him were his life-long friends and correspondent, Dr Joseph Black (1728–99), Professor of Chemistry in the University of Edinburgh, and James Watt (1736–1819), who later became a partner in the famous Boulton and Watt enterprise at Soho, Birmingham. It has been suggested that this attempted synthesis of soda was the cause of bringing Watt and Roebuck together through the intermediacy of Dr Black, whom Watt had known when they were both associated with Glasgow University. There is no evidence of production on a commercial scale, although T. S. Ashton speaks of Roebuck acquiring interests in coal mines and *soda works* at Bo'ness.[1] The high duty on salt militated against success.

One of Roebuck's and Watt's friends was more successful. He was James Keir (1735–1820) who like Roebuck was an Edinburgh-trained chemist. Keir engaged in glass manufacture (another industry that made large demands on the supply of soda) at Stourbridge from 1775 to 1778 in partnership with John Taylor and Skey of Bewdley, the latter of whom has already been mentioned as a manufacturer of sulphuric acid. Even at this time Keir was evidently interested in the manufacture of soda, for he opposed a patent application from Alexander and George Fordyce which would have secured to them the sole right to that manufacture.[2] In 1780, Keir joined forces with Alex Blair of Tipton, Staffs, and among the activities in which they engaged was the making of soda and soap, the soda being made from common salt by the use of sulphuric acid.[3]

The focus of activity once again returned to the Firth of Forth. When B. Faujas de St Fond was visiting Roebuck in 1784 he met Dr Swediaur, a European authority on venereal disease, who told him that he had purchased an estate at

[1] T. S. Ashton, *Iron and Steel in the Industrial Revolution* (1924), p. 50.
[2] *Journal of the House of Commons* (1778–80), vol. XXXVII, pp. 891, 912, etc.
[3] S. Timmins, 'James Keir, FRS', *Transactions Birmingham and Midland Institute*, vol. XXIV (1891), p. 1.

Prestonpans – the site of Dr Roebuck's vitriol works – where he intended to establish a manufactory for salt with the intention of separating the mineral alkali (soda).[1]

Dalmuir, near Glasgow, and Newcastle were two districts where the existence of glass and soap works offered a ready market for soda. Newcastle in particular was a large absorber of Scottish kelp (natural soda).

When financial difficulties drove Archibald Cochrane (1749–1831), 9th Earl of Dundonald, from Scotland to stay with friends on the Tyne he found in Newcastle two manufacturers, William Losh and Thomas Doubleday, experimenting independently on the conversion of salt into soda. Doubleday has already been mentioned. Through the agency of Dundonald a chemical works was founded at Walker in 1796, with Dundonald and Losh among the partners, though Doubleday seems to have dropped out. Helen Landell of Newcastle wrote to Matthew Boulton on 26 January 1796, saying that:

> Lord Dundonald had lived as a recluse in Newcastle for many months, and has at last exercised his chemical abilities to advantage, and will probably make a large fortune by his substitute for barilla. Our glass manufacturers are contracting with him, and have little doubt of his success.[2]

The details of Dundonald's patent operated by the works reveal that it depended on sulphuric acid.[3]

Further developments took place quickly. In 1808 a second Tyneside firm, Messrs Doubleday and Easterby of Bill Quay, began to make soda. It was they who got plans from Tennant, Knox and Co. of St Rollox and built a sulphuric acid plant, the first on the Tyne. They passed the plans on in turn to Messrs Cookson when the latter began to make soda at South Shields. Several other Tyneside firms had been founded before soda manufacture started in Lancashire.[4]

[1] B. Faujas de St Fond, *A Journey through England and Scotland to the Hebrides in 1784* (ed. Geikie, Glasgow, 1907), p. 173.

[2] H. Landell to M. Boulton, 26 January 1796 (Assay Office Library, Birmingham).

[3] Register of the Great Seal of Scotland (1795), vol. XX, nos. 584, 591.

[4] 'Newcastle: Chemical Manufactures in the District', *British Association Report* (1863), p. 701.

Contemporary developments of considerable interest took place in Scotland, where Dundonald persuaded Lord Dundas to operate his process at an old candle works at Burnfoot of Dalmuir. After much tribulation Dundas achieved success after, we believe, abandoning Dundonald's process. The inventor of the successful process, acting as sole manager for seven years, received a house, £150, and 5 per cent of the profits, under forfeit of £5,000 if he revealed the secret of the process. Profits up to 1809 were reckoned at £18,000, of which £10,000 went to Lord Dundas. The workmen, of whom there were about twenty, were paid 2s. per day, eked out by the provision of house and fuel by the proprietor.[1]

Within a few years of the starting of factories at Dalmuir and Walker, soda was being produced in Scotland at Rutherglen Bridge, Port Dundas, and Camlachie, usually in association with sulphuric acid manufacture. In 1816 the market price of the new synthetic soda was £60 per ton, but when one remembers the low soda output of kelp, or for that matter the best imported barilla, the price is understandable.

In Great Britain, Lancashire and Cheshire, with their vast resources of salt, were the natural focus upon which an extensive synthetic soda industry should converge. The founders of the industry in this area were James Muspratt (1793–1855) and Josiah C. Gamble (1776–1848). Both came to the Liverpool area from Ireland. Gamble, however, was educated in Glasgow, where he attended Dr Cleghorn's class in chemistry. During his course he obtained knowledge of the chemical inventions of Messrs Tennant, Knox and Co. of St Rollox. In 1812 Gamble established a bleaching works at Monaghan in Ireland. There he operated the Tennant process for the preparation of bleaching materials, purchasing the necessary oil of vitriol from Tennant, Knox and Co.

In 1822, Muspratt, having been a chemical manufacturer in a small way at Dublin, left Ireland and established himself at Vauxhall Road, Liverpool, in the following year. In 1828 Gamble followed his example, and they joined forces. So was laid the great cornerstone that chemistry contributed to the Industrial Revolution. The alkali manufactory at Liverpool

[1] *Session Papers*, F. 241:25.

flourished exceedingly, but acid by-products poured into the atmosphere and devastated vegetation for miles around, even crossing the watery, windswept estuary of the Mersey. The nuisance was so great that the Liverpool Corporation ordered Muspratt and Gamble to remove their works to a less populous district. They migrated to St Helens, and, after a two-year partnership there, Muspratt moved on to Widnes, leaving Gamble in possession of the St Helens establishment.[1]

By this time Tennant, Knox and Co. in Glasgow had also entered the soda manufacture. In 1825 the manufacture of soda ash was begun at St Rollox chemical works, and this works eventually became one of the greatest in Europe. About 1830 the firm opened an office in Liverpool under the name of Tennant, Clow and Co., to distribute their products to the textile manufacturers of Lancashire.[2]

Returning to Gamble, we find that he carried on at St Helens for some time without a partner. In 1835 he interested the brothers Joseph and James Crosfield, soap-boilers of Warrington, in the purchase of a defunct sulphuric acid works adjacent to his own alkali works and laid the basis of the Gamble and Crosfield association. In the following year Simon Crosfield, a Liverpool tobacco merchant, joined the firm, which then became Gamble and Crosfield. So capital acquired in West Indies trade was applied to establish heavy industry in Lancashire in a way similar to that whereby fortunes made by trade in sugar and tobacco in Glasgow helped to develop Lanark, Renfrew, and Dunbartonshire.

After the alkali industry was fully established, yet another field of application for sulphuric acid was opened up, that of artificial chemical fertilizers. It was to personnel in the alkali industry that Justus von Liebig (1803–73) turned in his attempt to commercialize a 'patent manure'. According to Fenwick Allen:

> When Liebig was making his researches and working out his theories in Agricultural Chemistry, and when he thought he had discovered the secret of the refertilization of the soil,

[1] J. Fenwick Allen, *Some Founders of the British Chemical Industry* (1906), p. 43.
[2] E. W. D. Tennant, *One Hundred and Forty Years of the Tennant Companies* (1937), p. 61.

the principal thing being to restore to the soil, as manure, the inorganic constituents which it was found by analysis of the ashes of the vegetation had been taken out of the soil by the plant, he got James Muspratt to carry out his ideas by manufacturing certain manures. This manufacture was carried on at Newton, about the years 1843–4. In this venture Muspratt was joined by Sir Joshua Walmsley, a gentleman of much ability and enterprise, who had only a few years before been Mayor of Liverpool.[1]

Liebig's patent mineral manure was a failure, but simultaneously vitally important researches were being carried out by one of his pupils, J. H. Gilbert (1817–1901) and by J. B. Lawes (1814–1900). Lawes and Gilbert between them, in little more than a decade, worked out sound manuring principles. One of Lawes's neighbours, Lord Dacre, directed his attention to the use of bones, which for some soils proved a valuable manure but were ineffectual for others. In consequence hundreds of experiments were set agoing, some upon field crops, others with pot plants, in which constituents of various kinds were tried as fertilizers. Of all the experiments those based on the suggestion originally thrown out by Liebig, that neutral phosphate of lime (in bone, bone-ash or mineral apatite) be rendered soluble by sulphuric acid and the mixture applied to root crops, had the most striking effects. Results first obtained on a small scale were subjected to more extensive trials round about 1840–1.

Lawes was quick to realize the implication of his scientific research, and took out a patent for the manufacture of superphosphate in 1842. This became an important industry in itself, and today is one of the chief absorbers of sulphuric acid. In 1843, he established a factory for the production of superphosphate near London. In the next year, 1844, manufacture of superphosphate was begun at Blaydon, in the north of England, by Dr Richardson. Among the raw materials used were bones, bone-ash from South Africa and America, as well as refuse animal charcoal from sugar refineries.

To be nearer bleachfields in Forfar and Fife, Charles Tennant

[1] J. Fenwick Allen, op. cit.

and Co. of St Rollox erected a small sulphuric acid works at Carnoustie, Forfarshire, output starting in 1836. With the introduction of artificial fertilizers they installed a bone-crushing plant in 1846, and supplied surrounding farms with superphosphate and fertilizers. The works have been modernized, and now form part of Scottish Agricultural Industries. A West of Scotland firm, Alexander Cross and Sons, founded in 1830, also owe their continued development to fertilizer production. In 1872 they removed to Port Dundas. At this date Lawes's factory alone was producing more than 40,000 tons of superphosphate annually.[1]

We conclude with a link-up of personnel who throughout a long period of sulphuric acid manufacture initiated parallel developments, viz. the Tennants and James Muspratt. Unwittingly, they together brought sulphuric acid into the sphere of international affairs. The source from which British manufacturers obtained sulphur was Sicily. To assure a supply of the vital raw material, John Tennant of St Rollox and James Muspratt entered upon a joint venture and purchased sulphur mines there. A feeling of jealousy resulted in the Neapolitans, and in 1836 a contract was drawn up between the King of the Two Sicilies and the house of Taix, Aychard and Co. of Marseilles in, it is said, an attempt to stabilize prices, which were fluctuating as a result of speculation. The contract gave a monopoly to Taix, Aychard and Co., who proposed to reduce the annual production of sulphur from 900,000 to 600,000 cantars. An export duty of £4. 7s. was also imposed, in consequence of which the price of sulphur rose from £5. 10s. to £15 per ton. The British government regarded the monopoly as a breach of the Treaty of Commerce and Navigation, signed in London on 16 September 1816, and, in the words of Liebig,

> As the price of sulphur has such an important influence on the cost of production of so many manufactured goods we can understand why the English Government should have resolved to resort to war with Naples in order to abolish the sulphur monopoly.

[1] E. W. D. Tennant, op. cit.; W. G. Armstrong, *Industrial Resources of Tyne, Wear and Tees* (1864), p. 175; A. McLean, *Local Industries of Glasgow and the West of Scotland* (1901), p. 190.

Thus there very nearly was a sulphur war, but the Neapolitans thought better of their association with Taix, Aychard and Co. and the monopoly.[1] Technologically, the short period of monopoly had a profound effect on the subsequent history of sulphuric acid manufacture, which, however, cannot be gone into here. Production went on expanding unabated.

The demand for sulphuric acid was increasing yearly, and with every improvement in manufacture the price fell, and with every fall in price the sale increased.[2]

[1] *Documents Concerning the Sulphur Monopoly, consisting of the Parliamentary Inquiry into the conduct of the Foreign Secretary* (1841).
[2] J. Liebig, op. cit., p. 24.

7 The Macintoshes and the Origins of the Chemical Industry

D. W. F. HARDIE

[This article was first published in *Chemistry and Industry*, June 1952, pp. 606–13.]

More than half a century has passed since the death of Ferdinand Hurter. The Leblanc System, on which, with George Lunge, he was a chief authority, has now long since ceased to be the basis of the heavy chemical industry. That we are met here to memorialize the name of Hurter is not merely a normal and fitting homage to that distinguished pupil of R. W. Bunsen but an expression of historical consciousness, an indication that we are not indifferent to the history of our industry. The choice of a historical topic for this lecture requires no other justification.

It is a facile and utterly false assumption that the history of chemical industry is merely that of the application of the discoveries and theories of pure chemistry and physics to technology, and that industry has always waited upon developments in the pure field. Such an assumption is nearer to truth today perhaps than it has ever been before. The chemical industry made its appearance and developed for over fifty years before the growth of pure science added significantly to its fundamental techniques. Indeed, we may recall that Hurter, who began his industrial career in Widnes in 1867, was one of the very first to apply rigorous physical chemical methods to an industrial process. Hurter's studies of the conditions of interaction of gases with liquids and solids[1] in this connexion, and his devising of instruments for the accurate control of large

---

[1] F. Hurter (1877), *Dinglers Polytechnisches Journal*, pp. 223, 224; (1885), *Journal of the Society of Chemical Industries*, p. 639; (1887), ibid., p. 707; (1889), ibid., p. 861.

volumes of flowing gases was even more the work of a pioneer than his remarkable excursion, with Vero Charles Driffield, into scientific photography. Industrial chemistry took its place in the Industrial Revolution before phlogiston and caloric were discredited or the modern notion of atomic matter was more than speculatively considered. The chemical industrialist of the first half of the nineteenth century used fire with the prehistoric abandon of his cave-dwelling forebears. The theories of Sadi Carnot, and the foundation upon them of the science of thermodynamics by Clapyron, Clausius, and Lord Kelvin, left contemporary industrial practice substantially unchanged. Research, in any modern sense, played no significant part in the chemical industry of this country and America[1] until the last century was far spent.

It is a strange contradiction that our country, which derived so much of its nineteenth century prosperity from the applications of chemistry and metallurgy, should have lagged behind the Continent in the study and teaching of scientific methods. So late as 1868, when Dr Hurter was coming to grips with the problems of the Deacon–Hurter process, bringing to his task the training he had received at Heidelberg, Matthew Arnold reported: 'In nothing do England and the Continent at the present moment more strikingly differ than in the prominence which is now given to the idea of science there, and the neglect in which this idea still lies here . . .'[2]

Historical understanding must be based on knowledge of origins. It is precisely in the records of its beginnings that the history of chemical industry is peculiarly infested with anecdotes, misunderstandings, and oft-repeated and frequently erroneous simplifications. Textbook writers generally hasten on from their 'historical introductions' to their technical chapters, having lit somewhat dim candles before the dusty busts of Roebuck, Keir, Leblanc, perhaps William Losh, and certainly James Muspratt. A small number of recently published papers, however, gives promise of an ultimate authorita-

---

[1] US 77th Congress (1941), 'Research – A National Resource. II: Industrial Research.' Document no. 234 (Washington, US Government Printing Office).

[2] M. Arnold, *Higher Schools and Universities in Germany* (London, 1874).

tive documentation of chemical industrial beginnings.[1] In what follows we shall be concerned with the historical moment of the Eve-like birth of the chemical industry from the textile developments which were the main factor in the Industrial Revolution. To give this period a human countenance and interest it will be described through an outline of the work of two men, a father and son, George and Charles Macintosh. There will, too, be considerable appropriateness in the fact that Charles Macintosh was the inventor of bleaching-powder, a substance to the manufacture of which Ferdinand Hurter made his own signal contribution.[2]

THE CHEMICAL REVOLUTION

The chemical revolution, like the wider technological revolution of which it was part, did not emerge suddenly. Transformation of the nature of matter into useful forms did not wait upon the factories of the chemical industry: salt, sulphur, lime, alum, sal ammoniac, saltpetre, soda, potash, borax, and tartar, to mention a few, were all substances with long records of utility; again, more than two millennia of hilarious history lay behind the use of a certain beneficent enzyme's action on carbohydrates!

The chemical industry was latent in certain developments which gathered momentum with the advance of the eighteenth century. Potash, in increasing quantities, was coming from the trans-atlantic Colonies, as the vast forests there fell before the axes of the westering pioneers. William Cullen of Edinburgh, in 1762, carried out a large-scale attempt to use the birks and bracken of Rannoch to supply a home source of potash.[3] Kelp from the Hebrides was growing in importance as a raw material for the soap-makers, particularly in Glasgow and Liverpool.[4] James Hutton, the great geologist, during the middle years of

[1] See R. Padley, *University of Birmingham History Journal*, vol. III (1951), pp. 64–78; A. and N. L. Clow, *Economic History Review*, vol. III (1942), pp. 47–58, and vol. XV (1945), pp. 44–55.

[2] D. W. F. Hardie, *Industrial Chemist and Chemical Manufacturer* (1951), pp. 502–5.

[3] A. Kent (ed.), *An Eighteenth-Century Lectureship in Chemistry* (Glasgow University, 1950), p. 63.

[4] A. and N. L. Clow, *Annals of Science*, vol. 5 (1947), pp. 297–316, and M. Gray, *Economic History Review*, vol. IV (1951), pp. 197–209.

the century was financing his scientific leisure by being sleeping partner in a sal ammoniac works, supplied with soot by the tronmen of Auld Reekie.[1] Also, in the mid-century, Dr John Roebuck had at Birmingham and Prestonpans, by the use of small lead chambers, laid the foundation of the vitriol industry. The discovery of Francis Home, the Edinburgh professor, that vitriol could be used as a 'sour' in the bleaching of linen stimulated the demand for that acid.

Vitriol was the first modern industrial chemical. Its manufacture on a factory scale developed during the second half of the eighteenth century; its production, however, did not reach large tonnages until the chemical industry, as a web of interrelated processes, made its appearance and became geared to the great growth of textile manufacture, which resulted from cotton displacing wool and linen from their long-established pre-eminence.

More than a decade before Nicholas Leblanc patented his process, considerable attention and activity were being devoted to obtaining a synthetic soda from common salt.[2] With the exception of Keir's, these synthetic processes attained little significance on an industrial plane.[3] It was not, as has hitherto been commonly supposed, the tax on salt that deterred early enterprisers in this field of chemical industry.[4] (The 'natural' alkali, barilla, was equally the subject of heavy tax.) The causes were twofold. Until Leblanc's method had been proved, a wholly satisfactory process for the large-scale production of a *good* artificial soda was not available. Soap-boilers and glassmakers could not use, without tedious purification, the various artificial sodas these early processes produced. Even more important as a deterrent to attempting the manufacture of synthetic soda was the fact that natural soda (i.e. kelp and barilla) was available in sufficient quantity and quality to meet the needs of the new textile manufacture for several decades after King Cotton began the spectacular ascent of his throne. Charles

---

[1] A. and N. L. Clow, *Nature*, vol. 159 (1947), p. 425.

[2] Lelievre, Pelletier, d'Arcet, and Giraud, *Annales de Chimie* (1797), pp. 58–156.

[3] R. Padley, op. cit.

[4] D. W. F. Hardie, *A History of the Chemical Industry in Widnes* (ICI Ltd, 1950), pp. 14–17, 137.

Macintosh, whose career will presently concern us, had, from 1806 onwards, his own extensive chemical works, but in his alkali department he continued to make soda ash from kelp. He was, as we shall see, fully acquainted with Continental developments and he prophesied the impending introduction of synthetic soda, yet, shrewd industrialist and business-man that he was, he did not assume in the direction of soda synthesis the role of pioneer; he did not attempt to anticipate a demand that lay in the future.

From France, then in a ferment of new ideas, there came, during the later eighteenth century, a philosophic interest in chemistry. The famous Lunar Society of Birmingham was a focus of this interest in England, and the great Joseph Black, who had connexions with the Birmingham group, expounded the new doctrines in Edinburgh. Lord Cockburn, in his *Memorials*,[1] tells us that when he was a young man, his elders in the stately drawing-rooms of eighteenth-century Edinburgh sent him shuddering to bed with their talk of revolution. 'It was a relief', he writes, 'to hear some younger persons talk of the new chemistry which Lavoisier had made fashionable . . .'

It is a commonplace that the instruments which made possible the fundamental technological revolution of the late eighteenth and early nineteenth centuries were the textile inventions of Hargreaves, Arkwright, Crompton, Whitney, and Cartwright. It is not so commonly understood that the revolutionary power of these inventions depended upon a great social experiment in the New World – the introduction of organized praedial slavery on a scale unknown in history. This turning of the wheel backward on one side of the Atlantic sent the wheels speeding forward on the other. The slavery of the plantations of the American South enabled the production of cotton to be increased at a rate that would otherwise have been impossible. An immediate consequence of this disturbance of established economy was an increased demand for dyes, mordants, and, above all, an efficient and rapid bleaching agent. It was to meet those first demands that the first modern chemical industry arose. In this phase George Macintosh, and, much more so, his son Charles, were important pioneers.

[1] H. Cockburn, *Memorials of his Time* (1856).

GEORGE MACINTOSH

George Macintosh was born in 1739 in the parish of Alness on the Cromarty Firth. He was the fourth son of Lachlan Macintosh, tacksman in the farm of Auchenluich. His family was of unmixed Gaelic descent, tracing its particular branch to Badenoch, the country of the notorious 'Wolf' and of the now legendary ospreys of Loch-an-Eilean. Before George Macintosh's generation, the family appears to have made no mark in history, even locally. Their name and fame are unknown in Alness today. George was not the only one of his father's sons to go into a wider world. His brother William, after amassing £60,000 in the West Indies, for a time wandered in the East, finally becoming a Bourbonist conspirator and a British secret agent in Revolutionary France, where he enjoyed the intimate favours of the Scots lady who was first the mistress then the wife of the notorious Talleyrand. William Macintosh incurred in some mysterious fashion the enmity of Napoleon, and met his death as a result of imprisonment expressly at the Emperor's orders.

Nothing is on record of George Macintosh's youth. We first hear of him as a junior clerk in a Glasgow tannery on the banks of the Molindinar, the beautifully-named stream where St Kentigern and St Columba exchanged pastoral staffs. Besides tanning leather, the works where young Macintosh was employed mass-produced shoes for the Colonial American market. Despite the affiliating 'Mac', popularly associated with romantic futility and Gaelic ineptitude in the practical concerns of life, Macintosh soon showed his mettle in industrial Glasgow. Before many years had elapsed he had sufficiently established his circumstances to marry Mary Moore, the daughter of an episcopal clergyman. This Miss Moore was the aunt of the John Moore the particulars of whose burial are known to most schoolboys ('We buried him darkly at dead of night . . .'). On her mother's side Mrs Macintosh was a descendant of the Andersons of Dowhill, a family that played a long and notable part in the history of Glasgow, its achievements including the saving of the Cathedral from the zeal of Knox's 'purifying' vandals, and the establishing of one of the first soap-making ventures in the city. By his wife, Macintosh had at least seven children, of which the second was Charles, born in 1766.

Nine years after his marriage, which probably took place in 1764, Macintosh was in business on his own account as a large-scale manufacturer of shoes, his five hundred soutars outrivalling the output of the tanwork on the Molindinar. Glasgow shoemaking and leather-goods manufacture for the Colonies was at that time an industry having about four times the annual value of the entire iron trade of the city.[1] In 1776 the Colonial market was suddenly closed by the revolt of the Americas. George Macintosh had to find a new outlet for his industrial capabilities.

Some time in the 1750s a certain George Gordon, from Banffshire, was following in London the trade of coppersmith. Gordon was called to repair the boiler of a firm engaged in the preparation of vegetable dyestuffs. The observant coppersmith was surprised to find that the process employed resembled the dyeing with crotal, which he remembered from the days of his Highland youth. Cuthbert Gordon, a relative of the coppersmith, was a merchant and probably also an apothecary in Leith. On hearing of the London manufacture, he set about attempting to produce an improved dyestuff from various lichens native to Scotland. 'After great study,' to use his own words, 'application, pains and expense, both of time and money, in trying various experiments', he succeeded in producing 'a most beneficial dye'. His new preparation he called 'cudbear', that being a Scots by-form of his own Christian name, Cuthbert. The patent, taken out in the names of both Gordons, is dated 26 October 1758 (BP 727/1758).

From Classical times, and probably earlier, it had been known that numerous lichens, when exposed to ammoniacal substances (e.g. urine) and air, yield a purple colouring matter capable of dyeing wool and silk. Peasants in later times were widely acquained with its use. Federigo, a fourteenth-century Florentine, derived his fortune and family name of Roccellari from his extensive manufacture of a dye of this kind from the rock moss *Lecanora rocella*. The Virginia merchants of Glasgow,

[1] G. Stewart, *Curiosities of Glasgow Citizenship* (Glasgow, 1881), pp. 67, 68, 72, 88.

probably using Leith cudbear, dyed their duffle coats purple as a mark of their mercantile aristocracy.[1]

Gordon's process, if he employed the method described in the specification, does not appear to have been a very inventive contribution to the art, and would certainly not justify his claim that the product 'was totally unknown to mankind'. Perhaps today he would have had to have been satisfied with registration of the name 'cudbear'.

In recent times it has been shown that lichens, from which dyes of the cudbear type may be made, contain orcinol (3·5-dihydroxytoluene), a compound which reacts with ammonia and air to give an amorphous brown powder, entirely similar to the dyestuffs formerly prepared from lichens.

For a number of years the Gordons, in partnership with William Alexander and his son, carried on a small factory at Leith for the manufacture of cudbear. Technically, they appear to have been successful; their weakness, like Dr John Roebuck's at his Prestonpans vitriol works, was on the financial side of the business.[2] Like Roebuck, too, they sought the financial aid of John Glassford of Glasgow. Glassford was at that time one of the City's most powerful Virginia merchants. It was probably a condition of Glassford's taking an interest in the bankrupt Leith cudbear works that his friend George Macintosh should join him in the undertaking. This Macintosh did, assuming active control of the business. Glassford's role in this, as in the vitriol works, was merely that of financial backer: that flamboyant gambler, merchant, shipowner, and moneylender was not a creator and administrator of industries. Macintosh moved the scene of cudbear manufacture to a site he had purchased in what was then the rural outskirts of Glasgow, but is now the populous district of Dennistoun. The Gordons were retained for a time to superintend the process, which evidently involved a considerable amount of 'know-how'.

The cudbear works Macintosh erected must have been one of the strangest factories in the records of industry. To ensure

---

[1] G. Stewart, op. cit.

[2] Cuthbert Gordon filed his petition for sequestration in April 1776, having failed, because of the 'dillegence of some of his creditors', to recommence the manufacture of cudbear, which it appears had been in abeyance for some months.

secrecy, a ten-foot wall encircled the site; within this were not only the factory buildings but the dwellings of the workers. On the highest part of the ground Macintosh erected his mansion of Dunchattan (i.e. 'The Hill of Macintosh'), which served not only as his residence, but as the administrative building and counting-house. The workers were practically all Gaelic-speaking Highlanders. All were solemnly sworn to secrecy as to what went on within the girdling wall. They lived under almost military discipline, having to answer nightly to a Gaelic roll-call, 'a ceremony that was never neglected'. A strangely isolated community it must have been. Many of its members lived and died within the factory wall, without ever attaining the power of expressing themselves in English.[1]

The Dunchattan factory, which began production about 1777, continued to produce cudbear until it closed in 1852, and its remaining Gaels were pensioned off. After George Macintosh's death the works were carried on as George Macintosh & Company, first by his son Charles, then by his grandson George. In its early days the factory treated some 250 tons yearly of Scottish lichens, using urine collected in the City at an annual cost of £800. Later, native Scottish sources of lichen failed, and other various lichens were imported, to a total value of hundreds of thousands of pounds, from Scandinavia and Sardinia. Cudbear, although used as a dye by itself, found its chief outlet for admixture with indigo and other vegetable colours. The change of fashion to drab tones, which in the early nineteenth century quenched the chromatic exuberance of the preceding one, and the cheapening of indigo and the lac dyes had a limiting effect on the demand for cudbear. Cudbear manufacture at Dunchattan ceased only four years before William Perkin put his mauve, the first aniline dyestuff, on the market. Cudbear was manufactured by others, and used for modifying the tones of various synthetic dyes almost to the end of last century.[2] The litmus of our laboratory test-papers appears to be the last survival of this dyestuff with a history half as long as civilization itself.

[1] G. Stewart, op. cit.

[2] *Journal of the Society of Chemical Industries* (1888), p. 67.

CHARLES MACINTOSH

While George Macintosh was establishing his cudbear industry, his son Charles was being most carefully prepared for a career in industrial chemistry. After studying under William Irvine at Glasgow University, he sat for a time under the great Joseph Black at Edinburgh. Young Charles entered upon his vocation equipped with the best training that the 'pure' chemistry of his day afforded. In order to give his son a grounding in business and mercantile matters, George Macintosh sent him to work for a time in his friend John Glassford's counting-house, through which, it was said, there annually passed business to the value of half a million sterling. It is significant of Macintosh senior's acumen that, while he employed his nephew-in-law, the future victor of Corunna, in his office at the cudbear works, he sent his own son to be trained elsewhere.

While still a trainee in Glassford's counting-house, and barely twenty years of age, Charles Macintosh embarked upon his first chemical industrial venture, his partners being his father and Dr William Couper, a Glasgow physician. Young Macintosh and Couper manufactured sal ammoniac from soot by the method Dr Hutton was using in Edinburgh. Their main object was probably to provide an additional source of the ammonia required by the cudbear factory; the sal ammoniac was also sold to those engaged in the tinning of iron, copper, and brass. The Glasgow sal ammoniac works was carried on for about six years, being closed in 1792 as unprofitable.

As the son of the cudbear manufacturer of Dunchattan, it was perhaps not surprising that Charles Macintosh developed an interest in vegetable dyestuffs. Some of his leisure was spent examining native plants for a possible source of a blue colouring matter to replace indigo. In 1786 Charles was sent to the Continent as probably one of the first chemical industrial commercial travellers in history. His mission was to find customers for Prestonpans vitriol and for cudbear. It is not known how successful he was in pushing these commodities, but his visit to the Continent was by no means fruitless in other respects. For a time he lived in the Champagne region, where he combined study of the French language with continued search for an indigo substitute, turning his attention to *Iris primula*, a plant indigenous to and abundant in the district. Although, to his delight, he obtained a blue colour with alum mordant, he does not appear to have followed up his results.

From France the young chemical missionary went to Holland. He visited a sugar of lead works, and was amazed to learn that the Dutch were importing their lead, coal, and malt from Britain, to which country they exported their lead acetate. Returned home, Macintosh informed his father of this situation, and, with paternal assistance, he set about finding the remedy. Before very long the Macintoshes were exporting to Holland lead acetate of as satisfactory quality as the product received from that country. In due time, sugar of lead, which was in increasing demand as a textile mordant, became an important export of Glasgow.

In 1789, Charles Macintosh, who had once written that lime was his 'favourite nostrum', started the manufacture of acetate of lime. He put this new commodity on the market as a substitute for the more costly sugar of lead, a substitution that brought down the cost of 'red colour liquor' (the product of the interaction of acetate and alum) from three shillings to less than sixpence a gallon. This notable innovation in the mordanting process was not patented by Charles Macintosh, although it is certain he could have obtained valid protection for it. The use of lime acetate was speedily adopted by others.[1]

To what extent the activities of the Macintoshes, father and son, were independent at this period is difficult to discover. Macintosh senior engaged in a number of industrial and other activities, including a remarkable attempt, of fourteen years duration, to introduce cotton spinning and weaving at Spinningdale in Sutherland. George Macintosh had great shrewdness in business, but he did not have either his son's training or inventive capacity in the technical field. After the account which will now be given of the establishing of the British Turkey red industry, he is not of further interest to us from the point of view of chemical industrial history.

By the 1780s cotton was a rapidly increasing import to the Clyde. The techniques of its fabrication were engaging the

[1] *New Statistical Account of Scotland* (Lanark), vol. VI, pp. 165-7.

weavers and spinners, whose experience had hitherto been in the linen and woollen manufacture. The transition phase was concretely represented by the so-called 'blunks' then being made; these were coarse handkerchiefs with linen warps and hand-spun cotton wefts. In 1780 James Monteith of Anderston, one of George Macintosh's intimates, warped the first web of pure cotton woven in Scotland.[1] A few years later, Arkwright, who had been invited to come north by the Clydeside manufacturers, met Macintosh's friend David Dale, a prosperous lawn and cambric merchant, interested in cotton manufacture. Dale persuaded Arkwright to become his partner in the establishing of water-power cotton mills on the Clyde near Lanark (1785). The Dale–Arkwright partnership did not long survive, but the genial and undaunted Dale, said to be the prototype of Scott's Bailie Nicol Jarvie, carried on the enterprise at New Lanark. Eventually, when Dale forsook industry for preaching and philanthropic pursuits, his son-in-law, Robert Owen, carried out in these mills his famous, and, to his contemporaries, dangerous, experiment in benevolent industrialism.

While cotton manufacture was making its rapid expansion on the Clyde and south of the Border, in Lancashire, in the 1780s, very little was known in this country of processes for dyeing the fabric, in particular the use of Turkey red (madder) for that purpose. On this subject David Dale conferred with his friend George Macintosh. At that time the centre of Turkey red dyeing on the Continent was at Rouen. It was from that city that a certain Papillon came to Glasgow as an invited expert to instruct Macintosh and Dale in the complicated mysteries of the madder vat. As proprietor of the secrets of the process, Papillon, in 1783, entered into an agreement, to which Macintosh and Dale were also, presumably, parties, with the Commissioners and Trustees of Manufactures in Scotland, by which, in return for a ten-year monopoly and a financial consideration, the process should be put freely at the public disposal in 1803. Professor Joseph Black received on behalf of the Commissioners an account of the secrets of which Papillon claimed to be the repository. Either from guile or inability, Papillon failed to impart much of industrial importance to the 'illustrious

[1] G. Stewart, op. cit.

Nestor' of Edinburgh. Before very long Papillon was dispensed with by Macintosh and Dale. In 1787, George Macintosh wrote to his son Charles: 'Papillon has now left us entirely.[1] We could not manage his unhappy temper. I have made a great improvement in his process. I dye in twenty days what he took twenty-five to do, and the colour better. We paid him his salary up to October, so as to be quite clear of him.' The Turkey red works Macintosh and Dale established in Glasgow was the first in Britain. Their dyeing is said to have been inferior to that of the Continental factories, because of their use of 'inferior alkali' (presumably, Scottish kelp), instead of good barilla.[2] In 1805, the process having entered the public domain, Macintosh being advanced in years, and Dale having deserted industry for his spiritual calling, the Turkey red works at Dalmarnock was sold to Henry Monteith of Carstairs, who was to equal and even outrival the skill of the Continental madder dyers.

In 1788, after a stormy passage from Sunderland to Rotterdam, Charles Macintosh was again on the Continent. He visited the Leipzig Fair, and later proceeded to Berlin, where he solicited unsuccessfully a contract for the supplying of cudbear for dyeing the blue clothing of the Prussian army. At this period, young Macintosh was probably still very much under his father's tutelage. In 1790, Charles married Mary Fisher, the daughter of a Glasgow merchant, with the blood of James II of Scotland and of the Bruce in her veins. Marriage no doubt freed him from the industrial fortress of Dunchattan, and, before very long, he became the leading partner in an enterprise entirely separate from his father's cudbear, Turkey red, and other interests.

The expansion of cotton manufacture and the development of the art of dyeing cotton fabric greatly increased the demand for alum mordant. With his friends James Knox, John Finlay, John Wilson, and Charles Stirling, Charles Macintosh set about manufacturing alum from aluminous shale at Hurlet, near Paisley. This appears to have been the first alum works in

---

[1] After leaving Macintosh and Dale, Papillon became manager of a nearby rival Turkey red works. See *Statistical Account of Scotland*, vol. XII, p. 113.

[2] G. Macintosh, *Biographical Memoirs of the late Charles Macintosh* (1847), appendix 1, p. 121.

Scotland. The shale was a waste material from coal-mining operations in the district, being removed from between the lime and coal strata. At Hurlet the shale excavation was 1½ miles long and three-quarters of a mile wide. Between 1768 and 1782, unsuccessful attempts had been made by others to make alum from this expanse of waste; Charles Macintosh, in 1795–6, 'by proper application of the principles of chemistry', had succeeded. The shale consisted of a mixture of iron sulphide (pyrites), alumina, and silica, together with lime and coal. On exposure to air the pyrites in the shale oxidized slowly to sulphate. By a series of reactions between the sulphate so formed and the alumina, aluminium sulphate ultimately resulted. Potash was added to the lixivium from the oxidized shale. Finally, the solution was evaporated to small bulk and allowed to crystallize. In connexion with this evaporation of the alum solution Macintosh invented a special type of reverberatory furnace, in which the flame swept over the surface of the liquid, and the 'watery parts' were carried off to the chimney. This evaporating furnace was later widely adopted in the chemical industry for the concentration of soda; it seems highly probable that it was the origin of the common practice of the Leblanc manufacturers of using the flame from their black ash furnaces to evaporate the liquor from the Shanks vats.

BLEACHING-POWDER INVENTION

The year 1797 is an important one in the history of the early chemical industry. In that year Charles Tennant,[1] an enterprising young linen bleacher, came to Glasgow to exploit his invention of using a suspension of lime in place of a solution of potash in the chlorine bleaching vat. He had acquired a site for his new operations at St Rollox, and was joined in his venture by Charles Macintosh, Macintosh's alum-making partner Knox, and Couper, who had managed the Macintosh sal ammoniac works. It was while he was a member of this partnership that Macintosh made an inventive contribution to the chemical industry which alone would justify ranking him

---

[1] E. W. D. Tennant, *A Short Account of the Tennant Companies 1797–1922* (privately printed, 1922), pp. 12, 13, and W. Alexander, *Chemistry and Industry* (1943), p. 411.

among the first half-dozen important pioneers of the chemical phase of the Industrial Revolution.

Powered by the waters of the Clyde, by the streams of Lancashire, and by Watt's improved steam engine, the cotton industry in the 1790s was overtaxing the capacity of the bleachers' greens with the inexorable miles of fabric poured forth. Traditional bleaching required many weeks of tedious exposure of the textile to sunlight and moisture: no acceleration was possible by modification of this process. This slowness of the bleaching stage threatened to set limits to the rate of growth of textile manufacture. After 1790, chlorine had been used for bleaching in this country, but its objectionable character when used as the gas, and the obvious difficulty of generating it at the bleaching sites, had restricted its application. It afforded no significant relief to the congested economy of the textile industry. A new means of applying the halogen was urgently required. On the solution of that chemical problem further expansion of the cotton industry almost solely depended. Charles Tennant had moved part of the way to solving it with his wet lime process (BP 2209/1798), but this still had serious disadvantages which prevented its wholesale adoption. It was Charles Macintosh who solved the problem completely with his process for absorbing chlorine in dry lime – the first gas–solid reaction to be technically exploited. The bleaching-powder process is one of the simplest and certainly one of the most momentous inventions in the history of industrial chemistry.

Because the bleaching-powder patent (BP 2312/1799) bears only the name of Charles Tennant as the true and first inventor, it has been widely accepted that this was indeed the case. Contemporary evidence is to the contrary. In a letter, dated 30 June 1831, Macintosh is quite explicit in stating his claim to be the inventor: 'You are aware of the extensive nature of Mr Tennant's manufactory of dry chloride of lime (at first established by myself, and *who invented the substance*) . . .' Again, among Macintosh's papers there was found, after his death, a draft of the patent specification in his own handwriting, with amendments inserted by his friend and former fellow-student, Major John Finlay, with whom he was in the habit of discussing his scientific work. It was the view of Macintosh's son (in his *Biographical Memoir* on his father) that the bleaching-powder patent was taken out in Tennant's name only in order to avoid collision with the earlier wet lime patent (i.e. BP 2209/1798), of which the St Rollox company was also the proprietor. Writers in Macintosh's lifetime gave him the unshared credit of his invention.[1]

In 1800, while bleaching-powder manufacture was still on the 50-ton a year scale at St Rollox, an obscure crisis occurred in the affairs of the firm.[2] Each of the partners put in a sealed tender for the purchase of the works. Tennant, with the financial backing of his father-in-law, Wilson of Hurlet, made the highest bid and obtained financial control. Thereafter, although he appears not to have severed relations finally until 1814, Macintosh took no notable part in the St Rollox enterprise. The exploitation of bleaching powder ultimately brought Tennant world fame and great fortune. There is no evidence that Macintosh was disgruntled with the fact that others had reaped where he had sown, or that there was any estrangement between him and the fortunate Tennant. Macintosh's son, however, seems to have felt that fate played foully by his father, and calculated that, between 1799 and 1846, the use of bleaching powder had effected a total financial saving in the linen and cotton industries of £423,667,014 2s. 1d.!

Whatever the actual dimensions of the saving directly derived from Charles Macintosh's simple invention in the textile industries, it is to be remembered that it also brought about an extremely profitable revolution in the chemical industry itself. Bleaching powder was the key commodity in the nineteenth-century manufacture of chemicals. Vitriol, the original industrial chemical, had its importance first greatly advanced because it was essential to the manufacture of the chlorine required for bleaching powder. In the history of the first seventy-five years of the chemical industry it is almost impossible to overemphasize the significance of chloride of lime. Once the acceleration of bleaching opened the flood-gates of textile manufacture, the demand for soda became so great that it could only be met by its large-scale synthesis from salt.

---

[1] *New Statistical Account of Scotland* (Lanark).
[2] E. W. D. Tennant, op. cit.

The key role of bleaching powder in maintaining the tottering economy of the Leblanc System in the face of the Solvay process, in the last decades of the nineteenth century, must also be remembered.[1]

It was impossible, of course, in 1799, that the St Rollox partners could have any conception of the epoch-making nature of the invention to which Charles Tennant put his name as a mere matter of prudent expediency. Indeed, more than a decade later, they were attempting to obtain through political channels a financial return for the invention. They prevailed upon the Glasgow Chamber of Commerce (of which Tennant was a member) to petition the Government to purchase the invention outright for disposal to the public. A direct approach was also made to the party in power in London, where the efforts of Sir Robert Peel (himself an interested party in the textile industry) were exerted on their behalf. Fortunately, as it turned out, the men of St Rollox were condemned to earn their reward by their unaided private enterprise!

An action by Tennant in Chancery, in 1800, against eleven Lancashire bleachers for infringement of the bleaching-powder patent was dismissed on the ground that the defendants had shown chlorine to have been fixed by means of lime and used for bleaching by a certain Robert Roper as early as 1791-2. Like all epochal inventions, bleaching powder had its crop of claimants to anticipation or, at least, simultaneous discovery. The history of chloride of lime in the earlier stages of its impact on the old bleaching industry has yet to be written.[2] That the Lancashire men, cited in Tennant's action, were able successfully to plead prior use of lime in connexion with chlorine bleaching does not necessarily imply any precise anticipation of Macintosh's invention. Certainly, the scale on which these English bleachers were working could not, before 1800, have been of much significance; at most their use of lime for fixing their chlorine must have been restricted to rough-and-ready production of small batches of bleach for immediate use. It remained to the St Rollox company to make bleaching powder

---

[1] D. W. F. Hardie, *A History of the Chemical Industry in Widnes.*

[2] This is no longer true: see Musson and Robinson, *Science and Technology*, chap. VIII.

manufacture part of the chemical industry and to supply it as a commodity to the textile manufacturers.

George Macintosh, the cudbear-maker of Dunchattan, died in 1807 in an inn at Moffat, in the south of Scotland. He was overtaken by sudden illness while returning from a visit to London. As chairman of the Glasgow Chamber of Commerce he had been on a mission to the southern capital to obtain redress of certain grievances which were then afflicting the trade of the Clyde, among these being the 'shamefully unequal' reliefs on the rock salt duty in the two kingdoms. This apparent breach of Article VIII of the 1707 Treaty of Union[1] was causing 'prejudice and loss to the Scotch manufacturers employed in making the much prized bleaching powder'.[2] Thus, in his last hours, was George Macintosh engaged in the affairs of the infant chemical industry, and the changes which his son's activity had brought about in that field.

In 1805–6, Charles Macintosh and his partners extended their alum manufacturing to a new site at Campsie in Stirlingshire. At Campsie a stratum of aluminous shale, from $1\frac{1}{2}$ to 2 feet thick, provided abundant raw material. In this new factory Macintosh did not confine his attention merely to alum manufacture, but set about making a number of the chief chemicals of that phase of the chemical industry. Annually, some 14,000 tons of coal were obtained in the course of mining the aluminous schist, as well as 450 chalders of lime. Part of the coal was used as fuel in the factory, and the remainder sold to domestic consumers in the surrounding country.[3]

At his Campsie works Macintosh made soda ash for the bleachers, his raw material being kelp, from which he also extracted the potassium chloride (muriate) required for his alum and prussiate manufactures. Copperas (iron sulphate) and iron ore were additional products of his new activities. Having iron sulphate available, Macintosh employed it in the making of Prussian blue, a pigment accidentally discovered by Diesbach of Berlin early in the eighteenth century.[4] The

---

[1] G. S. Pryde, *The Treaty of Union of Scotland and England, 1707* (1951), pp. 86–9.
[2] G. Stewart, op. cit.
[3] *New Statistical Account of Scotland* (Campsie), p. 256.
[4] Frankland, *Journal of the Society of Chemical Industries* (London, 1915), p. 307.

method used at Campsie for making this valuable blue was the already known one of calcining potash with a mixture of shredded hides, woollen rags, and animal horns in iron pots. The product of this crude procedure was extracted with water, and the pigment formed by addition of iron sulphate to the solution. Macintosh – and in this he was an industrial innovator – also manufactured potassium prussiate (ferrocyanide) in quantity by crystallizing the extract liquor from the original calcination. Before that time, potassium prussiate had sold at 6*s.* an ounce; Macintosh was able to sell it to the calico printers at 2*s.* 6*d.* a pound. He was also the inventor of the process of calico printing with Prussian blue, whereby the pigment was formed *in situ* on the fabric by dipping the textile, mordanted with iron sulphate, in a solution of potassium ferrocyanide. For many years Macintosh was the only manufacturer of prussiate in Britain. (In passing, it may be recalled that it was as a manufacturer of prussiates, with his partner Abbot at 14, Parkgate Street, Dublin, about a decade later than Macintosh at Campsie, that James Muspratt began his career as a chemical industrialist.) It is of incidental interest that it was in the course of his operations at Campsie that Macintosh devised the simplified form of the Baumé hydrometer, wrongly attributed to Twaddell, the Glasgow instrument-maker who first made it to Macintosh's specification.

After his father's death the control of the Dunchattan cudbear works was in Charles Macintosh's hands. In 1819, the year following the opening of Glasgow gasworks, Macintosh entered into a contract to receive quantities of tar from that source. This tar he distilled, and obtained, not only the ammonia required for the cudbear works, but considerable amounts of 'coal oil' (naphtha). Faced with the problem of finding a profitable use for this crude naphtha, he began to experiment with rubber solutions made with it. Its solvent action on caoutchouc was already a well-known property of naphtha. Macintosh, who was extremely knowledgeable on most contemporary technical matters, may have read the Edinburgh medical student (later the famous surgeon) James Syme's proposal to waterproof fabrics by treating them with naphtha solutions of rubber.[1] With his knowledge of scientific affairs on the Continent, Macintosh may also have known that Professor J. A. C. Charles, in 1783, had ascended from the gardens of the Tuileries in Paris by means of a silk balloon rendered gasproof with caoutchouc varnish. Again, the fact that most of the chemical products of his time found their immediate or ultimate application in the textile industry may have suggested to Macintosh such a utility for his rubber solution.

If Macintosh had gone no further than to coat fabrics with rubber solution, the immortality of his name in the English language would have been lost to him. Fabrics treated with the solution, in the manner suggested by Syme, were unpleasantly tacky and quite unsuited for making articles of wearing apparel. This very adhesiveness was what Macintosh made use of. His invention had again the striking simplicity of his bleaching-powder process. In his 1823 patent (BP 4804/1823) for water- and air-proof fabrics, Macintosh claimed:

> A manufacture of two or more pieces of linen, woollen, cotton, silk, leather, or paper, or other the like substances . . . cemented together by means of a flexible cement, the nature of which said manufacture is that it is impervious to water and air.

The flexible cement was, of course, the naphtha solution of rubber, which he made by dissolving ten to twelve ounces of shredded caoutchouc in a wine gallon of 'coal oil'. The adhesion of the treated fabrics to one another was assisted by application of pressure, and the naphtha was evaporated by exposing the united materials to a temperature of about 140° F.

After making his waterproofs for a time in Glasgow, Macintosh opened, in association with the Birleys, a new factory in Manchester, continuing to make the naphtha solution only at his original works in Scotland. In the 1820s railways still lay a short distance in the future. Travellers on horseback and on

---

[1] J. Syme, *Annals of Philosophy* (1818). Dr H. Sherer in his excellent paper delivered before the Newcomen Society on 13 February 1952, 'The Mackintosh: the Paternity of an Invention', gives a fully documented account of the pre-Macintosh development of the rubberizing of textiles.

the outsides of stage-coaches had to face the rigours of long, weary journeys in wind and rain; to them Macintosh's 'life-preservers', as they were called, came, like the well-known pen nibs, as a boon and a blessing. When Captain John Franklin, in 1824, set off on one of his explorations he took with him bags of Macintosh waterproof, which could be inflated for his men to sleep on – surely the first men in history to sleep on air! Three years later, the stores of Captain William Edward Parry's North Pole expedition were wrapped in Macintosh's patent fabric. Opposition to the 'life-preservers' came from two quarters: the tailors and the doctors. The opposition of the former caused Macintosh to set up his own selling agency, and it was in that way that his name came before his grateful public. The doctors' opposition was based on the overt ground that the garments prevented healthful perspiration; Macintosh's son attributed it to their realization that the new cloaks were 'a decided enemy to their best friends, colds and catarrhs'!

THE ORIGIN OF AN INDUSTRY

Fittingly, in 1823, the year of his second great invention, Charles Macintosh was elected a fellow of the Royal Society, a distinction more frequently then than now conferred upon men whose scientific achievements lie outside the pure and academic field.

We now come to a remarkable example of the play of chance in the origin of an industry. During the third decade of the last century a certain cultured widow, Madame Daubrée, was the proprietress of a very select *pension* in Paris. In her rooms Hector Berlioz gave instruction in music, and the romantic painter, Ary Scheffer, taught painting, incidentally finding time for a beautiful portrait of Madame. The Daubrée *pension* was much frequented by British visitors to Paris. Madame Daubrée's son, Edouard, met there a *'charmante écossaise'*, Elizabeth Pugh Parker, who soon became his wife. This Edouard Doubrée and his cousin, Aristid Barbier, were not-very-prosperous makers of agricultural implements at Clermont. In 1832 their business fell on evil days. It was then that Daubrée's young wife, the former Miss Parker, remembered how she had seen her uncle, Charles Macintosh, make balls of rubber to amuse her and the other children. She proceeded forthwith to make similar balls in a corner of her husband's factory. The demand for these toys astonished her husband and his cousin; they put her in charge of a number of workers engaged in this novel manufacture. In time, rubber fabrication at Clermont was extended to a variety of articles of utilitarian nature – tubes, belts, and valves. In the due course of history this enterprise at Clermont became the great Michelin concern of today. The writer of the unpublished history of that company[1] has well described the industry as the '*enfant de la balle*' – the ball that Charles Macintosh, in a playful hour, made for a favourite niece.

It may reasonably be assumed that Macintosh's interest in ferrous metallurgy in the early 1820s derived from two circumstances. He was mining a considerable amount of ironstone at his Campsie workings, and among his friends of this period was James Beaumont Neilson, manager of Glasgow Gas-Light Company. Neilson, who had made the city's gasworks 'the most perfect and beautiful establishment of the kind in the kingdom',[2] was, no doubt, by this time giving some thought to his own invention which was to revolutionize entirely the iron industry of this country.

In 1825, at his country home of Crossbasket, Lanark, Macintosh carried out extempore experiments in steel-making. Simple and gratifyingly successful experiments they were. Using an old gun barrel as his furnace and gas from an oil gas-lighting plant, Macintosh passed a stream of 'carburetted hydrogen' over heated rods of iron; within a few hours, instead of the days required by the cementation process, the conversion to steel was complete. Although, with the assistance and advice of his friend Dr Wollaston, FRS, he patented this invention (BP 5173/1825), Macintosh neither exploited it himself on any significant scale, nor succeeded in persuading others to do so. His son gives the somewhat vague explanation that the technical difficulties of constructing suitable furnaces were too great.

Macintosh's steel invention had an incidental and interesting

[1] Michelin Company, *De la Balle au Pneu Velo*. An unpublished history of the Michelin Company (Clermont–Ferrand, France, Robert Puiseux et Cie., 1951).

[2] *New Statistical Account of Scotland* (Lanark), vol. VI.

side-issue. Dr Hugh Colquhoun, repeating the process experimentally, observed that there were occasionally formed small amounts of 'metallic carbon of great hardness'[1] – this is the first recorded synthesis of graphite.

In 1828, three years after these steel-making experiments, Macintosh sponsored his friend Neilson's 'hot blast' invention (BP 5701/1828). Neilson had succeeded, where John Wilkinson the great English ironfounder had failed, in devising a means of supplying a hot air blast to iron furnaces. The importance of Neilson's invention was that it enabled the Scottish hard splint coal to be used in blast furnaces without previous conversion to coke, and effected a two-thirds reduction in fuel consumption. Macintosh, Neilson, and two others formed a partnership to develop the use of the 'hot blast', which was also worked under licence agreements by other ironmasters. In four decades the iron output of Scotland was increased from some tens of thousands to a million tons a year. Macintosh's great industrial ability was at the disposal of Neilson, and although his name is no longer associated with it, there appears to be little doubt that Charles Macintosh was the foster-father of this great development in iron technology.

OTHER CONTRIBUTIONS TO TECHNOLOGY

Charles Macintosh's principal technical interests have now been outlined; they by no means represent the sum of the results of his Leonardine curiosity and the application of his intensely capable and inventive mind to the technical problems of his time. It has already been shown that he was the first to bring coal tar, on a large scale, into the ambit of industry, if we except Lord Dundonald's activities in connexion with coal distillation at Culross in Fife, in 1782.[2] Macintosh's use of coal tar as a source of ammonia and naphtha did not, however, afford the relief the infant gas industry required from its embarrassing by-product. Coal tar was the subject of one of those peculiar reversals of technological importance, by which the by-product of a process becomes more important than the product for which it was originally carried on. Lord Dundonald had made

[1] H. Colquhoun, *Annals of Philosophy* (1826).
[2] A. and N. L. Clow, *Economic History Review*, vol. XIII (1942), pp. 47-58.

tar in considerable quantities as a protecting medium for the hulls of ships; incidentally he made coal gas, but seems to have dismissed it as a passing curiosity.[1] In the 1820s the gas industry was fouling the waters of the Clyde, Forth, and Thames with its rejected tar. A solution of the problem was imperative if the industry were to continue its expansion. With characteristic simplicity of approach, Macintosh devised a means of using the tar as a furnace fuel. No patent was taken out for this invention, which was first put into use at Manchester gasworks, of which one of Macintosh's partners in waterproof manufacture was a director. Tar was for a time widely used in this manner, and a saving of millions of pounds is said to have resulted from the expedient.

A number of examples of Macintosh's ingenuity and his technical activity in the public interest may now be given. Macintosh's brother, John, was for a number of years a captain in the maritime service of the East India Company. It may be assumed that it was this connexion that led Macintosh to put certain proposals before the directors of that company for the improvement of their affairs. Among these helpful suggestions was one for casting nitre into hexagonal ingots to save shipping space and to replace iron ballast, and another for the concentration of lime juice (crude citric acid), also to save space, and to prevent fermentation in transit. The first of these suggestions was rejected on the ground – so Macintosh was confidentially informed – that the company wanted not to decrease, but to *increase* the volume of the goods it shipped, so as to increase the patronage which the allocation of transport contracts involved – a curious sidelight on mercantile economics! The East India Company also rejected Macintosh's suggestion that they should mix copper salts and arsenic with tar to prevent fouling of their ships, and thus save the cost of the copper sheets with which they sheathed their hulls. This notion of preventing ship fouling by means of metallic poisons is a remarkable anticipation of present-day anti-fouling paints.

Macintosh put forward a method of making forger-proof banknotes. These notes were to consist of a 'sandwich' of Turkey red dyed cotton between two sheets of paper, the red

[1] Ibid.

cotton being 'watermarked' by means of bleaching powder. If the use of smalt for colouring banknotes and government stamps had not been previously introduced, it is not improbable that Macintosh's triple paper would have found official favour, and, who knows, banknotes and not waterproofs, might now have been known as 'Mackintoshes'!

Remembering, perhaps, what he had learned on his Continental visits of Guyton de Morveau's application of chlorine as a disinfectant at the time of the French Revolution, Macintosh at various times carried on an unavailing propaganda for its similar use in this country and in the Colonies, in particular for the protection of troops against fevers. The Army Medical Board informed Macintosh that it doubted whether 'the aqueous solution (of chlorine) could be safely regulated by the common soldier or sergeant. . . .'

In 1809, there was great public dissatisfaction in London at the unpleasant taste of bread made with brewers' yeast. The master bakers approached Macintosh and asked him to supply yeast free from 'beery' flavour. A factory was erected in the capital at a cost of £5,000, and Macintosh's brother, Captain John, put in charge. The brewers countered this attack on their yeast monopoly by throwing open their cellars to the journeymen bakers on the understanding that they should force their employers to return to the use of 'beery' yeast. The brewers' ruse was entirely successful; the masters capitulated to the pressure brought to bear on them by their bibulous workmen; Macintosh's London yeast works closed its doors.

Enough has now been said to establish beyond cavil Macintosh's position as one of the important pioneers of the first phase of chemical industry, that in which more or less integrated systems of processes were carried on in factories for the continuous supply in quantity of chemicals as commodities to the market, a market created chiefly by the great development of cotton manufacture. Macintosh's lifetime extended well into the second phase of the chemical revolution, the phase dominated by Tennant, Muspratt, Gamble, and the rest. He took no part in it. Indifferent health afflicted him to some extent during his later years and caused him to interest himself in agriculture, which, too, he approached in a scientific manner.

Charles Macintosh was not merely a local pioneer, organizing traditional or domestic techniques on a factory basis to bring them into step with the tempo of the age. His technical and intellectual horizons were much wider. Over a period of more than forty years he paid five visits to the Continent, meeting French scientists, such as Gay Lussac, Thénard, and Vaquelin. He saw for himself the technological and economic changes that stirred revolutionary Europe at the transition from the eighteenth to the nineteenth century. He brought to his native Clyde the influence of French technics and chemical philosophy. We can be in no doubt that his father's example, his pupilage to the great Joseph Black and to William Irvine (himself Black's pupil), and his view of Continental perspectives were the sufficient causes of his achievements and his success; the final cause lay in the need to express that happy combination of intuition and ability to give it concrete effect, a combination which defies further analysis and which is generally called genius.

Of Charles Macintosh's total personality, apart from his technical genius, little can be deduced from the record. In our modern term, Macintosh was an extrovert, a man whose conscious thoughts found immediate issue in action. His son found no diary or autobiographical material among his father's papers. Neither did Macintosh make any extended record of his scientific and industrial activities. No inside story can be given of those flashes of inventive thought that tamed chlorine to the purposes of manufacture, or protected the bodies of succeeding generations from the lash and chill of the wind and rain. In politics, Macintosh was an outspoken Tory and Conservative, when these terms meant something rather different from what they do today. One feature of his character is brought to light by the numerous letters to him (privately printed by his son) – his great capacity for making and retaining friends, and of persuading others to his point of view. A portrait of Macintosh in his years of maturity, painted by John Graham-Gilbert, shows a beardless face with widely-spaced eyes, straight nose, thick brows, a large and somewhat heavy mouth, a forehead not notably high, and hair showing a tendency to curl; the expression is one of calm resolution; there is little of humour in it; perhaps, like Maclaren, the *Scotsman*'s first editor, Charles Macintosh joked 'wi' deeficulty'! Yet there must have been playfulness in the man who made that rubber ball for his niece.

Macintosh died of influenza, on Friday, 25 July 1843, in his father's former mansion of Dunchattan, within the walls of the old cudbear factory. Perhaps in his last hours he listened reminiscently to the soft Gaelic voices that had once answered to his father's nightly roll-call. He left the respectable fortune of £77,000; a comfortable reward, if not a commensurate one, from his contemporary world, which had accorded him some at least of the recognition and honour that were his due. Ironical circumstance has given his misspelled name to an invention that derived incidentally from his proper chemical industrial activities, and, with the injustice of which history can show so many examples, discharged posterity from more informed remembrance of him.

8 Bryan Higgins and his Circle

F. W. GIBBS

[This article was first published in *Chemistry in Britain*, vol. I, 1965, pp. 60–5.]

The late Professor T. S. Wheeler was a scholar born, as well as an industrious and lovable character who gave people credit for far more knowledge than they possessed. Our interests coincided in following the activities of chemists in the eighteenth century, chiefly in Great Britain and Ireland. Two of the more problematical figures at that time were Bryan Higgins, MD, and his nephew William Higgins. Both are remarkable for having attacked the leading chemists of their day. Bryan accused Priestley of plagiarism, maintaining that the latter's celebrated work on the gases owed something, to say the least, to Bryan's lectures and demonstrations in London, some of which Priestley and Benjamin Franklin had together attended at the time of the work on oxygen. William, on the other hand, argued that he, rather than John Dalton, should be regarded as the originator of the atomic theory of chemistry – the 'modern' theory as distinct from that of the ancients. Bryan's claims do not stand thorough examination, for Priestley's work on 'different kinds of air' had already earned him the Copley Medal before he heard of Higgins as a lecturer. Priestley squashed these claims in a book called *Philosophical Empiricism* (1775), but Dalton (being a man of a different stamp, as Partington says) did not answer William.

Professor Wheeler hoped that he might be able to follow up his researches on the life of William Higgins with a book on Bryan, and I agreed that this would be worth while, particularly if attention were given to Bryan's position among an interesting group of London scientists and literary men and to his work on topics that appeared to be physical and commercial rather than chemical. (Professor Partington has since given first-class accounts of the chemical contributions of both Bryan and William,[1] so that it is not necessary to cover the same ground again here.) This is how I became involved, and why Wheeler made me promise to point out aspects of Bryan's work to which more attention could be given.

Bryan Higgins came of an Irish family, several members of which had been medical men. Most of the biographical information we have about him can be traced through Wheeler's papers first published in the Dublin journal, *Studies*.[2] Like many of his compatriots, Higgins went to the University of Leyden in order to present a thesis for the MD degree. This explains how it was that he entered in October 1765, and graduated in the following month.[3] He then settled in London, and his first address, so far as I can discover, was in Chancery Lane. Of this period he wrote:

> A just sense of the utility of the Chemical Art, towards promoting Natural Knowledge, prompted me at a very early period of my life, to employ myself privately in the Practice of Chemistry, and to attend with the utmost diligence to the phenomena which occur in the processes of Chemists and divers other artists.

He was thus following in the footsteps of a group of chemists who had done much to stimulate interest in the development of chemistry so that it, in turn, could play a more important part in the growth of manufactures and the technical arts – men like Peter Shaw, William Lewis, and Robert Dossie,[4] the authors of the chief books on the subject at the time Higgins was a student.

Of this early period there exists a book on icebergs (1766)

---

[1] J. R. Partington, *A History of Chemistry* (London, Macmillan, 1962), vol. III, chap. 16 and index.

[2] In their final form these appeared as Part I of T. S. Wheeler and J. R. Partington, *The Life and Work of William Higgins, Chemist, 1763–1825* (Oxford, London etc., Pergamon Press, 1960).

[3] R. W. Innes Smith, *English-Speaking Students of Medicine at the University of Leyden* (Edinburgh and London, Oliver and Boyd, 1932), p. 117.

[4] The work of these men has been described elsewhere, e.g. F. W. Gibbs, *Endeavour*, vol. 12 (1953), no. 48 (Wilson, Shaw and Lewis); *Annals of Science*, vol. 7 (3) (1951), p. 211 (Shaw); vol. 8 (2) (1952), p. 122 (Lewis); vol. 7 (2) (1951), p. 149 (Dossie); *Plat. Metals Rev.*, vol. 7 (2) (1963), p. 66 (Lewis).

and a patent (1767) for an oil-lamp designed to look like a decorative candlestick. Altogether Higgins patented four inventions, the last in 1802, and this indicates the period of his main activities – when he was aged from about thirty to about sixty-five.

Probably when he was in Chancery Lane, Higgins became acquainted with J. Welland of King's Inn, and he afterwards married Welland's daughter and heiress, Jane. In 1772 his address was Orchard Street, Portman Square, and from there he wrote a paper on a chemical topic that was presented to the Royal Society by his physician friend, Richard Brocklesby, and read at two meetings in December 1772, and January 1773. Brocklesby had the MD of Dublin and of Leyden and had also studied at Edinburgh. By 1774 Higgins had moved to the fashionable area of Soho – then part of Middlesex – at 13 Greek Street. Just as physicians tended to congregate on the north side of Oxford Street, so men of science seem to have favoured Soho Square and its neighbourhood. Here was the London home of George Parker, 2nd Earl of Macclesfield, who became President of the Royal Society in 1752, the year in which he was instrumental in changing the calendar. He was the virtual author of the Bill, and it was against him that the cry of the missing eleven days was raised. Greek Street was the address Higgins used for his scientific work from 1774 onwards. He attempted to be self-supporting through his chemical activities, for at various times he made and sold chemical and pharmaceutical preparations (such as the red lead he made for Priestley's work on oxygen), undertook consulting work (such as analyses for the traders in mineral waters), and carried out research on practical topics, such as cements and the manufacture of rum, the work on cements leading to a well-known patent. He also acknowledged help from several patrons, some of whom may be mentioned first.

At that time scientists worked largely on their own and at their own expense and so, like other men of letters, they needed patrons to assist them with special projects, for example in meeting the cost of materials and books and in supporting their publications. Thus the Earl of Macclesfield helped William Lewis in his work on platina, for which he obtained the Copley

Medal. The first Duke of Northumberland was another such patron; he assisted Lewis, Higgins, and Priestley, among others. The Earl of Shelburne (an Irish peer and later first Marquis of Lansdowne) is perhaps better remembered by chemists as Priestley's patron than as Prime Minister of England in 1782. Field-Marshal Conway, another of Higgins's patrons, was formerly MP for County Antrim and became commander-in-chief with a seat in the Cabinet; he was one of the few notable people who retained office under Shelburne, and is remembered for the bridge he designed to cross the Thames at Henley. Sir Joseph Banks, President of the Royal Society for many years, became famous for his hospitality to scientists at his home in Soho Square. Philip, the 2nd Earl Stanhope, and his son Charles, the 3rd Earl, were also known as patrons of science. Several others are mentioned in the writings of Higgins and Priestley. An account of such patronage deserves a book to itself, but relatively little has been written about its contributions, however indirect, to the development of pure science, technology, and the manufactures during the earlier period of the first Industrial Revolution.

Part of the self-imposed duty of these patrons was to invite scientists to discuss questions of the day with men in other walks of life who were likely to be interested in their work. Thus it was at dinner with the Duke of Northumberland that Priestley got the idea for making carbonated water that quickly led to the manufacture of artificial mineral waters, based on chemical analyses of spa waters, such as those made by Higgins; and it was Northumberland who assisted Higgins in a project connected with the glass industry. Shelburne had large estates in Ireland (where at one time he thought Priestley might be settled), a family home in Wiltshire, and a town house in Berkeley Square, where Priestley entertained politicians and men of science, including Higgins and Brocklesby, by demonstrating his latest experiments.

There were also a number of clubs where scientists and literary men could meet for discussions. The nearest of these to Greek Street was Slaughter's, where several of Higgins's acquaintances met and where no doubt he also was to be seen on occasion. The members included Banks, Captain Cook, Dr

Templeman (Secretary of the Society of Arts), John Smeaton (who made Priestley's air-pump), Dr George Fordyce (another teacher of practical chemistry and a consultant), and Richard Levell Edgeworth. Higgins, like Fordyce and Dossie, also gained admittance to Samuel Johnson's circle, and he is mentioned by Boswell. Johnson, of course, was a friend of Lord North's administration and wrote pamphlets in support of its policies; for this reason, among others, the names of Shelburne and Priestley were anathema to him.

Nor should it be forgotten that the meetings of the Royal Society during the London 'season' brought many men from the provinces and that contact between them was much easier and more direct than is sometimes appreciated. The most important group outside London was centred on the informal Lunar Society of Birmingham, famous for the direct stimulus it gave to men like Matthew Boulton, the 'father' of Birmingham; his partner James Watt, and associate Captain James Keir, the chemist and chemical manufacturer; William Withering, the botanist, chemist and physician; Josiah Wedgwood, the pottery manufacturer; and several others. Higgins also had contact with some of them, though not so intimately as did Priestley, who was indebted to them as patrons as well as friends.

The closest of them all to Higgins were Wedgwood and his partner, Thomas Bentley, whom Higgins referred to in his writings as neighbours. The reason for this was that Wedgwood had his London showrooms for many years in Greek Street, where Bentley was resident manager before he moved to Chelsea, and where Wedgwood himself sometimes stayed. Higgins, like Priestley, was given apparatus of glazed and unglazed earthenware for his laboratory, for Wedgwood was the first to try to supply this rather specialized market, and the laboratories of Higgins and Priestley were the chief ones where materials of various compositions were tried out in use. All these men had chemical interests and contributed directly or indirectly to the work of the Royal Society. Among their papers may be mentioned Watt's on the composition of water, Keir's on glass, Withering's on barium compounds (of importance for Wedgwood's 'jasper' ware), and Wedgwood's on pyrometry.

But these are not the only names that might occur in any

o

book on Higgins and his circle in London. He acquired a certain celebrity through his lectures and courses of practical demonstrations, and through the subscription club he organized for the discussion of scientific questions, which provided one of the more serious occupations for Soho residents and their friends. This side of his work began in 1774 with the first of a series of courses on philosophical (i.e. theoretical), pharmaceutical and technical chemistry. His avowed purpose in running this 'school,' which later led to his being styled 'Professor of Chymistry', was to obtain money to enlarge his laboratory, and in this he was successful.

After giving three such courses he arranged the 'Meetings ... for the Purpose of Improving Natural Knowledge' which were supported by fifty subscribers. The first meeting was advertised for 13 November 1775, and was preceded by a special practical course for those who were not familiar with the subject.

Higgins said that his intention was accomplished. He already made small amounts of chemicals to supply other chemists, and eventually he redesigned his laboratory so that he could deal with technical preparations on a larger scale, almost a manufacturing scale. One of his operators or assistants, S. F. Gray, made a plan of the laboratory as it was when he worked there, and he reproduced this in his book, *The Operative Chemist*,[1] which is a rich store-house of practical information relating to the eighteenth and early nineteenth centuries. The laboratory was a good-sized room more than thirty feet long – presumably on the ground floor, as his chimneys were forty feet high. There was a central group of furnaces (with nine flues), including three melting furnaces, two reverberatory furnaces, and a group of sandbaths. The fires were blown by a stream of air led in at ceiling level and presumably heated by the flue gases on its way down. Air-ducts led from the fire to the sandbaths and other equipment. In one corner was a large still, and elsewhere a press for the extraction of natural oils, a tank for work on gases, a balance table, and a useful laboratory bench.

[1] S. F. Gray, *The Operative Chemist; being a Practical Display of the Arts and Manufactures which depend upon Chemical Principles* (London, 1828), pp. 72–4.

The chief chemical problems at that time were connected with the function of heat and light in reactions. This had been made clear by Sir John Pringle, President of the Royal Society. When presenting the Copley Medal to Priestley in 1773 he expressed the hope that he would go on from his work on gases to study and explain these other matters. It is therefore not a coincidence, merely, that the meetings arranged by Higgins were concerned largely with phlogiston and the 'elastic fluids' (gases), or that these subjects, which, he said, he was thought to understand better than any other parts of natural philosophy, were those that he decided to publish first. His book was called *A Philosophical Essay on Light* (1776). Those who wish to trace the development of his chemical ideas must turn also to the final chapters of his *Experiments and Observations* . . . on a large number of miscellaneous topics (1786) and the *Minutes of a Society for Philosophical Experiments and Conversations* (1795), which dealt largely with the theory of heat and the antiphlogistic theory of Lavoisier, which even then was not understood clearly by many, apart from experts. In fact, all Bryan's major writings, despite their titles, reveal his ideas on chemistry rather than on any other science.

It is sometimes forgotten that in the 1770s the terms atoms, molecules, and particles were in common use both in Britain and on the Continent. Higgins began his *Essay on Light* by defining *atoms* as the ultimate parts of any mass of matter. A body consisting of two coherent and heterogeneous atoms he called a *molecule*, 'after the example of modern chemists'. Small bodies composed of cohering atoms are 'by common consent' called *particles*. Elements he regarded as matter whose several parts possessed the same properties, and so elements and compounds were still not properly distinguished. To a modern reader it comes as an anticlimax to find him claiming that there are seven elements, namely earth, water, air, acid, alkali, phlogiston, and light. Priestley had already shown that air was 'compounded' and that its constituent parts were dissimilar, having different densities. Higgins did not accept this; he maintained that phlogisticated air (later called nitrogen) had a greater density than air, despite Priestley's finding that it was less dense. Different kinds of matter, Higgins said, contained different atoms. (Priestley later found examples of different substances which were composed of the same 'elements', and it was a contemplation of such substances that led Dalton to his atomic explanations.)

Higgins then developed his views on the structure of matter and on chemical theory, introducing ideas of polarity and of definite proportions to explain reactions, e.g. between lime and sand. He also distinguished between phlogiston and fire as the difference between a property and a process – inflammability and combustion. Thus properties and substance were still confused.

Like some others of his contemporaries, Higgins was always alert to the possible practical applications of his observations. As an example we may look at his book on calcareous cements (1780).[1] The behaviour of mixtures of lime, sand, and water was studied in his first course of 1774 to illustrate polarity. From this, it seems, arose his interest in the actions of alkalis and sand to give mortars and glass. His applied research began in 1775, when he was impressed by the fact that the cement used by the Romans had lasted in exposed aqueducts for 1,500 years and more.

Remembering the work of Joseph Black, he first examined the decomposition of chalk and limestone by heat, and showed that the greater the amount of fixed air (carbon dioxide) driven off the better the cement made with it. He then showed how this could be applied in common building practice. He next measured the *speed* with which lime absorbs fixed air from the atmosphere. By experiment he found that a large batch of mortar used a little at a time became progressively less efficient, although builders thought this was the way to get the best results, and he explained why they were wrong. By changing the proportions of lime and sand he searched for the best mixture, and recommended one measure of lime to seven of sand, mixed preferably with lime-water.

Later he tried to find an ideal mixture for plastering and

---

[1] The full title was *Experiments and Observations made with the view of improving the art of composing and applying calcareous cements and of preparing quick-lime : Theory of these arts; and Specification of the Author's cheap and durable cement, for building, incrustation or stuccoing, and artificial stone.*

stucco work, and examined many materials. Most foreign matter spoiled the mortar, but in 1777 he found that a small amount of bone-ash helped it to set, and this formed the basis of his application for a patent, which was granted on 8 January 1779. Already in 1778 he had persuaded James Wyatt, the fashionable architect of Queen Anne Street, and his brother Samuel Wyatt of Berwick Street, Soho, an equally fashionable builder, to get the plasterers to use his mixtures and to judge their merits. By 1780 he was able to list several buildings, mainly private mansions, in which his mixtures had been used. This was the age of imitation in architecture, the age when older, especially classical, styles were followed without originality and when ruined temples were built from scratch. The Pelican *History of Architecture* speaks scathingly of Wyatt's work, but there is no doubt that he designed plenty of buildings in the London area and in many other parts of the country and that Higgins reaped some benefit from the arrangement. Higgins also produced mixtures in imitation of Bath stone and Portland stone which were used as facing materials. His book on this subject was considered to be of sufficient interest to justify an Italian edition.

The importance of the developing art of analysis was made clear in his lectures, for he devoted a separate section to 'vulgar analytical chemistry'. The best example of his work in this field is the series of analyses of well-waters and spa-waters that he made on behalf of John Ellison, a widely-known London supplier.[1] The demand for mineral waters was sufficient for Ellison to make a horse-drawn 'machine' for the delivery of all the common mineral waters on tap. His book containing Higgins's analyses carried the following advertisement:

Mr Ellison respectfully informs the Public, that his Spruce Beer and Mineral Water Machine sets out between Nine and Ten every Monday, Wednesday, and Friday, from Whitechapel; and proceeds by the way of Holborn, Red Lion, and Queen's Square, through Bedford, Cavendish, Portman, Grosvenor and Berkley Square, to his Warehouse in St Alban's Street.

[1] *Synopsis of the Medicinal Contents of the most noted mineral waters, . . . analysed by Dr Higgins, at the instance of John Ellison.* Editions of 1780 and 1788 are known.

Ladies and Gentlemen sending their Orders to the Three
Kings, Grange-Street, Bloomsbury, or to the King's Head,
No. 113 Oxford-street, at the corner of Bolsover-street, at
both which Places the Machine regularly stops, will have
them immediately executed.

Spruce beer had been made popular by the account of Cook's
voyages, for his men had been given it on the coast of Guinea,
and this, he thought, had been an important factor in helping
to prevent scurvy.

Higgins also dealt with the making of artificial mineral waters
in his discussion meetings, but it was not until 1793 that they
became available on anything approaching a manufacturing
scale from the domestic factory of J. J. Schweppe and his
daughter Collette in Margaret Street, Cavendish Square. It was
a remunerative business, for in 1797 they made a clear profit
of £1,200 from soda-waters and artificial spa-waters. In 1798
they formed a company, and in 1799 they retired, having
received £2,200 for 'know-how' and retaining a quarter
interest.[1]

During the 1780s Higgins carried out a considerable amount
of research, principally on alkalis, glass, and a series of topics
dealt with in his *Experiments and Observations on Acetous Acid
. . .* of 1786. His patent for soda and potash, dated 31 July
1781, was of some chemical interest. As regards soda, he suggested starting with brine or sea-water, which was first concentrated and then mixed in a definite proportion with sulphuric
acid to produce salt-cake. This was transferred to a separate
furnace and melted with charcoal to produce the sulphide.
Twice its weight of lead was then added while it was still fused,
and the mineral alkali floated over the 'sulphurated lead'. The
two layers were then separated. Instead of lead, one could use
iron or tin. This material was to be called 'British barilla' or
'patent mineral alkali'. Perhaps he rushed this, for on the following day a second patent for the same purpose was granted
to Alexander Fordyce of Harley Street, who fused Glauber's
salt, iron, and charcoal in stated proportions and pounded the

[1] The original Articles of Agreement, dated 14 May 1798, and Indenture of
14 February 1799, are preserved by Schweppes Ltd. For more details, see F. W.
Gibbs, *Journal of the Royal Institute of Chemistry*, vol. 86 (1962), p. 9.

product, leaving it in water for twenty-four hours. These patents were numbered 1302 and 1303, respectively, and it is of interest that Nos. 1306, 1320, and 1321 were a series of specifications dealing with improvements to the steam engines of James Watt.

One of Higgins's students was a second William Lewis who had come to this country from Jamaica and was interested in the manufactures of the West Indies, such as sugar and rum. He became secretary to the Society of Rectifying Distillers, and a member of the Linnaean Society in its earlier years. He regarded Higgins as one of the best chemists of his generation and thought his ideas and suggestions had done more for chemistry than the greatest discoveries of the period.[1] It was probably through this connexion that Higgins was elected to visit Jamaica, where he stayed for five years, in order to improve the manufacture of sugar and the process for rum-making. This was an important decision for him to make, as it involved selling up his apparatus and household effects, to-gether with his 'town chariot' and his scientific collections, advertised as a 'Systematic Cabinet of Mineralogy, Metallurgy, Vitrifications etc.'. The sale, which began on 30 July 1796, included 'All the valuable Stock of Materials for Experiments of Products of Analysis, of Pharmaceutical Preparations, and of Instruments, Chemical, Pneumatic, Mechanical, Optical, Electrical, and Technical, in Metal, Glass, and divers other Wares, several thousand flint glass and green Bottles and Vessels. . . .' The appointment that took him to Spanish Town was of sufficient interest for *The Times* of 4 October to mention that he was to have a salary of £1,000 a year from the West India Merchants and was to receive further benefits if he suc-ceeded in his mission which was 'to improve the distillation of Rum from the Sugar Canes, and particularly the offensive taste and smell of that article when newly made. There is every reason to hope that Dr Higgins will be successful.' On 14 December the House of Assembly set up committees for the improvement of Muscovado sugar and rum, and Higgins's work for them resulted in some publications which have become excessively rare. Apparently his work pleased his

[1] *Gentleman's Magazine*, vol. 93 (1823), p. 185.

employers, for *The Times* referred to his return to England on 14 September 1801, 'on leave of absence', adding that a 'very liberal provision has been settled on him'.

The Committee's reports indicate that his work was highly satisfactory, and his salary was raised to £350 a quarter retrospectively. In the sugar process he improved the design of the coppers to ensure greater fuel economy and accelerated the evaporation by pre-heating the liquor; he widened the flues and introduced bracing-bars across a 'terrace' of coppers so that repairs to brickwork could be effected without dismantling the equipment. His improvements in the still-house were said to have removed the offensive smell of new rum completely. 'The distiller, by setting his vats or cisterns by the hydrometer, and the scale adapted to it, acts with certainty and precision; . . . about a seventh or eighth of the sweets will be saved; and by the use of the ley of the stock-hole ashes . . . the spirit will be so rectified as to attain the perfection desired.'

In March 1801, the Committee 'lamented' that Higgins had to leave Jamaica because of the infirm state of his health and granted him a further £1,000 in addition to his salary.[1] Unfortunately, although the Committee sought to popularize the new methods, conservatism prevailed; they were not widely adopted, and most of the planters discontinued them soon after Higgins left.[2]

According to his biographer, Sullivan, Higgins retired to his estate at Walford, Staffordshire, where he died in 1820, aged 83.[3]

Had it not been for Higgins's complete break with Soho it is highly probable that more would have been heard of the Society for Philosophical Experiments and Conversations, which he founded in 1794 on the pattern of his discussion group of 1775. His proposals were issued in November 1793,

---

[1] *Journals of the Assembly of Jamaica*, vol. 9, pp. 551, 621; vol. 10, pp. 496, 576–7.

[2] L. J. Ragatz, *A Guide for the Study of British Caribbean History, 1763–1834*, p. 299. I am indebted to the Librarian, University of the West Indies, for this and the previous reference.

[3] Partington, op. cit., says 1818, and gives his date of birth as 1737 or 1741. Innes Smith, op. cit., gave *c.* 1732, but Leyden's records had *aet.* 24 in 1765. Following Sullivan, Higgins's dates would be 1736–7 to 1820.

and the Society was instituted in January 1794, when the number of subscribing members reached fifty. Meetings went on throughout the session of Parliament, and several politicians from both Houses attended. The members included Earl Stanhope, Field-Marshal Conway of Soho Square and Brocklesby, as well as others not apparently connected with the scientific world. Higgins called himself 'didactic experimenter', his talks were 'discourses', and he had a Committee of Publication which – as Partington could not resist mentioning – had a Mr Partington among its members. Higgins's lecture assistant was Mr Thomas Young, a relative of Brocklesby's. Topics were restricted to the physical side of chemistry and to the improvement of technical arts, the members having some say in what was done. Most attention was given to the works of Lavoisier and to the ideas of Crawford on heat. Higgins introduced the new chemical nomenclature in these discussions, but some members objected to this and made known 'their desire that it should be adopted no farther than might be requisite to express new subjects and doctrines'. He was thus forced to begin by expounding the new doctrines. In addition to this, experiments were carried out on the gases, and the members also inhaled some of them to note their effects.

The Minutes of the Society were published in the following year, and it seems to have been Higgins's intention to repeat or continue with the programme in the next session. But this was the only volume published, probably in view of his impending visit to Jamaica. By the time he returned the meetings were no longer necessary, for Banks and Rumford had already brought the Royal Institution into being, for the 'promotion, diffusion, and extension of science and useful knowledge'. Perhaps it was not merely coincidence that the Royal Institution also arranged discourses, and that its first 'professors' were the same Thomas Young who had assisted Higgins, and Humphry Davy, noted particularly for his knowledge of the gases and their effects on inhalation. This alone should ensure that Higgins is not forgotten.

Select Bibliography

The works listed below are a selection from books and articles relating to scientific–technological aspects of the Industrial Revolution (not including articles reprinted in this volume). For works on economic and sociological theory referring to industrial development generally, readers should consult the footnote references in the Introduction.

ARMYTAGE, W. H. G. *The Rise of the Technocrats* (London, 1965).

ASHTON, T. S. *The Industrial Revolution 1760–1830* (London, 1948; rev. ed., 1966).

BOUCHER, C. T. G. *John Rennie 1761–1821* (Manchester, 1963).

BOWDEN, W. *Industrial Society in England towards the End of the Eighteenth Century* (New York, 1925; 2nd ed., 1966).

BROOK, M. 'Dr Warwick's Chemistry Lectures and the Scientific Audience in Sheffield (1799–1801)', *Annals of Science*, vol. XI (1955).

CARDWELL, D. S. L. *Steam Power in the Eighteenth Century* (London, 1963).

CARDWELL, D. S. L. 'Power Technologies and the Advancement of Science, 1700–1825', *Technology and Culture*, vol. VI, no. 2 (Spring 1965).

CHALONER, W. H. and MUSSON, A. E. *Industry and Technology* (London, 1963), in Vista Books series, *A Visual History of Modern Britain*.

CLARK-KENNEDY, A. E. *Stephen Hales, D.D., F.R.S.* (Cambridge, 1929).

CLOW, A. and N. L. *The Chemical Revolution* (London, 1952).

CROWTHER, J. G. *Scientists of the Industrial Revolution* (London, 1962).

DAUMAS, M. 'Le mythe de la révolution technique', *Revue d'Histoire des Sciences*, tome XVI (Paris, 1963).

DICKINSON, H. W. *Short History of the Steam Engine* (Cambridge, 1939; 2nd ed., with introduction by A. E. Musson, London, 1963).

DONKIN, S. B. 'The Society of Civil Engineers (Smeatonians)', *Newcomen Society Transactions*, vol. XVII (1936–7).

FERGUSON, A. (ed.) *Natural Philosophy through the Eighteenth Century* (Commemoration number of the *Philosophical Magazine*, London, 1948).

FLINN, M. W. *The Origins of the Industrial Revolution* (London, 1966).

GIBB, SIR ALEXANDER *The Story of Telford* (London, 1935).

GIBBS, F. W. 'Itinerant Lecturers in Natural Philosophy', *Ambix*, vol. VI (1960).

GIBBS, F. W. 'Essay Review [of the Clows' book: see above]: Prelude to Chemistry in Industry', *Annals of Science*, vol. VIII (1952). See also other articles by Gibbs in *Annals of Science*, vols. VII, VIII, and IX (1951–3).

GILFILLAN, S. C. 'Invention as a Factor in Economic History', *Journal of Economic History*, Supplement V (1945).

GILLISPIE, C. C. 'The Discovery of the Leblanc Process', *Isis*, vol. 48 (1957).

GITTINS, L. 'The Manufacture of Alkali in Britain, 1779–89', *Annals of Science*, vol. XXII, no. 3 (September 1966).

HABAKKUK, H. J. 'The Historical Experience on the Basic Conditions of Economic Progress', in L. H. Dupriez (ed.), *Economic Progress* (Louvain, 1955).

HALL, A. R. *The Scientific Revolution, 1500–1800* (London, 1954).

HANS, N. A. *New Trends in Education in the Eighteenth Century* (London, 1951).

HARDIE, D. W. F. 'The Empirical Tradition in Chemical Technology', Davis–Swindin Memorial Lecture (Loughborough, 1962).

HARTLEY, SIR H. *Humphry Davy* (London, 1967).

HARTWELL, R. M. (ed.) *The Causes of the Industrial Revolution in England* (London, 1967).

HILKEN, T. J. N. *Engineering at Cambridge University 1783–1965* (Cambridge, 1967).

HUDSON, D. and LUCKHURST, K. W. *The Royal Society of Arts, 1754–1954* (London, 1954).

JEWKES, J., SAWERS, D., and STILLERMAN, R. *The Sources of Invention* (London, 1958; 2nd ed., 1969).

KENDALL, J. *Humphry Davy* (London, 1954).

KERKER, M. 'Science and the Steam Engine', *Technology and Culture*, vol. 2 (1961).

KRANZBERG, M. and PURSELL, C. W. (ed.) *Technology in Western Civilization*, vol. I (New York, 1967).

LANDES, D. S. 'Technological Change and Development in Western Europe, 1750–1914', *Cambridge Economic History of Europe*, vol. VI (1965), revised as *The Unbound Prometheus* (Cambridge, 1969).

LILLEY, S. *Machines and History* (London, 1948; 2nd ed., 1965).

LILLEY, S. 'Technological Progress and the Industrial Revolution', Fontana *Economic History of Europe*, vol. III (1970).

MANTOUX, P. *The Industrial Revolution in the Eighteenth Century* (English trans., London, 1928; rev. ed., 1961).

MCKIE, D. 'Mr Warltire, a good chymist', *Endeavour*, vol. X (January 1951).

MOILLIET, J. L. 'James Keir of the Lunar Society', *Notes and Records of the Royal Society*, vol. 22, nos. 1 and 2 (September 1967).

MUIR, J. *John Anderson* (Glasgow, 1950).

MUSSON, A. E. and ROBINSON, E. *Science and Technology in the Industrial Revolution* (Manchester, 1969).

POLE, W. (ed.) *The Life of Sir William Fairbairn, Bart.* (London, 1877; 2nd ed., with introduction by A. E. Musson, Newton Abbot, 1970).

POLLARD, S. *The Genesis of Modern Management* (London, 1965), chap. IV.

ROBINSON, E. and MCKIE, D. *Partners in Science: Letters of James Watt and Joseph Black* (Cambridge, Mass., 1969).

ROBINSON, E. and MUSSON, A. E. *James Watt and the Steam Revolution* (London, 1969).

ROSTOW, W. W. (ed.) *The Economics of Take-off into Sustained Growth* (London, 1963).

SCHOFIELD, R. E. *The Lunar Society of Birmingham* (London, 1963).

SCHOFIELD, R. E. 'Joseph Priestley, Natural Philosopher', *Ambix*, vol. XIV, no. 1 (February 1967).

SINGER, C., *et al.* (ed.) *A History of Technology*, vol. IV: *The Industrial Revolution c. 1750–1850* (Oxford, 1958).

SKEMPTON, A. W. 'The Engineers of the English River Navigations, 1620–1760', *Newcomen Society Transactions*, vol. XXIX (1953–5).

TODD, A. C. 'Davies Gilbert – Patron of Engineers (1767–1839) and Jonathan Hornblower (1753–1815)', *Newcomen Society Transactions*, vol. XXXII (1959–60).

University of Birmingham Historical Journal, vol. XI, no. 1 (1967). Special number on the Lunar Society.

USHER, A. P. *A History of Mechanical Inventions* (New York, 1929; rev. ed., Cambridge, Mass., 1954).

WHEELER, T. S. and PARTINGTON, J. R. *The Life and Work of William Higgins, Chemist, 1763–1825* (Oxford, 1960).

WILLIAMS, L. P. 'Michael Faraday's Education in Science', *Isis*, vol. 51, no. 166 (December 1960).

WOLF, A. *A History of Science, Technology and Philosophy in the Eighteenth Century* (London, 1938).

There are also a great many other relevant articles to be found in journals devoted to the history of science and technology, such as *Annals of Science, Ambix, Chymia, Endeavour, Isis, Technology and Culture, Transactions of the Newcomen Society*, etc.